Legacy

Book II of The Time Weaver Chronicles

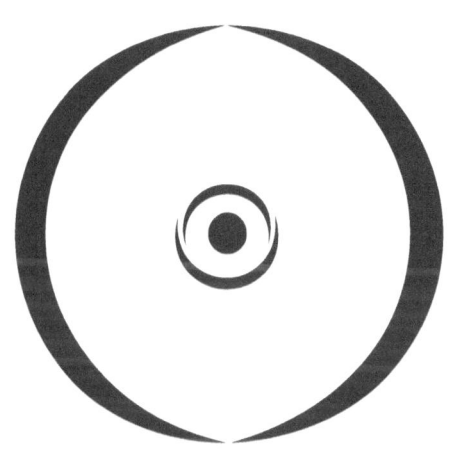

Thomas A. Knight

ISBN-13: 978-0986843730
DragonWing Publishing
ISBN-10: 0986843733

Credits:

Cover Design and Illustration © 2013, Claire Stratford

Edited By: Frederic Mora
Editing and Proofreading By: Claire Stratford
Structural Editor: Thomas A. Knight
DragonWing Publishing

Find the author at: http://thomasaknight.com

2013-02-09

Praise for Thomas A. Knight and The Time Weaver:

"I was caught up in this book from the moment I started reading it. It was so full of action, adventure, magic, mystery, evil, and a twist of romance that I couldn't help but keep reading."
- Angela, Angels are Kids and Furkids

"It starts good. I enjoyed it a lot. And as you read on, it gets better. And better."
- Will Knight, Bibliophilia, Please

"I haven't felt so at home inside of the pages of a fantasy novel in a long time."
- Megan Monell, Love, Literature, Art, and Reason

"Thomas A. Knight's, The Time Weaver is epic in every way. The world building is stunning and detailed, full of scary creatures, monumental landscapes and wonderful characters."
- Sallie Lundy-Frommer, Author, Yesterday's Daughter

Other books by Thomas A. Knight

The Time Weaver Chronicles
The Time Weaver
Legacy
Reprisal (Coming in 2014)

Visit http://thomasaknight.com for the latest news and updates on Thomas A. Knight

To my youngest daughter, Morgan,
who is a light in the darkness,
when no other light will shine.

Table of Contents

Chapter 1 – Awakening

A cool breeze blew in from the Rashean sea, bringing a chill to the wet, naked man lying in the sand. Sunlight flooded down through dark clouds that were breaking up, warming the sand on the eastern beaches of Arda. The waters of the sea were rough, but grew calmer as each minute passed. His involuntary shivers woke him and pain raged through his head, leaving him unable to concentrate. Another wave rolled in, splashing cold water up over his feet. He scrambled backward, expending what little strength he had.

Though his head felt like it was splitting open, he fought against the pain to look around. The sea stretched out before him, its green waters having settled to calm, lapping waves. He rested on a beach that stretched out to his left and right as far as he could see, and behind him a row of lush green foliage preceded a great forest. The trees stretched high into the heavens, with wide trunks and high branches that formed the canopy. He tried to think if he'd ever seen anything like it before, but remembered nothing.

Where am I? he thought, pushing himself into a sitting position and placing his forehead on his knees. The movement caused his vision to blur and his head to swim. He sat still for a long time, waiting for it to subside, when a voice jarred him from his rest.

"Are you well?"

The voice was clear and strong, but young, and it made his heart jump, as if with fear. He tried to lift his head, but failed. "No," he replied.

The young man, to whom the unknown voice belonged, approached him and said, "Remain calm and still. I'm a student of Philana. I can help you."

"Can you make the pain stop?"

A hand touched his shoulder, gentle and soothing. "You'll be all right so long as you remain still." The hand left his shoulder, and a moment later he heard the young man's voice again. "Restitas."

Warmth spread through him as a blue glow enveloped his body. He stopped shivering and felt his muscles relax. Bruises cleared and cuts sealed, leaving nothing but tiny scars in their place. He breathed a sigh of relief as the headache lifted and looked at the young man who helped him.

To his right stood a tall, thin boy, no more than seventeen or eighteen years old. His voice was mature, but his smooth skin, thick black hair, and a beard that wasn't quite filled in gave away his youth. He wore wood sandals with leather straps, blue pants and shirt woven with silver thread, and a blue robe that looked too warm for the current temperature. The boy offered a hand to him. "The name's Gladius. And you are?"

He opened his mouth to answer, but drew a blank. *Why don't I know my own name,* he thought, and searched for more memories. There was nothing. In their place, a single word echoed through his mind: *Krycin.*

"Krycin... I think," he said.

"Well, Krycin, let's get you somewhere you can dry off and get warmed up."

"Thanks, some clothes would be nice," Krycin said.

"Look, I'll level with you here. I'm staying in an Ardan village, and they're not fond of outsiders. But if you stick with me, you should be fine. Just listen to me and do as I say."

Krycin took Gladius's outstretched hand and pulled himself up. Dizziness overwhelmed him, and he staggered a few steps. Gladius steadied him until the feeling passed. "Sorry 'bout that," Krycin said. "This is a little embarrassing. I don't know who or where I am, or why I'm here. I can barely remember my own name."

Gladius handed Krycin his outer robe and said, "Speak not of it. You've obviously had some kind of ordeal. You remember nothing?"

"Nothing but 'Krycin'. I assume that's my name."

Gladius walked toward the edge of the forest. "Peculiar."

Krycin wrapped himself in the robe and followed.

"Ardans have a strict system of etiquette. Do not make eye contact with one you do not intend to challenge. Be respectful of their forest and their land, and above all else," Gladius stopped and turned to face Krycin to emphasize his point, "do not, under any circumstances, approach one with a hand outstretched. They seem like savages at first, but once you get to know them, they are great people."

"Thanks for the tips," Krycin said.

Gladius returned to his pace through the thick forest floor. All around them were massive tree trunks stretching far up into the sky. The trees grew thick, smooth bark and the air was fresh and clear, a contrast to the salty air near the shore. Krycin hadn't noticed it until he walked away from it and was able to breathe the air the forest had filtered and scrubbed. The forest brought a sense of peace that cleared away the confusion in Krycin's mind.

The pair walked in silence through the undergrowth. Krycin stepped with care, trying to avoid anything sharp that could harm his bare feet. Krycin broke the silence when he could no longer take it. "If the Ardans don't like outsiders, what brings you to their land?"

Gladius spoke without looking back, making him hard to hear through the sound of rustling vegetation. "I'm a student of magic. The Ardan people are mentoring me on the powers of earth. I could have gone to The Academy, but I would rather learn the secrets from the masters."

"That seems reasonable. What, exactly, is magic?" Krycin asked.

"Magic is what I did to you on the beach, when I made your pain go away," Gladius said as he paused and turned around. "You really did have your mind wiped didn't you?"

"Yeah. Every time I try to remember something, the headache gets worse."

"We will see one of the Ardan healers when we get to the village. It won't be long now. As far as magic goes, it's really hard to explain. It's a force that we can harness and control in different ways. Those different ways are called elements, and there are eight. Wizards are often adept at only one element. Mine is water. I'm one of the most talented water wizards seen on Galadir in many years." There was pride in his voice, but also a hint of arrogance that bothered Krycin. "There are a few lucky people who can control two elements, and some even more."

They resumed their walk toward the Ardan village, but no longer in silence as the two men became more comfortable talking to each other. "What can you do with water magic?" Krycin asked.

"Well, if one could draw enough magical energy without killing one's self, one could do almost anything. But there are few who can wield that kind of energy," Gladius said. "When I am finished my studies here, I'll go to work helping farmers all over the world prosper. Not my first choice of careers, but it's what I've got to work with, so I'm making the most of it."

Krycin sped up and walked beside Gladius. "What would have been your first choice?"

"Well, fire or shadow. But it's no use thinking about that. I can no more change my element than I can change my eye or hair color. If it can be done, the Wizard High Council guards the secret well." Gladius came to an abrupt stop and looked around. "This is it."

Krycin looked around. "There's nothing here."

"You need to look closer. Spot every detail of the world around you." He walked over to the base of one of the massive trees and grabbed something. Krycin spotted it as Gladius pulled it away from the trunk. A rope.

"Wait. We have to climb?"

A laugh escaped Gladius that echoed through the forest. "Of course. The Ardans live high in the trees. Grab a rope and follow me." He began walking up the side of the tree with ease, pausing to make sure Krycin was following.

Krycin found the end of a rope and did the same, placing his bare feet against the tree trunk and using the rope to anchor himself. The climb was hard, and Krycin had to stop to catch his breath more than once. About three quarters of the way to the top, Krycin lost his footing and slipped, landing face-first against the tree. Struggling to maintain his grip on the rope, Krycin looked down and saw the ground far below him.

A hand took hold of Krycin's arm, steadying him. "Skeiron help you if you fall from this height," Gladius said. "Short of a miracle, the sudden stop at the bottom would kill you."

"Thanks," Krycin said, regaining his footing against the tree trunk. "I owe you one."

"Don't mention it. Let's just get up there alive, right?"

"Right." Krycin smiled and tested his grip, then continued his ascent. Several minutes later he saw a wood plank floor above them with holes cut for them to climb through. Gladius made it first and set his feet down on the solid platform, then offered a hand to Krycin.

Once his feet were flat on the platform, Krycin let go of the rope and looked around. In every direction he saw massive tree trunks that were stripped of their branches and had similar wood platforms built around them. Wood plank bridges suspended between the platforms provided a means to travel from one tree to the next, and rope railings ensured their safety against an otherwise fatal fall.

Each tree with a platform had a door leading into a hollowed out area. The trees were large enough to provide a decent living space that protected the occupants from the weather. Krycin looked at the doorways and thought, *Not carved. Pressed into the trees.* He scanned the area once more before he came to a second realization, and this time said out loud, "Where are the people?"

Gladius looked at Krycin with an expression of exasperation that melted into amusement. "All around you. You need only look, my friend."

Krycin looked around once more and saw nothing. With a shrug he opened his mouth to say something, but was interrupted by Gladius. "Look again, carefully." He pointed to a few spots on the platforms. One by one, Krycin picked out tiny figures who appeared out of the background. They were about half the height of a normal human and thin, with feline features. Their noses were flat, with wide, narrow nostrils and they had a cleft upper lip up to their septum. When they opened their mouths, he spotted elongated canines. Their eyes were larger than human eyes and set wider on their face, giving them a broad field of vision. They wore earth tones that matched the trunks and leaves around them. Clawed hands allowed them to climb unaided up tree trunks and they wore no shoes. The exposed portions of their bodies were covered with a short, sleek fur that was the color of leaves and bark. Some had darker, greener fur, and others were pale, but all of them blended in to their surroundings with ease.

Once they caught his eye, Krycin couldn't figure out how he'd missed them before. "Why..." he managed to say, before Gladius cut him off again.

"Because they weren't sure what to make of you. Ardans have the unique ability to not be seen if they don't want to be. Remember what I told you: avoid eye contact, respect their land, and do not approach one with a hand outstretched if you value your skin."

Krycin nodded, keeping his hands down to his sides. Gladius smiled and led the way, giving polite nods to the tiny creatures as he made his way through the network of bridges and platforms. As he followed, Krycin made note of one feature he hadn't noticed on these people before: though they walked upright, they had a long tail that they used to keep their balance when moving from place to place in the trees. "Where are we going?" Krycin asked, trying to keep up.

"To see the chieftain and find out if they have any magic that might help you recover your memories," Gladius said. He continued up a ramp that led to the next level. "We also need to find out if they will let you stay here for at least the night. I'm not sure where you came from, but you must have had some wondrous journey to wash up out of the Rashean sea after one of the worst storms we've ever seen on this side of Arda. It's a wonder you're not dead."

"Yeah. I just wish I could remember it." Krycin followed Gladius up more ramps until they reached an enormous tree. Wrapped around the trunk of the tree and spiraling up was a narrow platform with another rope railing. The tree reached up above the rest and was the largest Krycin had seen yet. Gladius led the way up, and it took them another twenty minutes to climb to the top. A broad platform spread out at the top, supported by smaller branches, and created a lookout over the vast forest covering the island. The view took Krycin's breath away, with green treetops as far as he could see. The sky was clear and vivid blue with the sun just starting to descend on the western horizon. At the far end of the platform, an ancient looking Ardan stood hunched over a gnarled walking stick. Its tail made involuntary twitches as it stood in silence.

Gladius approached the tiny figure, who stood no higher than his knees in its hunched over state, and said "Chieftain Ranto, this is Krycin. I found him on the shore after the storm. He has lost his memories and I could not heal him. I wonder if you know a shaman who might help him?"

Krycin watched the old figure turn around and felt the Ardan's yellow eyes piercing right through to his soul. "Hmm," Ranto said as he approached Krycin, his voice carrying a vague rumble like the purr of a cat. "No memories, you say?" he asked in the common tongue.

"No, chieftain. I woke up on the beach with no idea where I was, or how I got there," Krycin said, kneeling down to the chieftain's level.

"I cannot help with your memory. That you will have to seek out on your own. When Torenna deems you worthy, you shall regain what you lost, and not before. But we will accommodate you until you find your way." Ranto looked at Gladius and said, "Take Krycin to the hut below yours. That should be big enough, and if it is not, have one of the shapers enlarge it for him." He hobbled back to the railing, and continued to watch the light fade as the sun set.

Gladius led the way down the ramp and escorted Krycin to his quarters. The "hut" as the chieftain called it was nothing more than a hole in the side of a tree. There was room for a bed of leaves and aromatic flowers that looked almost too small for Krycin to sleep in. "I know it's not much, but it's home," Gladius said with a smile.

"Thanks, Gladius. You've been so kind to me, and I have no way to repay you."

"Oh, not to worry. The real work begins tomorrow, when you can help me with my studies. Sleep well, you'll need all the rest you can get." Gladius walked away to a ladder that led to the platform above. When he was out of sight, Krycin crouched down and crawled into the living space provided to him. It was smooth and dry, and warm despite having no door. He curled up on the makeshift bed and used Gladius's robe as a blanket. Exhaustion set in as he closed his eyes, and he slept.

Chapter 2 – Lyecian

Morning came all too soon for Krycin as Gladius kicked his feet. "Come now, we can't have you sleeping all day. You're wasting daylight."

Krycin opened his eyes and squinted at the bright forest. Sunlight lit up the whole village, which was rife with activity. The angle of the sun and shadows told Krycin he had already slept later than he expected to.

"Okay, I'm up," Krycin said.

When he sat up, his muscles protested. Pain spread through his arms and shoulders, which ached from the climb up to the village.

"I'm not sure what I used to do, but I'm positive it didn't involve climbing."

Gladius let out a laugh and said, "We will have you in shape in no time. There is no end of climbing, swinging and jumping ahead. My studies will take us to the surface again today."

With a groan, Krycin stretched, then looked down at the robe covering him. He opened his mouth to say something, but Gladius cut him off. "Clothing, yes. I have some here."

He dropped a set of blue clothes on the floor in the doorway and turned around. Krycin took the outfit and put it on, then returned Gladius's robe to him. "Thanks. Appreciate that. You gonna teach me some magic today?"

"If I can, I shall. But it will depend on you."

"On me? Why would it depend on me?" Krycin asked.

Gladius looked toward the platform from which they first arrived, then back to Krycin. "Walk with me, and I shall explain how things work." Without waiting for a response, he walked toward the ropes that led to the surface.

Krycin followed without question. All around them, Ardans worked. Many of them appeared to be caregivers, tending to the young who frolicked and played in the treetops. Others were gathering fruit and nuts from the trees and storing them in more holes in the sides of the trees. When they reached the ropes, he saw still more working on trees that had no platforms. The Ardans clung to the sides of the trees and hummed, creating a throaty sound that captivated Krycin. Sections of the tree they clung to sloughed off its bark, sank in, and created hollow spots in the tree. Krycin wondered where the excess wood went and saw boards sprout out of the side of the tree and create a new platform for them to walk on. He looked at Gladius who was already watching him with some interest.

"You didn't hear a word I said, did you?" Gladius asked with a grin.

"Oh. Sorry. I was watching them work. Is that how this whole village was created?"

"Yeah. Some say they speak to the trees. They are connected to this forest, and live in harmony with it. Few are lucky enough to even see them. Fewer still are allowed the chance to live with them. You should consider yourself lucky. Most of the time, they simply toss outsiders over the side."

Krycin looked for the smile that would tell him Gladius was joking, but it wasn't there this time. "Seriously? They just toss them over?"

"They view outsiders as dangerous. Outsiders harm the forest, cutting wood and burning it for fire, and using dead wood to build with. This whole village is alive, and grows with the Ardans. They despise those who would exploit nature's gifts." Gladius motioned with an outstretched arm to the forest around them. "Take only what you need. Waste nothing. Kill nothing. Follow those few simple rules and you will get along just fine with the Ardans."

With a nod, Krycin licked his lips. "Speaking of what I need, I'm hungry, and thirsty. Do they have food up here?"

"I'm afraid not, my friend. The fruit and nuts that the Ardans eat are toxic to humans. If we want food or drink, we must go to the surface to find it. Let's go and find a decent meal." Gladius grabbed hold of a rope and stepped off the platform to lower himself down. Krycin followed Gladius as he slid down the rope, descending slower and being more careful than his friend for fear of falling. When he reached the ground, Gladius had already gathered some fruit that they could eat. He handed Krycin a large red fruit with soft flesh and said, "Here. That will keep you going at least until dinner time."

"Thanks." Krycin bit into the flesh and was surprised at how juicy and sweet it was. The flavor filled his mouth, releasing an aroma that he exhaled as he chewed. Fruit juice flowed down his throat creating a cooling sensation that satisfied his thirst. When he swallowed the flesh, it felt more substantial than it looked and abated his hunger. By the time he finished the strange fruit, he felt full and ready to work. Gladius finished just after him, and Krycin said, "So, you were saying about how things work?"

"Right," Gladius said. "There are eight basic elements that living things are aligned to. Fire, water, earth, air, life, death, shadow and time. Of those, humans can only hope to use seven. Only Lyecians can use time. Most living things can only use complex magic from a single element, your primary element. Some have more potential than others." Gladius led Krycin through the forest as he talked. "There are a lucky few who can use complex magic from more than one element. Simple magic of each element can be learned by almost anyone, though it comes easier to some. The simple spells usually gain much more power in the hands of somebody aligned to the element. My hope is to discover a way to use more powerful magic in an element other than water. If I could figure that out, it could change the way we look at magic."

There was a gleam in Gladius's eyes when he spoke of it that disturbed Krycin, so he changed the subject. "You mentioned time, and Lyecians. Who or what is a Lyecian?"

"Ahh, yes, time. The elusive element. Gifted by Lyecha only to her children. They are the gems of the magic world. Lyecians can control time, pause it, slow it down, speed it up. They can also use their magic without a focus, which makes them exceptionally powerful. Fortunately, there aren't many of them, maybe a few thousand in the world, and they have trouble reproducing. But they are always born with access to two elements, and require next to no training to use either one."

There was a bitterness to his voice that again bothered Krycin. They were a fair distance from the village now, and moving deeper into the forest. Curious about what they would be doing, he asked, "How far will we be traveling today? And what will I be helping with?"

"Finally, something worth talking about," Gladius said with a smile. "We're heading for a spring that feeds the Spira river to the west of here. The Ardans view it as a holy place, where two elements meet, earth and water. Our job today is to figure out why, in that particular place, the two elements can be combined to create new spells. I do not expect to return with an answer in only one day, but we will return here each day until we figure it out."

Krycin nodded. "Is it important to understand why? Why can't we just accept that it does?"

To his surprise, Gladius stopped in his tracks and whirled to face him. "See, now you're starting to talk like a Lyecian," he said. "Because blind faith isn't good enough. If I can understand why, then I can take that knowledge back with me to the Council and we can teach others to do it as well. New spells could be developed to make lives easier and save lives in the long run. Why should these people alone be granted this ability when others in the world have a need for it?"

Reeling from the verbal assault, Krycin shrank away from Gladius. "Okay, I suppose you have a point."

"Of course I have a point. This is the reason I was sent to Arda to begin with and I do not intend to return until I have figured it out. Even if it takes a lifetime to accomplish." Gladius stomped away, continuing west. Krycin followed in silence for another half hour until they heard the babbling waters of the spring.

Approaching the spring brought about a feeling of reverence. The air was calm, yet energized, and removed all fatigue Krycin felt from the walk there. Various Ardans rested on the rock ledge that surrounded the spring bubbling up from the earth. A small stream of water flowed away from the spring and continued west to contribute to the river. Flowers of all colors grew on the forest floor despite the near constant shade provided by the canopy above, and small, rough rock statues stood at intervals around the area. Gladius gave Krycin several orders to collect rocks, plants, sticks, and many other items as he set to work studying the area. They worked for several hours, stepping around the Ardans who came to worship their gods and pay respect to the holy land. For the most part, they tolerated the two men.

Krycin started to get hungry around dinner time, and heard a low rumble that he thought at first might be his stomach growling. He looked over at Gladius, who worked in silence for most of the day, and said "You must be as hungry as I am."

Gladius shifted his gaze from the rocks he examined to Krycin. "What?"

"I heard a growl. I thought it was your stomach."

The look on Gladius's face changed from indifference to fear in an instant. "Get down!" he yelled, and dropped to his stomach, flattening himself to the ground.

For Krycin, it was already too late. There was another growl, louder this time and the whole scene slowed as if time itself lagged. A creature with long, sharp claws flew through the air toward him. Its glossy black fur reflected what little light made it through the canopy far above and made it hard to look at, almost blurry. The animal's movements through the air slowed so much that Krycin was able to duck down underneath it and avoid its claws. The moment the immediate danger was past, time returned to normal and the creature plummeted to the ground, rolling over the rocks beyond. It hissed and snarled as it tried to stop itself, digging its claws into the ground.

It came to rest twenty paces from Krycin and spun around, searching for its mark again. When it spotted Krycin, it lowered itself to the ground and prowled forward. It let out a low rumble and sank its claws into the ground. Krycin backed up a step, staring into the creature's eyes, too terrified to move.

From behind him, Krycin heard Gladius yell. "Get down you fool!"

The sound prompted the creature to launch itself toward Krycin, who ducked and put his arms up over his face. He expected to be eviscerated by the creature this time, but after a few moments of silence, he lowered his arms. Krycin found himself staring into the creature's yellow eyes as it hung in the air inches from his face. Its long teeth were serrated and curved in, making them ideal for tearing flesh. Krycin shuddered at the thought and leapt out from in front of the creature. The moment he was out of harm's way, the creature flew head first into one of the massive trees and collapsed in a heap, unconscious.

The Ardans around the spring came to life and scrambled away up trees and into the forest. Krycin looked around, dumbfounded, and stared at the creature now lying on the ground before him.

Gladius stood up, brushed himself off, and walked over to Krycin, fuming. "Are you deaf? Or just incapable of following simple instructions? When somebody yells 'get down', it's a good idea to do it."

"I... I'm sorry," Krycin managed to get out before Gladius launched into a tirade again.

"You're sorry? Had you killed it, you would have gotten us both banished from the Ardan village, and spoiled any chance I had of learning the secrets locked away here. At least in its current state I can still heal it." He paused to take a breath, then said, "You did do one thing right."

"What?"

"You showed me something I didn't know about you before. Did you see time slow down or stop?" Gladius positioned himself in front of Krycin and looked into his eyes.

"I'm not sure, I think so," Krycin asked, his voice trembling.

"This isn't a complicated question, Krycin. Either you did or you didn't. Did you see time slow down or stop?"

Krycin leaned back away from Gladius and shuffled himself back along the ground. With a sigh, he replied. "Yes. Yes I did."

"Thank you. Now get down."

Without hesitation, Krycin laid down flat on the ground. Gladius walked over to the creature and placed his hands on its side. He closed his eyes and concentrated, then spoke a word. "Restitas."

His hands glowed with a blue light that traveled into the beast. After only a few minutes, it stirred, and Gladius backed away and laid down flat on the ground as he was before. The creature stood up and stretched, trying to shake off the remains of the injury that was now almost healed. It looked around once for its prey, then stalked off into the forest.

A few minutes later, Gladius stood up and again brushed himself off. "Crenshers are vicious hunters, but dumb as rocks. Flatten yourself to the ground, and they think you've disappeared." Gladius walked over to Krycin and offered him a hand. "My apologies for snapping at you. You have no idea how important this research is to me."

Krycin took his hand and stood up, brushing the debris from his clothes. "Don't worry 'bout it. You were right, I should have listened to you the first time." He thought for a second, then added, "You were saying you learned something about me?"

Gladius's eyes darkened as he spoke again. "Right. You said you saw time slow down and stop. From my vantage point, time did no such thing, which means *you* caused it. I believe you're a Lyecian. Which would certainly explain how your body survived the storm and washed up on shore. But that doesn't explain your lost memories."

"What do you mean?" Krycin asked.

"Well, Lyecians can be harmed and even killed just like anybody else, but it's exceptionally difficult. My healing spell should have repaired whatever damage was caused to erase your memories. If you still do not remember anything, then there are only two possible explanations." Gladius's voice dropped as he spoke this, lowering to a whisper.

Krycin's curiosity was piqued. "Which are?"

"Either you are suppressing your memories yourself, or..." his voice trailed off, reluctant.

"Or what?" Krycin asked, growing impatient.

Gladius looked around him, his eyes filled with suspicion. He appeared to be looking for someone, or making sure nobody could hear them. Satisfied that they were alone, he said, "Or one of the gods has removed your memories, in which case I must wonder: If it is the latter, what exactly did you do to deserve it?"

A look of confused innocence came over Krycin's face. "I don't know."

Gladius motioned for him to follow. "Come on, let's get back to the village before the sun goes down. Perhaps tomorrow will reveal more of your secrets." His tone was less than favorable, and there was a suspicion in his voice that Krycin didn't like.

"Yeah, okay. I'm getting tired anyway," Krycin said, and followed Gladius back. They gathered some more fruit from the surface, then climbed back up into the trees and ate before returning to their respective quarters and going to sleep for the night.

⊛

The next three weeks carried on much like the first day. Krycin and Gladius would get up with the sunrise, descend to the surface, and spend their days at the spring. Krycin did much of the footwork and lifting, while Gladius ran experiments on rocks, soil, water, and plants from around the area. Krycin still wasn't sure what Gladius was looking for, and Gladius didn't talk about his work except to himself and only in partial sentences. At the end of each day, they would return to the village, eat, and climb back up to sleep. Krycin grew stronger with each day, and complained less about aching muscles, but his occasional headaches didn't stop.

It was midway through the fourth week when Gladius made a breakthrough in his research. He and Krycin were working around the Ardans as usual, and the Ardans were conducting their prayers. There was another Crensher attack, and this time it managed to nab one of the little Ardans, delivering a mortal wound. The rest of the Ardans intervened and drove the creature away, but their companion was left lying on the rocks, dying.

The remaining Ardans surrounded the injured one, joined hands, and murmured a prayer. Soil crept up and around the injured Ardan, and his body was surrounded by a blue light. When they completed their prayers, the creature sat up, spoke a prayer in thanks to Torenna, and returned to the village. Gladius watched the whole process with keen interest.

When the excitement died down, he looked at Krycin and said, "I think I know what the key is now. The magic is not accomplished through this place. It is accomplished through these people. The Ardans carry the key, it's in their blood."

With a smile, Krycin responded, "So what does that mean, your work here is done?"

"Yes. Yes it is. I can take what I have learned back to the Council, and claim my reward. If you like, you can come with me. Maybe one of the members of the High Council will have an answer on how to restore your memories. We'll leave first thing tomorrow morning, if you think you're well enough." Gladius shot him a knowing smile and watched him out of the corner of his eye.

"It's not like I have anywhere else to be," Krycin said, returning the smile.

"Perfect. Let's rest and prepare for travel. We should pay Chieftain Ranto a visit to inform him of our departure."

The two men returned to the village early that day. When they reached the top of the ropes, Krycin noticed there was more commotion in the village than usual. "What's going on?" he asked Gladius.

With a shrug Gladius said, "I'm unsure. They are chattering so quickly, it's hard to understand them. Something about a 'dark one'. Come, let's go to Ranto and find out what the commotion is."

They walked through the maze of pathways and climbed the ramp to Ranto's platform above the treetops. Ranto stood at the far end of the platform as usual, looking out over the forest. Beside him stood a man-size figure cloaked in deep black robes that almost absorbed the light that struck them. Krycin felt a nagging despair and loneliness just looking at the thing. Its robes hung loose around it, and there was an almost non-corporeal look to it, like its robes were dissolving into the air and reforming. A deep hood covered its head and hid its face, and hanging on its back was a scythe, its arced blade gleaming in the sunlight.

Gladius opened his mouth to say something, but didn't get the chance as the dark figure moved to stand before them. Its movements were fast and fluid as it raised a pale hand up to Krycin's face. "You aren't supposed to be here," the figure said in a measured voice.

He shrank away from the figure's touch, and Gladius stepped between the two. "Explain your purpose, reaper. You have no business with this one, he is neither dead nor dying."

The reaper lifted its head and drifted toward Gladius. "This is no concern of yours. Remove yourself."

"No, I won't remove myself. And you shan't be taking this one anywhere. I will take responsibility for him. He is my concern, not yours." Gladius's voice rang out as he spoke, strong and true.

"He cannot stay," the reaper said.

Gladius took a step forward, now inches from the reaper. "I told you to leave." There was an edge to his voice that said more than his words conveyed. A blue glow surrounded his hand as he stared into the reaper's hood.

The reaper backed away. "I shall return for him." Its robes dissolved into the air and drifted away on the wind, leaving empty space where it stood.

"I don't know what you did," Gladius said, looking at Krycin, "but you have the attention of the Fates."

"The Fates?" Krycin asked, his voice trembling.

"I'll explain later. Let's talk to Chieftain Ranto first." Gladius approached the Chieftain who was now watching the two from across the platform. A few long strides and Gladius stood before the ancient Ardan. "Chieftain, we have concluded our research at the spring, and will be taking our leave tomorrow morning back to the mainland. I wanted to thank you for your hospitality and tolerance during this time."

Ranto looked up at Gladius and nodded. "The Council shall always be welcome in our lands, but that one must leave tonight, and never return."

"Chieftain, I don't understand. He has done nothing wrong."

"Do not be so certain of that. His memories elude him still, but that does not excuse past actions. The Fates do not pursue the living without cause. We cannot tolerate his presence any further. I am sorry." Ranto resumed his gaze over the landscape, indicating that these would be his last words on the subject.

"I guess we leave tonight then," Gladius said to Krycin.

He led the way back to their living quarters. It took Krycin only a few minutes to pack up his possessions. When he was done, he saw Gladius standing outside his quarters with a single pack slung over his shoulder. "So what's the deal with the Fates?" Krycin asked. "Who are they? And why do they want me?"

Gladius leveled his gaze at Krycin, speaking in a serious tone. "Most people believe the Fates control everything. Where you are going, what you do, what you accomplish in life. They measure out your life, and sever it at the end. The one we saw up on the platform is a reaper. A messenger of the Fates. We don't usually see reapers unless there are dead or dying present, and even then you might only catch a glimpse. The Council can tell you more about them, and may also be able to figure out why they want you. We should move as quickly as we can."

"Okay. I'm ready when you are," Krycin said.

Gladius led the way. "We'll have to take a ship to the mainland and go from there. There aren't any wizards on Arda capable of opening a rift, otherwise we could be there in an instant."

"A rift?" Krycin asked, taking hold of a rope and lowering himself from the Ardan village.

"Yes. Some of the more powerful wizards can create a hole in the fabric of space and pass through it. It can turn weeks of travel into minutes, but I don't know the necessary spells."

"How long will it take to get to the ship?"

"Three weeks," Gladius said. His feet touched the ground at the same time as Krycin's and he began walking. "If we make haste."

The two left the village behind and traveled west toward the only sea port on Arda. The travel was quiet except for idle conversation between the two. Most of it about Gladius or the forest around them. Gladius took the time to teach Krycin about the various plants that covered the forest floor and what they could be used for, and Krycin asked a great many questions. By the time they reached the sea port, they spoke to each other as old friends. Gladius used a few gold he had in his pack to obtain passage on a ship, and they both boarded in good spirits. Once they were aboard the ship sailing toward the port of Deshon, Krycin stood at the railing looking out over the sea. Gladius approached him, and with a smile said, "Copper for your thoughts?"

"What?" Krycin asked. He heard Gladius just fine, but the expression sounded off. Without thinking about it, he said, "Penny."

"What do you mean, 'penny'?"

"Penny for your thoughts. That's how I remember that expression. I know I've said it a hundred times, but I can't remember to who, or why."

"Ahh. I've never heard the word 'penny' before. But this is a good sign. If you remember that, then you are bound to remember more soon enough," Gladius said, nudging Krycin's arm. He flashed Krycin a grin when he looked up.

"You're right, of course. Where exactly are we headed?"

"Far to the northwest, to Ducain's Keep, where the Wizard High Council convenes. There we will hopefully find some answers."

Krycin stared down at the water that raced past the ship's hull. "Hopefully."

⊙

The trip across the Rashean sea was calm and quiet. Krycin was glad for that, as he had no interest in any excitement. His headaches worsened as the days went on, despite Gladius's best efforts to ease his suffering. The gentle up and down of the boat over the waves, and the calming sound of the water lapping against the hull of the ship helped Krycin relax. The air smelled of salt water and seaweed, and the gentle breeze and sunshine made for a perfect journey. So perfect, that the sailors even made comments on the pleasant weather.

When they reached the mainland, Krycin was almost disappointed that the sailing portion of their journey was over. "We have a long journey yet over land I'm afraid," Gladius said during a conversation that night.

"How long? I mean, are we going by foot? Or is there a faster way?" Krycin asked.

"We could hire a wizard to transport us there, but that's expensive, and I have little money left after the boat trip. Walking will have to do. Unless..."

"Unless what?" Curiosity filled Krycin's voice as he saw a glimmer of mischief in Gladius's eyes.

"Unless I call in a favor," Gladius said with a grin. "Follow me, we'll find a faster way there."

Gladius led Krycin to a tavern in the port town and left Krycin at the counter. The tavern was all wood on the inside and was decorated with various old fishing gear, large fish that were mounted on wood plaques, and the odd lamp that burned with a bright orange flame. Tables filled most of the floor space, but there was a spot at the far end of the tavern with a fire place where people could rest and warm themselves, and a counter with stools where people could get a quick drink after a long day of fishing and hard work. "Get some food and drink," Gladius said. "Speak to nobody otherwise. I'll be right back." He dropped a few silver pieces into Krycin's hand and walked off to a back room.

Krycin sat down at the counter and flagged down a barmaid. She was a thin, yet attractive young woman who wore a little too much face paint, and showed a little too much cleavage. "What can I get for you, darlin'?" she asked as she cozied up across the counter from him.

"A hot meal, and a cold drink, please," Krycin said with a smile.

"Oh, so polite. You must not be from around here. Just passing through?" She smiled, but it looked fake, and despite having a pretty face, her teeth were jagged and rotting.

Krycin fought the urge to cringe and replied, "Yeah, we're heading to Ducain's Keep."

Her brows lowered into a scowl, and there was a flash of anger or hostility in her eyes. "Oh. Right then." She walked away without another word.

That was odd, Krycin thought, but sat and stared at the bar waiting for his order.

The sound of the door opening and closing behind him told him another patron had entered the tavern. He lifted his head and scanned the room only to spot a big burly man walking through the room toward him. It was evident that the man was a fisherman, as he wore coveralls that were streaked red with fish blood, and large black boots that were treated to be waterproof. His frame was large and muscled, his arms being almost as big as Krycin's legs. Krycin turned back to the counter and tried to ignore the feeling of impending doom in his gut.

The barmaid looked up from her work toward the big man and made a hand gesture that Krycin didn't understand. Two thuds of booted feet behind him told Krycin he should turn around, but a voice inside him told him not to. He ignored the voice, and spun on the stool. Standing before him was the fisherman, his bloodstained coveralls standing out from the rest of his attire. "You're on my stool," the big man said in a gruff voice that matched his appearance.

Krycin shifted his gaze to the four empty stools next to him, then motioned towards them. "Couldn't you just use one of those?"

A hush fell over the entire tavern and Krycin became aware that every patron in the room was now staring at him. The fisherman lifted his big hands and grabbed the front of Krycin's shirt, giving him a shake. "What part of 'You're on my stool' do you not understand?" the fisher said, his voice filled with anger. Krycin got the distinct impression that he was either mentally unstable, or being paid to raise a fuss. Or both.

"There's no need to get pushy. If you insist on sitting here, I'm more than happy to move." He tried to get up from the stool but was forced back down by the man holding onto his shirt.

The barmaid made a half-hearted call across the room. "Now Dragga, there's no need to get violent."

All at once, Dragga erupted with an anger that Krycin didn't see coming. "Pushy am I? I'll teach you the meaning of the word pushy." He lifted Krycin off the stool with one hand and pulled the other back for a good swing at Krycin's face. He flinched in anticipation of the hit, but nothing came. When Krycin opened his eyes, Dragga stood before him, still clutching his shirt and holding a fist ready to strike. His face was contorted in a look of pure hate, but he didn't move. Krycin looked around the room and realized nothing moved.

Everyone in the tavern watched the scene, some with mild amusement, and some with a vague look of pity on their faces. Dragga was twice the size of Krycin, and thus there was no match between them. Had time not stopped, Dragga may well have killed Krycin. *Over a bar stool,* Krycin thought.

He tried to loosen Dragga's grip on his shirt and was able to free himself. With a quick sidestep, Krycin cleared away from Dragga's striking range. Without warning time resumed. The big man's fist smashed down hard against the counter, knocking him off balance and sending him crumpling forward. When he landed, it shook the whole building, rattling glasses and nearly knocking the entire counter over.

The barmaid looked on with shock, struck speechless. Whispers ran through the tavern, all saying the same thing: "He's a Time Weaver."

Dragga groaned and stood up. Krycin watched him, paralyzed with fear. "You're going to pay for that, *wizard*," he said spitting the last word out like it was an insult, or a curse.

He took a step forward but was interrupted by a sudden clear voice. "Congelascas."

A blue ball of energy flew from behind Krycin and struck Dragga in the chest, exploding in a hail of ice and frost and sending Dragga flying back against the wall. This time he hit his head, and slumped to the floor, unconscious.

Gladius's voice rang out clear above the murmur of the tavern, sounding much more mature than the seventeen-year-old he was. "Does anybody *else* want to get on the wrong side of my spells?"

The tavern was silent as people went back to their drinks and meals, pretending that nothing had happened. "Yeah, I thought so," Gladius said walking over to Krycin. "You all right?"

Krycin jumped at the sound of his voice. "Yeah. Yeah, I think so. Just a little shaken."

Gladius led him out of the tavern, but the door was only just closed before he spoke again as he walked ahead of Krycin. "I walk away for five minutes and you get yourself into a brawl? What were you thinking? What did you say that set the idiot brute off?"

"I don't know. He came into the tavern and just blew up on me."

"Only somebody with a death wish would act like that around here. Something must have been said or done to make him turn," Gladius said. He stopped in the middle of the road, facing Krycin. "What did you say? Everything, not just to him. Start before him."

"I was just sitting there. I ordered some food, and made light conversation with the girl behind the bar. What I wanted, where we were headed, stuff like that," Krycin said.

"You told her where we were going? You told her Ducain's Keep?"

"Yes. That's what I told her. I don't understand what the big deal is."

"The big deal? The big deal is this: We are both wizards. Whether you want to believe it or not, that's the reality. The difference is, I understand my potential and know how to defend myself. You, on the other hand, are only alive because of your instincts. Had you been anything but a Lyecian, your imbecilic behavior would have gotten you killed. Not everybody in this world is as accepting of wizards as the Ardans are. They are a race founded on magic, and are thriving on it. Others have seen magic cause nothing but death, and suffering, and destruction. Keep that in mind the next time you open your mouth."

Gladius stormed away without another word. Krycin would have let him go, but he had nobody else to turn to, and nowhere else to go. So he followed Gladius, breaking into a run to catch up.

Chapter 3 – Alkirk Manor

Krycin followed Gladius away from the port town for several hours in silence. When he thought Gladius had calmed down, he spoke. "Gladius?"

The young man stopped and turned to face him, an expression of mild disgust on his face. "What?"

Krycin recoiled from him, realizing that Gladius wasn't as calm as he looked. "Where are we going now?"

Gladius took a deep breath. "I've arranged for us to get a ride up toward Ducain's Keep. At least as far as the Arvok Caldera. After that it will be a week's travel."

"A ride? What sort of ride?"

A sly smile appeared on Gladius's lips. "You'll just have to follow me and find out, won't you?"

"Why don't I like the sound of that?" Krycin asked, happy that the mood between them had taken a turn for the better.

"Just follow me, and for Philana's sake, don't talk to any more strangers. You'll get us both killed."

The pair traveled for a day through the wilderness, heading north. They stopped for short rests and meals, but continued walking through the night by the light of a meager spell Gladius produced. The terrain was easy to navigate and the night air cool but not cold. Partway through the next day they found what Gladius was looking for: an old beaten path stretching east to west. "It won't be long now," Gladius said, breaking the silence. He turned west down the path and continued without saying another word.

It took another hour of walking to reach an old cave entrance covered over with vines. Gladius approached the opening, held up his hand, closed his eyes, and spoke a single word. "Congelascas."

A light blue bolt of energy erupted from his hand and flowed into the network of vines, freezing them solid. Frost spread over their surface causing leaves to wilt, wither, and die at the sudden extreme cold. When the spell had spread over the entire entrance of the cave, Gladius swung his fist forward into the vines and they shattered like glass and crumbled to the ground. A gaping hole filled with darkness remained. "Follow me," Gladius said over his shoulder as he walked into the cave.

Krycin followed him into the darkness, stopping only long enough to let his eyes adjust. As the darkness changed to dim light, a thought rushed into his head. It was a familiar voice speaking words he might have once heard.

"Krycin could only wield the time and life elements."

It hit him like a blow to the chest and caused him to drop to his knees.

Gladius stopped and looked down at Krycin who was now holding his head. "Are you all right?" he asked, though his tone was more impatient than compassionate.

"I..." Krycin said, as pain raged through his head. He fought against it and after a few moments it faded. "Yeah, I'm fine. I think I just remembered something else. A name. And a conversation I once had, or a fragment of a conversation."

Gladius knelt down beside him and put a hand on Krycin's shoulder. "Talk through it. Tell me about it. This is how you will regain all of your memories."

"Merek. The name was Merek. We were talking, but the only thing I can remember is 'Krycin could only wield the time and life elements'," Krycin said.

"Merek? He's the Arch-Magus of Findoor," Gladius said, and paused a moment to think. "We can test this easy enough. Cast a light spell."

"Cast a spell? I wouldn't know the first thing about casting a spell," Krycin said.

Gladius smiled and looked Krycin in the eye. "Three steps. Clear your mind. Visualize the desired effect to summon the energy. Speak the words to the spell to focus the energy into the desired effect. Being a Lyecian, you can skip the words, as you should be able to produce the desired effect by focusing your thoughts."

Krycin looked up at Gladius with an uncertain look on his face. "I don't know if I can do this. Even the memories I'm getting back are like they belong to someone else."

"Stop worrying, and just try it. Obviously your mind is still recovering from whatever trauma it experienced. It's no surprise that some of your memories might seem cloudy right now. But trust me. There is nothing you can do that will bring us harm here. Try it, you might be surprised."

With a sigh, Krycin nodded. "Okay, I'll try," he said, and lifted himself to his feet. He closed his eyes and put everything out of his head, thinking of nothing. Holding his hand out before him, palm up, he visualized in his mind's eye a ball of white light resting in his hand. It startled Krycin when the magical energy flowed through him and fulfilled his wish. When he opened his eyes, he saw a bright globe of light in his hand, and the cave was now lit up enough to see every detail.

Gladius let out a burst of laughter and patted him on the back. "Well done, my friend. So you can indeed wield Anam's gift. Regardless of how you feel about your recovered memories, they are obviously accurate in some regard."

Krycin smiled, proud of the ball of light that now provided a means to see their path in the darkness. "Where did you say Merek was from?"

"Findoor. Merek is the current Arch-Magus there, and a close advisor to the High Council. Perhaps when we are done at Ducain's Keep, you should transport yourself to Findoor castle. Maybe Merek will recognize you and be able to help you."

"Yeah," Krycin said, "that sounds like a great idea. But... transport myself?"

"You still have a lot to learn, my friend. Come, I'll explain later. We have a ride to catch."

Gladius walked deeper into the cave. Still holding the ball of light, Krycin followed. The walls of the cave were rough dirt that crumbled when touched. With no solid foundation, the cave appeared as though it could collapse at any second. The further in they walked, the more stale the air was. As they walked deeper, the walls changed from rough dirt to smooth stone, and there were fewer tree roots breaking through. Still they continued until the floor leveled off. Up ahead, Krycin could see a gold door gleaming in the dim light. Gladius sped up and approached the door without caution, like he'd been there dozens of times. When he knocked, the sound echoed up the hallway.

"Who lives here?" Krycin asked.

Gladius gave him another sly smile that told him he wasn't going to tell the whole truth, and said, "Our ride."

The door opened before them, though nobody could be seen inside. Gladius took a step back and knelt down. Krycin followed suit. Behind the door there was only darkness. From the depths of the room, a great rumble shook the floor and a powerful voice asked, "Who disturbs my rest?"

Without lifting his head, Gladius said, "A lowly wizard seeking a service for the High Council. Would you accept us into your lair?"

There was a long pause. Long enough for Krycin to start to doubt if there would be a response at all. He was about to open his mouth to say something when the voice boomed. "I did not think I would see the day that you, of all people, would call yourself a lowly wizard. What is it the Council requires of me?"

Gladius stood up and entered the room. The moment he stepped over the threshold, he disappeared, like walking through a curtain. Krycin followed. Inside the room was not what Krycin had expected. It was well lit and filled with mounds of gold and silver laced with gemstones and jewelery. At the center of it all was a massive gold dragon curled up with its right eye to the door. The slit of its pupil narrowed when Krycin entered with his orb of light. Seeing the amount of light in the room, he dismissed the ball and it disappeared.

Without hesitation, Gladius walked up to the dragon's head, stood tall before it, and said, "We need you to take us to Arvok Caldera. And before you ask, yes, the Council has already approved this. My friend here," he motioned to Krycin standing behind him, "is a very important person, it seems."

Krycin took a step forward to stand beside Gladius. "Morganath, this is Krycin," Gladius said. "And Krycin, this is Morganath."

Morganath took a moment to get up and stretch. "'Tis a pleasure to meet you, Krycin," the massive dragon rumbled.

With an uncertain smile, Krycin said, "And you. Are we really supposed to ride on your back to the caldera?"

"Why wouldn't you? Have you never ridden dragonback before?" There was a hint of adventurous glee in the booming dragon's voice.

"No, I don't think so. I mean..." Krycin's thought was interrupted by a ripping pain in his head that went from the front all the way through his head to the base of his skull. He cried out and dropped to his knees, holding his head.

After a moment, a voice cut through it, strong and clear. "Restitas." Krycin felt a pair of hands on his shoulders as his head cleared. When he looked up, it was Gladius who stood over him.

"Better?" Gladius asked.

"Yeah, I think so," Krycin said, trying to push himself to his feet.

Gladius helped him up and looked Krycin in the eye. "Tell me you're not going to do that while we're in the sky. None of us carry Skeiron's gift. If you fall off, you'll be a dead man."

Krycin thought about that for a moment and smiled. "I think I'm okay now. When do we leave?"

"Whenever you are ready," Morganath said.

The two approached Morganath. Krycin was cautious, but Gladius walked up and climbed onto the dragon's neck without a second thought. He offered a hand to Krycin, who accepted it and used it to pull himself up. Once Krycin was seated, Gladius said, "Let's go, Morganath."

"As you wish," Morganath said, and stood up to his full height, hunched back on his hind legs, and leapt. A few beats of his wings sent gold and silver coins rolling in every direction, but got him into the air. Morganath propelled himself through the cavern and toward a long, narrow tube rising up from the ceiling. As he flew, the light at the top grew bigger and brighter. They erupted from the cave just in time to see the sunset. All across the clear sky, pinks and oranges and yellows mingled and made it look painted. Only a few small clouds drifted by, and the first stars were just starting to shine.

Morganath leveled out his flight and made for the northwest, flying as fast as he could without knocking his passengers off. They flew well into the night before stopping to rest, and continued on the next day. For four days they traveled. Each night, the pair would hunt for small game to feed them, and Gladius would use his magic to produce fresh water to drink. At the end of their journey, they circled above a massive crater in the earth.

Gladius spoke up, shouting over the wind in their ears. "This is it, the Arvok Caldera. Legend has it, the crater was man-made. A wizard doing experiments with the fire element delved too deep into the earth, and the subsequent eruption and explosion left this caldera. We'll land and rest here a night before heading out. The wizard who lives here, Serrin, is said to be a direct descendant of the wizard who created the crater. He's a Lyecian, like you, but with fire in his blood."

Krycin smiled at the prospect of meeting one of his own kind.

One more circle around the crater and they settled down to the grassy ground at the edge of the landmark. Morganath landed a few hundred yards away from a stately manor built on the slope leading down into the center of the caldera. Most of the land inside the slope was simple grass pastures that grew well in the fertile volcanic soil. At the center of the caldera there was another larger building that looked more like a stone box than a house of any kind.

As Gladius slid down from Morganath's neck, a man came running out the front door of the manor toward them, his red robes fluttering in the breeze created by Morganath's landing. His hood was pulled back revealing short brown hair and a full mustache and beard. He was of average height and build, but his skin was tanned from working in the sun. By the time he reached the companions, he was winded, but still able to speak. "Gladius, I presume?"

Gladius approached the man and motioned for Krycin to follow. "Indeed, and you must be Serrin? Have you an extra room for a night? We could use a good meal and comfortable bed before we travel again."

"Indeed, I am Serrin," he said. "I was led to believe by the Council that you would be coming alone. Who is this fellow?"

"Apologies for the miscommunication. Serrin, this is Krycin. He's a Lyecian, like you."

A smile spread across Serrin's face. "Well then, welcome my friend. It is a real pleasure to meet you."

Krycin took a step forward and bowed before Serrin. "It's good to meet you."

When he lifted his head back up and looked into Serrin's eyes he stopped. His eyes were green, like Krycin's, and held a familiarity that Krycin couldn't explain. "Have we met before?" Krycin asked.

"Nay," said Serrin, "can't say that we have."

Krycin rubbed his eyes and felt another headache coming on. "Sorry, I guess I've just been on the road too long."

"Not to worry, my friends. My wife has a wonderful evening meal on right now. Come, rest your feet in the parlor, and I shall call you when dinner is served." Serrin led the way back to the manor.

Before Krycin followed, he turned to face Morganath, who looked like he was ready to leap back into the air. Krycin waved a hand at him to get his attention and said, "Thank you for the ride, Morganath. I owe you one."

Morganath blinked one large eye at him and made a motion with his head that looked like a nod. "It is my duty. You owe me nothing. Be well, young Krycin, and may we meet again."

"I'd like that." Krycin followed Serrin and Gladius at a run to catch up as Morganath leapt into the air and flew away.

Serrin invited the companions inside and bade them make themselves at home. The entryway was decorated with paintings and tapestries that seemed out-of-place, but Krycin was too distracted by the growing discomfort behind his eyes to notice anything beyond that. He followed Serrin in silence to the parlor. There was a couch at the far end of the room that Krycin headed straight for and laid down.

Gladius followed and stood over him. "Are you well?"

Krycin opened his eyes, an action he regretted the moment he did it, as the light in the room made the throbbing headache worse. "No. It feels like my head is splitting in half again."

"Get some rest, and perhaps it shall subside by dinner. I have matters to discuss with Serrin in his lab. If you need anything, Serrin's wife is in the kitchen."

"Thanks," Krycin said and closed his eyes.

⊙

The manor was still and quiet when Krycin opened his eyes again. The room was dark and it took a moment for him to remember where he was. His headache had eased up to a dull throb and he was able to sit up without feeling dizzy. *The sun's set, I must have been sleeping for a while,* he thought. The smell of food lingered in the air, but he could tell it was at least two or three hours since it was served by how faint the smell was. His stomach growled. *Maybe there's still some food in the kitchen.*

Krycin held out his hand, cleared his mind, and called on the power of light. A small glowing orb appeared in his hand, illuminating the room. To his surprise, standing between him and the door was a dark figure whose robes absorbed any light that hit it. He remembered the figure from the Ardan village, the reaper. Only this time, Gladius wasn't here to protect him.

Krycin opened his mouth to call for help, but nothing came out.

"Wait," the reaper said. He drifted closer to Krycin, but his hood hid his face even in the orb's light. The sound of his voice was like a shout in the silence of the room.

Krycin jumped and tried to back up, only to realize he was still on the couch.

"You must come back with me," the reaper said, continuing his advance.

Fear and panic took over as Krycin raised his hand and threw the glowing orb toward the dark figure, pouring magical energy into it as he did. The orb struck the reaper in the chest and exploded with a burst of light, sending him flying back. He struck the door behind him with a loud thud and dropped to the ground.

Krycin held out his hand and produced another glowing orb so that he could see the intruder. The reaper's hood was now back and Krycin could see his face, a young man with a shock of orange shoulder length hair, a clean shaven face, and blue eyes that stared back at Krycin with such intensity that it startled him. "Who are you? And what do you want with me?" Krycin asked.

"You must come with me. I've been instructed to return you to where you belong, and granted the power to do so. Come with me quietly, or by force, it matters not to me. But you will come." The reaper stood up and pulled his hood back up and over his head to hide his face. He reached behind him, took hold of a weapon and swung it out. A scythe with a long gleaming blade.

"I'm not going anywhere with you," Krycin said raising his hand to throw the second globe.

The reaper moved like the wind, drifting forward and swinging the scythe at Krycin. Time slowed, and Krycin was able to duck below the weapon. He thrust his hand forward and slammed the glowing orb into the reaper's torso. A second explosion sent the reaper flying backward again as time resumed its normal flow. Somehow, the reaper maintained his grip on the scythe, though he gasped for breath. "How?" he asked.

Krycin walked forward, holding his hand out to produce yet another ball of light. "How what? Did you think this would be easy? Did you think I was just going to follow you, without an explanation? I may not remember my past, but I'm not helpless. Gladius has taught me a thing or two."

"You misunderstand. I'm trying to help you," the reaper said as he stood up.

"You've got a funny way of showing it," Krycin said, taking another step forward. "Get out. I'll not be following you anywhere."

The reaper lowered his weapon and stepped forward. "You don't understand, you could ruin everything if you don't return." He reached out with his free hand and tried to take hold of Krycin's arm.

"I said, get out!" Krycin screamed at him. He thrust his hand forward once more and channeled more energy this time, slamming the orb into the reaper's body. An explosion of light sent both men flying in opposite directions. Krycin hit the far wall and landed on the couch he'd been sleeping on. The reaper smashed through the door and landed on the floor in the hallway. Instead of getting up, the reaper's body dissolved into black mist and dispersed into the air.

When Krycin caught his breath and looked up, both Gladius and Serrin were standing in the doorway staring at him. Gladius spoke first, taking a step into the room. "Krycin, are you all right?"

Krycin shook his head, trying to clear his thoughts. "I will be once this ringing stops."

"Who was that?" Gladius asked as he crossed the room.

"The reaper again. He tried to get me to come with him. When I refused, he attacked me. He said I could ruin everything if I don't return. What does that mean?" Krycin stood up and stretched.

Serrin entered the room and looked from one man to the other. "A reaper? You fought it, and lived to tell about it?"

"I told you he was powerful," Gladius said to Serrin.

"Why does he want me? And why is it a surprise that I'm still alive? Damn it! Somebody, give me a straight answer!" Krycin said, raising his voice in frustration.

"I don't know why he wants you," Gladius said. "There are stories, but they are more legend and myth than reality. The High Council is a better place to find these answers, and I am thinking tonight would be a better time to leave. As for fighting a reaper? Well, there are stories of those who fought death for a chance to keep living. But those stories always end the same way."

Krycin's face grew concerned. "How?"

"The reaper collects their soul, and they move on to the next life." Gladius lifted his head and looked Krycin in the eye. "As far as I know, nobody has ever fought a reaper and lived to tell the tale. Until now."

Chapter 4 – Teleportation

The three men regrouped out in front of Serrin's house. Morganath had returned and was lying with his massive body curled up over a volcanic vent, soaking up the hot air rising from it. Gladius collected their few things and brought them out while Serrin and Krycin made idle chat. When he was ready to go, Gladius approached Serrin. "I need you to teach Krycin how to teleport. If we are going to travel to Ducain's Keep with reapers in pursuit, I want to make sure that Krycin understands his powers. It may make the difference between life and death."

Serrin nodded. "After last night's events, I understand. I'll take him to my lab where he won't get hurt if he makes a mistake."

"Thank you, Serrin," Gladius said. "Morganath, are you staying here?"

Morganath snorted and said "You knew I would."

Serrin approached Krycin and motioned for him to follow. "Come with me, I'll show you around my lab and teach you some other things you can do as a Lyecian." Without waiting for a response, Serrin walked away toward the large gray building at the center of the caldera. Krycin was about to follow when Serrin blinked out of existence with a pop. Air rushed in to fill the space he once occupied.

There was a whoosh next to the lab door as Serrin reappeared and displaced the air. Krycin began walking there, but Serrin held up a hand. "No, don't walk. Jump here."

"I don't know how," Krycin said.

"Your body does, it's just your mind getting in your way. Ignore your mind. Visualize your destination in your mind, and will yourself here, the same way you draw the power for a spell."

Krycin closed his eyes and cleared his mind. Picturing the wood lab door on the gray building. He saw Serrin standing before him and willed his body there. There was a loud popping sound in his ears and it felt like the whole world twisted as he shifted from one place to another. Nausea surged through his body and he dropped to his knees. With one great heave, Krycin vomited bile out onto the grass beside the door.

Serrin let out a burst of laughter and knelt down beside Krycin. "Are you well? Do not be ashamed, it takes some getting used to. The first few times I did it, I also threw up. We will practice more of that once you've had a chance to see inside my lab."

With a sigh, Krycin stood up. "Sorry about that." He managed a weak smile before following Serrin into the gray building. The door opened into a small room where Serrin removed his outer red robe and donned a black robe instead.

He looked back at Krycin and smiled. "Follow me, we have a short time in which you must master this skill. Ideally, you won't vomit the second time."

"Yeah, sure," Krycin said. "Hopefully."

He followed Serrin into the next room which was a vast chamber with many tables, various equipment, and a pool of lava at the center surrounded by a short stone wall. The room was sweltering hot and smelled of brimstone.

Serrin walked to the other end of the room and said, "Now come to me."

Krycin nodded, closed his eyes and focused on Serrin's face again. There was another popping sound, and his head swam, but he felt fine otherwise. When he opened his eyes, Serrin stood before him with a broad smile. "Very good, my boy. Now, teleport yourself to the manor and back."

Without a word, Krycin did as he was asked, first disappearing from the lab and appearing in the parlor where he slept the night before. Once he established where he was, he focused again on the lab and Serrin's face and teleported back. When he stood before Serrin once more he smiled. "I think I've got it now. So can this be used for longer distances? Or is it short range?" Krycin asked.

"Well, that depends on the Lyecian. Some are more powerful than others and can move longer distances. Some can even traverse worlds. But you must understand that in order to teleport somewhere, you must have an excellent idea of where you are going.

Otherwise you risk teleporting into a wall, or the ground, or even into solid stone. Death would be instant, and unpleasant."

"Oh," Krycin said, with a grave expression on his face. "I'll keep that in mind." He looked around the lab once more. "So what do you use this place for anyway?"

Serrin didn't answer at first. His face was thoughtful as he stared at the center of the room, like he was trying to think of an answer. "Well, I do experiments here. Usually for the High Council, but occasionally for individual wizards as well. Lately, I've been working on a way to summon a dragon to my circle."

Krycin took one last look at the lava pool before walking toward the door. "Interesting. Have you succeeded?"

"Not as yet, but this is the reason why I asked for Morganath to come here. Should I be successful, it is likely that the dragon I summon will not be happy about it. Morganath is amongst the oldest and wisest of his kind, and will afford me some protection should things go wrong." Serrin paused a moment in thought. As Krycin's fingers wrapped around the door handle to leave, Serrin broke out of his thoughts and spoke up. "Krycin, a word of warning."

Krycin looked at Serrin before opening the door. "What?"

"Gladius is not who he seems to be. The Wizard High Council remains in power because of fear of what they would do to somebody who stood against them. In the case of Gladius, I wouldn't be surprised at all to know that he had some of his father's ability to manipulate people. He obviously thinks you still have something to offer him, or he would not be traveling with you. Be careful."

Krycin nodded. "Thanks, Serrin, I will." He exited the lab and met Gladius who was waiting outside.

"Come now, Krycin. We have precious little time," Gladius said. He walked to the northwest without sparing a glance back at Krycin.

After a few moments, Krycin followed him, still thinking about Serrin's warning.

Chapter 5 – An Appeal to the Council

The High Council chamber was peaceful and quiet. Eight chairs were arranged in a wide circle around a central platform where guests stood to address the Council. The room was large and circular, with black walls and gray stone floors. The circle in the center of the chairs had silver lines traced into it that formed intricate patterns and designs. Sitting in each chair was a powerful wizard, each having earned their position on the Council through an act of great skill, intelligence and power. One wizard of each element resided in the room and waited for their visitor to take a solid form.

A dark mist coalesced into a black robed figure who stood in the center of the eight wizards. His hood was drawn up over his head, hiding his face, but the scythe slung across his back marked him as a reaper. He took measured steps, turning in a circle so he could face each wizard in the room.

The gold-robed wizard Marius, representing Lyecha, spoke up first. "State your name and business before the Council." His voice was rich and smooth, and held an authority to it that was unmatched.

"I am Tyriel, a messenger of the Fates," Tyriel said. "I come before you to request the Council's help in apprehending a Lyecian who is on his way here."

A murmur went through the Council as they took in the odd appearance of a reaper before them. The red-robed wizard stood up and said, "Nothing is outside the Fates' control. Not even the gods. Yet, you would have us believe that a Lyecian is eluding you?"

Tyriel nodded. "I don't know how, but this Lyecian defeated me in battle. He must be returned to where he belongs."

Marius looked at the red-robed wizard. "Please, Lebriel, return to your seat."

When Marius spoke the name, Tyriel let out a gasp as though he had been injured and looked toward the red wizard with a sharp movement. "Lebriel?" he asked.

The red wizard pulled his hood back to reveal his face. A shock of red hair covered his head, and he had bright blue eyes. His pale complexion was that of someone who spends most of his time indoors, and his lips were pursed. He lowered his brows and said, "Do I know you?"

Tyriel took a step in his direction. "Not for a very long time," he said, pulling his hood back as well. The two men stared at each other as if there were a mirror between them. Marius looked from one to the other and saw the same man. "It's good to see you, brother."

Marius spoke up before Lebriel had the chance to speak. "What is it you wish us to do, reaper? If he is so powerful that he can defy the Fates, what can we do to stop him?"

There was a pause as Tyriel held his brother's gaze a moment longer before looking to Marius. "You must find a way to get through to him and get him to return to his rightful place in time. If he will not..." He paused, reluctant to speak the words he knew must be said.

Marius grew impatient. "And if he will not? Then what?"

Tyriel lowered his head. "Kill him. Even if it takes all of you combined."

"I don't understand," Marius said, his brows lowered so that the first signs of aging appeared at the corners of his eyes. "His rightful place in time? Nobody can travel through time, not even a Lyecian. I'm one of the most powerful Lyecians alive, and it's a task even I haven't figured out yet."

"I don't understand it myself," Tyriel said. "I'm just following orders. I've been told he's a threat. A threat to you, a threat to the gods, and a threat to the Fates themselves, though I don't think he knows it yet." Tyriel shifted from one foot to the other, showing his discomfort at being placed in such a sensitive position.

At that moment, the black robed wizard stood up. "When I spoke with my son not long ago, he told me of a Lyecian he was traveling with. Is that the one?"

Tyriel nodded. "Yes, Darson, they should be here within the week."

"Then I have a proposal: Allow Gladius to take on this task. He is more than capable, and has already befriended this Lyecian and gained his trust."

Lebriel shook his head. "No. Gladius is too young, and is still growing into his power. He lacks the wisdom and control required to perform a task such as this. If this Lyecian is as dangerous as the Fates say, allow me to confront him, talk to him, and convince him to go back to where he belongs."

"That's a lie and you know it," Darson said. "You're glory seeking, rather than accepting that Gladius is the best person for the job. He can do great things, if you'll only give him a chance."

"Talk about someone who is glory seeking," Lebriel said, raising his voice. "This is far too important for a pup like him."

Bareva, the white wizard, stood up and said, "I agree with Lebriel. Listen to reason."

"You would," Darson said, raising his voice above both men. "Sit down, before you hurt yourself, old man."

"Show some respect for the other Council members," Lebriel shouted back at him.

At that moment the entire room descended into chaos. Wizards of seven colors tried to shout over the other, and all insisting that they were right and all the others wrong. There was a sense of panic in the room that Marius hadn't felt for many years. When he grew impatient with their squabbling, he stood up and spoke with an amplified voice, "Order! I shall have silence and order in this Council."

The room settled and the other wizards returned to their seats.

"Thank you," Marius said. "We will vote. If greater than half the Council agrees, then it shall be done, and Gladius shall be given a chance. In an abundance of caution, a tied vote will be deemed a rejection of the proposal. Are we agreed?"

A chorus of voices filled the room, "Hear, hear!"

Marius looked at the gray robed wizard beside him. He raised his hand. As did the yellow and green robed wizards. Lebriel shook his head, rejecting Gladius. The blue robed wizard raised her hand. Darson sat with a smug expression on his face and raised his hand. Both the white robed wizard and Marius voted against.

"Five for, three against. So it is decided," Marius said with some concern in his voice. "Gladius shall be given the opportunity to convince this Lyecian to go away with Tyriel, or kill him otherwise.

Should Gladius fail, the task shall fall to you Lebriel, and all the rest of the Council members."

"Thank you for your aid in this dire situation," Tyriel said. "The Fates will not forget this." He pulled his hood over his head and dissolved into mist, dispersing into the air.

Marius addressed the Council. "I hope for all our sakes that Gladius takes this task to heart and does not allow his ambitions to get the better of him. There is little doubt that Gladius has the highest potential for power than any have had in a long time. Still, it is possible that Gladius could lose his life trying to complete this task. Are you prepared to lose your only son, Darson?"

"Ha! It will never come to that. Gladius is a grown man now, and a great wizard. If he fails in this task, it will be as a result of his own stupidity, and he will deserve whatever fate he claims." Darson's voice was serious this time, losing its mocking tone.

"I'm glad," Marius said. "This council is adjourned until such a time as Gladius and the Lyecian arrive."

"Understood," Darson said. He stood up and walked out of the room with his head held high. Marius motioned for Lebriel to stay and dismissed the remaining wizards.

When the last wizard exited and the door closed, Lebriel spoke up. "Is there a problem?"

"I didn't know you had a brother, and judging by your reaction to him, neither did you."

Lebriel lowered his gaze and said, "He died. Twenty years ago. I care not to talk about it."

"So long as this does not cloud your judgment," Marius said.

"It won't. You can trust me," Lebriel said. He thought for a moment and looked Marius in the eyes. "I don't trust Gladius. I think we've just made a grave mistake. There must be another way to stop this Lyecian. He's one of your people, couldn't you talk to him? Get through to him without the need for manipulation and violence?"

"Strange words coming from a representative of Ignith." Marius smirked.

"Ignith is only the god of war when war is required. We do not seek it, nor do we wish it," Lebriel said, returning the smile. "Talk to the Lyecian, privately. Make him understand."

"I shall. Until then, may the gods be good to you."

Lebriel stood up and left the room. Marius sat in the Council chamber alone for many hours by himself, thinking. And waiting.

Chapter 6 - Meet Cy Cooper

It took Krycin and Gladius six days to walk to Ducain's Keep, most of which they spent in silence. Once in a while Krycin would break the silence with questions about the landscape, plants, animals, or anything else that caught his attention. Gladius answered the questions, but did little more to stimulate the conversation. When they crested the final hill before the keep, Krycin saw the strategic value of the location right away. The keep was nestled in the middle of three sizable mountains arranged in a triangle, leaving limited avenues for attack if an army was to besiege it. It was built with solid granite and served as both the home of the Wizard High Council, and the largest academy of wizards in all of Galadir. Wizards of all elements and ages served and learned at the keep, many of whom were outside the walls practicing their latest spells when the pair drew near.

Gladius led Krycin straight through the front gates. The guards recognized Gladius right away and waved him through with his guest. Once they were inside, Gladius stopped. "I shall only tell you this once," he said, looking Krycin in the eyes. "You will be brought before the Council and questioned. Be honest. If there is anything you remember, be sure to tell them. Do you understand?"

"Yeah, I think I'm good." He took a deep breath to try and rid himself of the nervous feeling in his stomach, but it didn't help.

"Relax, Krycin, they aren't going to hurt you. If anything, they'll help you remember who you are and where you came from. This will be good for you."

"Think so?" Krycin asked, reveling in one of the few moments where Gladius seemed genuine and kind.

Gladius nodded. "Yes, I know so. Let's go."

He led the way to the heart of the keep and up several flights of stairs. At one point he spoke to a young boy and sent him off with a message, then carried on up to the highest point in the keep, to the Council chambers. When they arrived at the door, it was open and waiting for them. The two walked in to meet with the High Council.

They made their way to the center of the room where Tyriel had stood days before. Gladius stood facing Marius right away. Krycin looked around at each council member until Gladius nudged him and pointed toward the one in the gold robes. Marius stood, and with a smile said, "Welcome, my friends. I trust your travels were safe?"

"They were," Gladius said.

Marius looked Gladius up and down. "You've grown and matured since you left three years ago, Gladius. I trust the Ardans treated you well, and you learned what you were sent there to learn?"

"It was an interesting assignment," Gladius said. "Can we get to the point?"

A shadow fell over Marius's face at this comment, but he turned to Krycin rather than address it. "I've not met you before, which is unusual, because I never forget a face, and almost all wizards come through Ducain's Keep at some point in their careers. I am Marius, High Wizard of Lyecha, and you are?"

"My name is Krycin," he said.

"And you were found on the shores of Arda, after one of the worst storms of the last fifty years. Gladius tells me you have no memories?"

"That's right," Krycin said.

"Yet you remember your name?" Marius asked.

"Yes," Krycin said, but then thought about it for a moment. Marius must have read his expression because he waited for Krycin to continue. "Well, I can't actually be sure that it's my name. I remember a name. We assumed it was mine."

An amused murmur ran through the chamber that went away when Marius raised a hand. "I took the liberty of sending out runners with your name to all corners of the world to see if anyone anywhere has ever heard the name before. But nobody has. It seems that if your name is indeed Krycin, then you did not exist before you appeared on the Ardan beach."

Krycin frowned at this. "My plan was to head for Findoor, to meet with the wizard Merek. His is another name I have remembered during our travels from Arda to here. Gladius and I thought Merek might have an idea of who I am. Surely if I remember his name then he must have heard of or seen me before."

"That's a splendid idea," Marius said. "Gladius will escort you to Findoor and get you acquainted with the Arch-Magus. I am told you are a Lyecian?"

"Yeah, it seems that way," Krycin said.

"And you have Anam's gift over light and life as well?"

Krycin nodded and maintained eye contact with Marius, wondering where this was going.

"Then I shall also appoint a Lyecian to escort you to Findoor." Marius motioned to the opposite end of the room where another man had been standing unnoticed. "I'd like you to meet your new escort, a disciple of Grishtor. He will complement your powers over light and life."

The man stepped forward, approaching Krycin. He was dressed from head to toe in fine black silks and wore a broad brimmed hat. His skin was pale and his cheeks drawn in like he hadn't eaten in weeks. Krycin looked over the rest of him, which looked gaunt and thin. He had black hair and looked to be about the same age as Krycin. The man extended a hand and smiled. "The name's Cy, and it's a real pleasure to meet you."

His accent was strange, yet familiar to Krycin. He was about to extend a hand to Cy when another headache took him by surprise and raged through his skull, bringing him to his knees. The blue robed wizard on the Council stood up, but Marius motioned for her to return to her seat. "Are you all right, Krycin?" Marius asked.

The headache slipped away a little as Krycin raised his head. "Yeah, I think I'll live. Ever since I was found that morning, I've been getting headaches. I just need some rest."

"Cy, show Krycin to his room, and ensure he has anything he needs. Your journey to Findoor will begin as soon as Krycin is well enough to travel."

"Yes, sir." Cy said, and escorted Krycin out of the room, closing the door behind him. When they were a fair distance from the Council chambers, Cy spoke up again. "Some welcome, huh? 'Hi, bye, here's a new escort, get out of my face.'"

Krycin laughed as Cy did his best impression of Marius. "Yeah, I'm feeling pretty much like an inconvenience."

Cy nodded and smiled. "Don't you worry. Stick with me, and you'll do just fine. You should be with your own kind anyway.

Between you and me, I don't trust that Gladius. But we have to tolerate him because Daddy's on the High Council."

"Really?" Krycin asked, a little shocked at the revelation. "And they sent him all the way to Arda?"

"Yep. Nothing old Darson could do. Gladius got himself caught snooping around in the forbidden magics. Council voted seven to one to exile him until he could learn what it was like to truly work and strive for something. Darson fought it, but you can't win against seven Council wizards."

Krycin stopped in the middle of the hallway. "Exiled? Gladius told me he was on assignment."

Cy laughed. "On assignment? Gladius has a great sense of humor. It was a lesson he was to learn, about personal relations, diplomacy, and above all, patience. Had it not been for you, Gladius would still be there today, and likely for a number of years still."

"So," Krycin said, trying to put the pieces together. "Gladius not only lied to me, but he used me to get himself back here?"

"Welcome to Ducain's Keep." He slapped Krycin on the back and continued to walk. "Come on. We'll get you settled in to your room and then we can chat more. There are some things you need to know, but I don't think it would be wise to go over them out here where the walls have ears." He led Krycin the rest of the way to his room, which was only twenty more paces down the hall. "Here we are."

Cy pushed the door open and motioned into the room. Krycin walked in and looked around. The room was simple, with a rug on the floor beside a single bed. A small wardrobe rested opposite the bed, and a west facing window was in the middle of the far wall. Cy followed him in and closed the door behind him.

"Here's the deal," Cy began, sitting down on the side of the bed and motioning Krycin to join him. "Marius explained a little something about you to me. I know you've lost your memories, and you were hoping we could help you, but nobody here can. The thing about us Lyecians is, if we don't want to be healed, we won't be. We're hard to control in that respect. It's one of the things that makes us superior to all the others. If your memories haven't come back yet, it's because you don't want them to. When you're ready, they will come."

"So what you're saying is, I'm doing this to myself?"

"You catch on quick, boy." Cy flashed him a crooked smile and continued, "There's always a power struggle going on here. If you know what's good for you, you won't get involved with it. Heading to

Findoor is a good thing. I'm almost glad to be getting away from the mess for a while. Oh, and one more thing..." He paused and looked around, like he was making sure nobody was listening. "Once we arrive at Findoor, distance yourself from Gladius. He's bad news. Yes, he used you to get back here. He's an ambitious one, and will do what he sees necessary to accomplish his goals. Whether it means escorting you to Ducain's Keep and beyond, or putting a knife in your back."

Krycin looked at the floor for a long time, trying to comprehend Cy's words. "How do I know I can trust you?"

Cy laughed, revealing crows feet at the corner of his eyes. "Now you're catching on. I assure you, if I wanted you dead, you would be dead. I serve Grishtor, the god of death."

"So the opposite of me then?"

"If your element is life, then yes. That's likely why Marius put us together. Get some sleep, morning comes fast. We'll be heading out at first light." Cy stood up and walked to the door.

"Thanks, Cy. I'm looking forward to Findoor now. I don't want to be here anymore."

⊙

When Cy and Krycin left the chamber, only Gladius remained before Marius and the rest of the Council. Gladius shifted from one foot to the other as he felt all eight sets of eyes bearing down on him. After a long wait in silence, Gladius said, "Was there something else?"

Of all the Council members, Marius's gaze was the most intense. Gladius grew uncomfortable and felt as though Marius was peering straight into his soul. "Six days ago, the Council was contacted by a reaper," Marius said. "It seems the Fates have noticed a certain Lyecian you have been escorting around."

"Krycin?" Gladius asked, now interested in the conversation.

"Yes, Krycin. It appears the Fates think he's dangerous." Marius's face held a look of concern. "After meeting Krycin myself, I find this hard to believe. He seems pretty oblivious to what's going on, and genuine about his memory loss."

Gladius smirked. "Oh, he's genuine. But he also made quick work of the reaper the Fates sent to capture him, and that was without any combat training. If Krycin learns how to use his full potential, he could be one of the most powerful Lyecians who ever lived."

"And that," Marius said with some hesitation, "is why you are still here before us. We've been asked by the Fates to convince Krycin to turn himself over to their control, so they can return him to where he belongs. I don't yet know what the implications are of Krycin remaining here, but if the Fates themselves are worried, then I believe we have reason to worry as well."

Gladius stood silent, his eyes transfixed on Marius. After a few moments of deep thought, he said, "And why choose me for this task? Why not send a Council member after him?"

"The Council was divided on that decision. Those who think you're capable of this task feel you can leverage the trust you already have with Krycin to convince him to go peacefully."

"He's my friend. Of course I can convince him to go peacefully. But why would I want to?" Gladius asked.

"I believe if the Fates are involved, this goes beyond this world, and beyond anything the Council can control. If the Fates are afraid of this man, Lyecian or not, then he could be more dangerous than you could ever imagine." Marius paused to allow that to process. "Friend or no, he must be convinced to turn himself over."

"And if he refuses to go?"

Marius lowered his eyes to avoid Gladius's gaze. "Kill him."

"Understood." Gladius said, his expression troubled. He left the room without hearing anything else the Council had to say.

Chapter 7 – Betrayed

Krycin woke up the following day after the longest and deepest sleep he could remember. When he opened his eyes, Cy was standing over him. Startled, he sat bolt upright. "What the hell?"

A grin spread across Cy's face. "Hell? You are a strange one. It's about time you woke up. I've been trying to break you out of your sleep for an hour. Get up, change your clothes, and come have some breakfast. Then we're off to Findoor."

After Cy left the room, Krycin got up and walked over to the window. The day looked clear and bright, and the angle of the shadows told him it was already mid-morning. He checked the wardrobe and found extra clothes to change into. A light pair of black trousers and a white shirt, clothing typical of a runner, but not a wizard. With a shrug, he washed up, changed into the clean clothes, left his dirty travel clothes in a pile on the floor, and made his way to the common area that Gladius showed him the day before. Cy was waiting there, sitting at a table eating a light meal of bread and fruit. Krycin grabbed a plate and joined him. "So how far is it to Findoor anyway?"

"Weeks on foot. But we're going a different way."

Krycin looked surprised. "Oh?"

"If it were just you and me, we could be there in an instant. But since we're traveling with *Gladius*," Cy said, his tone sounding almost derogatory, "we'll need to use a more conventional method."

"Oh. When do we leave?"

"As soon as Gladius is ready," Cy said.

Krycin sat and ate in silence for a few minutes. When he couldn't take it anymore, he spoke up just to make conversation. "What is

Findoor like? I mean, the name rings a bell in my head, but I can't remember what it looks like."

"Rolling hills filled with green grass, blue skies, and a massive castle with an outlying walled city," Cy said, his tone nostalgic as he described Findoor castle.

Krycin stared at nothing and pictured in his mind's eye the castle, nestled at the bottom of a wide valley, gray stone walls surrounding a vast city, and at the center, a castle with spires that reached into the sky. His head began to throb. "And a flag," Krycin said, "a red flag, with a gold crown, and a sword through it."

Cy stared at him, dumbfounded. "So you *have* been there before."

"What?" Krycin said with a start.

"You've been to Findoor. You must have if you know their standard."

"But I don't remember being there. I just remember that image, in my mind." Krycin said, staring at the table, confused.

Cy was about to say something when Gladius approached their table and interrupted. "Time to go."

"Well then, that's that," Cy said, getting up from the table.

Krycin got up as well and followed Cy and Gladius out to the training grounds where the Council stood ready. In the center of the training grounds, gleaming under the midday sun, was a great gold dragon. "Morganath!" Krycin shouted, a smile spreading across his face. Morganath was sporting a new riding harness that he didn't have the first time Krycin rode on his back.

Morganath lifted his head and looked at Krycin. "Greetings, friend. It's good to see you again."

☉

The three companions traveled west on Morganath's back for several days, landing only to eat and sleep. Krycin spent most of his time looking around at the unfamiliar landscape and taking in the scenery. It was around midday the fourth day of travel when the first drops of rain hit Krycin's face. He looked up at the sky before them and saw towering storm clouds rolling in fast. "Shouldn't we land and take cover? That looks like a nasty storm," he shouted into Gladius's ear.

"Nay. Why would we waste time doing that?" Gladius replied. He looked forward and shouted, "Morganath, take us up above the storm. Push on."

The voice of the massive dragon rumbled beneath them. "As you wish."

Krycin felt a distinct push from underneath him as Morganath pumped his wings and took the trio higher into the sky, trying to outrace the storm that rushed toward them. The rain pelted faster and harder as they flew and the drops grew bigger. After only minutes, Krycin was soaked through and shivering from the cold. Cy sat behind Krycin and leaned closer to speak. "Lean in close to the dragon's hide. He's a creature of fire and will keep you warm as we go higher."

Krycin nodded and watched Gladius as he leaned down and flattened himself against Morganath's neck. Without hesitation, he followed suit and tucked himself down close to Gladius, trying to ignore the ice shards that now pounded them as they passed into the first of the massive storm clouds. The wind howled around Krycin and it took all his strength to hold on and keep from falling out of the riding harness.

A sound in front of him was only distinguishable by the vibration the voice made in Gladius's chest. He shouted something, but Krycin couldn't hear it. When he chanced a glimpse forward he saw what he suspected Gladius was trying to tell them. Despite all of Morganath's strength, he was losing the battle with the wind and the rain and was being driven down into the heart of the storm. Wind hit them in wave after wave, causing Morganath to list hard to the left one moment, and to the right the next. Krycin closed his eyes, wrapped his hands in the leather straps that kept him on the dragon's back, and prayed that they would hold out. His only reassurance was Cy, pressed against his back behind him.

The roar of the storm was all Krycin could hear for what felt like an eternity. The three men swung back and forth in their harnesses at the mercy of the wind and the rain. Morganath worked his wings with all his strength, fighting to get above the storm, but couldn't make it. Krycin could tell his strength was fading as the shifts through the air became more violent and it grew harder to hold on. He opened his eyes for only a split second and thought he saw a flash in front of him. Before he could question what was going on, the straps that held him in place went slack, and the whole world came to a stop.

Rain stood still in the air reflecting light like tiny crystals. Bolts of lightning hung in the air burning lines into Krycin's vision and creating bursts of steam as the intense electricity flash boiled millions of raindrops. No wind flew past his face as he tipped backward and lost his balance. He grasped for something to hold onto as panic filled him. Cy scrambled to hold onto him as well, but his weight had already shifted too far to the left, and with no riding straps, Krycin slid from the harness. Cy caught Krycin's sleeve just before he fell. "Don't you let time start again," Cy shouted, holding on with all his strength.

Krycin thrashed in the air, trying to turn himself around and grab hold of anything that could get him back up on Morganath. His cloak was too loose to hold him for long and he could already feel it slipping as his weight pulled at the sleeve in Cy's hand. "Help me," Krycin said, his heart racing so fast it was all he could hear. The silence of the world around him made it sound that much louder.

"Calm down, Krycin. Stop struggling and grab my hand. Focus on what you want."

Pain tore through Krycin's head. A voice boomed in his ears. *Clear your mind and focus on what you want.* Krycin screamed and grabbed his temples, letting his weight fall dead on the sleeve of the cloak. The material gave out, time resumed, and Krycin fell away from the dragon and his companions, screaming.

⊙

The wind and rain resumed and almost blew Cy from his own seat. He scrambled to grab the edge of the riding harness to keep himself on the dragon. "Morganath, we've lost Krycin!"

Gladius shouted back, "If Morganath changes course now, the storm will tear him apart, and we'll all die. Krycin will be fine, he's going back where he belongs."

"What do you mean? He belongs here, with me, and his people." Cy squinted through the driving rain and saw the satisfied look Gladius wore. "What did you do?"

"Exactly what I was asked to do. I've handed him over to the reapers." Gladius paused to replace his knife in his belt, then continued, "He doesn't belong here, Cy. He's a danger to us, and a danger to our world. The reapers will send him back."

A flash of light below them caught Cy's eye, and as he focused on where it came from, he saw another. "He thought you were his friend," Cy said without shifting his gaze from the white flashes. When he looked back up at Gladius, he spat one last word at him. "Human."

Cy let go of the riding harness and launched himself into the air in the direction of the flashes, hoping he wasn't too late, and hoping this wouldn't be the end for both him and Krycin.

For a few seconds, all Krycin did was scream. Darkness enveloped him, rain drove at him from every direction, and wind buffeted him around like a rag doll. He flipped and tumbled in the air and forgot which way was up. Thunder claps shook him to his core and made his head ache even worse. He fell for what felt like an eternity when he heard a whisper in his ear. "Come with me, and all will be right."

Krycin's reflexes moved faster than his mind. He summoned the power of light and created a shining ball of energy in his hand. With a jerk of his torso, he spun himself in the air and saw the source of the voice. Floating along with him was a black cloaked figure who was only semi-corporeal, a reaper. The storm didn't appear to affect him at all. In his hands was a long wooden shaft with a curved blade at the end. A scythe that reflected the light from every flash of lightning.

With a thrust of his hand, Krycin buried the ball of light in Tyriel's chest. It exploded on impact, sending both men flying in opposite directions and creating a brilliant flash of white light that lit up the sky. Tyriel recovered faster than Krycin thought possible and came flying toward him with the scythe raised for an attack. Time slowed again as the blade of the scythe crashed down on Krycin. He reached up and grabbed the shaft of the weapon, deflecting it to his left in slow motion.

When time resumed, Tyriel was disoriented, but managed to swing the scythe again. Krycin held up his right hand and called on his power again, creating a glimmering sword of light that blocked the attack. Without thinking, Krycin pulled the sword back and swung it wide at Tyriel. It should have been a mortal blow, and would have been to any normal man. Tyriel's body dissolved as the sword struck it and allowed the blade of light to pass through it without harm.

"You can't beat me, Krycin. Let us end this. Allow me to return you to where you belong." Tyriel steadied himself in the air, continuing his descent along with Krycin.

After a moments thought, Krycin replied. "Why should I? What makes you think I'm not exactly where I need to be? I may not remember who I am, or where I came from, but I know I came here for a reason, and I'm not about to leave until I find out why." His voice trembled as fear welled up inside him. He was aware of the ground below them growing ever closer as they fell. With his left hand, he summoned another ball of light and prepared to throw it, but before he could, a figure clad in black slammed into Tyriel, knocking him off his guard.

It took only a split second for Krycin to realize that Cy had come after him and was now wrestling in the air with Tyriel. Shouts went back and forth between the two entangled men, and the scythe flew away from Tyriel's hand and disappeared into the storm. Cy gave him one final kick to the chest and broke free, giving Krycin a clear shot at him.

Without hesitation, Krycin channeled all his power into one last shot and threw the ball of white light at Tyriel. It struck him in the back and exploded, sending Tyriel flying away, and blinding both Cy and Krycin for a second. When they regained their composure, Cy had managed to get himself to Krycin and grabbed his arms. "We must teleport. It's our only chance," Cy said, looking straight into Krycin's eyes.

"Teleport where?" Krycin asked, starting to panic again.

"To Findoor. Remember the castle. Remember the standard, and jump."

Krycin nodded and closed his eyes. He felt Cy's grip release him and heard the rush of air as Cy disappeared. With a vision of the green fields and gray stone of Findoor in his mind, and the flag with the crown and sword, Krycin drew in the power of time and space and willed himself to teleport.

⊙

Sunlight blinded Krycin as he opened his eyes. There was no impact. One moment he was plummeting to his death, and next the warm ground was beneath him. When his eyes adjusted he could see laid out before him, at the bottom of a hill, the city and castle from his mental picture. Cy ran toward him with a wide grin and laughed. "You made it! I knew you could do it. Are you all right?"

Krycin smiled at Cy and sat up. "I'm fine, thanks to you. Wet, but fine." He looked down at his drenched clothes, still shaken from the fall.

"I thought we were both about to meet Lyecha for a minute there. I told you not to trust that rat of a wizard. Gladius cut the strap. That's why you fell." Cy reached down and offered Krycin a hand to get up.

When Krycin was on his feet again, he could no longer contain his emotions. "Why would Gladius try to kill me? He's my friend. My only friend, other than you, and I barely know you. I've spent weeks with Gladius, learning from him, getting to know him. I can't believe he would do this."

"Believe it, boy," Cy said with a bit of a drawl. "He wasn't trying to kill you. He was probably under orders from the High Council. Friendship and loyalty don't matter to those filthy human wizards. He tried to turn you over to that reaper we fought. I'm amazed we both came out alive."

The words hung heavy in Krycin's head. *Filthy human wizards,* he thought as he looked at Findoor castle once more. After a few moments, Krycin said, "So what do we do about Gladius?"

"Nothing. He's not powerful enough to take on a Lyecian. Few humans are, and none could take on two Lyecians," Cy said. "He'll almost certainly report back to the Council that his job is complete, and then he'll get his reward, or not. The reapers didn't get you, and the gods only know why they're after you. We should talk to Merek."

Krycin nodded and said, "This place, it looks so familiar."

"Come on, let's go and see if we can get a meeting with Merek today. He's a very busy wizard, but he might spare some time for somebody he knows." Cy led the way down the hill to the city gates. The heavy wood doors were propped open and appeared welcoming. People moved in and out, many of them merchants and farmers. A few bored guards stood waving people by. When Cy and Krycin approached, one of them lifted a hand to halt them.

"You two, state your purpose here," the burly guard said.

Cy walked over to him and said, "We're here to see the Arch Magus, my friend."

"Is he expecting you?"

"No, but I don't think he'll mind seeing us. I escort an old friend of his, Krycin." Cy motioned to Krycin standing behind him.

"And you are?" the guard asked.

"Cy Cooper, I've been here before, though it's been a long time. If you need to, send a runner to the Arch Magus and check if he'll see us."

"That won't be necessary," the guard said, motioning them to go by. "Just making sure we have a record of who comes and goes."

Cy gave them one of his best smiles as he led Krycin through the gates and said, "Good work, men. You're doing your kingdom proud."

They made their way straight through the bustling city and to the front doors of the castle proper. Again, the doors were propped open and welcoming. They entered the castle without question and made their way to the inner chambers. When they reached a waiting room outside the throne room, a runner stopped them. "Halt, court is currently in session. Do you have business with King Valerra?"

Again, Cy stepped up and did all the talking while Krycin remained quiet behind him. "Nay, my good boy. We have business with the Arch Magus. Could you inform him that Cy Cooper is here for an audience, escorting Krycin?"

"Right away. Wait here," the runner said and disappeared into the throne room.

Cy sat down in a comfortable looking chair and motioned Krycin to do that same.

"They're all about procedure here. Always with the 'do you have an appointment' and 'is he expecting you'. They don't understand the ways of Lyecians. Impulsive, abstract, free spirits. I don't do well with rules."

"But Cy, aren't we just like them? I mean, humans can wield magic from the other seven elements, so they aren't that different right?" Krycin asked.

Cy looked at Krycin with offense, like he'd been physically injured by the words. "Not that different? Krycin, we can control time. We can move from place to place in the blink of an eye. There's a reason that a Lyecian is sitting at the head of the Council, and it's not because he has the best robe. We are far more powerful than normal humans, most of which can hardly master a simple spell, let alone something as complex as stopping time. And we do it without even thinking about it. We don't even require a focus for our magic. Not that different? No, I would say we are drastically different. It pains me to even have to interact with them. But we must."

"Cy, that seems like a narrow-minded point of view. I mean, you would put us above them?" Krycin said, his face concerned with this revelation about Cy.

"Yes. Yes I would, and you should too. No matter how hard they try, humans will never be as fast, as smart, or as powerful as us."

Krycin was about to respond when the runner opened the door and addressed them. "The Arch Magus will see you now."

"Well, that's our cue I guess." Cy got up and led the way in. Krycin followed close behind, now troubled by Cy's general view of the races.

As they walked into the throne room, Krycin looked around at the Council. The left and right sides of the room were lined with benches that were filled with people. At the far end of the room was a large throne with a proud looking dark-haired figure sitting in it. A gold crown topped his head and his dark eyes followed Krycin as he walked forward. Beside the king stood a man in gray robes with long brown hair that he wore tied back out of his face. His robes were threaded with silver that glittered in the magical light thrown from wall sconces around the room. Cy walked ahead of Krycin and straight to the Arch-Magus, avoiding the king. "Merek," Cy said. "It's good to see you again." Krycin heard an edge of contempt to his voice and assumed it was because he was speaking with another human wizard.

Merek looked down at him from the platform. "Cy, I never thought I'd see you here again. I presume this is Krycin, the man you brought to see me ? It is only out of curiosity and respect for the High Council that I grant you this, otherwise I would have had you escorted from the castle."

"Shame on you, Merek. Still holding a grudge? No matter," Cy said with a small amount of satisfaction.

"Get on with it, Cy," Merek said.

"Very well then. Yes, this is Krycin." He motioned for Krycin to step forward.

Krycin walked toward the wizard. As he did, he examined Merek's face. Krycin's voice was distant when he spoke. "I don't understand. You're so much younger than I remember."

Merek looked surprised by that revelation. "Younger? My boy, do not age me before my time. The Council led me to believe you have no memories of your past. Has that changed?"

"Not my past," Krycin said. The beginnings of another headache crept into his temples. "Just my memories. I don't understand it. A dream maybe? You were an old man, and you helped me." He paused for a moment and rubbed his eyes. "You helped me close a rift to another world." A burst of pain flowered behind his forehead. Krycin lifted his hands to his temples and held his head. A single droplet of blood fell from his nose and landed on the floor. "The dead world."

Krycin cried out and dropped to his knees. Lights flashed and danced before his eyes and the whole room tipped. He felt a pressure on his left arm and side before everything went dark.

Chapter 8 - Banished

Gladius held tight to Morganath and his harness and waited out the last of the storm before lifting himself up. When the wind died down enough, Morganath pumped his wings hard to get them above the clouds. Sunlight flooded over them as they broke through and Morganath settled into a lazy glide that had him skimming over the surface of the clouds. When Gladius was sure all was settled, he spoke up. "Morganath, we've lost Krycin and Cy. Krycin fell from the harness during the storm, and Cy jumped to rescue him. I think we should turn back and report to the Council what has transpired."

"Fallen? How could they? My harness is well made and strong," Morganath said, his voice booming through his hide.

"A strap on one side broke during the storm. Do not worry though," Gladius said with an edge to his voice he hadn't intended. "They are both Lyecians and are sure to have found a way to avoid an untimely end. It is shorter to turn back to Ducain's Keep than it is to keep going to Findoor. We must report this to the Council as soon as possible."

There was a long pause that made Gladius uncomfortable on the dragon's back. When Morganath did reply, there was a sadness to his voice. "Very well then. I do hope young Krycin is well. I shall return you to Ducain's Keep so you can make your report, and then set out to search for Cy and Krycin."

Gladius strapped himself down tighter into the riding harness. "Make haste, Morganath. Time is of the essence."

"As you wish," Morganath said in return. His wings pumped faster and the wind picked up. With his eyes closed again the wind, Gladius leaned forward and pressed himself flat against Morganath's neck. The pair stopped only when necessary, and made it back to Ducain's Keep in two days. When they landed in the courtyard, Gladius watched a runner take off into the keep ahead of him.

"Thank you, Morganath," Gladius said over his shoulder as he ran toward the keep. By the time he stepped through the front doors, Morganath was gone, flying off into the west. Gladius smiled to himself and made his way to the Council chamber where he knew the High Council would be waiting for him.

The doors to the Council chamber opened as he approached and the runner walked out. Gladius caught a smug look on the runner's face and seized him by the collar of his tunic. The runner gasped in surprise as Gladius slammed him against the wall. "You think it's funny to tattle on powerful wizards like a child?" Gladius asked him.

"N... No," the runner said. Fear washed over his face as he tried to avert Gladius's gaze.

Gladius pulled him away from the wall and shoved him down the hall, sending the runner crashing to the floor in a heap. The runner scrambled to his feet and ran away as Gladius stepped through the Council chamber doors.

Inside the chamber, the eight wizards were resting in their usual seats. In the center of the circle was a black cloaked figure who watched Gladius as he walked in. "Tyriel, it is good to see you again. I trust you took care of Krycin?"

There was a long, uncomfortable pause as Tyriel stared at Gladius from under his hood. A chill washed over Gladius, and he fought the urge to shiver. "I did not," Tyriel said.

Marius shifted his gaze toward Gladius. "Krycin appears to have gained some allies. Cy aided his escape from Tyriel. As of this moment, Cy Cooper, Krycin, and anyone else who aids them or harbors them in any way are enemies of the Wizard High Council, and will be dealt with accordingly. Gladius, you are to be returned to the island of Arda, having failed in your task. You will resume your research there until you have mastered it, and only then may you return."

Gladius looked from Tyriel, to Marius, and to each member of the Council. Outrage welled up inside him. "You would exile me?" He looked to his father. "Even you? Cast away your only son like a common criminal?"

Darson stood up with anger in his eyes. "Don't you dare speak to the High Council in this manner. It was because of your incompetence that you failed, and now you shall accept the word of this Council as law. Do not presume to know the extent to which you have failed not only me and this Council, but the entire world of Galadir. Tell him, Tyriel. Tell him what you have told me, so that my impudent son might understand the gravity of this situation."

"I have come before you today to inform you of the Fates' decree. Krycin is a danger to this world, and all worlds, and must be returned to his proper place. Every action he takes disturbs the delicate balance of time and space. If he is not returned to where he belongs, he will unmake existence as we know it. The Fates have spoken. Capture or kill Krycin by season's end, or they will destroy all of Galadir in order to contain him."

The news shook Gladius to his core. "Destroy..." he said, trying to come to terms with the news. "Season's end is a mere month away."

Darson walked in a semicircle around Gladius and Tyriel. "So you understand then, why we must now defer this task to the more powerful wizards. You had your chance. Your friendship with Krycin gave you an advantage, but that advantage is now lost. You will accept your fate and return to the island of Arda while the Council cleans up this mess."

"And if I refuse? Father, you know I can help. You know I can do this. Do not send me away like some hedge wizard. I'm part of this world too." Gladius followed after his father as he returned to his seat. "Please..."

"Stop begging. You sound like a child." Darson put his hand up before him, motioning Gladius to be silent. "Enough. In three days time, you will be sent by rift back to Arda. You will serve the Council as instructed, or I shall exile you myself to the Eastern Badlands and the Narshuks can have you."

Gladius opened his mouth to protest once more, but stopped himself. *If they will not allow me to do this, then I shall do it on my own,* he thought. *And when I capture and destroy Krycin, I will prove to them my power.* He opened his mouth once more and spoke, "Very well then, father. I shall return to Arda as you command." With that, he stormed out of the Council chamber.

⊛

Late that night, Gladius emerged from his room. His blue robes were tied tight around his waist to keep them from snagging on anything while he walked, and he wore blue leather slippers on his feet instead of his usual boots. His dark hair was tied back in a tight braid to keep it out of his face.

He made his way deep inside the keep to the second basement level and found the door he was looking for. A heavy oak door with silver runes traced up one side and down the other stood before him. He tried the door and found it locked. Drawing the power of water to him, he whispered a single word. "Exsiccatas."

A stream of blue light flowed from the door into his hand. As it did, there was a crackling sound as every trace of water evaporated from the wood and deep lines formed on the surface. Seconds later, the light faded and the spell ended. Gladius pushed one hand against the door and the wood gave out, crumbling to the floor in a series of dried chunks.

The smell of old leather bindings and paper flooded from the room the moment the door was removed. Gladius inhaled, taking in the sensation he longed for since he started studying magic. "With the power I find in here I'll be able to take care of Krycin, and then the Council will have no choice but to recognize my strength. Perhaps I can even replace my father on the Council." He smiled to himself as he stepped into the room.

Shelves filled the room from one end to the other. Books of every shape and size, both new and ancient, filled the shelves. To an untrained eye, it appeared a mess of various topics. To Gladius, each element was divided up by strength, author, subject. There was a complex filing system that was meant to deter the younger wizards from finding the most powerful magics even if they did stumble into the protected library of the High Council.

"I need the power of Lyecha," Gladius said to himself as he walked to the far corner of the room. "Nobody has any hope of slaying or capturing Krycin if they can't overcome his ability to stop time."

There were at least a half dozen shelves in the back corner of the room that housed books on Lyecha and her gifts. Most were written in high Lyecian scripts which Gladius had no hope of reading in the short time he had. He was about to give up when a single book caught his eye on the bottom tier of the last shelf in the corner. The cover of the book was white leather and the pages were gilded in gold. He reached down and pulled the book from the shelf. On the front there was a symbol of Lyecha pressed in gold. Gladius knelt down and opened the book, steadying it in one hand.

The pages were pure white and looked fairly new compared to some books in the library. Each page was filled with high Lyecian script that ran from edge to edge. He flipped through the pages until he reached one that had only a few simple lines on it, written in common:

> *Gifted by all the gods, the Traveler*
> *shall open the way to the Crossroads.*
> *A Time Weaver's soul is beyond the reach of time.*

Gladius stared at the lines for a long time, mesmerized by the way the letters curled on the page, the way the black ink bled into the white paper, and lost in the possible meanings of the words. He wasn't sure how long he stared at the page, but looked up when a figure appeared at the end of the aisle.

A red robed, red haired wizard stood at the end of the row with his hands on his hips. There was a moment of silence as Gladius's dark eyes met Lebriel's intense blue eyes.

"Gladius, you have some explaining to do," Lebriel said as he took a step forward.

"Why, Lebriel, whatever do you mean?" Gladius asked.

"You know well what I mean. Breaking into the restricted area? What were you thinking?" Lebriel asked.

"I don't understand," Gladius said. He stood up, closed the white book and tucked it into his robes.

"Don't play dumb with me, Gladius. Hand over the book and come with me at once. You'll have to face the Council for this crime. You'll be lucky if all they do is banish you to Arda."

Gladius scoffed at him. "I have no intention of going to Arda," he said, smoothing his robes out. "Or anywhere else for that matter. I'll not sit idly while a threat to this world runs free. You know the Council, they'll take forever deciding what to do, and by then, it will be too late. I won't sacrifice Galadir for the sake of their bureaucratic squabbling."

Lebriel shook his head. "So you're going to make another attempt? Don't you get it, Gladius? You had your chance. Now it's time to walk away and let the adults handle this. What hope does a child like you have of defeating a normal Lyecian, let alone one as powerful as Krycin supposedly is?"

Gladius took a step toward Lebriel and stared at him eye-to-eye. "A child, am I?" Anger flared up inside of Gladius. "You haven't any idea what you're talking about, Lebriel. I have a job to do, and if you stand in my way, things are going to get ugly."

"I'm standing in your way, Gladius. What are you going to do?" Lebriel asked. Fire burned in his bright blue eyes.

Gladius shrank away from the red robed wizard. "Fine," he said, "have it your way."

Lebriel relaxed and backed up a step, motioning Gladius to lead the way out of the library.

Without warning, Gladius spun around, held up a hand and shouted, "Congelascas!"

A bolt of blue energy fired from his hand and struck Lebriel in the chest, knocking him back off his feet. Frost covered his body and he shivered for a moment until he recovered from the attack. Lebriel didn't waste time getting up. He held up his hand and called back, "Incendras."

Fire flew from his hand toward Gladius. The blast struck him and knocked him back ten paces, taking out the sides of several book shelves in the process. He heard Lebriel's feet pounding the floor and coming after him. There was a brief window in which Gladius tried to move before a foot connected with his ribs, knocking the wind out of him. He gasped for breath, trying to clear his mind to call on another spell. Another kick to the ribs, higher this time, shattered a bone and sent pain searing through his chest.

"Did you really think you could take on a Council wizard?" Lebriel said, getting ready to drive his foot at Gladius again. "Did you think you were stronger than me? Faster? Smarter?" His foot connected with Gladius a third time, snapping another rib. Gladius felt the end of the bone puncture his lung. "You're nothing more than a hedge wizard, who got a little too big for his shoes. Your father can deal with you. He'll be down momentarily."

Lebriel walked back toward the door, and Gladius saw his chance. It took all his will to put his injuries out of his mind in order to call on the power of water. He drew all the power he could and gasped out the word, "Exsiccatas."

A blue light formed around his hand and extended away from him, reaching out across the room. Lebriel whirled in time to see the beam coming right for him. He tried to duck, but wasn't fast enough. The beam struck Lebriel's leg, connected, and formed a bond between the two men. Lebriel collapsed, screaming with pain as his leg shriveled under the assault of the spell. Gladius smiled to himself as he used his magic to sap the life from Lebriel, and restored his. The two broken ribs snapped back into place, and the internal damage healed. Gladius rose to his feet and watched Lebriel writhe on the floor.

Gladius moved toward him, continuing to feed power into his spell. "How does it feel to be helpless? How does it feel to be at the mercy of someone stronger than you?"

Lebriel tried to find breath enough to utter a curse at Gladius, but all that came out was a whimper.

"What's the matter? Can't speak? Too bad. I would have loved to hear your voice one last time before you die." Gladius once again called on the power of water. Focusing all his strength on one last spell, he spoke the words, "Merguntas."

A ball of water formed in his hand. He lifted it up to unleash the drowning spell on Lebriel, when a black mist appeared before him and coalesced into a black robed figure with a deep hood. Gladius threw the spell anyway, but Tyriel swung the scythe off of his back and swiped at the ball of water in midair. The blade hit the water, and vaporized it.

Tyriel moved like lightning, spinning all the way around and lashing out at Gladius with the scythe. Gladius didn't have time to flinch before the tip of the scythe buried itself in his gut. Pain bloomed there and coursed up through his abdomen as the razor sharp blade carried through, leaving an eight inch gash in his torso. He stumbled back and fell to the floor, and watched in horror as Tyriel drifted over to Lebriel. He was lying still on the floor gasping for breath. Tyriel looked toward Gladius and pulled the hood back. Bright red hair and blue eyes met Gladius's gaze.

"Not my brother," Tyriel said, "not now." He pulled his hood back up, picked up his brother, and both men disappeared into black smoke that drifted away.

Gladius gasped, holding the wound in his gut with his hands. With magic still in his mind, he cleared his thoughts again and spoke a word, "Restitas." Blue light surrounded his hands and sank into his wounds. They closed on their own leaving only a thin scar on the surface. Another quick spell and his robes were mended. He was about to leave the library when he spotted his father standing in the doorway.

"Move another step, and I'll vaporize you," Darson said, his brows lowered over his dark eyes in a scowl.

Gladius froze and stared back, his heart pounding. "I'm hurt, father. Why would you say such a thing?"

"Breaking into the forbidden area, rifling through forbidden books, attacking a High Council member, and for what?" Darson paused a moment, his gaze fixed on Gladius and his hands held at his side in a ready position. Gladius shifted his gaze from his father long enough to see that he was about to cast a spell. He tried to draw in power of his own, but the magic resisted his already drained body.

"You don't understand, father. I can do this. I can defeat Krycin and return him to the Fates. You think I've failed, but I've barely begun. Give me one more chance, and I will make you proud." Gladius took a small step forward, his hand clutched at his chest, holding the Lyecian book hidden under his robes.

"I understand perfectly. I have a son who is not only a failure, but a traitor. You have betrayed me, and betrayed the Council. You are hereby stripped of all rank, and banished to the Eastern Badlands. Never again shall you enjoy the luxury of instruction from a trained wizard. You are dead to me." Darson raised his right hand and pointed at Gladius, a soft glow surrounding it as magical energy built up around it. The last thing Gladius heard was his father's voice speaking words of power. "Relegatas seponasa excidai."

He felt a wrenching sensation in his gut and the library around him melted away into a rocky, desolate landscape. The shelves were replaced with barren tree trunks and the sky flashed with dry lightning from thick black clouds. Dried, nearly dead plants clung to walls and crevasses where they looked like skeletal hands reaching to the sky in prayer for a few drops of rain. Gladius checked his robes and breathed a sigh of relief when he felt the Lyecian book still tucked away. "I'll show you, father. Just wait and see."

Chapter 9 – Miracle Worker

When Krycin opened his eyes, he was lying in a bed with warm blankets and a soft pillow. The room was well lit, quiet, and smelled of incense. He tried to lift his head, but pain raged through it the moment he moved it. Letting out a groan, he rolled onto his side.

At the far end of the room, Merek sat in an old wooden chair watching him. He closed the book that he'd been reading and placed it on a small table next to him. He smiled and said, "You gave us quite a scare, young man."

The sound of Merek's voice reverberated through his head like a string of thorns being pulled through it. Krycin reached up and held his head. "What's happening to me? The headaches keep getting worse."

"I'm unsure, but I have a theory. You say you have no memories from before you woke up on the beach in Arda?" Merek asked.

Krycin opened his eyes wide, surprised at the level of knowledge Merek had already. "How do you know that?"

A hearty laugh escaped the gray robed wizard. "My boy, I've already been in contact with the Council, and I had a chat with Cy after you fainted. I was informed that various healers have tried to restore your memories, but failed. I think something is suppressing your memories. Your own body is in turmoil, because your conscious mind wants your memories to return, but there is something in the way. Your body is at war with itself, and like any war, each side will continue to escalate."

Krycin lifted his head from the pillow, ignoring the pain. "And what happens if neither side gives up?"

"Well, each side will use more and more fierce attacks, doing more damage in the process, and eventually, you will die."

"Die?" A look of shock and horror came over Krycin's face. "I don't want to die. Isn't there anything you can do? A healer that could fix me?"

Merek shook his head, his face growing sad. "I'm afraid not. This is a challenge only you can face and overcome. Something truly terrible must have happened to you for this to happen."

"I... I just don't know. All I get is hints. Vague glimpses inside my own mind. It's like there's a wall there, and I keep working to chip it away, and sometimes I make a hole and get to see what's on the other side. Then something fixes the hole, and I have to keep working at it."

"I have a proposal for you. Stay here and work with me, and I shall do my utmost to help you break through that wall and recover your memories." Merek gave him a warm smile.

"That's very kind of you, but I really have nothing to offer in return."

"Nonsense. Surely you have a secondary element. All Lyecians do. What is yours?" Merek asked.

"Life. That's one of the things I did remember."

"Then you can work with the healers. Now and then there is need for a strong wizard of life to cure diseases. I shall research your condition and get back to you. You have my word that I shall do what I can to help you."

"Thank you," Krycin said, pushing himself up into a sitting position. The pain in his head was easing up, and he didn't want to stay in bed anymore. "When can I start?" He managed a meager smile for Merek.

"Right away, if you feel up to it," Merek said. "Meet me at the front gates in twenty minutes, and we will visit the healer hall."

◉

Krycin spent most of the afternoon working. There were dozens of patients who were battling complex illnesses, some so advanced they had only hours left to live. The first patient he was assigned to, he felt an instant connection with. It was a young man, not even twenty yet, who had contracted a disease that rotted his flesh away faster than they could heal it. None of the wizards had been successful in curing the disease that devoured the boy's body.

He knelt down beside the bed and looked over the boy's unconscious form. His flesh was bruised from the inside, and large areas were black and red with rot. Pus oozed from every wound.

"We call it quickrot. Very rare, and thus far incurable," the head healer, Ryvis, said to Krycin. "All we can do is make the poor wretch comfortable. Those afflicted with the disease never live long enough for us to study the illness and find a way to cure it. Our top disciples of Anam have tried and failed to find a way."

Krycin looked up at Ryvis, a kind old man with gray peppered black hair, and said, "I've seen this before."

"Yes, we've all seen it before, son. It's curing it that's the problem."

"No. I mean, I know how to cure this." Krycin looked from Ryvis, to the boy in the bed. "I've done it before, I'm sure of it."

"If you want to try, you can. He has nothing left to lose. He will die regardless of whether you fail or don't try at all." Ryvis backed away, and watched Krycin stand up and take a deep breath.

Krycin cleared his mind and focused on the boy in the bed. Drawing the power of life, he channeled it into his hands. *Don't heal his body, eliminate the disease,* he thought as he placed his hands down on the boy's chest. A white glow surrounded first his hands, then his entire body as he drew in the magical energy required to destroy the infection raging through the boy. Krycin closed his eyes and saw the boy in his mind, the infection coursing through his body appeared as black specks that infested him. With all his strength, Krycin targeted the specks with the white, life-giving energy, and began killing them.

The white light transferred from Krycin's body into the boy as he drew all the energy he could. Bruises faded and blackened flesh revived to red, and then pink as the infection cleared his system. Krycin used his magic to fight the infection, but each time he thought he got all of it, more would appear. His arms ached from the magic flowing through them, and his hands burned. The energy cleared the last of the infection and brought life back to the boy. When the job was done, Krycin collapsed to the floor, his hands smoking and charred from the magic. The boy lay in bed in a peaceful, healing sleep.

Ryvis gasped and began shouting for others to come, claiming that Krycin had performed a miracle. In no time, all the other healers on duty were crowded around looking the boy over and marveling at his sudden recovery from the otherwise fatal condition.

"Dear Krycin, are you all right?" Ryvis asked, crouching down to help him up.

"I think so," Krycin said, looking down at his hands. "I think I need a healer though." He smiled at Ryvis, who cast a restorative spell on him to heal the burns.

"Magic like that would have killed us," Ryvis said, shaking his head. "I had no idea Lyecians could draw such power."

Krycin rose to his feet and looked down at his hands. Scars covered them where the skin had been healed. "Neither did I," he said with a smile. They spent the rest of the day going from bed to bed. Krycin healed everyone he could, but grew more exhausted with each one. The draw of magic took its toll on his body around dinner time when the room spun around him and he collapsed.

Ryvis again helped him up. "Go now, Krycin. You've done well today. If you push yourself further, I fear you will cause lasting harm to yourself."

"But there are more patients who need my help," Krycin said, shaking his head and trying to clear the fog in his mind that clouded his judgment.

"There will always be those who need your help, Krycin. But they shall be here tomorrow, and you can help them better after a long rest. I will escort you to your room myself."

"Okay, you have a point," Krycin said, relenting to the fact that he was too exhausted to cast anymore spells.

Ryvis walked him to his room and bid him rest well. Krycin was asleep the moment his head hit the pillow.

Chapter 10 – Soul of Death and Darkness

The skies over the Eastern Badlands were cloudy and dark, with the sunrise doing little more than making the gray, barren landscape visible. Jagged mountains provided many natural caves and holes for the dark creatures that lived in the inhospitable lands. Gladius found one such cave and slept the night on the cold, solid ground to restore his strength. He was awakened by the sound of creatures prowling around the opening of his cave. *Narshuks,* Gladius thought, remembering the giant wolf-like creatures that stood on two legs.

He scrambled to his feet and pressed himself against the wall, afraid of what they would do to him if they found him. His heart pounded as the Narshuks deliberated outside the cave for several minutes, though it felt like hours. After a small squabble that ended in one of the Narshuks falling to the ground outside the cave, the rest of them moved on.

Gladius waited until the rest of the Narshuks were on their way, and then approached the fallen Narshuk. It drew ragged breaths as it lay on the ground, a pool of blood growing beneath it. This Narshuk was smaller than most, and its black fur was streaked with gray. There were several gaping wounds in its side that were spouting a steady stream of blood. Even being smaller than the average Narshuk, this one would still stand nine feet tall.

As he stepped into the creature's field of vision, it growled at Gladius and said something in its native tongue that Gladius didn't quite understand. He shook his head at the creature and said, "Do you speak Common? I don't understand a lot of Narshuk."

The Narshuk winced as it drew another breath and spoke a single word. "Help." The word came out as more of a growl than actual syllables, but Gladius understood it well enough.

"Help you say? It seems we both need something. You need my talents in order to live longer than the next few minutes. I need your size and strength in order to live longer than the next few days. Fortunately, I'm in a charitable mood. Pledge me your life and soul in service to me alone, and I shall mend the wounds you are dying from. Anything less than that, and I shall walk away and let you die. Do we have an accord?"

There was a long pause while the creature thought about it, and fought against the pain of its wounds. Gladius kept a close eye on the creature, and after a long pause, it looked up at Gladius and sneered. "Agreed," it said, struggling with the common pronunciation.

"Excellent," Gladius said, "I'll hold you to that."

He moved around to the side of the creature with the largest wound and focused his mind. Calling upon the power of water, Gladius reached out and pressed his hands against the wound. When he made contact with the Narshuk, he whispered, "Restitas."

A blue glow surrounded his hands and flooded into the wound. Muscles grew and reconnected, knitting back together where they had been torn. Flesh spread over top of the wound and closed, leaving only a small scar. Other, less serious wounds closed as well, leaving the Narshuk alive, but weak. Gladius stood and backed up a step to give the creature some space. After a few minutes, the Narshuk rolled onto its side and pushed itself up. When it got to its feet, Gladius looked at it in awe.

It stood upright, but hunched over. Its arms were long and hung low until its claws were almost dragging on the ground. The Narshuk had a head like a wolf's but with exaggerated features. Elongated canines poked out below its lips and its eyes were large and dark. It wore leather straps covered with bone trinkets and had a knife made of bone in a sheath that hung from one of the straps.

Gladius smiled as he looked over the Narshuk. "Magnificent," he said. "Do you swear your loyalty to me, and me alone?"

The Narshuk bowed its head and managed a single word, "Yes."

"Very good. I'm Gladius, a wizard of Philana. Do you have a name?"

"Scrag," the Narshuk said without lifting its head.

"I have a need for more allies like yourself. Lead me to your people, and you shall have revenge on the one that did this to you.

While we walk, you can teach me your language, so that I can understand when they speak to me."

Scrag nodded and motioned him to follow. The two walked for two days. Scrag went over many of the basics of the Narshuk language with Gladius, who picked it up with ease. When they reached the edge of the camp where Scrag's tribe lived, they stopped. Gladius looked up at Scrag and said, "You're supposed to be dead, and I'll be dead if you don't protect me. Use Narshuk law, and challenge the one who did this to you. Offer my services to the tribe, for I'm sure you're not the only one who has ever been injured around here."

"What makes you think I can defeat him? If I fail, we will both die."

"That's a risk I'm willing to take. Without protection from you and your tribe, I'm as good as dead anyway. This will guarantee that I either live, or die quickly," Gladius said with a smile.

"I like the way you think." Scrag led the way down into the camp with Gladius following close behind. Other Narshuks saw them, but did not approach. Scrag made his way to the center of the camp and approached the largest of the Narshuks who worked on combat training there. Without warning, Scrag inhaled until his entire torso swelled up, and let out a long, powerful howl that shocked all the other Narshuks present. The sound of the howl radiated out in a wave from Scrag that washed over Gladius and incited rage within him. Gladius fought back the urge to attack, but Scrag's target stopped what he was doing and looked Scrag in the eye.

Gladius wasn't sure whether the look on the larger Narshuk's lupine face was fear, shock, or rage, but he saw a faint red glow in the creature's eyes and knew enough to back away from the pair before the fight began. All the other Narshuks around them backed away as well, leaving only Scrag and the larger beast in a circle together.

"You dare show your face here again," the larger creature said.

"I will have my vengeance, and destroy you for your treachery," Scrag said, and let out a second howl that was less powerful than the first, but just as deafening.

Gladius covered his ears, but remained attentive to what was happening before him.

The red glow in the larger Narshuk's eyes flared up with the second howl and caused him to fly into an unfocused rage. He lashed out at Scrag with a strength and speed Gladius hadn't expected.

Scrag appeared to be prepared and had a hand on a small piece of bone that hung from his belt. It looked like a snake skull.

The first attack from the larger Narshuk missed and he stumbled past Scrag spitting and snarling. Scrag crushed the skull in his hand and closed his eyes for a split second, then opened them and lifted his other hand to embrace the second pass of the larger creature. Scrag's hand was surrounded in a black haze, and though the larger creature buried his claws in Scrag's shoulders, Scrag managed to rake his claws across his attacker's chest. Both of them tumbled onto the ground and rolled to the edge of the circle. When they came to a stop, Scrag was on top and got himself to his feet. The larger creature lay wide eyed and gasping as black lines spread out from the flesh wound, which seemed superficial at first. It festered and spread to cover his entire chest in seconds. Black rot consumed the creature as he growled and snarled in pain, convulsing on the ground. After a few moments, his movement stopped and his head lolled to the side, black foam bubbling out of his mouth.

Gladius stepped into the circle and approached Scrag. Drawing the power of water once again, he placed his hand on Scrag's arm and whispered, "Restitas." Scrag's wounds closed and he breathed a sigh of relief.

Another Narshuk from the circle stepped forward and growled at Scrag. "Murderer," he said, and took a step forward.

"Justice is served. I made a challenge, he answered it, and lost. Grachen paid for his treachery with his life. You were there, Marg. You saw how he attacked me," Scrag said.

Marg paused and looked from Scrag to Gladius. "Who is this runt? Bringing outsiders into the tribe? Perhaps he's a gift? A snack," Marg said, taking a step toward Gladius and licking his lips.

"No," Scrag said, "This is Gladius, a blue wizard of Philana. He has won his place in our tribe. You will treat him as one of us, or suffer my wrath."

Many of the Narshuks gathered around the circle went back to their previous business. Gladius watched Marg look around and then back to Scrag. "We'll see about that," Marg said with a huff, and returned to his own business.

"Keep your eyes open," Scrag said to Gladius. "Don't turn your back on that one. He'll kill you if he has the chance."

"Thanks, Scrag. Perhaps there's something I can do around here to earn my keep? You're obviously trained in magic. Are there others?"

"Follow me," Scrag said, walking toward a small group of shacks built out of dried wood and thatch. They were decorated on the outside with various totems and fetishes and several objects carried the symbol of Grishtor, the god of death. Gladius followed Scrag to the shacks and entered the first behind him. Inside was dark and dreary. Several old Narshuks stood over beds with others in them, waving objects around and growling what Gladius presumed were chants of some kind. One of them paused as they entered.

"Scrag, you bring an outsider?" the old Narshuk asked.

"He is my lord, and welcome here. He is also a healer, and needs work," Scrag said.

"Work we have. Come." Scrag motioned Gladius to follow the Narshuk as it went out the back door and led Gladius to another, bigger hut. The moment the door opened, Gladius smelled death in the air.

This is where they go to die, Gladius thought as he walked through the door. A putrid stench hung in the air that Gladius had to force himself to ignore. The smell was of festering wounds and dying Narshuks.

The old Narshuk motioned to the hulking bodies lying in the beds. "Start anywhere. Finish when they are all well, or dead." It walked out of the room, leaving Gladius alone.

Gladius spent the remainder of the day casting healing spells in order to thin the number of patients in the hut. He healed the easiest first in order to free up some beds, and then worked his way up. Partway through, the old Narshuk came in and told Gladius to make note of the ones that were beyond hope of healing. When he was exhausted, both physically and mentally, he exited the hut and found Scrag still working in the first shack he passed through. He approached Scrag, ready to pass out from the stress of casting spells all day.

"Scrag, why are there so many?" Gladius asked, following Scrag to where he could get some sleep.

"The tribes are at war. They have been for many years. Resources are limited in the Badlands, and so we fight for everything we have. It is why we honor and obey our superiors, and why the strongest hold the highest ranks."

Gladius thought about this for a few minutes as they walked. "Why was I asked to mark the ones that are beyond hope?"

"Rest well, Lord Gladius. I will wake you when you are able to see the answer for yourself."

They arrived at a small hut at the edge of the tribe, away from the higher traffic areas. Gladius ducked his way in through the front opening, which was covered only by some dried reeds hanging from the top of the door. Scrag followed him in and motioned at a pile of light grasses and reeds on the far wall. "Sleep. I will wake you when it's time."

Gladius nodded and looked around the hut once Scrag left. The hut was small, only big enough for one Narshuk. There was nothing in the way of furnishings but the pile of bedding on the ground at the other end of the room. The floor was cold, hard stone and the walls were patched together with whatever sticks, twigs or scraps of wood that could be found. The roof of the hut was thatch, but wouldn't have kept out even a light rain, and a light breeze traveled through the walls without breaking. *Narshuks live like this?* Gladius thought as he walked over to the bedding. He knelt down and tested it with his hand. *More comfortable than I would have guessed.*

As he lay down in the bedding, he closed his eyes, and was asleep in seconds.

⊚

There was a low frequency rhythmic vibration that woke Gladius before Scrag came to get him. *Drums,* he thought, and lifted himself up off the bedding. *Why drums?*

He got to his feet and stepped out the door of the hut only to be assaulted by more, louder drums, and what sounded like howls of delight that came from the center of the village. His head still ached from the exhaustion, but at least he had recovered some strength and was now curious about what was going on.

Light blazed from the center of the camp and lit up the clouds above. A massive fire was burning and Gladius could see the tips of the flames shooting up above the tops of the huts. *Fire? In a tribe starved for wood?* He walked faster toward the light and sound, unable to contain his curiosity. He was close to the center of the tribe when Scrag stepped out in front of him and blocked his way. "I told you I would come and get you. It is dangerous here."

Gladius came to a halt at Scrag's feet and looked up, meeting the Narshuk's gaze. "Why is it so dangerous? And why are you burning so much wood when there are huts that are barely standing?"

There was a strange look on Scrag's face that Gladius couldn't place. He thought it might be anger or annoyance, but the more he wondered, the more he thought it was amusement. After a brief pause, Scrag said, "Be quiet and follow me. Do not be seen, as these rituals have never been seen by outsiders who lived to tell about it."

Scrag led the way without waiting for a response. They were at the edge of the tribal circle when Scrag pointed Gladius to a shadow. Gladius hid himself and was surprised at the view he had. Scrag continued into the circle and joined in the ritual.

Laid out before Gladius was a wide circle of Narshuks all growling and howling a chant that went along with the beat of the drums. Two Narshuks at the far end were the source of the drumming and they played through the night without taking a single break. At the center of the circle was a massive fire that flew up from the ground, but what surprised Gladius was that there was no wood fueling the fire. Instead, one Narshuk shaman danced around the fire, summoning a red glow to its hand and howling over it to create a massive gout of flame that kept the fire going without fuel. Gladius could feel the magic in the air, raising the hairs on his arms and the back of his neck. The beat of the drums, which was harsh when he first woke, was now lulling him, soothing his mind and enticing him to get up and join. He fought back the impulse, but it was strong.

Other shamans danced in the circle as well, each performing their own magics. An opening was made at one end of the circle and the first of the hopelessly ill and dying Narshuks were brought in, supported by others. A Narshuk shaman in the center of the circle raised his hand into the air and howled a long, keening howl. At the opposite end of the circle, a massive Narshuk pushed through the edge and joined the ritual. The newcomer dwarfed the rest of the Narshuks in the circle and made the ground shake as it danced.

The shaman lowered its arm and a black flame erupted from its hand. In one smooth motion, it thrust its arm forward and plunged its hand into the dying Narshuk. Moments later, it pulled back and took a black orb that pulsed with living energy from the creature's body. There was no wound, but the dying Narshuk slumped to the ground. The shaman walked over to the giant Narshuk and pushed the black orb into its body. The energy of the orb infused the giant Narshuk and made it shudder, and then howl with a rage Gladius had not known in all his life. When the ritual was complete, the giant Narshuk left the circle, and the ritual was repeated for other Narshuks Gladius had flagged earlier that day, each time with a new warrior on the receiving end of the energy.

After some time, Scrag left the circle and returned to Gladius who stood in awe of the power Narshuks wielded. "What are they doing, Scrag? And how are your shamans casting fire spells?"

"Empowering our warriors with the essence of the dying. We do not waste anything in the badlands," Scrag said, walking past Gladius and motioning for him to follow. "Some shamans have taken the essence of wizards they find wandering the badlands. Once they do, they can use the elements those wizards could."

"Why do you not leave the Badlands? This is no place for any creature to live."

Scrag stopped in his tracks and glared at Gladius with hate in his eyes. "You wizards keep us here. A single tribe alone cannot defeat an army of wizards and trained soldiers, especially if they have Lyecians. It would take all the tribes just to breach the Findoor border, and even then, they would drive us back."

Gladius took a step back, unsure of what Scrag might do. When he was sure Scrag wasn't going to attack him, he said, "I've seen the way you live, and you're right. I have a Lyecian to kill. When that task is done, I swear to you I will do what I can to help the Narshuks step out of the shadow of wizards and take their rightful place in the world. But I need help."

A growl rumbled up from deep within Scrag's chest that startled Gladius. "You cannot kill a Lyecian. No wizard can."

"What if I told you I found a way?" Gladius asked, reaching into his blue robes and withdrawing the white Lyecian book. "What if I told you I could change everything for the Narshuks?"

"If you could do that," Scrag said, "you would have all the help you need. But you must prove yourself to the tribe first. They will never accept you if they do not respect you. And they will never respect you if they do not fear you."

"Then I will make them fear me," Gladius said, and walked back toward the fire.

The rituals were still happening when Gladius broke the edge of the circle. Most of the surrounding Narshuks paid no attention to him as he pushed past them, but once he was in their circle, every Narshuks' eyes were on him. Marg stepped forward with rage filled eyes. "You dare break our circle, outsider. Nobody can protect you now. You're mine."

Marg ran at Gladius, snarling. It took only a split second for Gladius to summon the power of water. A blue glow surrounded his right hand as he waited for Marg to come within range of his spell.

When the Narshuk lunged at him, Gladius thrust his hand forward and shouted, "Congelascas."

Magic poured forth from his hand in a blue stream and hit the Narshuk who was too far into his run to stop or dodge. The energy of the spell pulled all the warmth from the Narshuk's body. Frost formed over its skin and its entire body froze solid. Gladius flicked his wrist as the last of the energy drained and created a pulse in the stream. When the pulse hit the frozen Narshuk, it exploded, raining chunks of frozen flesh across the circle and into the crowd.

Silence followed as all surrounding Narshuks stared at the frozen pieces on the ground. Gladius walked slowly around the circle, facing the shamans who were performing the rituals. "What you did for the warriors, you will do for me," he said, and addressed the rest of the tribe. "In return, I'll show you the meaning of might. I'll unite the tribes, and help you show the world that the Narshuks do not belong in the badlands. I'll show the world that the Narshuks belong in Findoor, in Caldoor, and as part of all the nations of Galadir. And if they will not accept you into their lands, then we will destroy them all, together!"

Gladius looked around at the tribe for any show of support, and at first was met with angry stares. Scrag entered the circle and stood before Gladius, staring down at him into his eyes. He stared back with no fear in his heart. After what felt like an eternity, Scrag bowed his head, then lifted it high and howled as long and as loud as he could. One by one, the other Narshuks joined him until the entire tribe showed their support. The drums began again, and the shamans danced, and Gladius waited as the next dying Narshuk was brought out.

A shaman slammed a hand into the Narshuk's body and removed its soul into a small black orb. A slight pang of fear crept up on Gladius as he stood waiting, unsure of what would happen, or how it would feel. The shaman didn't wait for approval, but instead bolted toward him and slammed the orb into his chest, sending him flying back through the crowd and out of the circle.

The energy of the Narshuk soul coursed through his body and merged with his own soul. He felt the new source of power open up to him as the last of the energy settled. With a deep breath, he opened his eyes, not realizing he had even closed them. Scrag stood over him with curiosity in his eyes and offered Gladius a hand. Gladius reached up and took the hand and was on his feet in one quick motion.

The world around him looked different. Darker. The clouds churned and rolled above them, lit up by the light of the fire. He spotted dead trees, brush, plants and even the dead bodies of the Narshuks who had given their lives to help the rest of the tribe. Everywhere he looked he saw death, a raw power that he couldn't control. "I must pay a visit to Findoor," he said to Scrag. "If I am to control this power, I will need knowledge, and Ducain's Keep is far too dangerous for me to sneak into. Merek keeps a private library at the heart of Findoor castle."

Scrag motioned to the shamans in the circle. "There is one that can send you there."

"Then we leave at once," Gladius said and followed Scrag back to the circle.

Chapter 11 - Enemy of the Fates

Krycin awoke the next morning to a firm pounding on his door. He took a few seconds to clear his head and look around before getting up and answering it. Standing in the hallway was Merek and Cy, both with serious expressions. Merek was in his usual gray robe with gold embroidery on the edge. Cy wore black traveling clothes that were a bit worn but clean. "Something the matter?" Krycin asked, looking back and forth between the two men.

Merek stepped forward and gave Krycin a warm smile. "May we come in?" he asked, and stepped into the room without waiting for an answer. Cy followed and closed the door behind him. "Krycin, if there is anything you can tell me about your past and your memories, now is the time to do it."

"I remember nothing before I woke up on the beach in Arda other than small glimpses. Like looking at a large picture through a small keyhole," Krycin said. "But you know this already. What is this about?"

"I received a communication from the Wizard High Council late last night. The news," Merek said, his expression darkening, "was not good. The High Council has declared you an enemy of the Council, and an enemy of Galadir. You are to be taken back to Ducain's Keep, where you will be turned over to the Fates. My orders are clear on this."

Krycin stepped back away from Merek and Cy, a look of shocked horror washing over his face. "An enemy of Galadir? What did I do to deserve this?"

"I am uncertain, but what I do know is that this is likely linked with the events that occurred in the sky on your way here," Merek said.

"What? What events? I won't go. You can't make me. I've done nothing wrong, why should I be the target of some kind of witch hunt?" Fear and anger swam through Krycin's mind as he looked back and forth between the two men.

Cy stepped forward and raised a hand. "Calm down, Krycin. Nobody here is going to allow this. I discussed our journey here with Merek last night and told him all about you and Gladius and what happened in the sky before we arrived here in Findoor. If you think I'm going to allow one of *them* take one of *us* away like a common criminal..." Cy laughed at this prospect.

The wave of anger slowed when Krycin heard this. "So what now? Why are you here?"

"I came to you today to get you to safety," Merek said with a warm smile. "Until we can sort out who you are and what happened to your memories, Cy is going to take you somewhere safe. I shall inform the Council that you have escaped and your whereabouts are unknown."

There was a moment of silence between them as it all sank in. When Krycin got things straight in his head, he looked up at Merek and said, "Why? I mean, I appreciate what you're doing for me, but why take risks for me?"

Merek laughed and replied, "I seldom see eye-to-eye with the High Council. Bureaucracy is something I have little tolerance for. If they do have a good reason for this order, they are keeping it to themselves, and thus I am not inclined to follow it. Go with Cy, and I will do my utmost to get this mystery solved. The Council will not find you where Cy is taking you."

"Thank you, Merek," Krycin said. He looked at Cy who was wearing a smile that he tried to use to hide something he was thinking, but Krycin could see the trouble in his eyes that gave away his concern. "When do we leave?"

"As soon as we can," Cy said. "We expect the High Council will be here any time now to take you away. We must be gone before they get here. Gather your things and meet me at the front gates."

Merek stepped forward and put a hand on Krycin's shoulder. "Don't worry, Krycin. I will get this sorted out for you. It's not the first time the Council has made a mistake. Make haste, there is not a moment to lose." Merek left the room with Cy following close behind.

⊙

Krycin stuffed his few things in a pack that a runner had brought him and walked out to the front gates of the castle where Cy waited for him beside two horses. He looked at the horses and then back to Cy. "I don't remember ever riding a horse before."

Cy looked at him like he was crazy, but gave him a quick lesson once the two mounted up, and then headed out on the road. The day started out clear and sunny, but that changed as the sun reached its peak. Dark clouds rolled in and the wind picked up. Cy slowed enough to let Krycin catch up beside him. "We had best hurry, or we'll get caught in the storm."

"Where are we going?" Krycin asked, shouting over the wind whipping past him.

"It's a surprise. Just follow me, and stay close."

The two men rode another several miles before Cy veered off the path. There were some rocky hills in the direction he headed and a small mountain just past them. Cy headed for a path that led between the hills. Several minutes passed as they drew closer to the valley that led to the mountain, when the rain started to fall. There were only a few drops at first, but it increased to a steady downpour.

Cy pushed his horse harder, racing across the fields and into the valley. Krycin followed him, trying to keep up the best he could, but he fell behind, unable to maintain Cy's speed and still remain on the horse. It took them another twenty minutes to reach the foot of the mountain, and a small cave entrance where they could find shelter. They were both drenched through and freezing cold but Cy laughed anyway. "That was a heck of a ride, huh?"

"Yeah. Not really my idea of fun," Krycin said, taking off his shirt and wringing it out.

Cy gathered up some dry wood inside the cave and lit a small fire, and the two men stripped down to their underclothes and hung their wet shirts and pants in the warmth to dry. Krycin sat down cross-legged beside the fire, trying to keep warm. "Narshuk claws," Cy said, breaking the silence. He pointed at several old scars down Krycin's thigh, two distinct lines and a single opposing line that matched them.

"What?" Krycin asked.

"On your leg. It looks like Narshuk claws would have made those wounds."

Krycin looked down at the scars and examined them. "What's a Narshuk?"

"Twice the height of a normal man, covered with fur, head of a dog. Sharp teeth, sharp claws, and only two fingers and a thumb on each hand." Cy made a gesture with his hand, mimicking the way a Narshuk hand would have grabbed onto Krycin's leg.

"Sounds terrifying."

"Just pray you never meet one. We're lucky they are a disorganized bunch. They live far to the south, in the western badlands. But there is always so much infighting and tribal rivalry that they never rally to form anything more than a minor nuisance on the border."

Krycin took one more look at the scars on his leg and felt the beginnings of a headache coming on. "Can we talk about something else? Where are we going anyway?"

"We're going to a special place. You'll love it, I promise. They'll provide you with a safe place to stay while Merek deals with the Council," Cy said, checking his clothes to see if they were dry.

"They? Who are 'They'?"

"Old friends of mine. They live on the other side of this mountain range. I figured since you are gifted with the element of life, and seem pretty powerful with it, that you would want to meet those who are Anam's children. You'll see. Soon."

Krycin watched the fire dance for a while longer, and must have nodded off, because the next moment he knew, Cy was shaking his shoulder. "Come, Krycin. Our clothes are dry. Let's go."

His rest left him feeling refreshed. They dressed themselves and made sure the horses were tied up as they wouldn't be able to navigate the caves. Cy led the way deep into the mountain. There was little light and the air was dank and humid, but not stale. A breeze drifted through the cave that carried with it the smell of fresh greenery and flowers. Once Krycin produced an orb of light to carry, he was able to keep up without a problem. They traveled several hours more through a series of twisting tunnels before they emerged into a vast clearing.

The sky above them had cleared up and was now a network of stars. A bright full moon lit their way, revealing a clearing filled with lush vegetation. A rush of water told Krycin there was a river nearby, and possibly a waterfall. Cy stopped at the exit of the cave and said, "We should set up camp here. They don't take kindly to night visitors. We will present ourselves in the morning."

It took little time at all to find a good place to sleep for the night. When Krycin lay down, he was asleep in minutes, as was Cy. They awoke with the first light cresting over the rocky ridge that surrounded the place. With sunlight washing down over the whole area, Krycin was able to see that it wasn't so much a clearing as it was an old crater that had grown over with trees, shrubs and other greenery, making it an ideal home for all sorts of wildlife.

Along the sides of the bowl, hanging off the rocky slopes that led down into the forest, were many small pods made of branches and leaves. They all looked empty, but a quick glance up revealed that the residents of these pods were high in the sky, circling the area. Man-sized creatures flew in circles on wings of silver and gold feathers. They had arms and legs, and looked like humans with wings except for their heads. Their heads were covered with the most beautiful feathers Krycin had ever seen. The feathers in their crests glittered and glowed in the sun, creating all sorts of colors that shimmered and danced on their heads. Their face was that of a bird, with a large beak, and eyes that were set forward like a predator.

In his awe, Krycin barely heard Cy speaking. "I give you the Fioraden."

He smiled and walked ahead of Krycin down a path that led to a giant waterfall. Krycin followed and watched the crashing water flowing from a wide river at the top of the ridge. The water fell into a deep hole at the center of the crater and then ran away underground. Cy approached a stone platform that overhung the hole and blew out the loudest whistle Krycin had ever heard. Several Fioraden noticed them right away and circled down to meet them.

When the creatures landed on the platform in front of Cy, they made almost no sound. Their beauty and grace left Krycin staring as they made their greetings to Cy, who already appeared to know them. Cy motioned for Krycin to approach, which snapped him out of his daze. He stepped onto the platform and bowed before them like he'd seen Cy do before the king of Findoor. "Ferron, Tersca, this is Krycin," Cy said, presenting Krycin to them like a dignitary. He looked at Krycin and said, "Krycin, this is Ferron, the lord of the Fioraden, and Tersca, his wife."

Ferron was tall, with black feathered wings and mane, and blue eyes that captivated Krycin. Tersca stood several hands shorter than her husband, and had a mix of iridescent blue and white feathers. Her eyes were brown and left Krycin feeling like she was looking right through him. Krycin smiled at them both and said, "It's good to meet you."

As it is you, a strong male voice said in Krycin's head. It took Krycin off guard because it sounded like a man before him speaking, but Ferron's beak didn't move when he heard it. The Fioraden lord must have seen the confusion on his face, because he heard the voice again, *Do not be alarmed. We do not speak the same way you do. Our minds are linked in a single consciousness, which allows us to communicate without speaking.*

There was a word that came to Krycin's mind, that he said before he could stop himself. "Telepathy."

Yes, a female voice said in his mind, *Telepathy is the proper name for it. Though this is more complex than just telepathy. A single shared consciousness that allows our individual minds to speak to many at once.*

Cy looked at Krycin and shook his head. "Sometimes you surprise me. I brought you here because I thought you could learn something from the Fioraden. And with their enhanced mental abilities, they can keep you hidden from the Council and perhaps help restore your memories."

There was a pause as Krycin considered this. "Thank you, Cy. Are you staying as well?"

"I'm afraid not. The Council will be suspicious if I'm not there as well to confirm Merek's story, so I must go. But don't worry, I'll take care of the horses." Cy turned back to the Fioraden who watched with patience. "I'll leave him with you then, and come back when things blow over." He gave Krycin a wink and then disappeared with a pop before Krycin or the Fioraden could say anything further.

Krycin looked up at the two before him with a nervous expression. "So. You can help me remember?"

We're going to try, Ferron said. There was a strange glimmer in his blue eyes that Krycin wasn't sure was sadness, or pity. *I offer you no promises, though. Come, we will take you to the inner chambers and show you where you will sleep during your stay here. Then we can start learning from each other.*

"Sounds good to me," Krycin said with a smile.

Chapter 12 - Threat of War

Merek was working deep in the basement of Findoor castle in a secret chamber. A pool of water rested in the center of the musty room. The smooth surface acted like a mirror in the dim light, creating a perfect image of the rocky ceiling. Merek stepped around the pool, calling on the power of shadow to fuel a complex divination spell. When he made a complete circle around the pool, he stopped and held his hands out above it. A gray glow surrounded his hands and he spoke ancient incantations, channeling the energy into the water. The gray light formed into a ball and left his hands, plunging into the pool.

The dim light flared to life under the water, stretching and warping into images. First a series of hills with a rocky mountain slope behind them. Then a cave that led into a large crater. Merek commanded the spell to seek out Krycin. The image shifted and honed in on the large hole at the center of the crater. Krycin stood at the edge of the platform speaking with two Fioraden nobles.

When Krycin appeared in the image, a dark mist appeared at the far end of the room. The mist moved into the shape of a man and coalesced into a dark cloaked figure opposite Merek. It was enough to distract Merek and break his concentration, causing the image in the pool to disperse. "Blast it!" he said, looking up at the figure. "Tyriel."

He said the name like it was all that needed to be said. Tyriel responded in turn. "Merek."

"Don't you have work to do?"

The reaper pulled his hood back to reveal his face. "You have the Lyecian," Tyriel said, his tone level, but serious.

"I do not. He fled when he heard the Council was after him."

"There is a problem, and Krycin is the source. I must speak with him," Tyriel said.

"I neither know where he is, nor do I have any interest in helping you find him. He is an innocent, that I know, and is being unfairly targeted by the Council. What ever the problem is that you and the Fates have with him, you will have to solve it without my help. I'll have no part of it."

"Merek, you must understand, there is more at stake here than just my life or Krycin's." There was an urgency to Tyriel's voice that Merek couldn't ignore, but as he was about to say something more, a small bell at the entrance to the room rang, telling him somebody had entered his lab.

"If you'll excuse me," Merek said, walking toward the entrance to the chamber that was camouflaged on the other side, "I must attend to a visitor. If you are here when I return, we shall discuss this further."

Without waiting for an answer, Merek returned to the main lab. He was just closing the secret entryway to the back chamber when a knock came at the door. He crossed the room and checked to see who was there. The moment he opened the door, a young runner with long brown hair barged into the room. "Arch-Magus Merek, you have been summoned by King Valerra to attend an emergency council meeting immediately."

"Thank you, young man. Now get out of my lab. And do not enter again without an invitation."

The runner got a sheepish expression on his face, nodded, and left at a full run. Merek followed at a much slower pace, navigating through the castle and to the upper region where the throne room was. When he arrived, the doors were closed and he could hear arguing going on inside. Without knocking, he pushed open the doors.

Silence fell as they opened. Inside, seven of the eight wizards of the High Council stood at the front of the room. Three were on each side of the king, with Marius sitting in Merek's seat looking the most severe. None of the Council members looked at all happy to see him.

"Your Highness, Council," Merek said in greeting, putting on a casual air.

"Merek," Valerra said, "my most trusted advisor. The Council tells me that our fair kingdom is harboring a fugitive. Is this true?"

Merek lowered his gaze to the floor and said, "It was. But it is no longer. He fled when he heard the Council was seeking him."

"There you have it," Valerra said to Marius. "The man you seek is no longer here. You will have to seek him elsewhere."

"I know you're hiding him somewhere, Merek," Marius said, standing up and stepping down from the king's platform. "There are forces at work here that none of us understand. The Fates themselves cannot control this Lyecian. An ultimatum has been issued. Find a way to get the Lyecian under the Fates' control, or they will annihilate our world to contain the damage being caused. So I will ask you one last time, Merek, where is the Lyecian?"

There was silence in the room as the king, the court, and all the other Council members watched Merek and Marius stare each other down. Merek opened his mouth to say something, but a voice behind him broke the silence instead. "Don't be silly, Marius. I'm right here," Cy said, his voice echoing through the chamber.

Merek spun to face him and looked relieved when he saw Cy. Marius sighed and said, "King Valerra, do not allow this madness to continue. We will take Krycin peacefully, or we will take him by force. It's your choice. You have one week to produce the Lyecian. If you refuse, I will bring the Council and every able-bodied wizard at Ducain's Keep here, and dismantle your castle brick by brick until we find him."

When Marius went to leave, Merek stepped back to allow him to pass, which left Marius face-to-face with Cy. There was a darkness in Cy's eyes that surprised Merek and Marius both. "We're better than this, Marius," Cy said, all the humor drained from his voice. "You think having seven human wizards is going to be enough? You think an army will be enough? Krycin is our kind. Don't turn your back on him. If you attack him, you attack all of us. If I call them, they will listen, and they will come. The last thing you want is Lyecian blood on your hands."

"I do not want a war, Cy. But if you force the issue, that's what you'll have. Krycin will not be harmed. The Fates will return him to where he belongs, and our lives will carry on." Marius stepped around Cy and walked toward the door with the rest of the Council in tow.

Cy kept his dark eyes on them as they left. Before Marius walked out of view, Cy called after him, "Is that what you told him when you sent Gladius after him, that he wouldn't be harmed? When you had Gladius pose as a friend, and throw him from a dragon's back

89

mid-flight? I guess you've already chosen your side, then. If you return, you will be met not by one Lyecian, but all of us. As many as we can muster."

Marius paused in the hallway and listened to Cy, then walked away without looking back.

Chapter 13 – Breaking In

It was midnight in Findoor when Gladius emerged from a rift just outside the city. All was quiet except for a few night insects that sang to the moon. The air was crisp and cool, but still warmer than the badlands, and the grass beneath his feet was a welcome change from cold stone. He walked down the hill toward the city's front gate, which was closed and barred for the night. When he arrived at the gate, he rang the bell that hung on the wall to get the guard's attention.

"Who goes there?" said a guard from behind the gates. There was a smaller door in the larger gates that would allow individuals to pass through without opening them, and a slot in this door slid open. A pair of eyes looked out at Gladius, though he couldn't see them well in the darkness.

"A traveler seeking a warm room and a comfortable bed. Nothing more," Gladius said, putting on his most charismatic smile. The silver trim on his blue robe glittered in the moonlight as he bowed before the gates.

"A blue wizard? What are you doing out at this hour?" the guard said, suspicion filling his voice. His eyes narrowed in the slot as he waited for an answer.

"I travel from Ducain's Keep. I would have stopped and set up camp, but I was close and the prospect of sleeping in an actual bed rather than on the cold ground was motivation enough to keep walking through the night."

There was a pause as the guard backed away from the door for a moment. Gladius heard some indistinct murmuring through the slot.

He presumed the guard was checking with his superior. After a few more seconds, the guard returned to the slot. "Name?"

Gladius felt his heart jump in his chest at this question. *Fool*, he thought, *you knew they would ask this.* He thought fast and came up with a false name. "Thatcher. Quinn Thatcher," he said, trying to steady his voice so as not to sound nervous.

A loud click pierced the air, and made Gladius jump. There was a sound of wood sliding on wood, and then the door opened, revealing a soldier in full armor. "Sorry about that," the guard said. "It's not often we get one as young as you traveling so late at night, and by himself no less. We have to ask questions. The Silver Steed Inn is just up the main stretch there. They'll likely still have some rooms open, and their food can't be beat."

"Thank you, kind sir," Gladius said as he walked by. He heard the guards close the door behind him as he walked away and headed straight for the Silver Steed. He'd heard rumors about the Silver Steed, that one could meet with the less scrupulous members of society there without fear of the authorities. He couldn't be sure if those rumors were true, but it was the best chance he had of accomplishing his goal, and he hadn't the time to come up with a better plan.

The Inn was quiet, with only a few patrons taking late-night meals or drinking themselves sober. Gladius walked up to the bar and sat down. When the barkeep approached, Gladius looked up and spoke before the rotund old man could get a word in. "I need a good stiff drink, a hearty meal, and somebody who can get me into a place I'm not supposed to be." His voice was hushed so that only the barkeep would hear.

"Why, you're not in but your eighteenth year. Why would you want to be gettin' yourself into trouble like that?"

"That's none of your concern. Can you help me or not?" Gladius glared at the barkeep with an icy stare and tossed a small bag on the counter that jingled when it landed.

The barkeep took the bag and checked its contents, then pocketed it and said, "Ay. I know a man. Comes 'round once in a while. Keeps to himself. We ne'er ask questions as he pays well. But he carries the tools o' the trade, so to speak. Some think him a rogue or a common thief. I think he's an assassin. Not many thieves carry an outfit like he's got." The barkeep turned around to fill a mug of ale for Gladius.

"Will he be around tonight? My business is of the utmost urgency," Gladius said to his back.

The gruff barkeep didn't speak again until he set the mug down in front of Gladius. "Maybe. Maybe not. He's funny like that. Sometimes we don't see him fer weeks at a time. But he always comes the same time. If you stick around, it'll be 'bout another hour, if he comes at all."

With a nod, Gladius picked up the mug from the counter. "Thank you, my good man. I'll take up a place at the hearth and be no further trouble to you." He dropped a few coins on the counter, stood up, walked over to a chair at the hearth, and made himself comfortable. It wasn't long before he drifted off to sleep without intending to.

Gladius awoke with a start as somebody kicked his chair. His heart jumped in his chest and his reflexes told his mind to seek the power of water. A blue glow surrounded his hand before his eyes had even snapped open.

Before him stood a tall, lean man wearing a loose brown cloak over a basic tunic and trousers. Several leather belts crossed his frame that held four daggers, a small case used to hold bolts, and a crossbow that was like nothing Gladius had ever seen before. The man had black hair, a trimmed black mustache and beard, and dark eyes that Gladius could tell had seen death many times over. His leather boots went up mid-calf and one held yet another dagger.

The man bent down and looked Gladius in the eye. His gaze darted to the blue glow surrounding Gladius's hand. "Put that away before you hurt yourself," he said. His voice was cold and confident and made Gladius doubt himself for even considering contacting him.

With some effort, Gladius calmed his nerves enough to disperse the energy without hurting himself. When he looked back up at the man, he was met with another look that Gladius found hard to read. The man had a half smile on his face, and a look in his eyes that sent a shiver down his back. "Who are you?" Gladius asked.

The man bent down, bringing his face within inches of Gladius and whispered, "Are you sure you want to know?"

Gladius froze, staring into the man's emotionless eyes. The eyes of a cold-blooded killer. Everything he had thought up, all of his plans disappeared from his mind. His heart raced, until he broke his gaze from the man's eyes.

"What's the matter? Can't handle what you're getting yourself into? I don't blame you. Go home. Forget you ever saw me. Forget what you were going to do, because even if I do get you into somewhere you're not supposed to be, you'll likely just end up getting yourself killed. If you can't face me, your heart ain't in it, kid." The half-smile on his face morphed into a smirk as he stood back up to his full height and moved to walk away.

"I've come a long way," Gladius said. "I won't turn back now. I have no home to go back to. So either you help me, or I'll find somebody who will."

The man stopped, tilted his head and chuckled. "I never said I wouldn't help you. But it'll cost you. I don't work for free. Are you sure you can afford me?"

"Name your price, I have plenty of gold," Gladius said, sitting up straight.

"Gold?" the man said with a scoff. "You think I want gold? If I wanted your gold, I would slit your throat and take it. But then you wouldn't be much good to me, would you?"

Gladius shot to his feet, anger rushing through him. "Do not threaten me. I've killed Narshuks far larger and more powerful than you."

The man remained calm, his face returning to the half-smile that hid his thoughts. He stepped forward and looked into Gladius's eyes. "Narshuks got nothing on me, boy. The name's Taraxle, and that's all you need to know. I help you, you help me. That's the way it works. I say what, when and how. If you don't hold up your end of the bargain, I'll kill you. Simple enough?"

"Yes, simple enough," Gladius said, hoping Taraxle would back off. Taraxle took a step back and Gladius was able to survey the room for the first time since he woke up. The whole place was empty other than the two of them and most of the lanterns had been dimmed for the night. A plate of food had been left on the table next to his chair. "Where is everybody?"

"I sent them away, in case things got ugly. Not because I was concerned about their safety, but because I don't like there to be witnesses if I have to kill someone. I wouldn't want to have to kill my favorite bartender," Taraxle shot him a sideways glance, the same half-smile on his face. "So, where do you need me to get you into? Let's get this over with, you're already costing me money."

Gladius almost said something about the last statement, but thought better of it. Instead he said, "I need to get into Findoor castle without being detected. The bottom floor, as close to the Arch-Magus's library as possible."

Taraxle raised an eyebrow. "Undetected? Understand that if you are caught, you're on your own. There is no honor or obligation between us. I'm doing a job, and if things go sour, I'll not be sticking around to see you hang."

"Understood," Gladius said with a nod.

"Good. Come with me then." Taraxle walked through the door to the kitchen and toward the back door of the building. Gladius followed as fast as he could, but Taraxle was quick, and light on his feet.

Gladius made it out into the alley behind the inn where Taraxle was already waiting for him. "Try to keep up," said Taraxle, his tone impatient. "I'm on a strict time line. Do step carefully, you're making more noise than a Narshuk in an antiquities shop."

Taraxle continued walking through side streets and alleys until they reached the outer wall of Findoor Castle. His steps were calculated and silent, where Gladius walked with a heavy foot and bumped into things as they progressed. No matter how he tried, the noise Gladius made rang out through the night.

"You'll never make a good thief, but I suppose that's not really a problem for you, is it?" Taraxle asked.

"No," Gladius said, glaring at Taraxle. "My only concern is getting into that library. After that, getting out will be simple. Just do your job."

There was an awkward pause as Taraxle gave him another of his half smiles, and then shrugged. "You're the boss." He walked forward, taking careful steps and examining the wall. After a few minutes, Taraxle stopped and pressed a hidden switch. A section of the wall fell in and slid to the side, revealing a tunnel that led down into the castle. Taraxle stepped back and presented the tunnel to Gladius. "There you have it. One way to get you into somewhere you're not supposed to be. Just remember our deal. Some day I'll come to you for a favor. I expect you to honor that."

Gladius narrowed his eyes at Taraxle. "And just how do you propose to find me? Once I leave here, I have no intention of returning. You don't even know my name."

There was a flash of steel as a dagger appeared at Gladius's throat. Taraxle took hold of his robe and slammed him against the wall. "Don't ever make assumptions about what I do know and what I don't, Gladius of the blue robe, son of Darson of the black robe. Or shall I call you Quinn Thatcher? That is what you told the city guard, is it not?"

A look of astonished shock washed over Gladius's face. He opened his mouth to say something, but Taraxle cut him off. "How? That's the question everybody asks. How is simple. I listen to people, and watch people. I know you're a blue wizard because you wear it right up front. It's not a ruse because when I startled you, you resorted to your native element. All you wizards do. You're powerful, because you knew how to let magical energy go without hurting yourself. Shall I continue?" Taraxle paused only for a split second and looked into Gladius's eyes. "You've been banished. It's the only way you would have confronted a Narshuk. You wizards love your luxury, and the High Council has gone to great lengths to ensure that the Narshuk population stays at war with themselves. None of you would put yourselves in harm's way unless forced to do so. The only blue wizard to be banished in recent weeks would be you. The only thing I haven't figured out yet, is how you got here from there. By all sense and logic, you should have been dinner for one of those animals." A smug smile washed over Taraxle's face as he held Gladius at knife-point.

Gladius struggled against Taraxle's grip, but he couldn't move without risking injury. "They aren't animals," he said once he resigned himself to his situation.

There was a pause as Taraxle appeared to consider these words. "'They aren't animals'? Here you are, being held at knife point, seconds from having your blood spilled all over your pretty blue robes, and all you can muster in your defense is 'They aren't animals'?"

"Yes. The Narshuks. They aren't animals. Their tribes are scattered and at war, but they have strength, and magic the likes of which us wizards have not yet discovered. When I unite their tribes, the world will tremble before my army."

Taraxle burst out in laughter with such force that he dropped his dagger from Gladius's throat and turned around. "Oh, that is rich," Taraxle said once he calmed himself. "I like you, Gladius. You're almost as crazy as I am. Go now. Fetch what you need to fetch, unite your tribes, and *if* you survive, be ready for my task. At least I'll know where to find you."

With that, Taraxle walked away into the night.

Gladius breathed a sigh of relief to be rid of the rogue. He pulled himself away from the wall and stepped into the tunnel. Three steps into the tunnel he felt a stone shift under his foot and the door slid closed behind him, leaving him in total darkness. The tunnel was narrow enough that Gladius was able to walk with one hand on each wall. He felt moss growing on the walls and the dank musty air made it hard to breathe. Spiderwebs strung from one side of the tunnel to the other broke and stuck to him as he walked. He lost track of time in the blackness of the tunnel, but eventually made it to a dead end. He felt around for any kind of protruding stone or latch that would open the door but found nothing. After a few minutes of searching in the dark, panic began to fill his heart. *That thief has led me to a trap,* Gladius thought as his heart pounded. He lifted his fists and slammed them on the wall at the end of the tunnel. "Blast it all!"

When his fists impacted the stone, the wall shifted and slid to the side revealing the back of an old tapestry. Dim light streamed through pin holes in the tapestry and brought relief once again. Gladius pushed the edge of the tapestry to the side and peeked out into a gray stone hallway that he recognized as the first lower level of Findoor castle. He waited and listened for a few minutes to make sure there was nobody there before stepping out into the hallway, then looked around to orient himself. Once he knew where he was, he brushed off the dust and webs from his robe, and made his way toward Merek's library with his hood pulled up over his head.

He recognized the door the instant he saw it. A heavy oak door with silver runes spread over it and steel bands reinforcing its structure. The stonework around the door was also reinforced with steel. *This one won't be as easy as the last one,* Gladius thought. *If I break it down, Merek will know someone is here.* He examined the door once more, closer this time, and found that although the structure of the door was solid, there was still a gap around and under it.

Gladius closed his eyes and gathered the power of water to him, infusing his entire body with the power and focusing his mind on one word. The hallway was silent as he finished drawing the power required for his spell. "Tabescetas," Gladius whispered. The spell dissolved his body in an instant and his form fell to the ground as pure water. With his mind and soul still intact, he willed the puddle that was now his body to move under the door.

Inch by inch the large wet spot on the floor flowed into the library. When the last of the water reached the other side of the door, Gladius released the power that bound him to that form and the water pulled together, reforming his physical body. He looked around and smiled to himself as he saw the many shelves of ancient books that represented all the knowledge of the Findoor Arch-Magus.

Chapter 14 - Acquisition and Death

Merek and Cy descended to the lab in the basement of Findoor castle. Tyriel waited there for them. As they entered the room, Tyriel approached. "You would rather start a war than turn over one Lyecian to the Fates?"

"We are protecting a good man who has done nothing wrong," Merek said, his tone level and unwavering.

"And if I told you this Lyecian was dangerous? He holds the power to destroy not only this world, but others as well," Tyriel said.

"There are many men who are dangerous, but until a crime is committed, until that potential is realized, I will not act. No Council can find guilt in the potential to do harm."

Cy stepped forward and spoke. "If our potential to do harm were a measure of guilt, then all Lyecians, and all wizards for that matter should be found guilty. Will you kill us all to get to one? I will not turn on my own kind, not even if the fate of the world depends on it."

"Then you are a fool," Tyriel said, turning to face the Lyecian with a jerk of his head. "And yet, you have a point. Every time Krycin crosses paths with someone, he changes their fate. We are unsure of why this is, but what the Fates do know is this: If he affects the wrong person, or he changes too much, all of existence could unravel. Our fears are not unfounded. But you are right, we should not pass judgment based on the potential to do harm. Tell me where Krycin is, and allow me to speak with him. Let him decide what he wishes to do, but allow him to do so based on all the facts."

"This is a serious matter," Merek said. "I will not turn Krycin over to the High Council for crimes uncommitted, but I cannot allow him to continue moving about this world without knowing the consequences of his actions. If what you say is true, then we must ensure that Krycin at least knows what he is capable of and allow him to decide. Is that acceptable to you, Cy?"

"How do we know if you speak the truth?" Cy asked, never shifting his gaze from Tyriel. "How do we ensure that you won't just whisk Krycin away the moment we tell you his location?"

Tyriel's hood dropped like he was lowering his head. Though neither Merek nor Cy could see his face, his frustration was evident in his voice. "Krycin has grown in strength each time I have encountered him. I fear I could not take him by force even if I wanted to."

"I will accompany you," Cy said. "Given your history with Krycin, you will need somebody to, shall we say, mend your relations with him?"

"Very well. If that's what it will take." Tyriel approached Cy and extended a pale hand with long slender fingers to him. "Take my hand, and tell me where we are going."

Merek backed up a step to give the men some space. "Be careful, both of you. Krycin is aware that the Council and the Fates are looking for him. He may believe you turned on him, Cy. Reassure him that you have not. We sent him to the Fioraden for training and protection."

Cy took Tyriel's hand, and the two men dissolved into black mist and dispersed into the air, leaving Merek alone in his lab.

Merek returned to his work, researching ways to improve the efficiency of his scrying pool when he heard a sound at his door, like somebody had entered, but the door made no sound. When he looked up to see what the noise was, he saw a young blue-robed wizard standing just inside the door. "Gladius," Merek said, surprised.

"Merek," Gladius said, taking slow measured steps forward. "I need your help."

There was a long silence as Merek considered his words. "If I help you, I will face the same fate as you. You shouldn't be here, young man. Or have I been misinformed about your banishment?"

"Oh that? It didn't take. I've made some new friends, and I want to help them out, but first, I need to know the meaning of something, and I'm sure you can help me with it." He reached into his robe and pulled out the white book with the symbol of Lyecha on the front. "I've found this book, and inside this book is High Lyecian script, except for two small passages written in common."

"You know I can't help you," Merek said, though his eyes drifted to the book and curiosity welled up inside him.

Gladius scowled at him. "Stop pretending like the Council has you in their pocket. I know very well that your research strays outside of what is considered good and decent. The Council only tolerates it because you do it quietly, and they get to reap the reward from it. You may have the rest of Galadir fooled, but remember who my father is. I know better."

"Perhaps you do. But what do you plan to do if I refuse? You're a young man, and an intelligent one at that. Know that I do not pass my knowledge out lightly, especially that which you seek. Become my apprentice, and I will have your past forgiven, and all charges against you removed. I'm in need of an apprentice of your aptitude. In return, I will help you."

Gladius took a step forward, opened the book and flipped through the pages until he found the one with the passages on it. "'Gifted by all the gods, the Traveler shall open the way to the Crossroads,'" Gladius said and paused, looking up at Merek. Merek didn't move or speak, so he continued. "'A Time Weaver's soul is beyond the reach of time.' What do you think, Merek? Who is the Traveler, and what is the Crossroads?"

"What you seek is dangerous knowledge, and what you've stolen from the Council is forbidden lore. I won't have any part of this, and you shouldn't have come here." Merek held his right hand palm down and called upon magical energy. He was about to speak the words to his spell when he heard Gladius speak first.

"Congelascas," Gladius said, and Merek felt a blast of cold strike him, interrupting his spell. The errant power rushed through his body, heating him up and causing pain over his whole body. Merek fell to his knees and tried to clear his mind to defend himself. He heard footsteps approaching him, but couldn't ignore the pain the magical energy caused him as it dissipated.

"I have a secret to tell you," Gladius said as he stood over Merek. "I've already learned what I needed from your personal library. I was hoping you would help me with this book, but it appears you're going to be unreasonable. Once I've gained the rest of the elements, I'll only need to learn one thing more. I need to know how to kill a Lyecian."

Merek looked up at the much younger wizard and shook his head. "The Council will never allow you to continue. Your life is forfeit."

"On the contrary, they don't have a choice," Gladius said, smiling down at Merek. "I'll be the hero of Galadir, saving the world from the one man who threatens to destroy it. Where is Krycin anyway? I owe him a visit. In fact, I owe him a lot more than that."

"You'll never find him, and you know I'll never talk, no matter how you torture me. Let this go, Gladius. Return to the badlands, and give up this grudge. Allow myself and the Council to take care of Krycin, and maybe I will be able to get you reinstated as my apprentice. I would still do that for you. It's never too late to redeem yourself."

"No!" Gladius screamed down at Merek. "Krycin was *my* responsibility. He was *my* discovery. I should be the one to do this, and if nobody will help me, then I shall do it on my own. Nobody knows Krycin like I do. Make no mistake, Merek, I will discover what this Traveler is, and I will own that power. The power of all eight gods."

Merek struggled to get up as Gladius walked away toward a nearby table. When he looked up, Gladius had his hand resting on an ancient sword constructed of black steel that Merek had been studying. "This," Gladius said as he picked it up, "will be the end of you." Merek watched him return, and as he raised the sword, he said, "Goodbye, old man."

There was a moment of silence, and then Merek felt the tip of the sword pierce his chest, sending a searing pain through his body. He fell back, sliding off the sword and landing on the floor on his side. As Gladius walked away, he gasped for breath, trying to stop the young wizard. The last thing he saw before he lost consciousness was a blue light flood the room as Gladius escaped through a rift, and then everything went black.

Chapter 15 - The Flow of Time

Krycin was receiving lessons from a Fioraden warrior when Cy and Tyriel appeared at the sidelines of the training grounds. Cy looked at Tyriel and spoke in a hushed voice, "Let me do the talking until I've convinced him that we're not here to harm him or take him away. One wrong move, and you'll have another battle on your hands."

Tyriel said nothing, but nodded his approval.

The warrior was teaching Krycin some basic sword handling as Cy approached. It took a few minutes for Krycin to spot Cy, but when he did, he raised his hand to the warrior to signal him to stop his advances. "Hey," Krycin said with a smile. "Back so soon?"

"I've brought somebody to talk to you, and I want you to listen to what he has to say." Cy motioned Tyriel to step forward. "I know you two have had your differences, but Tyriel has finally listened to reason and agreed to talk with you about what's going on, and why the Fates are after you."

Krycin's face went grave when he saw the reaper. "You. What do *you* want?" He shot an unpleasant glance toward Cy that said he wasn't happy about the situation.

"You have my apologies for my past behavior. The Fates do not normally encounter resistance when they interfere in mortal affairs. This is a somewhat unique situation," Tyriel said, giving Krycin a quick bow. "You are more powerful than any Lyecian we have encountered. You are also not in your proper place in time, which should be impossible."

"What do you mean, 'not in my proper place'?" Krycin asked.

"Time flows like a river, from the past to the future. Every person has a place in that flow, which the Fates determine. Even the gods have a place in that flow, and while Lyecians can slow down, speed up and even stop that flow, they cannot alter their place." Tyriel paused to let that sink in.

"Except me," Krycin said.

"Except you. Problem is, while you're out of your place in the flow, you are altering other people's paths. You're changing the flow of time, probably in ways you never imagined."

"I don't understand, how could I change my place, or anyone else's place in the flow of time?"

"We're not sure. What we do know is this: If you alter something that affects the reason you were here to begin with, you will create a paradox. An impossible condition that will not only halt the flow of time, it would destroy it." Tyriel watched Krycin's face carefully as he processed that information.

Krycin thought about it for a long time. "Destroy it?"

"Yes. All existence would end."

"Do you know my proper place in the flow of time?" Krycin asked.

"Sadly, no. But the Fates feel that it would be best to remove you from the flow until we can figure it out. Where you are from, and your reason for being here are locked somewhere in your own mind. You must remember everything eventually, or we will never figure out where to place you back in the flow. My question right now is this: Will you allow yourself to be taken by the Fates until that happens?"

Krycin looked from Tyriel to Cy. "What would you do?"

Cy shook his head. "I can't help you with this one. You are a Lyecian, of that there is no doubt. But you are also something more, something greater than all of us. I brought Tyriel here so that you could talk and make the decision yourself. You deserve that much. But I can't make that decision for you."

"I just don't know," Krycin said, walking away, his eyes lowered in deep thought.

Tyriel stepped forward and spoke. "Remember, Krycin. The more you disturb the flow of time, the greater the chance that you'll..."

"I won't go," Krycin said.

Both Tyriel and Cy stopped in their tracks for a moment. Cy wasn't sure if he'd heard Krycin right.

"I don't remember everything, but I have bits and pieces. I came here for a reason, and until I figure that out and accomplish it, I can't go back."

Cy nodded and approached him. "I understand."

"You don't know what you're doing," Tyriel said, his voice steady, but sad.

"That's a chance I have to take," Krycin said. "I can't go back. Not yet. Not until I know why I came here, and I won't know that until my memories return. Ferron and the other Fioraden are helping me with that, but it's going to take time. Ferron said there is damage to my mind the likes of which he has never seen before."

"Temporal damage," Tyriel said. Cy and Krycin gave him a curious look, and so he continued. "Agents of the Fates are sometimes granted the ability to move backward and forward through the flow of time, but it requires a tremendous amount of energy, and puts a large amount of stress on them. If they attempt to do it when they are already tired, the temporal stress could tear them apart, either physically or mentally. That may be what's happened to you, though that still doesn't explain how you accomplished such a feat to begin with."

"Will I get better?" Krycin asked.

"Maybe. It depends on the extent of the damage. There is no magic that I know of that will heal it, nor have the Fates been successful in restoring one who has sustained wounds from temporal stress. Some have recovered naturally."

There was a moment of silence between the men, then Cy spoke up. "We should get back, Merek will be waiting for us."

Tyriel gave him a quick nod and took a place beside Cy.

Krycin looked at both men. "I'm sorry. For everything."

Cy smiled back at him. "Don't blame yourself, kid. You've done nothing wrong."

Tyriel placed a hand on Cy's shoulder and they dissolved into black smoke and dispersed.

Chapter 16 - Soul of Earth

The Ardan village was quiet and still, with many of the residents just saying their prayers to Torenna as the sun went down. Chieftain Ranto was in his usual place high above the forest on a balcony on the tallest tree. He began his chants as he always did, his voice carrying on the breeze out over the forest for all creatures to hear. The sun was just settling below the tree line when the hum began. Ranto didn't notice it at first, as his own chanting drowned it out. But as the hum grew louder, he paused and listened, his ears turning to locate the source of the sound.

It came from behind him, at the top of the stairs leading down from the balcony. A flash of light caught Ranto's eye and he stopped his chants to see what it was. A line formed in the air above the balcony sending blue rays of light down to the floor and lighting up an area ten paces around it. Arcs of electricity jumped from the line to the balcony, carving small black scars into the wood. Ranto stepped forward, more curious than afraid, and watched as the line split into a man-sized tear in the fabric of the universe. Lightning spilled forth from the hole in cascades down the edges and into the wood below it. Inside the hole, a blue-robed figure stepped forward and out of the rift. Once he was through, the rift slammed shut behind him.

"Gladius," Ranto said, lowering his brow. "What is the meaning of this intrusion? You know the conditions of the treaty between the Ardan people and the Council; no rifts are to be opened within our forest."

Gladius returned his stare, a look of contempt on his face. "I'm not working for the Council anymore." He took slow, measured steps toward Ranto, keeping his hands hidden.

"Then you will suffer the penalties of our laws. Be gone at once, and never return to our land," Ranto said. He watched as Gladius drew closer and began drawing the power of earth to himself.

"Do you remember that research I was doing? I was trying to figure out how to expand my access to other elements. The research would be invaluable to the Council, had they known how close I was to figuring out the answer," Gladius said. The corner of his mouth tipped up in a slight smile, and his steps brought him within ten paces of Ranto. "Turns out, somebody else already knew the answer, and you'll never guess who. All I had to do was get myself banished, and the knowledge was there for the taking."

Ranto took a step back and focused the magical energy he gathered into a defensive spell. He felt the life force of the tree below him, its living energy fueling his spell. Gladius continued his advance even as Ranto made his attempt to cast.

A horrible pain pierced the Chieftain's abdomen just as the words reached his lips. Other, darker words echoed through his mind in Gladius's voice. "Vimvitas Mortai."

He looked down to see Gladius's hand plunged into his body. No blood spilled from his body, as there was no wound. Instead, Gladius grasped his life force and pulled, wrenching it from his body. He screamed as his soul was ripped from his body and the magical energy that he had drawn flooded through him in a backlash that cooked his flesh. As the last ounce of consciousness left him, he heard Gladius speak. "The Narshuks *will* rise."

⊛

Gladius pulled the last of Ranto's life force from his body and watched as it swirled into a green sphere of light in his hand. He closed his fingers around the sphere and focused his mind, willing the Ardan soul to enter his body and bond with his own. Little by little the energy of the soul gave in and streamed into his body. He shuddered and exalted in the newfound power as all the earth spells he already knew grew stronger, and new areas of the earth element became available to him.

When the light was gone, Gladius opened his eyes and looked down at the crumpled heap that was Ranto's body. Smoke rose in tiny streamers from his body and his flesh and fur were burnt from the failed spell. Gladius gave the tiny creature a good kick and sent the body flying off the edge of the balcony under the railing.

A commotion coming up the tree caught Gladius's attention and he spun to see several Ardan warriors racing up the stairs to see why their chieftain screamed. Gladius called on the power of water and formed it into a spell. His hand filled with a blue glowing ball that he tossed at the top of the stairs as he spoke the words for the spell. "Congelascas."

The ball of energy struck the floor in front of the stairs and flashed, releasing a torrent of energy that manifested as a wall of ice. When it was fully formed, it blocked the path onto the balcony. The approaching warriors paused only a second to consider the obstruction before they climbed over the railing and crawled along the outside of the balcony and around the wall using their claws to anchor themselves to the tree.

Gladius huffed and tried to think of another way to buy himself some time. As the first Ardan made it over the railing and ran at him, he called on his newly acquired power of earth and drew the unfamiliar energy to him. It flowed slowly at first, requiring more effort to harness the energy for his spell, but it manifested for him as he spoke the words to the spell. "Laxamentas."

The energy of earth coursed through him and into the tree. New branches sprouted and grew wild, crisscrossing in a tangled mess that blocked and entangled the Ardan warriors that were approaching. Gladius smiled at their surprised yelps and hisses as they were encased in branches from the trees they dedicated their lives to protect. When he was sure they were immobilized, he prepared his next spells.

He summoned magical power and chanted the ancient words to open a new traveling rift. The tear opened in front of him, spewing lightning and sparks all around it. Gladius stepped forward into the rift and willed it to close behind him.

❂

Gladius stepped out of the rift onto the Badlands just outside of Scrag's tribe. The air was still and quiet, with only the odd growl or howl echoing from the large plot of huts. He walked into the village and was met by various scoffs and growls from the residents. When he found Scrag, the Narshuk was stripping a dried branch of leaves and placing them in a small burlap bag. Gladius approached the Narshuk shaman with a wide smile. "Are you ready to unite the tribes? Are you ready for a new dawning for the Narshuk race?"

Scrag grumbled and continued his work without looking up.

"Oh come now. There are plans to make, tribes to gather, an army to prepare for war," Gladius said, approaching Scrag.

There was a long, awkward silence before Scrag looked up at Gladius. "You have big words, wizard, but now that the night has worn off, none of the senior members of our tribe believe you can do it. I'm surprised you even came back."

There was another pause as Gladius worked to suppress his temper and avoid exploding on Scrag. *Easy, Gladius,* he thought, *you still need this one.* After a deep breath, he focused his dark eyes on Scrag's and said, "Gather the Elders."

Scrag burst into a series of gasps and barks that Gladius guessed to be laughter. "The Elders have not gathered for many years. It can only be done under condition of full surrender of the hosting tribe, and you will never get this tribe to agree to that."

"And why not?" Gladius bellowed back at Scrag. "Why will they not do this? Surrender. Gather the Elders and surrender, and I promise you that by the end of the gathering, the tribes *will* unite." He stormed out of the shaman's hut and stomped his way to the center of the village. Many watched the display, but none moved or stopped their work.

Gladius reached the center of the circle where the Narshuks held their rituals and stopped. When he turned around, Scrag was standing at the edge of the circle, watching him. With his anger still fueling him, he shouted out, his voice carrying to the edges of the village. "Friends, come to me, and hear my plea. Too long have you lived in squalor and poverty. Too long have the Narshuks been forced to suffer a fate worse than death under the oppression of human wizards. Living in filth, fighting for food, dying at your brother's hands? That's no way to live."

Many nearby Narshuks looked up at Gladius as he spoke, some getting up to stand at the edge of the circle. Gladius smiled as he watched the beasts come to him. "So tell me this: do you want to exist, scraping by with whatever you can find in the wilderness, constantly battling the other tribes for what you need?" Gladius said, pausing to let his words sink in. "Or do you want to *live*, an equal to all the other races? Stand with me. Surrender the tribe, and call a gathering of the Elders. A full surrender might result in the end of this tribe, but not doing so dooms all Narshuks to live in the shadows. I guarantee that when the Elder gathering is done, the tribes *will* come together, or I will die trying."

A chorus of howls rose from the crowd around him. Gladius turned to face Scrag, who now approached him. "If you fail," Scrag said, "you will be a dead wizard."

Gladius looked into Scrag's eyes and scoffed. "I don't know how to fail."

Chapter 17 - Merek, The Great and Powerful

Ducain's Keep was quiet on the night before the High Council and their army of wizards was to set out toward Findoor. Every capable wizard was conscripted into service in order to pressure Merek and the king into turning over Krycin to the Council. Moonlight lit up the empty training grounds and the courtyard before the gates. In that silver stream shining down from the sky, a red wizard stood waiting, though his robe appeared dark gray. His hood was pulled back to reveal red hair, and though the light was dim, his blue eyes were unmistakable. Lebriel awaited his brother with what he'd heard was news of the Lyecian they'd been after. His eyes were still sunken in and his cheeks drawn back, as he wasn't yet fully recovered from his battle with Gladius, but he felt well enough to attend the Council meeting.

As he scanned the courtyard, he saw a black mist coalesce at the far end into a man-sized shape. It took only seconds for Tyriel to materialize. "Brother," Lebriel said. "I never got a chance to thank you."

Tyriel approached, his hood drawn up and his face hidden in shadow. "You still don't look well," he said, stopping several paces from his twin.

"I'm fine. What is this news I hear?"

Tyriel lowered his head and looked from side to side like he was checking for others who might be listening in. "I have spoken with Krycin, and he has refused to go with me. He claims he is here for a reason, and won't leave until he discovers and fulfills that obligation. Until his memories return, I'm afraid all we can do is wait. But the ultimatum from the Fates remains."

"I'll discuss this with the Council and see what they say," Lebriel said, his eyes darkening to reflect his mood. "People are afraid. They are afraid of what he can do. He challenged you twice and lived, which is something no man or Lyecian has ever done. He defies the Fates, who control everything. How do we deal with a threat like that?"

"You must find a way."

"Very well, I'll try. That's the most I can promise you." Lebriel walked toward Tyriel, sadness filling his eyes. "I've missed you. I never thought I'd see you again."

Though Tyriel's hood was drawn over his head, Lebriel could hear the pain in his twin's voice when he spoke. "I cannot stay. The Fates call."

The black robes dissolved into mist and dispersed into the night air, leaving Lebriel alone again in the courtyard. He walked back to the keep, each step feeling like a labor that was more than he could bear.

⊙

When Lebriel arrived in the Council chamber, the rest of the Council was already assembled. Marius watched him enter and take his seat while the rest of the wizards talked with hushed voices. When Lebriel was comfortable, Marius cleared his throat to get the Council's attention and began. "Is there any news from the Fates, Lebriel?"

"Yes. Krycin refuses to go with Tyriel, and their ultimatum stands," Lebriel said.

"What of the threat he posed?" Marius asked.

"The threat remains, though it seems even the Fates are powerless to prevent it. Even Krycin doesn't know why he is here, and won't until his memories return."

"What do you advise this Council to do?"

"Starting a war over one man seems rather drastic to me. I think we should wait, and see how events unfold. There really is nothing further we can do."

Darson stood up without warning and shouted, "The threat remains, but we should do nothing? Are you mad? This man has the power to end our world. To destroy the fabric of the universe, and Lebriel is suggesting we just leave him be to blunder about until his memories return? What if he hasn't lost his memories? What if this has all been a ruse? I say we put an end to these games Krycin is playing. We take him, by force if necessary, and lock him up until he tells us his purpose. The army is assembled, we have simply to march in and take him."

"I will not risk open war on Findoor if I don't have to," Marius said, shaking his head. He paused, looking thoughtful. "Yet, you have a point, Darson. The danger remains, and we must consider the needs of the many over the needs of the few. As a council, we have not faced a threat like this before. The potential that our entire world could be wiped out of existence by one man cannot be ignored, and thus I will put it to a vote. Those in favor of marching on Findoor, please raise your hands."

An awkward silence filled the room as several hands raised. Darson was the first, followed by the gray robe. The yellow and green robe followed, and when Farissa of the blue robe saw Lebriel remain still, she also raised her hand.

"That makes five for," Marius said, "and three against. We shall march on Findoor for the purpose of taking Krycin into custody, where he will remain until such time as his memories return, or we discover his purpose here. Prepare the army to march at first dawn."

The Council wizards stood up and left the Council chamber with the exception of Marius and Lebriel. Marius was lost in his own thoughts and didn't notice Lebriel's presence. Lebriel got up out of his seat and approached the Lyecian. "We're making a mistake," Lebriel said.

Marius started and met Lebriel's gaze. "I know, my friend. But the Council has spoken. Go now, get some sleep. You look weary."

Lebriel nodded and walked out of the room without another word. When the door closed behind him, Marius went back to his thoughts in the lonely, silent chamber.

⊙

When Cy returned to Findoor, he went straight for Merek's lab to talk to the old wizard. The basement of the castle was always cool and quiet, but as he approached the lab, there wasn't a single sound coming from the room, and the door was ajar. *Merek never leaves his door open,* Cy thought, and broke into a run toward the door. His own footfalls sounded like thunder in the quiet hallway, and as he entered the lab he stopped in his tracks, frozen with shock.

In the center of the room, a gray heap lay still on the floor with a dark pool around it. Nothing else looked out-of-place in the room, but Cy knew right away who was under the gray robe. He took a step forward, his heart pounding at the prospect of somebody powerful enough to slay the Arch-Magus of Findoor. Another step forward, and the scene before him melted away, like a mirage in the desert. One second there was a body in the middle of the room, and the next, the floor was clean and the body was gone. There was a rustle from the far side of the room, and a gray robed figure emerged from an unseen doorway, laughing.

"Merek! I thought you were dead," Cy said with a sigh of relief.

It took a second for Merek to stop laughing. "I would have ended the illusion sooner, but you should have seen the look on your face."

Cy scowled at the Arch-Magus, but didn't respond. He was still getting over the shock, and the anger at finding out it was just an illusion.

"On a more serious note," Merek said, calming his laughter and taking on a much more dire tone, "we have another problem. It seems that Gladius has found some friends in the Badlands, and has stolen not only some valuable spells, but also a valuable artifact from me."

"Gladius? I thought he'd be dead," Cy said, his surprise renewed.

"Indeed. The Council has underestimated Gladius. He seeks the power of the Traveler, and I fear won't stop until he gains it, though I'm not sure he can." Merek walked over to a shelf on the far wall and plucked a book from it before turning back to Cy.

"The Traveler?" Cy said. "I'm not familiar with that. Who, or what, is the Traveler?"

"A Lyecian legend, hidden away by the Wizard High Council. It was discovered many hundreds of years ago, a prophecy that read 'Gifted by all the gods, the Traveler shall open the way to the Crossroads. A Time Weaver's soul is beyond the reach of time'. The book, a Lyecian manual of magic, was placed in the forbidden zone because it contained some of the most complex and dangerous magic anyone has ever known." Merek paused for a moment, deep in thought, and then continued. "The Traveler is prophesied to be a Lyecian who can wield all eight elements of magic. But further to that, The Traveler can also open a doorway to The Crossroads, the place where the gods themselves convene in mortal form. If one could enter this place, one could conceivably slay the gods and take their place."

"And Gladius has taken this book from the forbidden zone?" Cy asked.

"I'm afraid, yes. It's the reason he was banished. He was caught in the forbidden zone, and then attacked a Council wizard and nearly killed him. The Council, and even myself, thought Gladius would not make it long in the Badlands. It seems we were incorrect in this assumption, and now he has friends."

"The Narshuks. But they're a bunch of animals," Cy said with a half smile. "What could he possibly do with one small tribe of them? There's no way the tribes will stop warring amongst themselves long enough to form any kind of real threat."

Merek closed his eyes and thought for a long time before responding. "Do not be so certain about that. Gladius is very much like his father. Ambitious, persuasive, and highly intelligent. I will discuss the matter with the king and send a scouting party to the southern borders to see if there have been any disturbances. In the meantime, I think it would be wise of you to gather what Lyecians you can summon, as I expect the High Council will be here soon looking for Krycin."

"Agreed. Those blowhards aren't going to give up without a fight."

Chapter 18 - Calamity

Under a full surrender, the tribal elders gathered in Scrag's village and waited for Gladius to speak to them. Each of the Elders was a hulking beast, having seen many battles and lived a good many years. Gray-haired, scarred, and impatient, they were just starting to get restless when Scrag and Gladius entered the circle. Just outside the circle stood several lieutenants of each Elder, ready with weapons in case things didn't go well.

Scrag took his place at the edge while Gladius walked the circle and measured up each of the Elders. "Such a fine group of Narshuks you are," Gladius began, with a half-smile on his face.

The oldest of the Elders spoke up with a gruff, almost unintelligible voice. "Don't patronize us, wizard. Save your silver tongue for your own kind. Tell us why we are assembled today before we make dinner of you."

All the other Elders let out a hearty laugh as Gladius prepared once again to speak. "Very well. You have a problem. Your tribes are fractured, and the Wizard High Council keeps you that way so that you will not be a threat to them. I can solve both of these problems, and elevate the Narshuks to a level not previously known on Galadir. But I cannot do it alone."

"Why should we help you, wizard?" another Elder said, spitting as he talked. "Why not unite the tribes on our own, and lead ourselves to victory?"

"Why not indeed. Go on then, bring the tribes together. Il's what you've all wanted. Except," Gladius said with a smirk, "who will lead the united Narshuk nation?"

A dumbfounded look came over the Elder's face. "I will lead them, of course." He stood up tall and proud and let out a howl.

Another Elder jumped to his feet and said, "You? Never! I should be the leader!"

Soon all the Elders were arguing and throwing threats around. The whole gathering almost descended into a blood bath when Gladius intervened with a shout that echoed for miles around. All the Elders went silent and looked up at him.

"I am neutral. I can lead all the nations without past injuries clouding my judgment. And most of all, when the High Council comes to confront your army, I will eliminate them."

Scrag started at this revelation and spoke up. "What about the eighth? What will you do about the Lyecian?"

A smile came over Gladius's face. "My friend, that's the beauty of my plan. I have a spell, a reality anchor that will prevent the Lyecian from using his powers. Gather the tribes, and while you do, I shall gather the elements. When all the pieces are in place, we will destroy the High Council and take all of Galadir by storm."

Gladius walked out of the circle to the sound of all the Elders howling their approval, and Scrag walking close behind him. When they were a bit further away, Scrag approached him. "Where are you going now?"

"To the Fioraden to gather life. I have four elements left to gather before I can cast the reality anchor. Until I have all seven, I need you to keep the Narshuk uprising as quiet as possible. If we show our hand too soon, I won't be able to stop the Council." Gladius placed one hand on Scrag's arm and looked up into his eyes. "I promised you the world, my friend, and I intend to deliver."

⊙

Krycin spent several more days with the Fioraden learning to control the white magic of life. His favorite place to study was at the top of the waterfalls, where he could practice his magic bathing in the light of the sun. From the top of the ridge he could spot every detail of the crater. The Fioraden had done their best, but even they could not bring back the memories locked deep inside his mind.

You are battling with yourself, Ferron said in Krycin's head. *When you resolve whatever struggle is raging inside of you, your memories shall return.*

The words didn't comfort him when he combined them with what Merek had told him. *Am I going to die?* he thought to himself.

It is possible, Ferron said, *though I have never seen somebody destroy their self for the sake of their memories. I find it much more likely that you will find what you are looking for, or do what you have to do, and then the battle shall be over.*

Krycin looked out across the beautiful landscape of the crater, contemplating the events that had passed. The sun was just lowering into the west. Thin clouds lit up red in the sky and bathed the crater in reds and oranges. Several Fioraden warriors were sparring in the sky above the crater and Krycin lost himself in their graceful movements. They swooped and dove at each other, spinning in the air and clashing. The Fioraden fought with more than just hand held weapons. Each of their flight feathers were tipped with thin steel blades that they could attack with in a spin that would be deadly to an unarmored foe. Their feet were also equipped with long steel talon extensions that they used when attacking ground based foes from above. Their training allowed them to focus on and attack opponents in any direction in the air.

It was during this moment of personal reflection that he spotted a blue light on the platform at the base of the falls. "What the..." he said as he watched the air over the platform split open. A figure in blue robes stepped out of the rift that struck a nerve inside Krycin. *Gladius,* he thought, when he finally recognized who it was. Ferron and Tersca were flying toward him in order to greet him and find out what he wanted. Krycin got a feeling deep inside him that he hadn't previously known. A churning in his gut that told him something was wrong with the scene before him. Gladius didn't move once he stepped out of the rift. The split closed, and Gladius was focused on something. *He's casting a spell,* Krycin thought, watching the water wizard with alarm.

Something about the spell caught Krycin's eye. Gladius's hand glowed with black energy. Death magic flowed through the air all around him. Krycin acted without thinking. He broke into a run and leapt off the edge of the ridge toward the hole at the center of the crater. Gladius pulled his fist back and spoke several words that Krycin couldn't make out in the rushing air. Krycin's body flew like a dart toward Gladius as he was about to strike Ferron. Krycin pulled in the power of light and life, forming it into a ball of light in his hand. He paid no attention to the ground that was approaching him. He threw the ball at Gladius and watched it fly at him as his fist flew toward the Fioraden lord.

Gladius thought this was going to be as easy as the Ardan soul was to collect. Everything went as planned. He appeared on the platform where the Fioraden greeted all of their guests and began to draw the power of death right away. He knew it would take no time for the Fioraden lord and lady to show up and he wanted to be ready. His spell came to fruition just in time. Ferron landed before him as the black glow formed around his fist. He spoke the words to the spell, "Vimvitas mortai," and swung his fist forward. There was a flash of light, and a searing pain in his side. He felt himself flying off the platform and into the forest around it. When he landed, he felt his arm snap under his weight, the bones cracking and piercing the flesh. His blood flowed out and soaked his robe as a severed artery spouted a fountain of crimson. A scream came from his mouth, though he wasn't conscious of it. His mind was clear, and separated from his body, something the Ardans had taught him.

The power of water flowed to him, coursed through his veins. "Restitas," he said and his wounds healed as fast as they had been inflicted. The bones in his arm cracked and snapped back into place, and the burns on his side where the light had struck him closed over and were left as nothing but scars.

It all happened in seconds, and when he managed to get himself back onto his feet, he looked around for the bird man that had thrown the attack. Ferron and Tersca still stood on the platform, staring at him in disbelief. Beyond them, a figure in white robes flew through the air, dropping out of the sky like a rock from the ridge above. Gladius let out a laugh as the lord of the Fioraden would not be lucky a second time. Two steps toward the platform and the figure falling from the sky blinked out of existence and reappeared between him and the Fioradens.

With a clear view of the white robed wizard, he recognized who it was. "You!" he screamed as he stormed forward.

Krycin charged another white light in his hand, the orb pulsing with energy. "Gladius, what are you doing?"

"I should ask you the same thing. You always seem to be exactly where you shouldn't be. Get out of my way so I can finish the job I've started."

"I can't let you do that, Gladius. I don't know what you're trying to prove here, but I can't let you kill them."

Ferron and Tersca looked from one wizard to the other with expressions of dread and took flight, leaping off the far end of the platform to escape.

"No!" Gladius screamed as he watched his chance for a life soul fly away. "You'll pay for that Krycin. The Council is against you. The Fates are against you. And now I'm going to show you a few new tricks and accomplish what I was sent to do."

Before Krycin could say a word, Gladius charged at him with his fist clenched and in a full swing.

⊙

Krycin slowed time to dodge the incoming attack. Time responded. The Fioraden in the sky, now on high alert, slowed to mere floating statues. The water behind him from the falls slowed, and then stopped. Each drop of water could be seen falling into the abyss below. Gladius stood frozen as well, rage contorted his face into a manifestation of pure hate. His fist was positioned so as to strike Krycin's face, but Krycin stepped to the side and started the flow of time once more.

Gladius tumbled forward off-balance and landed in the brush at the side of the platform. Krycin was ready to approach Gladius and offer him a hand when Gladius spoke several words. Krycin didn't hear the words, but the moment they were spoken the forest around him came to life and grew wild. Vines sprouted from the ground and wrapped around his limbs. Tree roots grabbed at him and writhed around him, squeezing the breath from his lungs. Krycin struggled against the grip of the animated plants and watched before him as Gladius prepared another spell. The black glow surrounded his fist and he spoke the words of the spell again, "Vimvitas mortai."

Gladius swung his fist down at Krycin. *Move,* a voice shouted in Krycin's mind. He willed himself to teleport and blinked out of existence again, leaving Gladius stumbling forward. He reappeared behind Gladius and fired another glowing orb of light at him, striking Gladius square in the back and sending him sprawling into his own animated plants. With a new target, the plants wound around Gladius and held him fast.

Krycin walked toward Gladius, drawing more power and flinging one, then two, then three orbs of light at Gladius, each one exploding on Gladius and making his body convulse in the tangle of plants. When Gladius stopped moving, he turned away from the blue robed wizard.

He realized his mistake when he heard Gladius's voice behind him, "Exsiccatas."

Searing pain ripped through Krycin's entire body all at once. Every nerve lit up with pain causing a scream to emit from his lungs as he collapsed to the ground. He felt his mouth go dry, and his eyes burned. His cheeks sunk in and his skin tightened over his entire body as the water drained from him. His muscles contracted, causing him to curl up on the ground as Gladius prepared to make the killing blow.

"Thirsty Krycin? I thought you would be harder to defeat. The almighty Krycin who even the Fates feared, brought down by a blue wizard."

Krycin tried to say something, but his throat was too dry, and all that came out was a strangled croak.

"Oh, there's no need for words right now. I think this is a first," Gladius said. "A human, defeating a Lyecian."

Panic overtook Krycin, and he did the only thing he could think to do. His body needed water, and so he blinked out of existence, and reappeared at the top of the waterfall, only to plunge into the water, and fall with it down into the massive hole in the earth.

The pain eased, and his focus came back. *Gladius is going to kill them. He's going to kill Ferron*, he thought, even as he struggled to swim to the surface of the underground lake with the water crashing down from above.

I am safe, Ferron's voice said. *Gladius must be stopped.*

Krycin got himself to the surface of the water and considered his options. An idea formed in his head, but he had to act fast.

⊙

Gladius watched the white robed form fall from high above down into the lake below. He smiled to himself and looked around for his next target. Several Fioraden, equipped with full battle gear were flying fast toward him. He readied the power of earth and spoke, "Laxamentas."

Vines flew up into the air from trees below the warriors. Their legs and arms were snagged, and Gladius watched as three of the four were dragged down into the forest right away. The fourth struggled against the vine's hold, swinging his sword at each new tendril that grabbed hold of him. After a short battle, even he lost as the vines wrapped around his wings and pulled back. He lost his balance and dropped backward, striking a large tree branch in the process. An ominous snapping sound told Gladius the soldier had met his match.

A sound behind Gladius startled him. It was the sound of wind rushing from an area suddenly occupied by something else. He spun around in time to see a gleaming white figure swing a sword of light at him. The sword connected, slicing through his left arm and leaving a wide gash. The instant the attack was done, the figure disappeared with a pop, and another rush of air hit Gladius from behind. He spun again, and was hit with a second sword strike, this time getting sliced across his chest. He gasped at the sudden pain and tried to summon the magic to fight back, but again the figure disappeared. A third rush of air hit him from behind.

When Gladius turned to face it, gaining control over his mind and focus, the sword of light was plunged into his gut, running him through. The spell in his mind had already begun, and so he drew the power of the earth, pulling everything he could until it felt like his head might explode. Smoke came from his ears and eyes as the magical energy started cooking Gladius from the inside out. Pain flared through his entire body, and a scream came from his mouth that he formed into a single word, "Tremefascas!"

With the sword still protruding from his body, he focused all the power he harnessed into a single strike. Green light flashed as Gladius drove his fist into the ground, pushing the magic into the earth at the center of the crater.

The ground trembled at first, then gave a violent heave as the stone and clay and sand beneath the crater gave out in a massive earthquake. Cracks radiated out from Gladius and stretched all the way to the edge of the crater, running up the rocky ridge and spreading wider with each passing second. The cracks created an intricate spiderweb across the floor of the crater, and began to cave in. The platform beneath Gladius and Krycin shuddered and cracked as it listed toward the hole in the center of the Fioraden's home.

Seconds later, the earth gave out and fell into a great pit that started in the center and spread out all the way to the edge. Krycin disappeared when the ground gave out, but Gladius fell into the hole along with the entire outer ridge.

(·)

Krycin felt the earth shift, then give out under his feet. The moment he started to fall he focused on a location just outside the ridge and teleported there. He was still catching his breath when the flock of Fioraden took to the air. Many of them carried the young or old in their arms, evacuating their home as it collapsed into an endless void in the earth. When the dust settled, the landscape was flat, and the entire crater, ridge, and outlying hills were gone. Nothing remained but a gaping hole.

"Why?" Krycin screamed.

Thousands of Fioraden were flying away from the pit, making their way to a field to the east where they could regroup.

He surveyed the devastation that Gladius created and couldn't catch his breath. He tried to scream again, but only managed a gasp.

A voice spoke in his mind, *We are safe, and most are accounted for. Do not blame yourself for this evil.* Krycin recognized it as the steady voice of Ferron.

He didn't have to destroy it. I would have died to prevent this, Krycin thought.

But you didn't, and he did. I no longer sense his mind or corrupted soul. We will find a new home.

It's not right, Krycin said, looking at the ground before him. He was on the path that once led into the cave where he and Cy had camped.

It's never right when darkness falls on the souls of men. What matters is, he shall never do this again, Ferron said. *You are a hero.*

"Hero?" Krycin asked out loud, not expecting an answer. "I'm no hero. I was just here at the right time. And this hardly feels like a victory. I traveled with him. He was my friend. He was there when I woke up, and taught me to use my powers. He taught me to use magic. No. I'm no hero. Not today."

If it weren't for you, my beloved Tersca and I would be dead now, and Gladius would be more powerful still. Heroic deeds never feel that way when they happen. You could have done nothing and allowed the atrocity to happen. Whatever you call it, your action saved our lives, and we shall be forever grateful for that.

Krycin opened his mouth to say something when he heard a sound behind him. There was a humming sound, and then the crackle of lightning as it arced out of the air and struck the ground. He looked up at it with his heart racing. The rift split open and he saw the blue aether that existed between worlds. A sudden pain raged through his head as a headache came on all at once. He gasped and grabbed his head, falling to the ground. Blood poured from his nose, eyes, and ears. Krycin laid on the path and screamed himself unconscious.

Chapter 19 - Open War

Findoor castle was quiet with the tension of war. A great many Lyecians had answered Cy's call and now lined up on the walls of the city and the field just outside it. The sun was starting to set as Cy walked through the front gates. Wizards emerged from rifts onto the field before him, with Marius and the High Council leading the way.

"I told you, he isn't here," Cy said, sidling toward them with a smile on his face.

"And I told you that we'll tear this castle apart to find him," Marius said, matching Cy's tone. "So here we are, at an impasse. We could continue with this madness, and lives will be lost, or you could simply tell us where Krycin is, and this ends now."

Cy scoffed at the ultimatum. "How can you look at this army before you and possibly believe you have a chance at victory? You're one of us, Marius. You know what we're capable of, and if we have to vaporize every one of your little wizards, we will. You won't be taking Krycin. Not tonight. Not ever."

Marius took a step forward and placed himself inches from Cy. He opened his mouth to respond, but didn't get another word in before the earth beneath his feet began to shake. A deafening thunder came from the northwest and the shaking intensified causing everyone on the field to lower their stance in order to keep their balance. A murmur went through both sides when the earthquake stopped.

Cy looked up at Marius and said, "Hold that thought."

Without warning, he blinked out of existence, leaving a void that the air rushed in to fill.

Merek was watching the confrontation from the battlements when the earthquake hit. He held tight to the wall as the entire castle shook beneath his feet and made him feel somewhat motion sick. When the shaking stopped, he turned around to go back to the castle and nearly bumped into Cy who appeared before him. "There was nothing natural about that," Merek said as he led the way into the castle and moved with all the speed he could muster down to his basement lab. Cy followed close behind him, but didn't say a word.

The hidden door to Merek's scrying pool was already open when they entered the lab, and both men entered the dark, dank room. Merek approached the edge of the water and summoned the power of shadow. He cast a light into the pool and focused on the source of the earthquake. The image that appeared before him shook him to his core.

The entire Fioraden ridge had collapsed into a great pit in the earth, burying a bright light at the center of it all. "Krycin," Merek said, and the image shifted to the edge of the hole where Krycin appeared. He looked in rough shape, but he was alive. The fact eased Merek's mind, but he still wanted to find out what had happened.

With a wave of his hand, Merek dismissed his spell and made his way back to the main room. He cast a series of spells to open a rift and when he looked around before stepping in, saw that Cy was already gone. Without further hesitation, he stepped through the rift.

When Merek emerged on the other side, Krycin was on the ground screaming and holding his head. Blood covered his hands and face, making it hard to see if he had sustained any serious injuries. Cy was at his side whispering soothing words in Krycin's ear. It took a few minutes, but Krycin calmed and fell into a deep sleep.

"What happened here?" Merek asked, looking to Ferron.

A dark wizard, Gladius, attacked us. Were it not for Krycin, Tersca and I would both be dead. We owe him our lives, Ferron said as he knelt down beside Krycin and faced Cy. His wings folded against his back and his feathered mane settled.

Merek looked from Krycin to Ferron. "What injuries has he sustained?"

When he saw the rift open, he collapsed. Before that, he looked as though he would be fine. He fought hard against Gladius, and in the end, the earthquake that Gladius caused consumed him. I am glad to say that I doubt we shall see him again.

"What of your home? Where will your people go?"

Tersca is leading them to the North, to the mountains there.

Merek looked around at the gaping hole in the earth. "Such devastation. I had no idea Gladius was this powerful. We must get Krycin to a healer."

Cy gathered Krycin into his arms and said, "Lead the way, Merek. We will have to take him back by rift."

Merek walked over to the ledge and looked down into the pit. Darkness hid any kind of bottom that might have been there. "What have you done, Gladius?" Merek asked, shaking his head and walking away from the pit. When he was a safe distance from it, he opened a rift and he and Cy returned to Findoor castle with Krycin.

⊛

Merek and Cy walked together out onto the field to confront the High Council. The last of the Council's rifts had closed and night had fallen on the kingdom. The temperature fell as the sun went down, causing a heavy dew to coat the grass. Merek motioned for Cy to be quiet as they confronted the Council.

"I'll be honest with you," Merek began, "I don't want a war. I know you've come for Krycin, but I can assure you, he is less of a threat to Galadir than Gladius is."

Darson stepped forward with a smug look on his face. "Gladius is no more a threat than a common hedge wizard. A total waste of talent if you ask me. I'd be surprised if he was still alive."

"You are a fool, Darson. You always were. The earthquake that just occurred, that was the entire Fioraden mountain range collapsing." Merek was interrupted by a number of gasps from Council members. Marius and Darson stood fast.

"A tragedy, I'm sure," Darson said, looking into Merek's eyes. "But what does that have to do with me?"

"It was caused by your son," Merek said with a cool, flat tone.

The rest of the Council backed up a step at this news. Darson looked at the ground without another word. Marius spoke up instead. "What of the Fioraden? Are they all right?"

Merek nodded. "They have taken to the northern mountain range where they will no doubt join their brethren. Ferron claimed they suffered minimal losses due to the valiant fighting of one man."

"Who do we thank for this? And is Gladius still alive?" Marius asked.

"Ferron feels that Gladius perished in the collapse. I'll not believe it until we find his body. The hero of the day is Krycin, though he has now suffered his own ill fate and is resting, unconscious, in the healer's hall."

Marius lowered his gaze to the ground now as well, and thought in silence for a long time. When he looked up again, Merek remained, waiting in silence. "Merek, we have been fools..."

"You do not honestly believe these lies, do you?" Darson said. "Merek would say anything to avoid a war now."

Marius looked toward Darson, his movements sharp and unrestrained. "Shut up, Darson. You've spoken enough tonight. I was never fond of turning on my own kind, and now I regret it even more. But it is, thankfully, a mistake I can now correct."

"You cannot defy the Council. Our vote is law, you know that," Darson said with a sly smile.

"You're right," Marius said, looking to the rest of the Council. "My friends, we are about to commit a grave injustice against a fine kingdom, and an innocent man. If there are any who remain true to their previous vote, stand by Darson now. Otherwise, there will be no war, and Krycin will remain a free man."

There was no hesitation for Lebriel. He walked to Marius and stood behind him in full support. Bareva of the white robe moved next, taking a place beside Lebriel. The remaining Council members paused for only a split second before joining Marius, leaving Darson to stand alone.

"If this is the Council's wish, then it shall be done," Darson said through gritted teeth. "But do not come to me if Krycin betrays you and brings about Galadir's destruction." With that, he stormed off into the mass of people in the field, shouting angry orders at the hapless wizards.

Marius looked at Merek and Cy and said, "It is a shame the Fioraden have lost their home. Will Krycin live?"

Merek nodded. "He is suffering from some kind of internal conflict, brought on by familiar sights and sounds. His memories are trying to come back, but at the same time, part of him is trying to suppress them. I fear that if he does not accomplish what he has set out to do soon, his own mind will tear itself apart."

"Please keep us advised of Krycin's condition, and if there is anything we can do to aid him, simply ask, and you shall receive it."

"Thank you, Marius," Merek said with a bow, "you are most kind."

Chapter 20 – The Might of a Nation

There was pain as the sword lodged in his gut dissolved into the air around him. Then falling. Endless falling into darkness. He didn't scream. There was no point. He waited, in too much pain to summon any more magic, and with an entire mountain falling down on top of him. It felt like he fell for an eternity, though it was only a few seconds. His hand found the hilt of the black steel sword he wore at his side, and the sensation of falling disappeared, the pain abated, and he lay motionless on a solid surface.

I must be dead, Gladius thought, and opened his eyes. He wasn't even aware that he'd shut them until that point. Darkness surrounded him, a blackness no light could pierce and no eyes could see through. It had a tangible quality to it, like floating in water, though he wasn't wet.

A strange voice echoed around him, one that wrapped him up and held him. "Gladius, arise."

He started at the sound of it. "Who are you?" he asked with a hoarse voice.

"Your destiny," the voice boomed around Gladius.

"I..." Gladius said, stumbling over his words.

"We need each other." There was a dark figure before Gladius, just beyond his range of clear vision.

"Who are you?" Gladius asked, trying to make out any kind of detail in the form.

"A long forgotten memory," the voice said.

"Don't play games with me," Gladius shouted at the figure before him.

"The games have barely begun."

Laughter boomed all around him, pressing in on him and shaking Gladius to his core. The figure before him disappeared and the sensation of falling resumed, followed by hard ground beneath him.

A cool breeze blew over Gladius and he once again opened his eyes. A dark, rocky landscape surrounded him. Campfires dotted the landscape that stretched out before him and he could make out a large number of hulking figures around these fires. Several of the creatures approached Gladius as he got his bearings, snarling and growling their feral language to each other. He tried to make out what they were saying, but his mind was filled with fog that refused to clear.

One of the Narshuks approached him and growled something that Gladius thought was "Who goes there?"

He planted his feet on the ground and got up, shaking his head to clear it. He tried to say something, but nothing would come out. The lead Narshuk didn't wait for Gladius to recover, but instead approached him, grabbed him by the throat and lifted him off the ground.

"Who are you?" the beast asked again.

Being lifted by the throat was all he needed to clear his mind. The magic flowed through him when he called on the power of death, and he spoke, "Obitas nexasa mortai."

A black glow surrounded his hand as he reached up and grabbed the creature's arm. Its eyes grew wide and a strangled cry came from it before its grip loosened, dropping Gladius. It was dead before Gladius's feet hit the ground, and it slumped over in a loose mass of bones and meat, its life snuffed out with a single touch.

"Who am I? I am your master, and you will address me as 'lord'." Gladius took slow, deliberate steps toward a second Narshuk, who shied away from him.

It took a step back, dropped to one knee, and said, "My lord."

"Take me to Scrag."

The Narshuk stood up and mumbled, "Yes, my lord." He led Gladius, twisting and winding his way through the maze of campfires and rocky outcroppings. When they reached the other side of the encampment, Scrag was there growling orders to several larger ones who accepted their tasks, though not without some reluctance.

"Well done Scrag. Well done. The tribes are coming together nicely. This is more than I thought possible in such a short time," Gladius said, clapping his hands and approaching with a strut that verged on cocky.

Scrag scoffed. "Short time? It has been weeks. I was beginning to think you were never coming back. The tribes are already growing restless."

Gladius stood and stared at Scrag, awestruck. "Weeks? Don't play me for a fool, Scrag, I've been gone a day at best."

The Narshuk shaman narrowed his eyes at Gladius. "You think I could gather the tribes like this in only a day?"

"A thousand Narshuks would take only a few days to gather. I'm no fool Scrag. If you are trying to make me look like one, I'll have your head."

"Come," Scrag said, and walked up a narrow pathway to a ledge above them.

He followed, looking out at the landscape around them as he made his way up the slope. When they reached the top, Scrag spread his arms wide and howled. The response back from the army surrounding them shook the earth as ten thousand Narshuks, spread out around the small hill for miles, howled back. Gladius looked out at the massive army in awe. "Glorious."

Scrag lowered his head and looked down at the human wizard. "An army worthy of a god. Grishtor will favor us, and give us victory. We do not need you."

Laughter escaped Gladius before he realized what he was doing. A great hearty laugh that echoed across the camp for all to hear. "You think Grishtor favors you? Do you have any idea what the High Council will do to you if they discover this?" Gladius said, taking a step towards Scrag. "You need me to dispatch them. That was the plan. I need four more souls to cast the reality anchor. I shall return in two days' time."

Gladius didn't wait for a response before opening a rift. Scrag snapped out of his stupor and took a step forward, but was too late. Gladius entered the rift, and disappeared.

$$\odot$$

The room in Findoor Castle where Berel the runner sat was calm and quiet. He loathed being put on this shift because it meant he had to sit and watch the mysterious stranger that did nothing but breathe and sleep. He'd done this shift many times, always with the same result. He would get bored, fall asleep, and then the Arch-Magus would catch him, scold him for being lax on his duty, and he would fight to stay awake for the remainder of the shift.

Today wasn't much different. The brown-haired stranger lay in the same bed, sleeping as always. He sat in the chair by the door and watched the stranger. If his memory served him right, the stranger had laid there in that spot for weeks. Staff at the castle tended to the man, changed his bedding and clothing, and healers ensured he remained otherwise healthy. But he never woke up. Nobody but Merek knew who it was, but they all knew it was a Lyecian.

The boredom was getting to Berel and his eyelids were getting heavy when he saw the man's fingers move. With a shake of his head, Berel's eyes snapped open and he took another, more careful look at the man's hand. *There's no way he could wake up now.*

He watched the stranger's hands as the fingers twitched again, and then he ran in a panic out the door. "Merek!" he screamed at the top of his lungs as he ran through the castle corridors and made his way to the throne room. "Arch-Magus Merek!"

When he reached the throne room, Merek was already making his way out. "What is it boy? Half the castle heard your screams."

"Merek," Berel said through breaths. "The stranger, he moved. Come quickly."

He led the way without waiting for Merek. He knew the Arch-Magus would follow. When he got back to the chamber, he opened the door for Merek. A dark figure was waiting inside that made his heart jump into his chest. He almost cried out for the guards, but Merek put a hand on his arm, shaking his head. "There is no need for alarm, he is a friend," Merek said to Berel. "You may go now, you are excused from duty."

Berel nodded and walked away without another word.

Chapter 21 - Waking Up

A murky darkness surrounded Krycin. The pain in his head was gone, but he couldn't see anything through the mist surrounding him. It was almost liquid in the way it moved, churning and rolling, creating various shapes and then dissolving before his eyes.

"Hello?" he called out, but received no response.

He turned in what he thought was a circle, and saw nothing in any direction. *Where am I?* He thought, trying to get his bearings and figure out what was happening to him.

There was a whisper in the darkness, a female voice with a Findoor accent. *"My apologies. I would have liked to have introductions on better terms..."*

Krycin didn't catch the rest as the voice faded into the distance. He followed it, running as fast as he could, but no amount of speed could help him reach that voice again. *There's something I need to remember. Why can't I remember it?*

Another whisper reached him, this time coming from his left. *"What makes you think we are going to Findoor?"*

It faded as fast as the first one did, but Krycin tried to follow it. "Who are you?" he called into the darkness. "Where are you?"

"Indeed, you are right. But I fought hard for my placement in the army, and Merek helped a lot," the female voice said.

"What am I forgetting?" he asked out loud.

"At the rate it's growing, our worlds won't last the night," another whisper said. It was a voice much like Krycin's, and it opened a floodgate. Images assaulted his memory of a young man being assaulted by a Narshuk, of waking up in a strange land. Hundreds of sharp images flooded his memory. A strange masked man who

helped with a journey. A great wizard in gray robes. *Merek,* Krycin thought. He watched as more images went through his mind, scattered and out-of-order. Narshuks attacking again and again, and a man in black. A relentless man in black.

Cy. How can it be?

One final image burned into his mind before the assault stopped. A great rift, larger than any he'd seen before, threatened to destroy two worlds.

"The rift," he said, taking a step back. The memory appeared before him. "It was closed, but it wasn't enough. The damage was done."

Krycin watched the scene play out, as if it were happening right in front of him.

He was between two worlds, the blue aether swirled around him. A man before him wearing crystal armor was working magic to stabilize the two worlds, but there was too much damage, and he was failing. The armor was disrupting his efforts, so he sent it back to Galadir, along with a very special gold necklace to let his friends know he was okay. Both worlds were crumbling around him and it took every ounce of strength he had left to stabilize them.

"There had to be another way," Krycin said, and watched as the man before him buckled under the strain of his work. "Prevent the damage before it happened."

He opened his eyes, not realizing he had them shut. Bright light in the room caused him to blink and squint until his eyes adjusted. He was lying in a comfortable bed with blankets tucked in around him. A calm, peaceful feeling filled his heart, and he relaxed. Gray stone walls, cool, but not cold air, and somebody Krycin could sense next to the bed. A friend.

"Krycin?" a voice said to his right. He looked toward the voice and saw two figures looking back at him. Merek wore his usual gray robes with gold trim. The second figure was cloaked in black robes from head to toe and had a deep hood pulled up over his head. Tyriel.

"I've seen the future," Krycin said. "I know what I have to do."

Merek and Tyriel looked at each other with curious expressions, and then back to Krycin. Merek smiled and said, "We were all very worried about you."

Krycin looked toward the window and saw bright colors over the trees like a vivid painting of fall. Reds and oranges and yellows and greens blended together in a bright flurry of leaves that rustled in an afternoon breeze. "It's autumn," Krycin said. A torrent of emotions welled up inside him, but he fought them back. His heart felt like it was breaking, though he couldn't remember why he would feel this way.

"Autumn?" Merek asked.

"The leaves are changing."

"Yes, Krycin," Merek said in a soothing voice. "The harvest is upon us."

"How long did I sleep?"

Krycin looked at Merek's face and saw it full of conflict. "You must understand, Krycin, you've been asleep a long time."

"How long, Merek?"

With a sigh, and a long pause, Merek looked into Krycin's green eyes and said, "Weeks, my friend. You've been asleep for weeks."

The words hit Krycin with all the force of a hammer blow to the head. For a long time, the only sound in the room was the whisper of leaves coming in the window.

Krycin looked up at Merek and said, "Why?"

"Nobody knows, Krycin. But I have ensured that you have been tended to all this time. We've been waiting for you."

"Thank you, Merek."

Tyriel stepped forward and said, "It is of the utmost importance that I talk to you, Krycin. I know you are disoriented, but the lives of many depend on you."

"Yes," Krycin said. "I know." He paused and looked out the window one more time, then back to Merek. "The Fioraden, how are they?"

"Settled in to their new home nicely and managing just fine. Had it not been for your fast thinking and valiant actions, it would have been much worse for them," Merek said.

"And Gladius?" Krycin asked, not sure he wanted to know the answer.

"Dead. Or presumed so. We have neither seen nor heard of any trace of him since that day."

Krycin breathed a sigh of relief. "Then perhaps my task is done."

"You said you knew the reason you were here now. What is it, Krycin? What is, or was, your task?" Tyriel asked.

Krycin sat up and made an attempt to get to his feet, but his legs wobbled beneath him and he fell back onto the bed. With a sheepish smile, he said, "You'll have to excuse me." He cleared his mind and called on the power of life. The white magic filled him up and restored strength to his body. He made another attempt to get out of bed, and managed it this time. A few steps later his balance returned, and he was able to cross the room. He turned around and took a second to clear his thoughts before speaking. "I've seen the future, or what was to be the future," he said, his voice shaking with his nerves. "There's a rift, bigger than any I've seen. It isn't stable, and continues to grow long after the creator of the rift has gone. It threatens Galadir, and another world. A young man works to close it, but he's too late. The damage is done, and the barrier between worlds collapses, destroying both worlds. I think I'm supposed to prevent this from happening."

Merek nodded, but his expression couldn't be read. Tyriel ran a hand through his red hair and looked concerned. "Who created the rift?" Tyriel asked.

"Cy, aided by Gladius, or rather, Gladius's consciousness. But if Gladius is dead, and Cy is still here in Findoor, there is nothing to fear. The future that would be has been prevented," Krycin said with a smile. His smile faded fast when he saw Tyriel shaking his head.

"It's not that simple," Tyriel said. "You're not from this time, Krycin. Everything you do, everything you touch, every life you affect is being changed from its original place in the flow of time. There are certain events that *must* happen or it will create a paradox, and destroy everything. I suspect what you saw, your vision, was actually your memories returning."

"So if Gladius is really dead, then the future could already be destroyed?"

Tyriel raised a hand and looked like he was deep in thought. Krycin watched the conflict in his blue eyes and then the troubling expression that washed over his face. "I must go," Tyriel said. "I can interfere no longer."

Krycin approached him, his brows lowered over eyes lit up with anger. "That's it? You can interfere no longer? That's all you've got? Tyriel, I'm confused, and still don't know who I am or where or even *when* I'm from. The balance of time is resting on my shoulders, and you're going to leave me?"

There was a look on Tyriel's face that spoke louder than any words could. "Merek, could you excuse us for a few moments to talk alone?"

"Certainly," Merek said, retreating through the door. Over his shoulder he said, "Send a runner for me when you are finished, Krycin." He closed the door behind him.

Tyriel approached Krycin, and in a hushed voice said, "I am sorry, Krycin."

"Sorry for what? If what you say is true, if these visions are my memories, then I did this to myself."

"Indeed, but time is seldom that simple. Certain events led to you coming to this particular place and time. You cannot change those events without destroying everything. Gladius lives. He must if he had a hand in creating the rift you speak of. "

Krycin braced himself against a dressing table, his knees suddenly weak. "So what now?"

Tyriel shook his head. "I can tell you no more. Your memories must return on their own. But please, heed my warning. Gladius and Cy must live, no matter what you do."

The black robes began to dissolve into mist, signaling the end of Tyriel's presence, but Krycin stood up and approached him, anger in his eyes. "No! You can't leave me like this. I don't know what to do."

Tyriel continued to dissolve, but said one last thing to Krycin before he disappeared. "Trust your instincts."

Krycin watched the last of the mist disperse into the air, and then walked over to the bed, sat down, and got lost in his thoughts.

$$\odot$$

It was several hours before Krycin emerged from the room, composed and focused on a new task. He sent a runner to summon Merek to the throne room and made his way there. Court was in session, so he waited in the lobby until Merek arrived.

"Goodness, my boy, I'm glad you're all right. What did you want to discuss?"

Krycin stood and approached the gray wizard. "You must call the High Council to a meeting here immediately. Travel by rift must be stopped."

Merek's mood changed in an instant from pleasant to serious. "That's a high order coming from a man who was just recently considered a fugitive. The Council will not easily agree. Why would you request such a thing?"

"Rifts are damaging the space between worlds. The rift itself closes, but the hole in the aether between worlds does not. It's part of what caused the damage in the future. Eventually, you will put so many holes in the space between worlds, that the boundary that surrounds our world will collapse, destroying Galadir and everything on it in the process."

"By the gods," Merek said, taking a step back. "Can you prove it? I may take you at your word, but the Council will not. We will have to have proof."

Krycin took hold of Merek without warning and focused on transferring them both to the space between worlds. The lobby disappeared and was replaced by swirling blue aether all around them. Now and then, electrical arcs would jump from one point to another, letting out a dull crackling sound. Other than that, there was silence. Krycin pointed out to Merek the areas in the aether where it was riddled with holes and the boundaries were getting weak. A look of shock washed over Merek's face, but he could not speak. Krycin didn't wait a second longer, and transferred them back to the lobby outside the throne room.

Merek gasped for breath, but regained his composure quickly. "I have little doubt now," Merek said. "It will be done. I shall assemble the Council, and all travel by rift shall be banned, effective immediately."

Chapter 22 - Soul of Life and Light

Gladius emerged from the rift at the northern-most tip of the Astaran desert and broke into a sweat before he had taken a single step. The sun beat down on him as he stood on a wide plateau of sand and nothing more. Waves of heat rose from the ground all around him, causing ripples in the landscape. There wasn't a cloud in the sky, making it easy for Gladius to see why the place was one of the most feared locations on Galadir. *Just a day in this heat would be enough to drive a man mad,* he thought as he walked away from the rift which closed behind him.

He walked east as far as he could tell by the sun and scanned the ground for tell-tale signs of his prey. After only a few minutes, he pulled his hood up despite the temperature. The sun beating down on his head was giving him a headache, and he knew if he walked too long without protection, he would end up with a nasty sunburn.

The air he breathed was starved for moisture and drew water from his lungs, leaving Gladius thirsty, but without drink. His mouth grew sticky, and then dry over the course of minutes while he continued to walk east. He was looking for a particular landmark, and knew many existed in the desert. What he didn't know was how far apart they would be.

Each step grew more and more difficult as the heat drained his energy and the hot air robbed him of his moisture, leaving him with cracked, dry lips. He stopped and surveyed the landscape. More sand, in every direction. Miles of it. The only way he knew what direction he had come from was by looking at the footprints he left as he walked, and those only lasted a few minutes as the steady breeze filled them in and smoothed the sand out.

There must be a colony here somewhere, he thought, and carried on walking east.

Several hours later, he was about to give up his search, when he spotted something in the ripples in the distance. He thought he was seeing things at first, as the mirage masked it quite well. As he drew closer, it became clear: this is what he was looking for.

Ahead stood a tall column of packed sand that looked like stone. It was at least the height of an average man, but narrow, and designed to blend into the mirages that the desert heat created. *Clever little beasts,* Gladius thought. *I might have walked by dozens of them and never known.* In fact, Gladius had passed by several of these columns, but could see them no more than he could see the wind.

Standing outside the column was a tiny creature, about one hand tall. Four transparent wings like the wings of a dragonfly, only shorter, grew from its back. Though it stood on two legs, it had six limbs total, four of which it used as hands. It had a tough exoskeleton, and compound eyes that were positioned to give it near perfect vision in every direction. Its only blind spot was directly behind and slightly below it. The creature standing outside the column held a bladed weapon that looked like a tiny halberd. It was so small that Gladius might have used it as a razor.

"At long last," Gladius said, and approached the column. The creature spotted him right away and held its weapon at the ready. "Good sket, I mean you no harm," he said. He bowed down before the column and concentrated on drawing the power of death. "I've been looking for you."

The creature tilted its head and let out a string of clicks and buzzes that sounded like speech, but Gladius didn't understand it. He continued to draw power as the creature took a step forward, lowering its guard. Its wings came to life and it lifted up off the ground into a hover level with Gladius's face. It let out the same string of clicks and buzzes, and continued to watch Gladius.

He pulled his hands into his sleeves just before the black fire erupted from his right hand, and said, "You'll have to forgive me, I don't understand your language."

His spell was almost complete when the creature moved back toward the column. "Wait," Gladius said, and caught the creature's attention. "Vimvitas mortai," he said, and thrust his hand at the creature. It was fast, but not fast enough. Gladius caught its hind legs in a tight grip and felt its soul resist the magic. He drew more energy

142

and pushed it into the spell that would separate the creature's soul from its body.

The yellow energy glowed as it began to separate from its physical form, but the creature spun its weapon and stabbed it down into Gladius's hand, leaving a deep gash between his thumb and index finger. Still he held on.

Just before the sket succumbed to the spell, it let out a deafening screech that hurt Gladius's ears. The yellow energy of its soul flowed from its body and formed into a ball of light in Gladius's hand. He let the limp body of the creature fall to the ground as he absorbed the energy into his body. His task was almost complete when the column before him burst to life with hundreds of the little creatures flooding out of every opening. Gladius finished his work and backed up away from the column.

The swarm grew larger still and pursued him, moving like a great living cloud.

Gladius spun back toward the swarm and called on his newly acquired power of air. "Adglomeras," he said, and manifested the energy as a steady wind that blew at his back and toward the swarm. He lacked the power to create a gust strong enough to disperse the swarm, but it slowed them enough to allow him to gather his thoughts. With the power of air fresh in his mind, and his native element water, Gladius combined the two into a powerful spell, drawing all the energy he could without hurting himself. He raised his right hand into the air and called out, "Tempestas."

Clouds rolled in above the desert and grew dark, winds picked up, and thunder rolled across the sky as the first strokes of lightning arced. Rain fell, gentle at first, and then growing into a torrential downpour. The skets were forced to land for fear that the gusting winds and driving rain would blow them from the sky. Lightning flashed over and over. Some struck the column and caused explosions that tore large chunks of it off, but most hit the sand all around them, melting it into glass. Thunder deafened them, and darkness fell as the thick clouds blotted out the sun. The storm was violent, and would last many hours. None of the skets noticed when Gladius cast another rift and escaped through it.

⊙

Gladius emerged from his rift back in the badlands and cast a healing spell on his hand to repair the injury he sustained. Darkness still cloaked the land, though the sun would be up soon. He looked around at the jagged mountains and rocky terrain and smiled to himself. *Sunrise will be my only chance to catch one of the lumbering Mordos in the open,* he thought. The black skinned giants were all but invisible under the cover of night. He could be standing right in front of one and not realize it. A quick look around revealed a hiding place from which he would have a good view of the terrain around him. There, he waited for the first rays of sunlight to break through the clouds that always covered the badlands.

When it happened, Gladius was surprised at how close the Mordo was. The light hit the creature, and reflected off of its skin, revealing it to Gladius. It was twelve feet tall and shaped like a giant human, with hair, eyes and skin the purest black Gladius had ever seen in a natural creature. *It's no wonder they are the subject of legends,* he thought as he crept out of his hiding place.

Trying not to be seen, Gladius moved step by step toward the Mordo, who looked like he was just out for a casual stroll. When Gladius lost his footing and made a rock snap against the ground, the Mordo spun, looked him in the eye, and then disappeared. "Blast it," Gladius said, and focused his mind on drawing power from three elements at once. Earth, water and air flowed to him, stressing his limits and causing his head to ache. It took a second for him to find the words through the pain, but when he did, they rolled off his tongue. "Tremefascas merguntas tempestas." The three elements combined into a whirling mud storm at Gladius's command and coated every surface in the area. The Mordo was left in the open, its natural defenses unable to protect it. Three others were in the area as well, that Gladius hadn't seen before.

"Come now," Gladius said, "you'll have to do better than that."

His target faced him head on, its black eyes staring at him with such intensity that it made Gladius feel unsure of himself. It said something in a language Gladius could not understand, but its tone was hostile. It picked up a large boulder in one hand and hurled it at Gladius. He ducked, letting it fly past him and tumble on the ground behind him.

Startled by the sudden attack, Gladius took a moment to clear his mind. The Mordo took advantage of this and picked up a second boulder. When he hurled it, Gladius was ready and summoning the power of earth. He focused the power into a counter to the boulder attack and spoke the word, "Concutinas."

A concussive force struck the boulder in midair and shattered it into thousands of smaller pieces that were then sent flying back toward the Mordo. Some of the smaller pieces bounced off the creature's skin, but others pierced it or left bruises where they struck. A deep crimson stream flowed from the Mordo's wounds, and yet it continued its advance. More angry words came from its mouth. Its hands were balled up into fists and it was winding up for a strike when Gladius called on the power of death. He focused the energy in his hand, into a black glow and waited for just the right moment. When the Mordo was paces from him, he ran forward and plunged his hand into its gut, calling out the words to his spell as he did so. "Vimvitas mortai!"

Gladius took hold of the Mordo's soul and ripped it from its body as he dropped to the ground. He slid between the Mordo's legs, letting momentum carry the giant forward. It collapsed, rolling across the rocky ground, and came to a rest in a heap next to a great boulder. There was an ear-splitting roar from the other three who watched as Gladius integrated the gray soul into his own. Then the hail of boulders started.

One smashed down next to Gladius, and startled him out of his reveling. He scrambled to his feet only to have a second one crash to the ground inches from him. He looked up and saw three more large rocks flying through the air toward him, and more being launched. *Time to go,* he thought, and ran for cover behind several large rocks.

There were more crashing sounds that followed Gladius as he ran. He didn't waste time looking back to see how close they were. When he was under cover, he concentrated on opening a rift so that he could escape. The crashing of the rocks around him became more frequent as he worked his magic, and from the footsteps he heard, the Mordos were growing closer every second. He finished the spell, and the rift split open before him just as one of the large creatures made its way around the rocks behind which Gladius hid.

Gladius made a run for the rift, and the Mordo made a run for him. He leapt into the opening just as the large hand snagged his leg, stopping him half way through the portal. The magical opening began to close with Gladius only half way through, and the creature hauled on his leg to pull him back out. Summoning the power of water, Gladius spoke a word, "Exsiccatas."

A blue glow surrounded the Mordo and flowed from it to Gladius. Its screams were all Gladius needed to know his strike was true. He pulled hard, fighting the Mordo's grip on his leg, but the dessication spell caused it to squeeze tighter as the spell drained the water from its body.

The edge of the rift was closing fast, and Gladius felt the bones in his leg give out under the pressure of the Mordo's grip. Pain flared up through his leg and into his hip as he dislocated it trying to pull free. He gave one final heave, and moved back another couple inches before the rift slammed shut, severing the Mordo's arm at the wrist. He kicked the severed hand off with his other foot. The pain of the broken leg and the dislocated hip was blinding, but Gladius knew if he didn't get moving, he would get lost in the space between worlds.

He rolled over and saw a light at the other end to focus on. Dragging himself, and doing the best he could to ignore the pain, he inched his way through the blue aether. When he reached the other end, he tumbled through the hole into the bright light, and fell unconscious.

⊙

A kick to his leg woke Gladius up as pain seared through it and radiated up into his body. "Philana curse you," he screamed without opening his eyes. Whoever kicked him was going to pay for it once he managed to heal himself. Ignoring the voices of the men around him, he called upon the power of water. "Restitas," he said, and allowed the blue healing energy to flow into his leg. There was an audible snap as his hip moved back into joint and the tendons tightened up again. His tibia in the same leg straightened and grew back together, setting into place. It took a lot of his remaining strength just to channel the power required to mend the bones, but when he was done, the pain went away, and all he was left with was fatigue.

Gladius opened his eyes and looked around. Four soldiers surrounded him, pointing their spears toward him. The tips of the spears were inches from his head. Each soldier wore a chest plate with the symbol of a crown with a sword through it. "Is there a problem?" Gladius asked, pushing one of the spearheads away from his face.

The soldier that held the spear shook Gladius's hand off of it and returned it to its position near Gladius's face. "You are on Findoor land, and using restricted magic. We are required to take you in for questioning."

"Restricted magic? Whatever do you mean?" Gladius put on his best innocent smile.

"The rift you used to travel here. By the order of the Wizard High Council, travel by rift is no longer permitted. The spells used are now classified as forbidden." The soldier backed up a step to allow Gladius to get up.

When he got to his feet, he brushed himself off. His temper boiled inside of him, but Gladius acted casual, trying to hide his anger at the insolence of the soldier. "You must understand, I have leave from the Council to use forbidden magics," Gladius said in a calm, level voice.

"That will be up to the Arch-Magus to decide. Move it. If you do have leave, then you have nothing to fear." The soldier prodded him with the tip of his spear, which pushed Gladius to the tipping point.

He walked, as directed, but as he did, he focused his mind and drew the power of air, despite the pain of doing so when he was already fatigued. He pulled in a much larger amount of power than he needed, and felt it burning inside of him. The soldiers talked amongst themselves as they walked, and didn't notice the painful grimace on Gladius's face until it was too late.

Gladius spun on his heels and shouted, "Adglomeras!"

A powerful burst of air spread out from Gladius in a circle, knocking the soldiers back away from him. He used just enough magic to get them away so that he could do his next spell.

"Incitatas," Gladius said, and focused the last of his strength on the spell that pushed him into the air, into flight. There was a burning pain in his head that no spell would heal, but the ground fell away as he flew north to the mountain range.

He was out of range of the soldiers spears before they got back to their feet.

Gladius flew as far as he could with what strength he had left. He could see the patrol lines of the Findoor soldiers, which were marked by faint wear lines in the fields. When he was a safe distance from them, he returned to the ground to rest and took cover in a small forest at the foothills of the mountain range. Sleep took him fast.

He woke up to large water drops soaking his robes. The trees held back the rain for a little while, but once the leaves were saturated, the water ran off in large drops and splatted against him. Gladius stood up, feeling better after a rest despite the wet clothes. He walked toward the mountains, continuing on his quest for the remaining two elements.

The Fioraden must have come to these mountains. There is nowhere else they could have gone, he thought.

For several hours he walked, trying to conserve his strength for what might prove to be a longer battle than he had for the first five elements. Getting a shadow soul nearly got him killed. The sun was starting to set when he reached the base of the mountains, and as he suspected, the side of the mountain was covered with small swells made of sticks and thatch. He smiled to himself and kept walking.

When he was close enough to the mountains that the Fioraden might be able to spot him, he found a boulder to take cover behind and thought. *I need more than just these robes to protect me from the Fioraden weapons.* Gladius rested his hand on the hilt of the black steel sword he had taken from Merek and felt it was warm to the touch. He was trained in the use of basic weapons, the longsword included, but had never fought with one. *Why is it warm,* he thought, drawing the sword from its scabbard.

The entire weapon was forged from black steel and was perfectly weighted for his grip. The sword felt lighter than it should have, and when Gladius swung it, trails of flame and smoke followed it. "Warm indeed," he said out loud without realizing it. "Now I just need some armor."

A nagging feeling in his mind startled him as magical energy pushed into him from the sword. It burned for a moment as he resisted it, but when he realized the sword wasn't going to let up, he opened his mind and allowed it to control him. The sword's own power of fire coursed through his body and seared off his robes, leaving him exposed to the elements and holding only the sword. It drew upon his own power of water and attracted rain drops to him, forming a layer over his entire body except his eyes, nose and mouth. Earth energy came to him and radiated into the ground, drawing small pieces of iron from the ground to cover his entire body. Fire again flowed over his body, melting the iron into interlocking plates that covered every inch of his exposed flesh. Even his head was covered with a black helmet. The water sizzled and evaporated as steam from under the armor, but did not burn him. By the time the last of the water had disappeared, the armor was finished and cool to the touch.

The armor was black, like the sword, and fit well. Gladius tried moving in it and found his actions unhindered by the new armor. He looked down at the chest plate and said, "Beautiful, if not a little plain."

There was a jolt in his sword hand, and a spark appeared on the chest plate, carving a pattern into it. "Something to represent renewal, and rebirth," Gladius said. The sparks moved over the chest plate, creating a design that would satisfy his request. A lily with a snake wrapped around the stem.

"Perfect," Gladius said, and felt a wave of approval from the sword. Gladius looked down at it one more time before placing it in the sheath at his hip and said, "Who would have thought that Merek would have you stowed away."

With full battle gear now in place, Gladius called on the power of air once more and said, "Incitatas." A moment later, he was aloft and ready to complete his task.

A quick scan of the mountainside showed him some easy targets: Fioraden people who were sound asleep in their nests. The black armor concealed his approach until the last second, when he dropped down on a nest with a single Fioraden female in it. When he landed, he plowed his fist into the creatures head to ensure that it stayed unconscious. Drawing the power of death, his fist flared up with black fire. He spoke the words, "Vimvitas mortai," and plunged his hand into her torso. He felt the white hot energy of her soul struggling against him, and so he channeled more energy into his spell. The female's eyes shot open and she let out a blood curdling scream as Gladius wrenched her soul free from her body. The light from her soul, a ball of white energy in his fist, flooded out of the nest like sunlight. Movements outside the nest told Gladius he had to move fast. He regained his focus in order to absorb the Fioraden soul and integrate it with his own. The energy flooded into him, filling him up and intertwining with his own soul. As they became one, the light faded, and then disappeared.

Gladius heard the whispering whine of the arrow before he saw it. It flew at him and glanced off his armor as he leapt out of the nest into the air, taking flight. More arrows flew at him as the tribe alarms were raised to wake up the rest of the warriors. Gladius paused in midair and drew upon the power of shadow. "Indespectas," he said, and drew a cloak of night around him, hiding himself from sight. Once he was invisible, he flew as high as he could muster and opened a rift.

The Fioraden warriors below him were confused until they saw the blue light of the rift shine down. By the time they reached that altitude, Gladius was gone and the rift closed.

Chapter 23 – Soul of Fire

"This is highly unusual, Merek," Marius said from a seat in the Findoor throne room. "What is the meaning of this?"

All eight Council members were present at this meeting, along with Merek, Krycin, Cy, and King Valerra in his throne.

Merek gave Marius a plain, emotionless smile and spoke. "It appears events are unfolding around us as we sit in our comfortable castles and ignore them. The Fioraden have reported an attack on their people by a wizard in black armor. The Astaran desert has been struck with a monstrous storm like nothing Galadir has ever seen. It rivals the storm that raged over the Rashean Sea the night Krycin was found. There is a disturbance in the Western Badlands where the fabled Mordo are said to live in peace, and the Ardan chieftain Ranto has been murdered. Runners from the south are reporting that the Narshuk tribes are on the move, heading south, deeper into the Eastern Badlands, and yet, when I look around at this Council, and this kingdom, even myself, I see nobody worried about these events."

Marius stammered, struggling for words, but Merek raised his hand to stop him. "I am guilty as well. Life, air, shadow and earth. That's my count so far. And if you include the Narshuks themselves, and his own native element, that would be six of the eight elements Gladius has collected."

"Impossible," Darson shouted, jumping to his feet. "My son doesn't have the strength or the knowledge to remove a living being's soul, let alone absorb it. And besides, Gladius was reported dead in the Fioraden mountain collapse. How can he now be doing as you suggest?"

"I don't know, but I suspect somebody in this room *does* know." Merek looked to Krycin, and every other person in the room followed suit.

Krycin shifted in his chair and cleared his throat. "Gladius lives." A gasp ran through the room as the news sank into each Council member and all others in attendance. Krycin continued despite their visible shock. "I'm not certain what he's doing, or why, but I know it's him."

Merek walked up the middle of the room, looking at each person with his dark eyes. "Gladius confronted me before he went to the Fioraden mountain. He was looking for information on The Traveler. He was carrying a stolen tome of Lyecian magic, and may have managed to translate some. He also stole magic from my personal library, so we have no way of knowing what spells he has, or what he is capable of."

"We know he is collecting the elements to make himself more powerful," Marius said. "The next he will be after is fire, which he will need a dragon for. Those are in short supply these days. Many appear to have disappeared from the world, and those who are left are near impossible to find."

Krycin's face lit up and he stood to make himself heard. "Serrin!"

Marius whirled in place to look at Krycin. "Serrin?"

"Serrin was working on a way to summon a dragon," Krycin said, his voice filled with excitement.

"Indeed. Then we should go there, as I suspect that is where Gladius is heading next."

"I'm already there," Krycin said, and disappeared.

⊙

Serrin's lab was quiet and still when the rift opened and broke the silence. Gladius stepped out and looked around. Everything was as it had been the last time he'd been there. In the center of the room, the bubbling pool of lava radiated waves of heat. Various tables and lab equipment were lined up around the outside of the room. On the floor around the lava pool was a circle traced in silver, and marked with many hundreds of intricate runes.

"Thank you, Serrin," Gladius said to himself as he walked to the edge of the circle. He knelt down and traced a finger over the edge of the circle and a few of the runes. "Draconic. That's the key, isn't it?" He gave a sly smile and stood up.

Gladius began walking around the edge of the circle. As he passed each rune, he spoke the name of it out loud. One by one the runes lit up around the circle until he had walked the entire edge of it. When the circle was complete, the silver line glowed with a white light that spread into the middle.

With a broad smile, Gladius looked toward the lava pool. "Cyrilathelimusaktimarius, I summon you!" Gladius said, and watched as the white glow of the circle became red and the pool of lava bubbled up over the edge. The lava spread out through the circle, covering the floor and radiating wave after wave of heat. He stepped back away from the edge of the circle. The temperature in the lab increased with every second. Gladius's black armor protected him from what would be an unbearable temperature for a normal human.

The lava reached the edge of the circle, and the ground began to shake. The center of the circle swelled, rising up from the ground in a great mound. When it reached Gladius's height, it split open, and a great clawed foot reached out of the hole and grabbed the edge of the circle. Sharp black claws at the end of red scaled toes dug into the stone floor and hauled a head, body, wings and tail from the pit. It came to rest just outside of the circle, shaking off bits of molten stone that flew and hit the walls and tables of the lab. Small fires broke out, but went out when the massive red dragon stretched its wings and shook off dust and debris. Its red scales gleamed in the dim light of the lab, and its dark eyes looked toward Gladius who was watching the majestic creature with great interest. Black spines grew in a great mane from its head, and black ridges ran down its back. The tip of its tail was barbed with a large bone spur that could pierce any armor. Two great black horns grew from the dragon's head and pointed forward. It opened its mouth to speak and Gladius got a view of its hundreds of razor sharp teeth that were designed for tearing flesh, and smelled the brimstone on its breath. "You summoned?" the dragon asked.

"Cyril, greatest of the great red dragons, I call upon you today to help me fulfill my destiny."

"And why would I want to do that? What would you offer me in return?" Cyril asked.

Gladius smiled and said, "A chance to become part of history. To be known as the dragon who made me the most powerful wizard in all the history of Galadir. Grant me your soul, and this process shall be painless for you." As Gladius spoke, he walked around the red dragon. It followed Gladius with its eyes.

"Grant you my soul? Not on your life, wizard." Cyril almost spit the word out as it backed up a step, retreating toward the circle once more.

There was a moment of silence between them as Cyril measured up the wizard standing before him. Gladius spoke after a long moment, "Have it your way then." He broke into a full run at the dragon, summoning the power of air as he did. With his arms outstretched before him and his palms open and facing the dragon, Gladius shouted, "Fulmenas!"

Lightning erupted from his hands and struck the sides and chest of the dragon, leaving black scorch marks everywhere it touched. Cyril let out a great roar that echoed off the walls of the lab and would have burst a normal man's ear drums. Gladius poured magical energy into the spell, the electricity paralyzing Cyril as his muscles contracted. His claws dug into the floor and he let out another scream of rage. Portions of his scaled flesh broke up, forming large wounds that poured crimson blood out onto the floor.

With all his might, Cyril fought back against the spell and swung his tail forward at Gladius. His aim was true, and the bone spur hammered Gladius in the chest, sending him flying back against the wall. The lightning stopped, but Gladius got back up and stormed forward, readying another spell. He called on earth power this time, aiming the spell at Cyril's front left leg. "Concutinas," Gladius said, and a wave of green energy plowed forth from his hands. The concussive force struck Cyril's leg and shattered the bones, knocking the dragon off balance. He tipped forward as his front leg crumpled underneath his weight, causing him to let out another painful scream.

Gladius didn't relent. He called forth more energy of the earth, and repeated the spell on Cyril's back leg, again shattering his bones. With nothing left to hold him up, Cyril rolled onto his left side and moaned. "Giving up already? I expected more fight from one as great as yourself," Gladius said, taking slow measured steps towards the now whimpering dragon.

Cyril's eyes filled with rage, and he began drawing in a great breath. Gladius saw this and smiled, calling on the power of light and life. He uttered the words, "Clypas custodiasa tuitai."

Just as Cyril finished drawing in his breath, white light erupted from Gladius's hands and spread out before him. Cyril exhaled a slow, steady and focused stream of the most intense fire he could muster in his wounded state. The flames hit the white light in front of Gladius and deflected around it, leaving Gladius unharmed.

When the flames cleared, Gladius broke into a run at Cyril and summoned the power of air once more. "Incitatas," he said, and leapt into the air. The magic flowed, lifting Gladius higher into the air and helping him land on Cyril's chest which now heaved with labored breaths.

"Any last words, dragon?" Gladius asked as he lifted his hand into the air.

"You're insane, wizard," Cyril said, trying to shake Gladius off.

"Oh no. I'm not insane. I know perfectly well what I'm doing and why. You are the last, dragon. The final element. I will take your soul, like I did all the others, and consume it. And when I do, nobody will be able to stop me, not even the Lyecians."

Gladius channeled the power of death, focusing the power into his hand. Black fire erupted in his palm and spread up over his hand and up his arm. "Vimvitas mortai," he said as he plunged his hand into the dragon and took hold of the red soul inside him. There was more resistance this time as Cyril bucked and convulsed, trying to shake Gladius off. He almost lost his grip on the dragon's soul and poured more energy into his spell, severing the bindings that held it to Cyril's body. Bit by bit, the soul let go, and Cyril's movements slowed, and then stopped as his strength gave out. Gladius gave one last pull, and the dragon's soul came free, a great ball of red light that flashed and danced in his hand. He closed his eyes and reveled in the power as he consumed the soul and made it one with his own. The red light faded, and then disappeared as the last of it was absorbed.

Cyril laid his head down on the floor, his body now a dead empty shell, and closed his eyes on Galadir for the last time.

A hush fell over the wrecked lab as the circle closed, the gateway to Cyril's lair now sealed forever. Gladius was about to jump down from Cyril's back when the front entrance to the lab exploded in a cloud of splinters. In the doorway stood a woman, her face was twisted in anger. Gladius watched her scan the room until she spotted him atop the dead dragon. "Gladius!" she said. "What have you done?"

He smiled back at her with a smug expression that changed her face from startled and surprised to enraged. "What every wizard wishes he could do, my dear Catrina."

Without warning, he held his hands up and launched a massive fireball at Catrina that exploded in the doorway, taking the front of the building off with it. When the dust cleared, Catrina was already gone. He spun just in time to see her behind him. She threw a glowing ball at him that splattered on his chest plate. The substance was sticky and white hot, and as Gladius tried to brush it off it spread and grew. He tried to summon the power of water but was interrupted by a concussive force that exploded on his chest, sending him flying back and knocking the wind out of him. He landed in the rubble of the building and scrambled to get up.

He got to his knees and she was already next to him, holding her hands out to blast him again. The substance on his armor smoked and scalded as he tried to regain his focus. Some seeped down into the seams in his armor and began burning his flesh. He ignored the pain and called the power of water, drawing all the moisture in the nearby air to him in a large bubble. It coalesced in front of him just in time to put out the burning fire that spread over his body, and to block Catrina's next attack. Her jet of flames sizzled against the water, but did little more.

When he let the water go, they stared at each other. Her intense green eyes drilled into him, like she was hunting his soul for something. He gave her another smile and said, "A lovely set of powers you have there, but I really must be going."

He lashed out at her with a stroke of lightning that arced toward her. She disappeared, but at the same time, Gladius launched himself into the air and flew as high as he could so as to be out of her reach. He looked down in time to see another figure running from the manor, his red robe flying out behind him. *Serrin,* Gladius thought. Before Serrin could see where he was, he opened a rift and escaped through it.

⊛

Krycin appeared just outside the manor in the Arvok Caldera and was just in time to see Serrin running toward a woman who stood near the front of the lab. The lab was destroyed, with the entire front of it blown off and an enormous dragon lying inside it, his red scales covered with crimson blood. He reeled at the scene as it made him sick to his stomach and tried to hear what was being said by the couple, but everything sounded like it was coming through a long tunnel. *I'm too late,* he thought as his eyes glazed over with tears.

He tried to take a step forward, but his knees gave out and he fell to the ground instead. Anger flooded through him, and he raised his hands to the air and shouted as long and hard as he could. "Gladius!"

There was a long period of clouded silence before Krycin felt a hand on his shoulder. The touch was gentle and comforting, not what Krycin had expected. When he looked up, a woman he recognized was looking down at him. *Mom?* Krycin thought. His heart jumped and he fell back catching himself on his hands in a sitting position.

Serrin's voice came from behind him. "Easy, Krycin. It's safe now."

Without waiting for his head to clear, Krycin said, "No. No it's not. Nobody is safe now. He has seven. Gladius has seven of the elements. I came here to prevent it, but I failed. I'm too late."

Catrina knelt down before him and spoke. "It is good to finally meet you, Krycin. I've heard so much about you. About how promising your abilities are. So long as we have Lyecians like you defending Galadir, all will be safe."

Her voice was familiar to Krycin, and her face as well, though she appeared much younger. It was a face he remembered from his childhood. He was about to say something, but stopped himself. "My memories..." he said.

Serrin walked into his field of vision and helped Catrina up, and then offered Krycin a hand, which he accepted. "Your memories," Serrin said. "What about them?"

"I've got them back. Most of them, anyway. Though I'm not the same person I once was. When I think about what I've done, and what I've seen, it's like watching a movie."

Confusion washed over both Serrin's and Catrina's face. Serrin spoke up, "A movie? What's a movie?"

Krycin realized his slip all too late. "Never mind. It's like watching somebody else's memories, though they are all there."

"Ahh, I understand," Serrin said. "There is still a wound that needs to be healed, inside your mind. It will take time."

"And rest," Catrina said with a smile. "Come, I'll prepare a hearty meal for you, and you can stay in a guest room for the night." She didn't wait for a response before she headed back toward the manor. When she turned, Krycin noticed for the first time Catrina's swollen abdomen.

He looked to Serrin and asked, "Is she..."

"Pregnant? Why yes. And we have high hopes. It's not often you get two Lyecians with all eight elements between them. Our child might wield all of them." Serrin beamed with pride.

"How does it work? How is a child's element determined?" Krycin asked.

"Sometimes it's luck. Sometimes it's random. In some rare cases, a child will inherit all of both parent's elements. Both myself and Catrina can wield five elements. Powerful even by Lyecian standards. But between us, we have all eight, and we're hoping that our child will inherit all of them."

Krycin froze as another thought occurred to him. *Dad?* He shook his head, trying to clear his mind. "You called her Catrina. I thought her name was Marie?"

Serrin seemed surprised at this question. "No, my boy. I've not heard that name before. My wife's name is Catrina, and you have my apologies for not making a formal introduction. Our first encounter with each other was marred by the reaper attack, and now this," he said, motioning to the destroyed lab. "I wish our encounters could be on better terms."

"Same here. I could use the rest though, so I think I'll take you up on your offer of a room for a night. We don't yet know what Gladius is up to or even where he is now, but I do know that we can't fight him exhausted." It wasn't until that moment that Krycin realized how tired he was. His stomach grumbled for food, and his head ached from fatigue.

⊙

Gladius emerged from the rift on the platform overlooking the Narshuk encampment. In every direction, thousands of Narshuks worked at arming themselves and readying for the promised battle with the rest of Galadir. He smiled to himself and walked down into the camp looking for Scrag.

He found Scrag in a command tent reviewing written orders and disputes. He continued to work when Gladius walked in and didn't look up.

"Bravo, Scrag," Gladius said, clapping his hands.

The sudden human voice startled Scrag and he snarled in Gladius's direction before he realized who it was. Once he did, he calmed himself and went back to his work. "You have returned," he said.

Gladius laughed and said, "Yes. Is the army ready? Are the tribes ready to march on Findoor?"

"As ready as they will ever be," Scrag said.

"Good. Then in one day's time, we go, and claim our place in Galadirian history."

Scrag scoffed at this, but said nothing more.

A flare of anger surged through Gladius at this. "Do you not believe we can do this? Do you still doubt me, after all I've done for you and your people? I told you I would save your life, and I did. I told you I would unite the tribes, and I have. Now I say we shall march on Findoor and conquer it. Do you yet doubt that I will follow through with this?"

"And what of the Lyecians?" Scrag asked, looking up from his work. "How can you be sure your spell will work? How can you be sure that the Council will come? Narshuks have never breached the Findoor border, and it is because Findoor uses Lyecians to defend it. How do we fight that?"

Gladius took a deep breath and calmed his temper. "The Council will come, and when they do, I will be ready for them. I have the seven elements I need, and once I do away with them, I'll have the eighth. After that, you leave the Lyecians to me. Come, we have work to do, and it's a long march to Findoor."

Chapter 24 – Impending Doom

It was several days before Krycin returned to Findoor to make his report. When he did, he appeared on the battlements of the castle at sunrise. He sat on the edge of the wall and watched the brilliant colors fill the sky for the second time that day and smiled to himself. Serrin and Catrina were pleasant hosts, and Krycin had decided to stay and help Serrin rebuild part of his lab. The memories he regained of his father's abandonment seemed far away compared to having the man by his side, even if he couldn't reveal their true relationship. It was during this time that Krycin gave up his white robes for some more conventional clothing, and now wore plain black trousers and an off-white tunic.

As he reveled in the sunlight and greenery that was the Findoor landscape, he was surprised by a voice behind him. "You look like a peasant."

It was Merek's voice, and Krycin didn't care to turn to greet him. "I'm more comfortable in these than I ever was in wizard robes."

Merek approached and placed a hand on his shoulder. "What news is there from the Arvok Caldera?"

"By the time I got there, Gladius was already gone. A great red dragon lost its life to him," Krycin said with a note of sadness in his voice. "I don't know where he is, or what he's up to, but I know it's nothing good. I stayed to help Serrin put his lab back together."

There was a long pause, and then Merek again spoke. "You understand that this makes Gladius one of the most powerful wizards who ever lived."

"I know," Krycin said. "And I know what he's capable of. I've seen the results of his power."

"You don't seem yourself anymore," Merek said, sitting down beside him so that his legs hung on the inside of the wall.

"I feel more myself than I have in months," Krycin said.

"Is something the matter? Something bothering you?"

"There's a lot that's bothering me," Krycin said, swallowing a lump in his throat that grew with each word, "but not much anyone can do. Tyriel is right, I'm not supposed to be here. But I am now, and I have no choice but to stay. I've seen the future, the end result of all this. I know what's going to happen. I know what *must* happen. I can't stop it, Merek. Terrible things are about to happen to Galadir, and I can't do anything about it."

"We all have a part to play in this," Merek said in his most comforting voice. "When darkness falls on the world, we must all be heroes in our own way, even if it means doing nothing so that the sun may rise again another day."

Anger flashed in Krycin's eyes. He spun on the wall, rose to his feet and turned back to Merek. "Heroes? I wanted to be a hero. I came back so that I could be a hero in my own time, so that I could save the world. So I could save Galadir. Instead, I've ended up setting in motion the events that caused the biggest atrocity this world has ever known, and I'm told I'm not allowed to do anything to stop it. Nothing. So you know what? I don't want to be a hero anymore." He was yelling now, loud enough for people around the castle to hear and stare. "If being a hero means losing myself in the process, then I want no part of it."

Merek sat staring in shock throughout Krycin's tirade, and spoke up only after a lengthy pause. "Surely there is something you can do."

"Ha!" Krycin said, his breathing coming faster now as the anger continued to boil. "Something I can do? Absolutely. I can watch. Gladius is the most powerful wizard who ever lived, and when the killing starts, I get to stand back and watch it happen. I'd rather die, but I can't even do that, or it will ruin everything. Where I come from, they say 'ignorance is bliss'. I wish I hadn't gotten my memories back. I wish I could go back to being naive and stupid Krycin. It was far easier than *this*."

Krycin watched as Merek appeared to be searching for the right words. When Merek opened his mouth to say something, he was cut off by a runner who charged out onto the battlements at a full run. He came to a stop ten paces from the two men and spoke right away without waiting to be addressed. "Arch-Magus Merek, King Valerra requests your presence in the throne room, urgently."

Without waiting for a response, the runner bolted back the way he came. Merek stood up to follow, but as he walked past, Krycin took hold of his shoulder and said, "Right here, right now. This is how it begins."

Merek let out a sigh and headed for the throne room with Krycin in tow.

⊛

When they arrived at the throne room they could hear shouting coming from inside. Many voices were all trying to be heard at once, but none of them were distinct. Merek pushed open the doors without knocking and led the way in.

The room was packed with more people than usual. All seating to either side of the center aisle was filled with councilors and pages and runners waiting for instructions. The center aisle held regional lords and their respective aids, and at the front of the room was King Valerra, Cy, and Marius.

Almost every person in the room was shouting to be heard over the rest, but when Merek and Krycin entered, many of them fell to a hush.

"You summoned, your highness?" Merek said in his cool, composed way.

King Valerra raised a hand to the court and silence fell over the room. "An hour ago, runners from the south arrived with messages that a large number of Narshuks have been spotted approaching the southern Findoor border. We sent Lyecians to investigate the claims, only to have them confirmed. An army, ten thousand strong, is quickly approaching."

"Hadra have mercy," Merek said. "How did an army of this many Narshuks happen on our border without us knowing weeks in advance?"

Marius stood up to respond, a troubled look on his face. "The High Council has been monitoring Narshuk border activity for months, but nothing changed. They gathered in the south, and traveled north once they had amassed a sizable army. We would have had to post wizards all over the badlands to prevent this sort of incursion."

Valerra raised his hand again as the rest of the occupants in the room started to murmur words of blame back and forth. The room again went silent. "It doesn't matter whose fault it is. The reason I called this court was to discuss what will be done about it. If you have no worthwhile ideas, leave now."

A number of the councilors sat with sheepish expressions on their faces, but nobody left. Cy stood up and looked around. "I have an idea. It's really the only idea that makes sense. Assemble every Lyecian we can find, and wipe the invaders off the face of the planet. They don't stand a chance against an army of Lyecians. Fifty thousand Narshuks wouldn't be a match for us."

Krycin snapped his head toward Cy, his eyes wide. "No," he said, standing up. "Absolutely not. Why would you endanger our people like that? Wouldn't a combined effort make more sense?"

"Krycin, my friend," Cy said with a smile. "You can't honestly believe that these Narshuks are in any way a threat to us Lyecians?"

There was a long pause while everyone looked to Krycin. He stood for a moment, frozen under their gazes. "I do," he said. "And here's why." He walked out to the middle of the throne room, reached down to his left leg, and tore open the leg of his pants revealing the jagged scars on his thigh. "These were caused by Narshuk claws."

A gasp ran through the room, and Cy's face darkened. "Oh, come now. One Lyecian's injuries are not reflective of the entire race."

Valerra spoke up over the sudden murmur of the crowd. "I agree with Krycin. As powerful as Lyecians are, I will not trust my kingdom to the hands of one race. This kingdom is the home of many, and will be defended by all. Still, I will not deny that the Lyecians will be a great asset to the border defense, and thus I implore you, Cy. Summon the Lyecians. Marius, organize what wizards you can muster and join them. I will send runners out to call in every available company of soldiers and have them assemble in the Losteron Plains, and march south to meet what's left of the Narshuk army, if anything. Are there any objections?"

Silence filled the room, though when Krycin looked up at Cy, he was met with a cool stare.

⊙

"Why would you do that?" Cy yelled at Krycin later in private. "Why would you sow the seeds of doubt in the Findoor council?"

"I'm sorry. You can't expect Findoor to rely on the Lyecians for their defense forever. What would happen if we were all gone? Where would that leave Findoor?" Krycin was yelling back by the time he finished.

Cy scoffed at the idea. "We are superior in every way, Krycin. What has gotten you so scared? I don't know how a Narshuk injured you in the past, but it won't happen now. You and I, we will march into battle together and watch each other's backs. Like brothers." Cy smiled at Krycin as his voice calmed. "You'll have nothing to fear, and neither will I."

Krycin considered this for a moment, and nodded in agreement. "Okay. We march together."

⊙

Merek met with Marius in his lab in the basement of Findoor castle after the court was dismissed. The lab was quiet except for Merek's pacing.

"You wanted to speak with me?" Marius asked, interrupting the silence.

Merek looked up from his thoughts to Marius and nodded. "Yes. A runner arrived just as court was getting out. I received the message myself and thought it wise to keep it quiet. I want you and the rest of the Council to deal with this personally."

"What is it?"

"The army approaching the southern border is being led by Gladius. He made mention of meeting up with some Narshuks when he was down there. I had no idea he'd established such influence with them." Merek resumed his pacing, never lifting his gaze from the floor as he walked.

"By the gods," Marius said. "How did we miss this? He runs around collecting souls from each of the elements and destroys the Fioraden's home, all under our noses. Were they just distractions?"

"Perhaps. But there is another explanation as well. The only way Gladius could assume control of this many Narshuks would be with a great show of strength and power. It may be that he required the souls he took in order to show his strength to them, to make them follow him. Take the High Council, confront Gladius, and if he is indeed leading this army, you may have no choice but to slay him once and for all. Without a leader, the Narshuks should be easy to drive back into the Badlands."

Marius considered this for a moment in silence before responding. "Very well. We will take our leave immediately and deal with Gladius. The plan should not change though. Even without Gladius, this many Narshuks will be a dangerous army to face."

"Agreed. Return here once Gladius is dealt with, and we will decide what to do from there," Merek said, and went back to his work in his lab.

Chapter 25 – Soul of Time and Space

The Narshuk army was less than a day's travel from the Findoor border when Gladius called a halt to their advance. The Badlands sloped down into Findoor land and Gladius stood at the top of the slope looking at the lush green land beyond. Scrag stood next to him in silence, but wouldn't avert his gaze from the border.

"It's beautiful, isn't it?" Gladius asked.

"The Council hasn't come yet like you said they would," Scrag said.

"Patience. Did you wonder why I led the charge this last day by horseback? The border guards have seen me. The Council will come."

Scrag opened his mouth to say something more, but was distracted by a sound before him. Gladius smiled to himself as a white light appeared on the slope before them and stretched out into a dome. A light humming sound filled the air as eight figures appeared inside the dome. When the light receded, the entire High Council stood on the stone ground a hundred paces away.

Marius led the way, making the first step toward Gladius. Scrag stepped forward and blocked the way while Gladius began to chant. Arcane words came from his mouth as he drew first fire, water, earth and air and combined them into a white hot light before him. As he continued the spell, he called on the power of life and death, and shrouded the light before him in a swirl of black and white that pulsed with magical energy. His final words added the power of shadow which wrapped the ball of energy in a gray haze that caused it to disappear.

Gladius looked up from his work and focused his mind on the area the spell would affect, then through force of will, urged the ball of energy into the ground and shouted the final words of the spell. "Resanchoras diutirnai."

There was a flash of light that exploded from the ground before him which spread out in a circle that was a hundred paces in diameter. When it reached its maximum size, it burned a line in the ground and disappeared.

Marius walked toward the edge of the circle, but stopped several paces short of it. The rest of the Council remained behind him. "Gladius," Marius said. "What are you doing here?"

"Go on, Scrag," Gladius said to his second in command. "Get the troops ready to move out. This will only take a minute."

Scrag walked away without question, leaving Gladius to face the Council on his own.

"What am I doing here? Can't you see? I've raised an army worthy of a god, and I plan to accomplish what you never could. I'm going to eliminate the threat from Galadir once and for all." Gladius focused his mind on drawing the power of death, but didn't manipulate it into a spell.

Darson surged forward and stood at the edge of the circle, eying the blackened line with suspicion. "Step down, before you get yourself killed."

"Step down? Why would I do that?" Gladius laughed as he felt the magical energy flow to him. "Can't you see what I've done here? No other wizard has ever united the Narshuk tribes before. No other wizard has captured the ability to use seven of the eight elements. And still, with all of that, you can't find it in yourself to have even a little pride in your son?"

"What you've done here is start a fire you can't control. You think these animals will follow you to the end, but you're wrong. The moment you show any sign of weakness, they will eat you alive, and everything else in their path." Darson stepped closer to the edge of the circle, but didn't step into it. "Stand down, Gladius."

Anger surged through Gladius at the sound of his own name from his father's mouth. "You call me *son*," he yelled, stepping forward in the circle to meet Darson. "Get out of your Council chair for five minutes and acknowledge me as your son. Everything I've done, and everything I'm going to do is to prove to you that I can be a great wizard. Say it, *Darson*. Say you're proud of me, and I'll stand down."

Darson snorted. "A great wizard? All I see is a spoiled child having a tantrum. The only difference is, you're playing with much more dangerous toys."

The magic surged through Gladius as he lost control of his emotions and his spell. The power of death flew from his fingers in a black stream that writhed and twisted in the air. It slammed into Darson's chest, sending him flying backwards into the rest of the Council. By the time his body came to a stop, he was nothing but a lifeless corpse.

Bareva rushed to his side, his face frozen with shock at seeing one of his colleagues snuffed out like a match. "He's dead," Bareva said, looking up at Gladius. "You've murdered your own father. May Anam have mercy on your soul."

Gladius stepped backward into the middle of the circle, his thoughts clouded with mixed emotions. It was like a weight was lifted from his shoulders. A smile came over his face when he saw each of the Council members preparing their own spells.

There was a long silence as Marius stared hard at Gladius, his intense concentration obvious on his face. When he approached the edge of the circle, he spoke. "Last chance, Gladius. Stand down and disband this army, or face death."

"Have you forgotten already?" Gladius said. "I've already beaten death."

Marius shook his head and let loose a powerful fire spell that would have vaporised a lesser wizard. A massive gout of flames flew through the air, but instead of flying straight at Gladius, the flames were deflected around him and traveled along the edges of the circle, dissipating as it went. The display distracted the rest of the Council, and left Marius with a look of disbelief on his face.

"Yes, that's right," Gladius said, mocking the men and women standing before him. "You're going to have to do this the old fashioned way." He drew the black steel sword and swung it in the air, leaving a trail of flames that drifted up into black smoke.

Marius held his hand out to the side and cast a second spell. In his hand, a gleaming silver sword appeared and erupted with blue flames. He took a step forward into the circle, but paused when he heard Lebriel's voice behind him. "Be careful," he said. "We don't know what that spell is."

"I know. But what choice do I have?" Marius asked without taking his eyes off of Gladius. "It obviously disrupts magic, and we can't allow him to carry on like this."

Gladius took a step back, feigning fear as Marius took a second step and put himself all the way into the circle. The two men stared each other down as they drew closer together, neither willing to drop his sword for even a split second. When Marius was within striking distance, Gladius took the first swing. His sword came alive with fire and streaked through the air with more speed than Marius had been ready for. The black blade struck his left arm, cut through his robe and the outer bicep, and then pulled free. Confusion filled Marius's face as his blood spilled from a wound that he hadn't expected. Gladius laughed and swung again in the other direction, repeating the wound with the other arm and causing Marius to drop his sword. Gladius called on the power of shadow and cast a haze of gray magic at Marius, paralyzing him.

"What's the matter," Gladius asked, "time not obeying?"

Marius tried to speak, but couldn't, his eyes reflecting his panicked state of mind. Several more spells cast by the Council hit the circle and dissipated like the first.

Gladius walked up to Marius and grabbed his robe, hauling him forward off his feet. "Let me explain this to you slowly, so you understand. What you're standing in is a reality anchor," Gladius said, dragging Marius to the center of the circle. "No magic can penetrate its boundaries, and no Lyecian magic will work inside it. That includes their ability to control time."

A movement outside the circle caught Gladius's eye. When he looked up, he saw Lebriel carrying a long red staff and approaching the circle.

"I'll make this quick, so as not to disappoint," Gladius whispered into Marius's ear. He called upon the element of death and focused it into his right hand, causing it to burst into black flames. There were shouts and snarls and growls coming from outside the circle, but Gladius ignored them, seeing only his prize before him. He plunged his hand into Marius, closing his fist on the powerful Lyecian soul inside him, and wrenched it free from his body. The moment Gladius stood up with the ball of golden energy in his hand, Marius fell limp on the ground, his eyes blank and dead.

⊙

Lebriel watched in disbelief as Marius stepped into the circle and was subsequently struck with a sword he expected Marius to be able to dodge. The second hit prompted him to action and he cast his own spell, conjuring up a red staff in order to fight Gladius hand-to-hand. When he took off running toward the circle, he saw a company of Narshuks approaching and got a feeling in his stomach that told him they'd made a grave mistake.

It took him seconds to reach Gladius, but by the time he did, Marius was dead. Gladius stood up, a shining golden orb in his right hand and a black sword in the other. Lebriel lifted the red staff over his head and swung it down with all his strength, but Gladius batted it away with the black sword with little effort.

"Come now, Lebriel," Gladius said, mocking him. "Didn't you get enough the first time?"

Lebriel called on the power of fire, using his anger to fuel him rather than distract him. "Never," he said. "Not until you're dead." He focused the magical energy into a concentrated blast before him and called out the words to the spell. "Incendras!"

Fire burst from his hands and drove into Gladius's chest, sending him flying back onto the ground. Even as Gladius fell, Lebriel didn't let up on the spell, unleashing a storm of fire and heat on the much younger wizard. Flames swirled around Gladius causing waves of air to shimmer and rise away from him. When the spell was done, Lebriel gasped for air and leaned on his staff to keep from collapsing with exhaustion. Gladius lay on the ground before him and didn't move.

A battle raged outside the circle, but Lebriel only heard the sound of his own breathing and the beating of his heart. The golden orb remained in Gladius's hand, flashing and swirling with a living light. Smoke rose from the black armor and the emblem on the chest plate was blackened and distorted. Instead of looking like a perfectly formed lily, it was curled and dying. And instead of a loosely wrapped snake facing the flower, it was now a snake constricting around it and set to attack. Lebriel was ready to join his colleagues in battle when he saw Gladius's chest rise and fall with a breath.

The single breath became a laugh, and the laugh increased to hysterics. Gladius sat up, a wicked smile on his face as the golden orb sank into his hand. A golden light flared up from his skin leaving Lebriel blinded for a split second, and then disappeared.

"What have you done?" Lebriel asked, staring at him in disbelief.

Gladius walked toward Lebriel with confidence, the smile never leaving his face. "Oh it's not what I *have* done that will astound you most. It's what I have yet to do. What all of you lacked the nerve or the conviction to do. I'm going to kill that meddling Krycin and save all of Galadir. And once he's gone, I'm going to continue to lead my army all over Galadir, until every race, every kingdom, and every wizard bows to me."

"You're insane!" Lebriel said and summoned more power. The strain of drawing power while fatigued made his head ache, but he ignored the pain the best he could and focused the power into one more spell. "Illiquefactas incendrai."

A stream of liquid fire poured from Lebriel's hands and blasted toward Gladius. It wasn't fast enough though, as Gladius raised a hand and projected a shield of ice before him, deflecting the fire around him. Several Narshuks screamed as the liquid splashed onto them and ignited their flesh and fur. Black smoke and white steam filled the air between Lebriel and Gladius, making it hard to see. Lebriel stood by the strength of his staff, as the magic had drained most of his own. He backed up a step, trying to think of a way to beat Gladius, but was running out of options.

⊙

Gladius searched through the mist and smoke trying to find the red wizard. The battle hadn't gone quite the way he expected it thus far, but he wasn't disappointed. The sounds of battle, both mundane and magical, surrounded him and he could hear the shouts of the remaining Council wizards as they defended against a growing tide of Narshuks. He drew upon the power of shadow to enhance his hearing and searched for signs that Lebriel was moving.

To his left he heard a shuffling sound and labored breathing combined with the tapping of wood on stone. *There you are,* he thought and walked toward the sound. As he drew closer, he drew the power of death and focused it into his hand. Black flames burst forth from it, fueled by magical energy. He reached the hunched over form seconds later and spoke. "Oh, you won't get off that easily, my friend."

Lebriel stood up and spun to face him, his blue eyes filled with sadness. "I'm ready to continue my journey with a clear conscience," he said. "Can you say the same?"

Gladius smiled at him and shook his head. "You're a fool then, because this is the end of your journey."

He thrust his hand forward and attempted to take Lebriel's soul, but as he moved, black smoke coalesced into a human form between them. Gladius's hand entered Tyriel's body, but instead of finding a living soul, his hand closed on something else. It was cold, draining and sent pain up his arm like he'd just plunged his hand into an ice cold lake. He heard a scream and took a second to realize that it was his own voice. His vision went black and all he could see was a bright shard that might have been crystal or glass, but from which emanated a blinding white light. His hand was wrapped around the shard, and he couldn't let it go. His life drained away as his hand refused to accept his command. He pulled with every ounce of his strength and managed wrench his hand free, causing him to fall backward onto the ground.

Tyriel moved fast, like he was the wind itself and hovered over Gladius shaking his head. "Not him. I can't let you take him."

Gladius watched him drift back to Lebriel and place a hand on his shoulder. Both men dissolved into black smoke and disappeared.

There was still a battle going on around him and Gladius was losing his temper. He got himself to his feet and stomped to the edge of the circle where the air was clear. His hand still ached but he ignored it as he spotted the blue wizard, Farissa, blasting ice at a Narshuk. She had no sooner finished her spell than she spun face-to-face with Gladius. He had summoned the power of air and unleashed a stroke of lightning from his hands that struck her square in the center of her chest. Her blue robes ignited the moment it touched her and a gasp escaped her lungs as every muscle in her body tensed up all at once. She fell to the ground with the lightning still coursing through her, and burns covering her chest and face. When it stopped, she lay on the ground twitching, but her eyes were cold and lifeless.

A flash of green caught Gladius's eye and the power of water came to him without a thought. He focused it into a ball in his hand that he tossed at the earth wizard. The ball hit her with a splash and startled her, interrupting her next spell. The magical energy came anyway and burst through her skin, burning her from the inside out. Narshuks that she battled took advantage of her distraction and closed on her, sinking their claws and teeth into her flesh. Her screams turned to silence seconds later.

Gladius continued across the battlefield, looking for the remaining Council members. Shreds of bloody yellow and gray fabric told him those two wizards had met the same fate, leaving only Bareva to deal with. He walked toward the last remaining commotion where Narshuks crowded around a glowing dome, snarling and howling.

"Halt, back off," he shouted at the creatures and they did as they were asked, though not as fast as he would have liked. Under the glowing dome of energy was Bareva, cowering from the creatures and pouring every ounce of his strength into maintaining his defensive spell. "You're all that's left," he said to the white wizard with a smile. "Just give up and go quietly. It'll be easier on all of us that way."

Bareva looked up at Gladius, tears flowing from his eyes. "Never. You're a monster."

"A monster?" Gladius let out a burst of laughter that got the Narshuks nearby going again. Howls rang through the air and appeared to hurt Bareva as he flinched away from them. "You have no idea, do you? I'm here to kill Krycin, and that's what I plan to do. And along the way, if a few more die, then so be it. The ends justify the means."

"Listen to reason," Bareva said. "You sound like a maniac. Krycin is one man, and has been deemed no more a threat than any other Lyecian in the world. Would you kill them all like you would him?"

A sly smile spread across Gladius's face. "Yes," he said, and paused to take a breath. "Do you know why Marius locks all those books up in the library in the basement? It's because if he didn't, then everybody would know the truth. Krycin is not the only one who poses a threat. He's just the first. 'A Time Weaver's soul is beyond the reach of time.' That's what the book said. They all pose a threat, and will all be treated with the same punishment. Death. Now make this easy on yourself and drop the shield. I know you can't hold it forever."

Bareva shook his head and drew more energy into the shield, causing it to grow and push Gladius back.

"Have it your way," Gladius said. He drew his sword and swung it once, striking the shield. It glanced off with no effect. A few Narshuks nearby resumed their assault on the dome as well.

Gladius called on the power of fire and felt the sword draw the energy from him, channeling it into the blade. He swung the sword with all the force he could muster and slammed it into the shield. Flames spread out over the shield and a small crack formed in the dome. Without hesitation, Gladius drew more power and channeled it into the sword. A second strike left another crack, but did little more. He examined the crack and ignored the cowering wizard inside. *Death*, he thought. *I need the power of death.*

He focused all his efforts on drawing the power of death and forming it into a corruption spell that he fed into the crack in the shield. Black lines formed around it and spread out across the surface of the dome. Bareva cried out under the strain of keeping the shield intact. Gladius hammered the shield again with his fist and a much larger crack formed. With a shout, Gladius lifted his sword one last time and swung it in a full circle, slamming it into the dome where it was already cracked and weakened. There was a loud shattering sound as the spell broke and the sword carried through. A sickening thud told Gladius before he looked what he hit on the other side. Bareva lay on the ground with the black steel sword cleaved half way through his head.

Gladius placed his boot against Bareva's head and pulled his sword free, leaving the Narshuks to feast on his flesh.

Scrag waited for him at the edge of the reality anchor. "How long will it last?" he asked, watching Gladius approach.

"It's permanent," Gladius said with a smirk. "I needed to make sure it would last even if I lost concentration on it."

"You have earned the respect of all Narshuks on this day," Scrag said with an almost reverent tone.

Gladius looked around at the army and the field soaked with blood. "The best is yet to come."

Chapter 26 - The Lyecian War

The southern border of Findoor was quiet. The sky lit up with reds and oranges and yellows as the last gasps of the sun set behind clouds. Cool air moved in from the badlands, carrying with it the smell of long doused distant camp fires. Cy and Krycin waited in a stand of trees for the impending army of Narshuks to crest over the hill and rush the border. Hundreds of other Lyecians had answered the call and came at Cy's request to help defend the kingdom and were likewise waiting in hiding until the time was right. Krycin shifted every few seconds from one foot to the other as his nerves got the better of him.

"Would you stand still? You'll give away our position with all that jittering," Cy said with a reassuring smile. "We'll be fine. There's not a Narshuk on Galadir that can take on a Lyecian and win."

"Sorry. I just have a terrible feeling about this," Krycin said, forcing himself to stand still. "What if something goes wrong? I haven't seen any of Ducain's wizards yet. Aren't they supposed to be coming to help us?"

"Indeed. The Council likely lost its nerve. Stop fussing, we don't need them."

Krycin sighed and scanned the border again looking for any sign of movement. "I'm not so sure about that. I know you think Lyecians are invulnerable, but what if somebody found a way to make us vulnerable? What if the Narshuks are more than they seem?"

"They're nothing but a bunch of mindless beasts that somebody has riled up. The Council has been doing this for eons. Every so often, they get it in their minds that they're going to rally and leave the

Badlands, and the Council beats them down and disperses them every time."

Cy raised his hand to silence Krycin's next response as he spotted the first signs of the Narshuks coming over the hill. They moved at a fast, steady pace accompanied by a human dressed in black armor. It was like the ocean poured over the ridge as a black army crested and covered the entire hillside.

"Sweet Lyecha," Cy said as he watched the army of ten thousand Narshuks invade Findoor territory.

Krycin pointed to the figure at the front and center. "Who is that?"

The front lines of the army was at a hundred paces when Cy squinted to see who led the army. "By the gods," Cy said, astonished. "It's Gladius." He moved as though he was going to run out and meet the army, but Krycin grabbed his shoulder and stopped him.

"Stop," Krycin said. "Wait."

Cy shot Krycin a cool stare, but waited.

"We've still got the element of surprise," Krycin said. "We shouldn't blow that too early."

The army thundered toward them now, the sound drowning out all but their loudest shouts. At fifty paces, Cy gave the signal down the line to prepare their attacks. He and Krycin did the same.

"We stick together, right?" Krycin asked.

"Like brothers," Cy said, drawing the power of death to him and readying his first spells.

Krycin called on the power of life and with a nod to Cy, cast his spell out in a broad area. A wave of white light flooded out in a fan shape toward the Narshuk army, blinding them as they ran into it and searing their flesh when they failed to avoid its strike. Cy unleashed his spell as well, a wave of decaying rot that blistered and destroyed their flesh as they ran through it. The murky black mist that poured from Cy's hands coated their bodies and caused them to drop to the ground howling.

All down the Lyecian line spells erupted over the Narshuks, killing them by the hundreds. Undaunted, the army continued its advance, trampling the fallen without sympathy. The dark figure leading the army was untouched by the wave of spells and now approached one stand of trees. Cy tried to see what was going on as Krycin cast his second wave of spells, but all he saw were several bursts of golden light come from the trees. He was surprised when

Gladius emerged from the trees at a run shouting orders to the Narshuk army as he went.

"You're right," Cy said, his voice panicked. "Something's wrong."

They both looked in time to see Gladius reach a second stand of trees and disappear into them. Several more bursts of golden light came from it, and he emerged, shouting more orders. Hordes of Narshuks were now circling all the trees along the border, despite the steady stream of attacks coming from the Lyecians. Krycin noticed that no spells came from the two stands Gladius had been in.

He looked at Cy, his expression just as panicked. "He's killing them. Gladius is killing Lyecians."

A wave of Narshuks surrounded their hiding place and Cy released a new spell that moved out from him in a circle, traveling fast. A black ring of light moved through the Narshuk ranks, binding each Narshuk it touched with black strings that wrapped around them and reached for the ground. Several dozen were caught in this web when Cy waved his hand and the strings all constricted together, shearing and slicing Narshuks into pieces that fell lifeless to the ground.

Cy motioned for Krycin to follow him. "We need to take him out, once and for all," Cy shouted.

Krycin nodded and followed close behind him. They waded into the sea of Narshuks, using their magic to plow a path through them. Light and Darkness alternated as they moved closer to their destination.

The sounds of battle were all around them, clouding their senses, and so Krycin didn't hear the small group of Narshuks coming up from the rear. The world around him slowed, and he knew his instincts were kicking in. He turned in time to see a Narshuk with its claws raised to take a swipe at him. He moved to the side to avoid the hit, but Cy kept moving forward without him. In the blink of an eye, the two were separated on the field and Krycin was surrounded by Narshuks.

He held his hand out to the side and called on the power of light and life. A sword of pure light manifested in his hand and grew to cover his entire body with crystal armor. The sword blinded the Narshuks, who all shied away from the warrior now before them. Krycin didn't wait for them to adjust, and launched his first attacks, slaying several before they realized what was going on.

⊙

Cy continued forward, despite the slight disturbance in the flow of time. He was used to seeing disturbances like that and didn't think anything of it. It wasn't until he was a mere twenty paces from Gladius that he realized Krycin was gone. With no time to look for his friend, he continued forward and launched a bolt of black fire at Gladius, which was deflected away by his armor.

Gladius spun on his heels after feeling the hit and smiled. "Oh Cy," he said in a mocking tone. "So good of you to join the party. Aren't we all having a blast now?"

To emphasize his words, he released a sonic wave at Cy that struck him and knocked him back onto the ground. Cy didn't wait for a second blast, he stopped time in order to recover from the hit. Narshuks all around him were frozen with teeth bared and claws ready to rip him to shreds if they could just grab hold of him. He pushed himself up off the ground and stood up. When he turned to cast a spell at Gladius, a fist slammed into his face and sent him sprawling onto his back. The magical energy that he had drawn coursed through his body, but he was too distracted to form it into a spell. Instead, it sizzled in his body electrifying every nerve. He cried out from the pain of being partially cooked from the inside out and tried to focus on what had hit him.

Standing over him was a dark figure that he couldn't make out against the night sky, though the laughter gave him away. "How?" Cy said, trying to back away from Gladius along the ground. "How have you gained Lyecha's blessing?"

"I took it," Gladius said, kicking Cy hard in the thigh with a steel boot.

Cy grunted from the pain, feeling the muscles swelling and a bruise forming right away. "You're an abomination," Cy said. "An aberration of nature that shouldn't exist. No human can receive Lyecha's blessing. We're better than you."

Gladius walked around Cy and heaved another kick into his ribs. There was an audible snap as at least one broke, and more pain clouded Cy's mind. "See," Gladius said, kneeling down to look Cy in the eyes, "I've discovered something. It's incredibly easy to catch a Lyecian off-guard when they think they can stop time to avoid me." Gladius lifted his fist and slammed it into Cy's stomach. The impact caused Cy to gasp for air and sputter blood from his lips. "And if I inflict enough pain, you cowards can't teleport away."

The battlefield was quiet except for Gladius's voice and a few other Lyecians who were trying to figure out what was going on. Cy tried to say something, or even scream, but Gladius put a hand over his mouth. "Oh no. We can't have you calling your friends. I'm not finished with you yet."

Gladius braced his knee against Cy's ribs where he had kicked before and applied pressure until he heard another snap. Cy struggled under his weight and made a muffled cry, but couldn't clear his mind enough to summon any more magic or teleport. A haze of pain settled over him such that he didn't see the black fire erupt from Gladius's other hand.

"Now you die," Gladius said, and plunged his hand into Cy's chest. He felt the impact, but it didn't hurt at first. There was no physical injury from the spell. Gladius wrapped his fingers around the roots of the energy that was Cy's soul and pulled. Every nerve in Cy's body fired at once, like Gladius was ripping him in half on a cellular level. His consciousness split as he saw the golden light being pulled from his body. He tried to resist it, but was too weak. His vision faded as Gladius completed his task.

⊛

For every Narshuk Krycin slew, another two appeared and took their place. His muscles burned from the effort of swinging the sword and running, and his heart raced faster than it ever had before. Still the army continued its advance, and it seemed no matter how many he killed, it wasn't enough. He was about to teleport away when the field went quiet and all the Narshuks froze in place. *Time has stopped,* Krycin thought. *But it's not me.*

He looked around at the chaos surrounding him, and though it was frozen in time, he realized for the first time just how terrifying it was. *Cy,* he thought. *I've gotta find Cy.*

The silence worked in his favor this time, as he listened for any signs of movement on the field. He heard the voices of a few Lyecians calling to each other to regroup, but nothing else. Panic seized his heart as he thought the worst. He ran in the direction he thought Cy went the last time he saw him, but still heard nothing. Narshuks by the hundreds blocked his path, forcing him to duck and weave around their dangerous claws and teeth.

When a gold light flared up into the sky and time resumed its flow, Krycin gasped. The Narshuk army moved again and Krycin had to duck to avoid getting hit by a passing claw. His mind was so focused on Cy that he didn't notice the Narshuks now ignoring him.

There was a body on the ground ten paces away, dressed all in black. "Oh god, Cy!" Krycin said, running to his side. Blood that had run from Cy's mouth was beginning to dry and his dark eyes stared into the sky, a look of terror frozen on his face. "No, it can't be you. You can't die now. You weren't supposed to die now." Tears ran from his eyes as he knelt down next to Cy's body.

A familiar laugh was the only thing that cut through his grief. Krycin looked toward the noise and saw Gladius standing ten paces away with a smile on his face. "All of this," Gladius said with his arms outstretched. "All for you."

"What have you done?" Krycin said, trying to blink the tears out of his eyes so he could see Gladius.

"I came for you. All you had to do was return with the reaper. I don't understand why you didn't just go."

"You protected me once," Krycin said. "You were my friend." Rage welled up inside of him, clouding out all of his other senses. He could see and hear Gladius, but nothing else. "All this death, all these lives, for what? How can you possibly justify this?"

Gladius stared back with his intense eyes. "Me? You would blame this on me?" He stepped forward, pointing one hand at Krycin. "It's you that's to blame for this. You and that infernal meddler, Cy. This would all be done now if it weren't for him, but I took care of that already." He spared a glance at the body lying beside Krycin. "You're a danger to Galadir, and a danger to all existence. That's what we were told. The High Council was too caught up in its own politics to take you themselves, but I acted. And now, not only do I have the power to destroy you, but I have also righted a wrong that began hundreds of years ago."

His last words confused Krycin, and it must have shown on his face as Gladius swept his arms out in a wide circle to indicate the Narshuk army all around them, still pressing forward into Findoor land. "My glorious army was once a proud people, until the wizards formed the High Council. Then the Narshuks were alienated, subjugated, and eventually herded into the badlands and forced to live in squalor while the rest of Galadir thrived."

Krycin stood up and looked at the ground, his spirit fading fast. "It didn't have to be this way. We had a chance to make it better."

There was a long pause before Gladius spoke again. "There is nothing better than this."

"Then you truly are beyond hope," Krycin said, with sadness in his voice.

"Enough of this," Gladius said as he balled up his hand. He ran and swung his fist at Krycin's head.

Krycin's instincts kicked in and stopped time. The world around him froze and went silent. Narshuks stood like statues forever marching toward their goal. Even the wind stopped and the air resisted every breath he took. Everything stopped except for Gladius. His fist connected with Krycin's face and sent him sprawling backward onto the ground. His lip split open and swelled right away from the impact and blood dripped from the wound. The side of Krycin's face throbbed with a pain he hadn't felt since the last time they battled. He tried to gather his wits about him and recover from the unexpected hit when he heard Gladius laugh.

"How many of you foolish Lyecians do I have to hit before you catch on?" Gladius said as he walked up beside Krycin. "You can't stop time and run from me. Not anymore."

Clear your mind, and focus on what you want, a familiar, ancient voice echoed in Krycin's head, and he obeyed despite the foot that connected with his side. His conscious mind left his body and focused on calling the power of life. The magic flowed to him and he projected it up at Gladius in a concentrated blast that struck his chest plate and sent him flying up into the air and back into a group of frozen Narshuks. *This can't happen,* Krycin thought. *Not here. Not now.*

He scanned the area and spotted Cy's body mere paces from himself. Gladius was up and running at him with a spell ready but instead of defending himself, Krycin reached out and grabbed hold of Cy, then focused on the image of the Findoor banner flying high above the gray stone castle, and disappeared.

⊙

Gladius fired his spell at Krycin, hoping to distract his mind enough to disrupt his magic, but by the time the blast of ice struck, both Krycin and Cy's body were gone. "Blast it all!" Gladius shouted as the Narshuk army around him started moving again. With a thought, the power of air came to him and he lifted off into the sky to survey the area. All magic had ceased, and there was no sign of any more Lyecians. He looked to the front of the army and spotted Scrag leading the charge.

The wind carried him to the front lines where he set himself down next to Scrag at a full run. Scrag looked surprised to see him, but didn't stop moving. "What's our situation?" Gladius asked. "How many did we lose in the attack?"

Scrag grunted in response, but appeared to be doing some mental calculations. Moments later he said, "We've lost a thousand troops, but you've slain nearly all of their Time Weavers."

"Gather a list," Gladius said, motioning Scrag to stop his advance. When they came to a halt, the rest of the army followed suit and stopped to wait for orders. "I want a list of every Narshuk who lost his life today. Once you have that, we will send it back to the Elders to decide how to honor their deaths. Leave a garrison behind to gather their bodies. Tell them to do with the Lyecians as they please."

Scrag nodded and gathered a number of commanders to follow through with the orders. Gladius gave orders to keep moving into Findoor land, and the rest of the army followed him, marching toward the Losteron Plains.

Chapter 27 - Revival

When Krycin appeared in the courtyard of the castle proper with Cy's body, the sun had fully set and a full moon was on the rise. It provided more light than the few torches that were kept burning in wall sconces around the perimeter. A chill was in the night air, just enough to make Krycin's skin cool to the touch. He lifted himself up off the ground, knelt next to Cy's body, and began to sob.

"It wasn't supposed to be this way," Krycin said to the motionless form before him. "I thought I could at least change this one thing. You were supposed to end up my friend, not dead."

He heard light footsteps approaching his position and looked up. A young runner walked toward him, taking cautious steps. "Is everything all right?" the boy asked, trying to get a good look at the dark form on the ground.

"Far from it," Krycin said through his tears. "Go and get the Arch-Magus. Tell him Krycin has made a mess of things, and needs help to fix them."

The runner hesitated a moment, still looking at the dark form on the ground. "And if the Arch-Magus is retired for the night?"

"Then wake him," Krycin said to the boy, his voice filled with anger. "Go. There is more at stake here than Merek's beauty sleep."

"As you wish," the boy said, recoiling from Krycin, and ran inside the castle. Krycin heard his steps fade as he moved deeper into the castle.

He took a deep breath and tried to calm his nerves. Krycin's mind was reeling from the night's events. *How do I fix this now,* he thought as he looked once again at Cy's motionless body. "We were the perfect team, life and death. I hoped we could be friends, and change things. I know I'm not supposed to change things, but you were a different person the first time we met. The way you are now, that's the way you should have been. A mentor, not an enemy."

A cool breeze blew and caused the torches to flicker in the courtyard. A few leaves rustled against the paving stones, but no other sound disturbed the quiet of night. Krycin placed his hands on Cy's chest and bowed his head for a moment of silence. "I wish I could bring you back," Krycin said, thinking of his powers and how destructive the power of life could be.

He closed his eyes and resigned himself to his thoughts, and didn't notice the white glow that surrounded his hands. A voice spoke inside his mind. *Witness the power of life.*

The voice was calming and reassuring, and made Krycin feel like he'd been wrapped in warmth and love. He felt a presence surround him, though he didn't open his eyes. It melted away all of his fear, all his grief. His heart filled with joy and happiness and the warmth flowed from him, through his hands, and into the body beneath them. Thoughts of the approaching army and what Gladius had become left his mind, and all that remained was a pure source of magic. He saw in his mind's eye the brilliant light that was the source of all life magic, and never wanted to leave that moment.

The feeling was fleeting though, and faded as fast as it had appeared. He tried to cling to it, but the more he grasped at it with his mind, the faster it went away. The only thing that broke him out of his trance was the gasp for air that came from the body on the ground in front of him.

⊙

Merek had not retired for the night. Far from it. He was in the war room with King Valerra when the runner burst in. The sound of the door hitting the wall made them both jump as they focused on the maps before them. Reports of the failure of the initial defense of the kingdom had already begun making their way back, and they were both working on where to place the kingdom's units on the Losteron Plains for the best tactical advantage.

Valerra turned around to see who entered and shook his head at the young boy. "Don't they teach you runners manners anymore?"

The boy nodded, gasping for air. "My apologies, your highness," the boy said once he regained enough breath to speak. "Arch-Magus Merek, you are required in the main courtyard immediately. It's Krycin, and I think Cy, but I couldn't tell, it was dark."

"By the gods, boy, lead the way," Merek said, and followed the boy out of the room.

They walked through the quiet castle and to the main entryway. When they were at the door, Merek stopped and looked at the boy. "Go home, I will inform your commander that I dismissed you for the night."

The boy didn't wait for Merek to change his mind and took off running. Merek opened the door and took a step out into the cool night air.

Out in the middle of the courtyard, he saw Krycin in crystal armor kneeling over a dark form on the ground. Krycin's hands were pressed against the form, and it looked like he was saying something, though his words were too quiet to hear. A brilliant white glow burst out of Krycin's hands and lit up the entire courtyard. In the harsh light, Merek could see that the form on the ground was, in fact, Cy. He took a step toward the pair, but had to cover his eyes as the light around Krycin's hands grew brighter still. A warmth radiated from Krycin that Merek could feel coming in waves. It soothed him and made him feel welcome, though the light was now blinding even through his closed and covered eyes.

When the light faded, he heard a gasp for breath come from Cy. He dropped his hand away from his eyes just in time to see Cy sit bolt upright with a startled expression on his face. Krycin fell back away from him onto his back and looked startled as well. "Precious Anam," Merek said, rushing to the aid of the two men.

Cy looked around and tried to catch his breath. "What did I miss? Where is that swine, Gladius?"

Krycin stammered something unintelligible, but couldn't get a real word out through his shock.

"I'm unsure of where Gladius is. The High Council was supposed to take care of him," Merek said, and offered Cy a hand up.

"The High Council? Ha!" Cy shouted as he stood up. "Those cowards didn't even show. Not a single human wizard showed up to help several hundred Lyecians battle ten thousand Narshuks and a wizard gone insane."

"He's killing them," Krycin said from his position on the ground. He was making an attempt to get up and finally found the words to speak. "Gladius is killing Lyecians. Any that he can find. Hundreds died today because they weren't ready for this battle. Nobody was ready for what we faced today. Not even Cy."

Cy spun to face Krycin and glared at him. "Not even me? I would have done much better if my *brother* hadn't left my side. We were supposed to stick together. Instead, I got stuck facing Gladius alone. I'm not even sure how I made it back here."

Merek raised a hand to try to calm the situation. "Let's not point fingers at each other. We must be strong in the face of this darkness, and stick together."

"Indeed," Cy said in a dry tone. He looked at Krycin again, who was staring at a torch to avoid meeting his gaze. "How did I make it back here, anyway?"

"I brought you," Krycin said, shifting his eyes to the ground. "I brought your body back, because I couldn't bear to leave you to the Narshuks. Gladius took your soul, like he did so many others today. I tried to find you. I tried to help you." Tears rolled down Krycin's cheeks. "I was too late."

Confusion clouded Cy's face as he looked from Krycin to Merek.

"Cy," Merek said, placing a hand on his shoulder. "When I arrived here, Krycin was already casting a spell. He brought you back, with the blessing of Anam and the power of life."

"Brought me back? How is that even possible? There's no coming back from the dead." Cy's voice filled with anger as he looked back and forth at the two men next to him.

"I don't know how I did it," Krycin said. "But it's done. I couldn't see you die."

Cy took a deep breath, like he was trying to calm himself, then without warning, swung a fist out at Krycin. Merek watched as Krycin ducked to the right to avoid getting hit, which put Cy off balance. He fell forward into Krycin, who caught him and steadied him. Cy reacted with a violent shove away from Krycin. "And what was that? Are you so powerful now that you surpass me in all Lyecian skills?"

Merek stepped between the two men and faced Cy. "Come now, Cy. Krycin saved your life. You should be grateful."

"Grateful for what?" Cy roared back at the Arch-Magus. "For bringing me back into some kind of un-life? He hasn't surpassed my Lyecian abilities, he's robbed me of them. I'm no better than a human now. I would have been better off dead." He stormed away without a second look back.

Merek looked at Krycin who was watching Cy walk away. "Don't take his words to heart," Merek said with a calm, gentle tone. "They can hurt like dagger wounds, but in time he will come around."

Krycin let out a great sigh and lowered his head. "I don't think he will."

"Come," Merek said. "Have a hearty meal and give me your report on the attack. We must be properly prepared for the next confrontation. The Findoor army is assembling on the Losteron Plains and will require instructions on how to proceed."

Merek walked back toward the castle. When he reached the main entrance, he checked to see if Krycin was following. Krycin looked one more time in the direction that Cy had walked, and then followed Merek into the castle.

⊙

Krycin sat opposite to Merek at a table in the great hall and ate while Merek went over some papers that a runner had delivered to him from the king. At one point Merek looked up to see if Krycin was done yet, but went right back to his papers again. When Krycin was finished, he looked at Merek and said, "You were right. I do feel better after a good meal. Is there any news from the Council yet?"

"Not yet," Merek said. "I'm worried. I sent the Council to take care of Gladius before our armies met. Several scattered reports have come back from Lyecians, but we've heard nothing from the Council. If Gladius is still alive, it means either they have turned their backs on us, or..."

"Or they've met their end," Krycin said, staring at the table.

"Well, let us hope for the best, shall we?" Merek smiled and looked down at his papers once more, leaving Krycin to wonder what the best option actually was.

When Krycin couldn't stand the silence anymore, he looked up from the table and spoke. "Gladius was waiting for us," he said, his voice filled with sadness. "He was waiting for us, and knew just how and when to hit us. He wasn't afraid. He didn't even get hurt. I think he actually enjoyed it. I don't know how, but he's immune to our Lyecian abilities. I think it's because he's taken a Lyecian soul."

The last sentence caught Merek's attention. His head snapped up from his papers and he stared into Krycin's eyes. "The book," he said. "The last time I saw Gladius, he had a book. It was a Lyecian spell book, and an ancient one at that, though you wouldn't know it to look at it. He was asking about an inscription in the book, written in common, but there were a great many spells in the book written in High Lyecian script as well. I studied the book once, but could not translate it. If Gladius did find a way to translate it, then he could indeed have a spell that would help him accomplish what you've proposed."

Neither man noticed when the dark form entered the banquet hall until he was standing next to their table. Cy cleared his throat and startled both men. He gave Krycin a disdainful glare, then looked at Merek. "I apologize for my earlier behavior. I was out of line. I'd like to help in any way I can with the defense of the kingdom, even if it means I must cast spells the human way."

Merek smiled at Cy and nodded. "And help you shall. Krycin and I were just discussing the attack and how Gladius could have obtained the power he did. He has a book that we must get back. A white Lyecian spell book. We must find a way to get the book away from Gladius. Perhaps you could use your anger to better a bad situation?"

"What are you proposing?" Cy asked.

"Get close to Gladius. Find the book, and bring it back to us," Merek said with a sideways glance toward Krycin. "Your anger toward Krycin is still evident. Use that, and convince Gladius that you know our plans and that you can help him defeat our armies." Merek handed Cy a stack of papers with the Findoor seal pressed into them. "Take these as proof. They are maps, battle plans, army locations. When the time is right, return to us with the book, and we will try to finish Gladius once and for all."

Cy took the papers and nodded. "Dangerous. But just crazy enough that it might work. And if it doesn't, then he will likely kill me again, and that would only be doing me a favor," Cy said. "All right, I'll do it."

Krycin looked at Cy and finally spoke. "Cy, I'm sorry. I didn't mean for this to happen, you have to know that."

"I have to? You're the one who has supposedly seen the future. You're the one who is supposed to be our all powerful savior. But I see it a different way," Cy said, raising his voice in anger once again. "Had you never appeared, Gladius would still be on that island in the Rashean Sea studying rocks and eating berries, instead of leading one of Galadir's most dangerous armies on a rampage across Findoor land. So by my count, everything that has happened since you appeared, has been your fault. So no, I don't *have* to know that. I'm doing this for Merek, and for Findoor. Not for *you*."

He stormed away from the table, leaving through the main entrance. When he was out of the room, Krycin heard him shout for a runner and a horse.

Lebriel and Tyriel appeared in the center of the High Council chamber. The room was silent other than the occasional shout from a commander outside. The army of wizards was awaiting orders from the High Council before moving out. Lebriel leaned on his staff and gasped for breath while Tyriel helped him to his seat.

"Rest now, brother," Tyriel said. "You are safe, though I cannot say the same for the rest of the Council."

Lebriel sat for a moment staring at the floor. When he was rested enough to speak again, he looked up into his twin's eyes. "Could you not help the rest of them? Could you not slay Gladius and end this?"

"It is forbidden. Just by helping you, I defy the Fates, but I could not allow you to die. Gladius must live. Krycin must defeat him. There is no other way."

"There must be another way," Lebriel said. "Lives are at stake here. The army he's raised could destroy Findoor, and the rest of the world. It's the reason the High Council has worked so hard to keep the Narshuks in check."

Tyriel's voice was dry and flat as he spoke. "Many thousands will die. Findoor will be forever changed."

"Can we not fight this on our own? The Fates be damned, these are real people we're talking about." Lebriel raised his voice now, his strength returning to him as he rested.

"Too much has already changed. The Fates are trying to save this world. If some lives are lost to save millions, then the ends justify the means. Death is a natural part of life."

"Oh come off it. You come to me twenty years after your death and try to tell me this?" Lebriel stood up on his own and held his staff to the side, taking steps forward as he spoke. "If death is so natural, why didn't you stay dead? Why are you here now? And if too much has been changed already, then why continue to save me from death? By my count, that's twice now that I should have died, but haven't. Stop parroting the Fates and give me a *real* answer."

The two men stood in the center of the room, mirror images of each other. Lebriel stared into the intense blue eyes of his brother and gritted his teeth. There was silence between them as Lebriel waited for an answer. After a long pause, Lebriel broke the silence. "Yeah, I thought so," he said, walking away.

Lebriel was at the door when Tyriel spoke up. "Because I love you. Because you're my brother," Tyriel said. Lebriel paused, but didn't turn around. "And because the Fates don't always get their way."

With a long sigh, Lebriel left the room and went outside to find the commanders of the army. When he called a meeting, they assembled without question just outside the front gates of the keep.

"I've called you here to inform you that the Wizard High Council has been defeated," Lebriel said. "You are all brave men and women, but the threat we face now is greater than any we have fought before. The blue wizard Gladius is out of control and has killed the other seven members of the High Council."

Gasps and murmurs went through the small crowd of commanders. Some of them sounded as though they doubted the news, others spoke in disbelief. One particular commander stepped forward. He stood taller than Lebriel and wore his brown hair long, but tied back with a leather thong. His face was covered with stubble and his eyes were a deep brown. Other commanders backed away a step as he approached. "Even Marius? How do we know this isn't some kind of trick? Nobody here has ever seen a Lyecian die. I didn't even know they *could* die. What if this is just some kind of ploy of yours to take control of the army?"

Several other commanders shouted jeers of support for the black-robed wizard who now stood tall with a defiant look on his face.

"Come now Garrick, this is serious business. Yes, Marius is dead. Gladius killed him. I don't know how he accomplished it, but I think it was some old form of Lyecian magic that he used. The bigger concern is that Gladius now marches on Findoor, and without the rest of the Council, we have no way to transport this many troops to their aid. We must go the old fashioned way, and hope they can hold out until we arrive."

Garrick looked at Lebriel with suspicion. "Where did Gladius get an army large enough to march on Findoor? He could never muster that many men."

"He doesn't have an army of men," Lebriel said. "He has an army of Narshuks. Gladius has united the tribes and leads an army ten thousand strong. If we don't stop him, he will wash over the land with them. Nothing will survive in the wake of an army that big."

"Grishtor save us," Garrick said, astonished. "Why should we run to the defense of Findoor when only a few short weeks ago, we were marching on them? What happened to this Lyecian that was deemed so dangerous?"

"Krycin is no longer a threat." Lebriel raised his voice to address as many wizards as he could from his position. "Right now, Gladius and his Narshuk army are marching on Findoor. But if he succeeds in taking Findoor, where do you suppose he will go next? Caldoor? Arda? The outer regions? I think not. He will come here. And if this keep is lost to Gladius, then all of Galadir is lost. And so I implore you all, lend me your support. March to Findoor, and help defend it as if it were your home. Because if you don't, pretty soon they *will* be marching on your home."

Another murmur ran through the crowd surrounding Lebriel. Garrick raised his hand for silence, and then spoke. "If the rest of the Council is indeed defeated, then appoint a new Council. You must, as this army will not accept the authority of a single red wizard. Bring us a Council of all the gods, and we will march."

Lebriel thought about this for a moment, and said, "Very well. Garrick, you are my first, appointed to the position of Black Wizard on the High Council. I am willing to accept suggestions for the remaining Council members, though I recommend that we appoint Serrin Alkirk to the position of gold wizard on the Council. He is by far the oldest and most experienced of the Lyecians we know of."

Garrick smiled. "I agree. Let us assemble the new High Council, and then move out."

Chapter 28 – A New Council

Serrin and Catrina Alkirk were just waking up when the knock came at their front door. The sound echoed through the hallways and reverberated off the walls, startling Serrin, as they rarely received company in the Caldera. With a grumble, he got up from his bed and walked to the door. He didn't expect what he saw on the other side when he opened it.

"Can I help... you?" Serrin said, trailing off as he opened the door. His tone went from calm to surprised when he saw five wizards waiting outside his door. "Lebriel," he said to the red robed wizard who led the group, "to what do I owe the pleasure?"

Lebriel had his brow lowered, creating wrinkles around his eyes, and wore a frown that wrinkled his cheeks around his mouth. Sadness filled his mannerisms as every move he made, and every word he said was reluctant. "Serrin, my friend. It is with great regret that we must inform you that Marius, child of Lyecha, and gold wizard on the Council is now dead, along with all other members of the High Council."

Serrin backed up a step, stunned at the news. "How? I mean, Marius was one of the most powerful Lyecians who ever lived. What trickery is this?"

"There is no trickery, no games," Lebriel said. "May we come in?"

"Please, forgive my manners. Come in, we can meet in the dining hall," Serrin said, motioning down the hall to a door at the end.

"That would be splendid. We have much to discuss, and a comfortable seat would be welcome to all of us."

Serrin held the door for them as they entered. When they were all inside, he motioned down the hall. "The dining room is that way. I'll be with you in a moment."

The group went to the dining room while Serrin walked to the kitchen. Inside, Catrina stood at the counter peeling and chopping vegetables for their morning meal, her long brown hair tied up at the back. Serrin approached her from behind, moving through the kitchen like a ghost, yet when he reached her, she said, "Company, my love?"

He could almost hear the smile on her face. "I don't know how you do it. Yes, the High Council, or what remains of them, have come to discuss some matters of great importance. Would you join us?"

She turned around and extended her arms toward him. From the back, her figure was average. Not thin, but not overweight, and only just having the proportions that would measure as moderately attractive. When she moved to face Serrin, he saw her protruding belly and beamed. Though he had watched her grow over the last thirty-five weeks as her pregnancy progressed, he never stopped appreciating what he considered unending beauty. She smiled and said, "Of course. What remains of them? Has something happened?"

"Yes. Come, all shall be explained." Serrin led her by the hand to the dining room and they took seats next to each other so they could both face the Council. "You had matters to discuss?" Serrin asked.

"Yes," Lebriel began, "we have decided unanimously, that you should join the High Council as the new gold wizard."

It took a long time for Serrin to respond to this. He stared at Lebriel, trying to comprehend what he had been asked. And then looked at the table before him, considering the position and what it would mean to his family. When Lebriel gave a polite cough to remind him that they were still waiting for his answer, he looked up and said, "How did the others perish? What warrior or magic could slay one as strong as Marius?"

Lebriel's face darkened, a forbidding expression washing over him. "Gladius, son of Darson. He used an ancient Lyecian spell to prevent Marius from using his magic, and ripped his soul from his body."

"By the gods," Serrin said, glancing at his wife. "I knew Gladius was getting powerful, but I had no idea he had grown into such a monster. We had a confrontation with him here not too long ago, where he did the same with a dragon. Krycin helped us clean up the mess. Why make a move so quickly? I can see you have appointed new High Council members. Should this not be done the usual way, with a contest?"

"There is no time," Lebriel said. "I've begun appointing a new Council so that we might rush to the aid of Findoor. Gladius leads a massive army of Narshuks, ten thousand strong, and will wash over all of Galadir if he is not stopped."

Serrin made another long, thoughtful pause as he considered his options. "I will come and serve as gold wizard on the Council, but on one condition. I bring Catrina with me."

Lebriel nodded. "Very well. Catrina, you are welcome to come along, just know that we are heading into dangerous territory. We have no idea what else Gladius can do at this point. He has collected all eight elements, though we can't be sure if he can actually use the element of time."

"I am more than capable of taking care of myself," Catrina said. "I drove off Gladius once, I'm sure I could do it again if required."

"If that's settled, we must make haste. Findoor was expecting our wizards with the initial attack, but without a Council to lead them, the wizard army wouldn't move," Lebriel said, shooting a sideways glance to Garrick. "We're already late, and we're going to be even later as we no longer have enough wizards who know the transport spell to move the army all at once. We must march."

Serrin stood up from the table, followed by Catrina. "Then what are we waiting for? Let's stop wasting time talking about it, and get our troops moving. It sounds like Findoor can use all the help they can get."

Lebriel stood up as well, along with the rest of the newly formed Council. "Serrin, I have one last favor to ask of you. I need you to go to Findoor castle and inform King Valerra and Merek of what has happened to the Council. Talk to Merek about sitting on the Council as the Gray Wizard, and let them know that Ducain's Keep has not abandoned them. We are coming."

"A very good plan," Serrin said. He took his wife's hand and led the wizards out of the dining hall and down the hall to the front door. "I shall report back to you once I have spoken to Valerra and Merek."

Serrin held the door for the Council and watched them gather on the grass in front of his home. Catrina followed them, but stopped several paces short and waited for Serrin to join her. He closed the door, walked to her side and gave the Council a wave. "I shall see you all soon," Serrin said, and he and Catrina disappeared.

They reappeared in the field in front of Findoor Castle. The sun hadn't yet risen, but would soon. It was quiet other than a few early morning sounds, like night birds settling down to sleep, and early morning birds waking to sing the sun up. Serrin led the way, walking toward the front gates of the city. Catrina followed close behind him.

The city guard allowed the couple passage into the city without question and they walked straight to the castle proper. There were few people awake at that hour; only those bakers and butchers who were setting up for the day's markets. Inside the castle, only servants and runners roamed the hallways. Serrin flagged down a runner as he passed. "Young man, please inform King Valerra and Arch-Magus Merek that Serrin and Catrina Alkirk are here to see them with a matter of utmost urgency."

The runner said nothing, but nodded and ran into the inner chambers of the castle. Serrin and Catrina made their way to the waiting area outside of the throne room and took a seat. Merek appeared in the room minutes later, followed by Krycin.

"My apologies," Merek said. "King Valerra will not be joining us. He's decided, against my counsel, to join the Findoor army on the Losteron Plains. It is good to see you again, Serrin." He looked at Catrina, took her hand, and gave her a low bow. "And this must be your wife, Catrina. It is a real pleasure to meet you, even under such dire conditions."

Catrina blushed at the attention but gave him a polite smile. "You as well, Arch-Magus Merek." She looked toward Krycin and said, "We meet again."

"I've been helping Merek plan the castle defense," Krycin said with a polite nod.

"I don't mean to be rude," Serrin said, cutting in, "but our business is urgent, and we must speak with Arch-Magus Merek alone. I hope you understand, Krycin. I am glad you are well."

Krycin opened his mouth to say something, but was cut off by Merek. "Nonsense," he said. "Krycin has as much right to be here as anyone." Merek's tone became serious as he opened the doors to the throne room. "Come in, everyone, where prying ears can't hear. What news do you have for us, Serrin?" He walked into the throne room and took a seat beside the king's throne. The others followed him in and sat in the front row of the court's benches.

"The reason we've come to you today," Serrin began, "is to bring you news of the High Council. I am sorry to be the bearer of this news. As you know, the Wizard High Council confronted Gladius last night in an effort to stop his insanity. With the exception of Lebriel, the entire High Council has been slain, including Marius." Merek flinched, like he'd been physically struck by the news. Krycin's face darkened and he looked at the floor. Serrin continued. "Lebriel has begun appointing a new Council, and asks that you serve as the Gray Wizard."

There was a long pause as Merek appeared to think the proposition over. "I appreciate the offer, but I must respectfully decline," he said. "I will tell you what I told the previous High Council when they offered me the position once before. My heart belongs to Findoor, and to my research. I have no desire to take up a career in politics. Have they gotten you involved now?"

Serrin nodded. "Indeed. I have been appointed Gold Wizard on the Council. I will lead it the best I can. I'm sorry to hear you decline, you would have made a wonderful addition, but I understand your point of view. The Ducain's Keep wizards are on their way to Findoor on foot to aid in the defense of your kingdom. We had promised aid in the border defense, but with the untimely death of most of the High Council, we had not the resources to transport that many wizards without using rifts. Many wizards are still learning the new transport spells. I assume we will be joining the Lyecians on the Losteron Plains then?"

He saw a strange look on Krycin's face, but kept his attention on Merek, who also appeared troubled by his question. "You haven't heard," Merek said.

"Obviously not," Serrin said. "What other news do you bear?"

"I'll let Krycin relay the news, as it is more his news than mine."

Krycin cleared his throat and blinked a few times. His face was sad, and Serrin thought he looked to be holding back tears. "He was ready for us, Serrin. He was ready for the Lyecians. He knew what he was doing, and how to hit us the hardest. Gladius killed hundreds of us last night. The remaining Lyecians have scattered."

"Lyecha save us," Serrin said. Catrina gasped at the news and huddled close to her husband. Krycin gave them a funny look, but Serrin assumed it to be because of his state of mind. "What do we do then? How do we defend against Gladius and his army of Narshuks?"

Merek shook his head. "King Valerra has gone south to rally the troops on the Losteron Plains. Those few Lyecians that are brave enough to stay have joined him. I suggest you direct your army to head that way as well. They will need all the help they can get."

"And if they can't hold back Gladius?" Krycin asked without being prompted.

Serrin looked at Krycin with a grave expression. Merek looked worse. "If we can't hold him back, we will have to fall back to Findoor castle. This castle has never fallen to siege before. We can hold out against Gladius for weeks while we look for an answer."

Krycin looked at Merek like he was insane. "Just fall back? That's your answer? Fall back and let Gladius walk all over us? Let me ride out and meet him. Let me try to defeat him. It's me he's after, and you know it."

"I cannot," Merek said. "You're too important. I won't put you in harm's way again. Not now that I know Gladius has the ability to take your life."

"You won't put me in harm's way?" Krycin said, getting up from his chair. He spun to face Merek and stared into his eyes. "God damn it, Merek, stop acting like my father. You don't need to protect me, I can take care of myself. If I want to go to battle, I will go to battle, and there's nothing you can do to stop me."

Serrin stood up and approached Krycin, placing a hand on his shoulder. "Come now, Krycin. Nobody is trying to tell you what you can and can't do. Merek is simply trying to act in your best interest. Nobody here wants to see you die at Gladius's hand."

Krycin looked at Serrin and heaved a sigh. "There are so many things I want to say to you," he said. "But I can't. Not yet. Just understand that this isn't easy for me, for reasons you could not possibly fathom." He walked toward the door, opened it, and stepped through, leaving the other three in silence.

There was a long pause before Serrin turned back to Merek and said, "Should I go and talk to him in private? Perhaps another of his kind would be better to counsel him?"

"Perhaps. I think we're done here anyway," Merek said. "If you go look for him, check the battlements. He likes to sit up there when he wants to be alone."

⊙

Krycin sat on the edge of the battlements overlooking the rest of the castle and the city. The sun was up by the time he left the throne room, but the scenery around Findoor castle was still beautiful, even without the red and orange light of early sunrise. He watched little smoke trails rise from chimneys throughout the city as shops and households prepared for the day. When he heard footsteps behind him, he didn't turn around, but said, "I wondered how long it would take you to come after me. I don't want to talk to you."

He wasn't expecting Serrin's voice. "Come now, Krycin. Tell me what's on your mind."

Serrin had crossed the battlements halfway before Krycin swung his legs toward the inside of the wall to face him. "I expected Merek to come after me. I'm sorry. I didn't mean to be rude."

"Don't mention it," Serrin said with a smile. Krycin's heart jumped as he remembered that smile from his youth.

"When I was young, my father used to read me stories about a hero, and all the great things he did. I would listen in wonder, and dream about one day being that hero. About fighting the forces of darkness and dealing out justice with my sword of light. It's amazing how far real life can be from the stories we tell."

Serrin let out a chuckle. "It's amazing how simple life can seem through a child's eyes. Things are not always so black and white, but I should very much like to read my child the stories of Krycin, and how he defeated the Dark Lord, Gladius." He made a mocking dramatic tone when he said Gladius's name that brought a smile to Krycin's face. "But that won't happen if we don't win this war. Even heroes need help, Krycin. You can't fight this war on your own."

"I know. And yet, I feel like it's my responsibility. Cy is right. Had I never appeared, none of this would have happened," Krycin said, shifting his gaze toward the stone floor.

"Time is a funny thing. You can wonder and postulate about how things might have been, but one things remains true," Serrin said. He reached forward and placed two fingers on Krycin's chin to lift his face and look into his eyes. "You cannot change the past. What's done is done. You can drive yourself mad wondering what might have been, or you can accept this inevitable fact and live to forge the future."

Krycin relaxed when he heard those words. "You're right. I can't change the past, no matter how hard I try."

"So let's build a future for Galadir, and battle Gladius together."

"We need help," Krycin said. "From an old friend." He smiled to himself and felt a little better for the first time since he returned from the battle in the south.

Serrin smiled back at him, but had a curious expression on his face. "An old friend?" he asked.

"Yes. With any luck, I should be just in time for the battle on the Losteron Plains. But don't wait up for me. Destroy him if you get the chance." Krycin concentrated for a moment and disappeared, leaving Serrin on the battlements alone.

Chapter 29 – Betrayer

Cy rode hard for days to reach Gladius and his army before they reached the Losteron Plains. When he crested a hill south of the plains he saw the army moving over the land like a swarm of ants in the distance. The rumble it created was like thunder rolling in before a storm.

He tried to tell himself he had nothing to fear as he made a beeline for Gladius; that even if Gladius did kill him, it would be doing him a favor. In truth, he had no interest in dying just yet and that left his guts feeling like they were twisting themselves up inside of him.

The ride to meet Gladius was shorter than Cy expected. Gladius raised a hand to halt the Narshuk advance and, minutes later, strutted up to meet him. "Didn't I kill you?" Gladius said with a snide tone.

"You tried. Apparently the gods have other plans."

Gladius narrowed his eyes and peered at Cy for a moment, and then smiled. "Those plans don't include your Lyecian powers."

"Sadly, no," Cy said. He looked to either side of Gladius where Narshuks stood waiting.

"So why *are* you here then? Give me a reason not to snuff you out and feed you to my army."

Cy reached into his saddlebags and pulled out the papers Merek had given him. "I have information for you."

There was a moment of silence between them, and then Gladius burst into laughter. "You ride up here, back from the dead, and expect me to buy that? All right. Let's just say that I believe you. Why shouldn't I kill you and take your precious papers?"

"Because I have far more information than just this. Face it, you'll need somebody on the inside to take Findoor Castle," Cy said. He didn't believe his words for a second, and it must have showed on his face, because Gladius walked up to his horse, pointed at the papers in his hand and sent a spark into them, lighting them on fire.

"That's what I think of your information," Gladius said as Cy dropped the burning papers to the ground. Before Cy knew what was happening, Gladius reached up, grabbed hold of him, and hauled him from the back of the horse. His back hit the ground hard, knocking the wind out of him, and the sudden motion spooked the horse and sent it running down the Narshuk line. Gladius leaned down over him and looked into his dark eyes. "He brought you back without your powers. I know how you are, Cy. Krycin has turned you into a human. Turned you into something you hate, and you're going to do his bidding?"

Cy gasped for breath, but couldn't form the words he wanted. He shook his head instead.

"No?" Gladius leaned in closer so that his mouth was next to Cy's ear. When he did, he leaned his knee on Cy's torso and pinned him to the ground under his weight. "Oh let me guess. For Findoor?" Gladius whispered the words, which drifted into Cy's ears and infected his mind. Cy could feel it spreading like a disease that took every ounce of his strength to fight.

"Yes," Cy said. "For Findoor."

"You're going to do something for me," Gladius said, still whispering. The magic ran through Cy's head and down his spine, causing him to shiver. "I want you to carry something for me. A little piece of myself to keep you company."

Cy fought against the spell infesting his body, but without his Lyecian abilities, he had trouble drawing even a small amount of magic.

"Forget about Findoor. Don't fight it. You hate him. I may have robbed you of your life, but Krycin brought you back against your will. He forced you into this un-life. This *human* existence." Gladius let go of Cy and stood up. "Surrender to me and I'll make sure you get power."

The spell gripped Cy's mind and spread throughout his body. He stopped fighting it and let it take over, but rather than seizing control of his body, it slowed and settled. Cy relaxed and stood up. "What kind of power?"

"Limitless," Gladius said with a wicked smile. He stepped back and held his hand out before him. In his palm, a ball of black energy formed. Swirling around in the ball were all of the other colors of magic. Gladius stepped toward Cy and pressed the ball into Cy's chest.

The energy sank into his body, filling him with a second presence that coexisted with his own consciousness. It took a few minutes for Cy to get used to it, but once he felt the magical energy flow again, he smiled. "How?" he asked, looking into Gladius's eyes.

"It's a piece of my soul. A simulacrum if you will. It won't bring your powers back, but it will enhance what you have. And you will always carry a piece of me with you, to be my eyes and ears. Once I have eliminated Krycin and the rest of the Lyecians, I will find your power, and you will have your reward."

"They're expecting me back with the Lyecian book," Cy said.

"Take it. I have no further use for it." Gladius motioned to Scrag to bring the book forward. Scrag pulled it from a satchel at his side and handed it to Gladius, who in turn held it out to Cy. "If you betray me, I'll know. But you won't, will you? I can feel the hate inside of you."

"You have my word," Cy said, and walked away.

⊙

King Valerra and his royal guard arrived at the rendezvous point on the Losteron Plains when runners reported Gladius and the Narshuk army approaching. Without rift magic, there was no easy way to transport the vast numbers Findoor held in reserve, and so what lined up on the hills surrounding the plains now were a meager defense for the kingdom.

"Two thousand men? That's all we could muster?" Valerra asked.

"There aren't enough wizards who know the new spells yet," one commander said. "We've pulled together what we could, but the Narshuks move so fast, and stop for such short times. Nobody ever anticipated they would invade in such numbers."

Valerra shook his head and shifted his worried eyes toward the south and the rumble of the approaching army. Stress and age had begun etching lines in his face around his eyes and now they were more pronounced than ever. "What do we do? How do we fight them?"

A commotion came from behind the group as several Lyecians appeared on the field behind them. Krycin led the way into the huddle. "You fight them with us," Krycin said, motioning to the field as several dozen more Lyecians appeared. "There's not many of us left, but we're here to help."

There was a moment of silence as Valerra watched more Lyecians appear. When they were all present, he counted at least a hundred. "By the gods, Krycin. Have you any other tricks up your sleeves?"

"A few. I'm going to call on an old friend. I should be back before the battle starts."

The growing rumble in the distance didn't leave Valerra with hope in his heart, but he accepted the help with grace. "Thank you, Krycin. For all you have done already."

Krycin looked over the Lyecians in the field behind him. "Remember, when the battle starts, do not try to confront Gladius. He's immune to our time weaving, and much more powerful than any one of us can handle on our own. If you spot him, move, and attack from another position."

The group acknowledged his orders, and then he disappeared, leaving only the rushing sound of air to fill the space he was in.

⊙

When Krycin reappeared, his eyes met a familiar sight. The mouth of a cave on the side of a mountain. There was a rough path that led up to the cave coming from a swampy forest. He could see for miles around.

A voice startled him out of his daze. "It's quite a stunning view, isn't it?"

Krycin whirled toward the voice. He acted on reflex and called on his magic to produce a glowing orb in his hand and readied it to throw. Standing just inside the cave was a familiar sight. A tall, lean man wearing loose fitting traveling clothes, black leather boots and a black cloak. The most familiar feature though, was the black mask the man wore that covered most of his face. He could see the man's thin lips and chin that was covered with just a slight shadow of stubble. "Cedric?" Krycin asked, surprised.

The man narrowed his eyes behind the mask, as if he were trying to figure something out, or remember something. "I'm afraid you have me at a disadvantage, which is a rare occurrence. Well played, my friend." He looked from Krycin's face to the glowing ball of light, and then back to his face. "Were you going to do something with that? Perhaps go exploring? It's quite dark in there." He motioned to the cave behind him.

Krycin looked at Cedric in stunned silence. Thoughts whirled through his mind trying to come up with an answer as to why his friend was standing before him in the wrong time. "You're truly Cedric?"

A smirk appeared below Cedric's mask. "Indeed. But use caution, as you might wear out my name, and it's such a bother to find a new one," Cedric said, his tone half mocking and half genuine humor. "Speaking of names, I don't believe I caught yours, or have you worn that one out too?"

Krycin almost spoke a name from his memories, but stopped himself. The pause was noticeable, but he carried on anyway. "Krycin."

"Krycin? Are you sure? You don't sound very confident with that name. You seem like a nice lad, but you need to get your head on straight. How do you expect anyone else to know you, if you don't even know your own name?"

Krycin took a deep breath and tried to clear his head. "Krycin Alkirk. Sorry about that, I just didn't expect to see you up here." He dismissed the orb of light and offered his hand to Cedric.

"The feeling is mutual," Cedric said with a smile, shaking Krycin's hand. "Why, do I not belong here?"

"I don't know," Krycin said. "I'm confused. Maybe you're not the person I think you are."

Cedric took a step forward, the smile disappearing from his face. "Perhaps. It will take some thinking to figure this out. One of us is somewhere we're not supposed to be, and one of us is pretending to be somebody he's not. I can assure you that my name is, indeed, Cedric, but whether I'm the Cedric you think I am, that I can't answer." He took another step toward Krycin. "The real question is, are you sure you are who you think you are? Because if you're not sure about that, how can you be certain of anything?"

There was a brief silence between the two men before Krycin spoke up. "I don't know. I don't have time to sort this out right now. I have an old friend to speak to." Krycin sidestepped around Cedric and entered the cave.

"Be careful," Cedric said. "Something tells me your friend isn't going to be happy to see anyone right now." He walked down the path toward the forest without looking back. Krycin watched after him, still confused.

When Cedric disappeared into the forest, Krycin made his way into the cave. He hesitated just inside the entrance. Memories of Narshuks frozen in time haunted him. When he proceeded, he remembered where Malia and Cedric had made their stand, and how

Malia had been injured. *Why did I come here,* he thought. When he was almost at the inner chamber, something occurred to him. *Where is the crystal?*

All around him were dirt and stone walls. There was no barrier protecting the entrance to the inner chambers, and the crystalline walls that had fascinated him the first time he was there were nowhere to be seen. He continued walking deeper into the mountain until he came to a large room with a black void on the far wall. As he stepped into the room, he heard a rustling come from the void, and then felt the temperature rise quickly as hot air rushed past. He put his arms up in front of his face as a reflex and a glowing white shield emanated out in front of him.

Liquid fire burst into the room striking the shield and flowing around it like a river flowing around a rock. Everything the fire touched super-heated and glowed red, but inside the shield, Krycin was safe. He focused his mind on maintaining the shield until the blast of fire let up.

"Morganath, stop!" Krycin shouted above the crackling and shifting rocks around him.

The black void disappeared and the cavern inside lit up. Vast piles of gold and treasure filled the cavern, sparkling in the dim light. Morganath sat high on one of the largest piles and looked at Krycin with one eye. "My apologies, Krycin. I thought you were the thief returned to claim yet another prize."

Krycin stepped forward to the edge of the circle he now stood in. "Thief? You mean the bard, Cedric?"

"Bard? That would explain the mask. He stole something quite valuable from me, and I want it back." Morganath's voice boomed in the closed in cave and hit Krycin from every direction. "What is your purpose here, Lyecian?"

"I came to ask you for help," Krycin said, choosing his words carefully. "Findoor is under attack by a vast army of Narshuks led by the wizard Gladius. There wasn't enough time for Findoor to raise a proper defense, and now they'll be overrun if we don't do something to help them."

The massive dragon shifted his head to face Krycin with both eyes. He gave a huff to clear some smoke from his nose and said, "Then go and do something. I have a treasure to guard. Never again will I allow a thief to get the better of me."

"What?" Krycin asked, astounded.

"You heard me, Lyecian. Human matters are their own. I've seen many a kingdom rise and fall in my lifetime. If Ignith deems them worthy, they will survive their trial by fire and live on."

"How can you say that?" Krycin asked, yelling now. "How can you sit there on a mountain of treasure and cry about a thief, when you have enough gold here to fund half a nation? People are dying out there, and you would be this selfish?"

Morganath stepped toward the ledge that led out into the treasure chamber and stared Krycin down. His gaze was intense, and made Krycin doubt his position. "Do not presume to know what is and is not best for this world and the nations within it. The gods have a plan, and I shall not interfere with that unless it involves us dragons."

"The gods have a plan? That's the best you've got? And what will you do when they come this way? When the Narshuk army overruns Findoor and spreads throughout the rest of Galadir? This already involves every race on Galadir. Gladius made sure of that when he took the souls of one of each. And now he's killing Lyecians. You have to help." Krycin's voice was forceful, but desperate. He was running out of ideas to spur the monster before him into action.

Morganath's eyes narrowed. "Took the souls? Gladius has killed dragon kind?"

"Yes. I saw it myself, at the Arvok Caldera. Gladius took the soul of a red dragon to further his own ends. You can't ignore this, not even for your horde."

"You are right," Morganath said with a great sigh. "And yet, I must ensure that no thieves can return for the rest of my treasure."

An idea came to Krycin's head. He looked around at the cave and again remembered the blue crystal that had covered the floor, walls and tunnel leading out. He recalled the barrier that had protected the cave. "I can ensure the safety of your treasure," he said to the great gold dragon.

"How could you make such a promise?" Morganath asked.

"Watch," Krycin said with a smile. He called on the power of life, drawing everything he could and focusing it into protective magic. When he reached down and touched the floor, the energy flooded through him and into the cave. The floor beneath him changed to crystal and spread out to the walls, ceiling and down the tunnel. Krycin continued drawing energy and directing it into his spell until the tunnel sealed off with an energy barrier that could only be passed by another Lyecian. When he was done, he looked up at

Morganath and smiled. "There. Nobody will disturb your treasure while we're gone. And when Findoor is safe, you can return."

Morganath made a satisfied grunt and asked, "How long will this last?"

"I don't know. Hundreds of years maybe? As long as there is magic in the world, it will remain."

"Very well then. Get on, and we will go." Morganath lowered his neck to the ledge so that Krycin could get on. Once Krycin was seated and holding on tight, the dragon stepped away from the ledge, gave a mighty leap, and a few strokes of his wings later, they were air-born and heading toward the rear entrance to the lair.

The pair burst out into sunshine and warm air and flew toward Findoor. "Where is the battle happening?" Morganath asked, his voice rumbling through his hide.

"The Losteron Plains," Krycin said.

"It will take days to get there. The battle will be done."

"Not if I can help it." Krycin closed his eyes and focused. The flow of time around them slowed, and Morganath picked up his pace. "Go as fast as you can. Don't worry about me, I can hold on."

"Very well then." Morganath pumped his wings faster still and picked up speed. The pair rocketed through the air toward the impending battle.

Chapter 30 - The Battle of Losteron Plains

General Jhet Corsair served in the Findoor Militia for most of his adult life. Like many other soldiers, he married and had children, but his one true love was his country. In all the years he served Findoor, he had never seen a sight like what laid before him. It was a nightmare he couldn't wake up from. His troops were outnumbered and outmatched by the massive Narshuk army they now faced and they had little magic support other than a handful of Lyecians who had volunteered.

He led the left flank of the Findoor army, with orders to surge ahead and funnel the Narshuk advance into a narrow column that could be met by the main army. It would be easier to fight the Narshuks if there were fewer of them in narrow lines than the mass they currently faced. As he looked out over the army rumbling toward them, he realized this would be a much bigger challenge than he thought. The Narshuks marched in straight lines, ordered and disciplined, a stark contrast to what Jhet had expected from the beasts.

"Archers ready!" He shouted to his troops behind him and gave the signal to the flag man who raised a green flag with a bow embroidered on it. His troops responded with practiced precision as the Narshuks came within range. "Remember, fire for the outer flanks. Aim!"

Archers shifted their aim to hit the outer flank on their side in the hopes it would drive them into the narrow inner column. Jhet watched the other flank of the Findoor army for the archery flag to raise. When it did and he knew both sides were ready, he called out in the loudest, most forceful voice he could muster. "Fire!"

The archery flag dropped, arrows were loosed, and the sky filled with the deadly projectiles. They flew toward the Narshuk flank with the first arrows striking wide, hitting only a few of the beasts. As more found their mark, Jhet expected them to panic and flee to the inner ranks.

The Narshuks kept running in their ordered lines, ready to destroy anything in their paths. A few lucky shots hit eyes or chests and felled them, but most grazed their arms and legs. Those Narshuks without lethal injuries continued their run without even a flinch.

"That's not possible," Jhet said, in shock at the display of power before them. Narshuks with arrows sticking out of them continued their run. Those that fell were trampled and forgotten about. "Fire at will! Get more arrows into these beasts," Jhet shouted at his troops behind him.

Many of the archers sped up their rate of fire, creating a steady stream of arrows flying into the Narshuk lines. Still they ran, though more fell, and the numbers in the front lines thinned. As each archer ran out of arrows, they dropped their bows and drew their swords. Jhet glanced back at his men and saw the anxious looks on their faces. The flanks of the Findoor army were thinner than the main bulk of it and they had hoped that by herding their enemies into a more focused path they could avoid a direct confrontation on the flanks. Now they faced the possibility that they would have to fight for their lives and hold the flank against the beasts.

"Hold your ground," Jhet shouted. "Lyecians, ready. Focus on the edges, get these monsters to break their lines." A dozen individuals stepped forward, unarmed and unequipped. They all wore robes of various colors, but each had the symbol of Lyecha on their backs embroidered in gold. "Go, fire. Destroy as many as you can."

All of the Lyecians disappeared at once and reappeared in amongst the Narshuks. Spells erupted within their lines, exploding with fire and ice and lightning. One yellow robed Lyecian cast a chain lightning spell that arced forward, struck one in the chest and forked, chaining from creature to creature. The spell spread across several hundred Narshuks who all dropped to the ground convulsing from the electricity.

Another Lyecian launched a massive fireball into the Narshuk flank that spread out and incinerated several dozen of the creatures in an instant. Jhet watched with some small amount of relief that for the first time in the confrontation, the Narshuk lines began to falter and move into the center. When the bulk of the spells were finished and the Lyecians had vanished, Jhet raised a hand. "Infantry ready!"

The flag man raised a blue banner with a sword embroidered on it. Every soldier in the Findoor line slammed his sword hilt against his shield several times while stomping his feet. The resulting beat echoed across the battlefield and drew cheers from all the Findoor men.

"No prisoners, no mercy. Findoor, attack!" Jhet shouted and led the charge forward.

(⦿)

King Valerra led the main force of Findoor against Gladius and the Narshuk army. He watched the flanks and worried as the archers had little to no effect on the Narshuks. "Findoor at the ready," he shouted as the front lines of the Narshuks drew near.

Gladius broke away from the rest of his army and ran ahead at an inhuman speed. Valerra drew his sword and did the same, leaving the rest of his army behind. His charge caught his men off guard, but he didn't care. The challenge was made and would not go unanswered. He closed in on Gladius and readied his sword for his attack at a full charge.

It took seconds for the distance to close between the two men. Valerra saw Gladius draw the black steel sword but paid little attention to it. When they clashed, Gladius was ready for his attack and parried it like an expert. Valerra didn't wait for him to return the attack and instead spun and swung a second time which caught Gladius off guard. The king's sword screamed through the air in a vicious attack that should have cleaved Gladius in two. Instead his sword struck the black armor plates that Gladius wore and shattered from the force of the attack.

The vibration sent shoots of pain down Valerra's arm. He cried out and backed up a step, holding his shield up in front of him to protect himself from Gladius. He had enough time to reach his short sword and get it drawn before Gladius hammered down on his shield with the black sword and sliced through it. Valerra felt the heat from the sword as Gladius closed the distance between them. Another attack came which he tried to parry with his short sword. The blazing hot black sword carried through the blade of the short sword and knocked it from Valerra's hand in two pieces. A booted foot slammed into Valerra's chest and sent him flying back onto the ground, the wind knocked out of him.

Valerra tried to get up, but Gladius's hand closed around his throat. The weight Gladius applied cut his next breath short and sent panic rushing through him. He struggled against the much younger man's grip, but fell still and silent as he heard Gladius's voice in his ear. "Hush now, dear king."

"You might take my life, but you'll never take Findoor," Valerra said with labored breaths.

"Oh, don't be so sure about that," Gladius said with a smile. "Remain still."

Valerra had no intention of doing as he was told, but the magic in Gladius's voice infected him. No matter how he resisted, he couldn't move.

Gladius stood up above Valerra with his back to the Findoor army. He raised his hand and Valerra felt his body rise into the air.

"Any last words, old man?" Gladius said.

"Krycin will destroy you," the King said. "You and your disgusting army of animals."

"Animals? I'll show you animals. Watch, as your army falls apart before your eyes."

Gladius raised his hand and made a signal to several Narshuks approaching in the front lines. They each let out a long, crooning howl that sent shivers down Valerra's spine. He fought harder against the enchantment holding him in place, but couldn't break free of Gladius's grip.

Further down the Narshuk lines, more of the creatures let out howls which spread back through the army. The Findoor advance on their flanks faltered and the Narshuks pushed back, slaughtering men by the dozens at first, and then by the hundreds. Calls were made by both flank's generals to fall back and the Narshuk lines spread out again and surged forward.

"No," Valerra said as he watched his army lose control of the battle.

"Yes," Gladius said with a laugh, "and now you die." Valerra's eyes grew wide as Gladius thrust a hand toward him, creating a shock wave that shattered the steel plates protecting his body. He felt his bones break and pain flash through his entire body. His vision blurred and faded, as did the sounds all around him. He felt a hot slash across his abdomen that sent pain coursing through him once more. Something opened up in his gut, spilling down the front of him. Valerra lost focus on the battle around him as he struggled for life. Breathing got easier, but he could feel his blood spilling out and his entrails hanging down from his body. The sound of his heart beating grew slower and quieter as he felt his feet touch the ground once more, and then his head.

The world grew quiet, and the silence of death overtook him.

(∗)

General Jhet watched in horror as his king was magically hoisted into the air, stripped of his armor and humiliated in front of his own army. Gladius slashed a wide hole into his gut and eviscerated him before letting him down to the ground. The Narshuks pushed back fierce and hard, slaughtering his men around him. Every stroke of his sword took one of the creatures down only to have it replaced by two more. He'd already made the call to fall back, but his men couldn't get enough cover to fulfill the order.

Lyecians appeared up the line and blasted the Narshuks once more and knocked them back long enough to allow Jhet and his men to regroup and fall back to the main army. He watched in wonder as they appeared, cast spells and disappeared, only to repeat the process in another location. Three or four of them had taken on Gladius at the same time, each keeping their distance from him and blasting him with everything they had, repeating the same pattern of teleporting and casting. Nothing they hit Gladius with seemed to faze him. A white shield around Gladius took the brunt of the spells and deflected them around him, but while he was busy with the Lyecians, he couldn't control his army.

The Narshuk army faltered again in the face of the Lyecian attacks, giving Findoor more time to regroup. "Hold the lines and defend if required," Jhet said to one of his commanders. "I'm going to head to the front with the rest of the generals. Don't let any of those beasts through."

He didn't wait for a response as he knew the order would be followed. Panic had come over the front lines of the main army at seeing their king's horrid death. Jhet intended on taking control of the army and getting them back in line.

As he made his way to the main army, a blast in the center of the battlefield caught his attention and made his ears ring. He looked in time to see four Lyecians vaporized by a strange wave of black energy that radiated away from Gladius. When he got to the rest of the Generals, they were bickering amongst themselves and leaving the rest of the army in a confused state.

"Enough," shouted Jhet above the rest of them. "We have no choice, we must fall back with the entire army. Reinforcements will be arriving at Findoor castle soon, and we can make our stand there."

One general looked at Jhet and nodded. "Understood. How do we make a retreat with an army like this on our tail?"

Jhet looked out at the Narshuk army being held at bay by Lyecians. There was another blast and several more Lyecians fell to the black fire that spread away from Gladius's hands.

"We have to leave some men behind," Jhet said. "My men will stay and do their best to hold the monsters at bay. Get the army back to the castle."

Shouts ran across the battlefield as the Findoor army reorganized. The main army fell back to the north toward Findoor castle. The remaining men from the flanks filed in and made their stand before the massive army of Narshuks.

"Hold your ground, men. No matter what, hold your ground." He beat his sword against his shield and smiled as the action was echoed back to him by all the troops behind him. "All of Findoor depends on us."

⊛

Krycin and Morganath arrived at the Losteron plains in time to see the bulk of the Findoor army retreating to the north. A small group of soldiers made a stand before the much larger and more powerful Narshuk army. Gladius walked with slow, measured steps toward the Findoor army, holding the Narshuks back from a full attack. It looked like he was shouting at the leader of the Findoor army, but Krycin couldn't make it out from his distance.

"Take us in, Morganath. We need to push back those lines to give our men a fighting chance at getting away," Krycin said to the massive gold dragon.

"As you wish," said Morganath, who tucked his wings back and dove toward the front lines of the Narshuk army.

Krycin saw Gladius battling with the General of the Findoor army, their swords clashing as they traded blows. The general's movements were quick and fluid. Every step and sword swing was intentional and calculated. Krycin watched as he matched every movement of Gladius with an equal movement of his own and even scored a few hits that pushed Gladius back.

"Blast those Narshuks, and get me close to Gladius," Krycin said, preparing himself to launch into battle. Morganath inhaled as he swooped down causing his chest to puff out and his body to swell. When he was within range, he let out the breath in a slow, steady stream, raining fire down on the Narshuk lines. Their screams of pain and panic rose up as hundreds of them died instantly and many more were set aflame and were forced to focus on putting out the fire rather than advancing to battle.

When Morganath approached the center of his run, Krycin leapt from his back toward Gladius. He held his hand out in the air and called on the power of light and life. Energy flowed from his hand, forming a sword of light. The light flowed down his arm and covered his body, hardening into crystal armor plates. The ground and Gladius rushed up to meet him as he fell.

Krycin landed hard against Gladius's back, sending him crumpling forward toward the Findoor general. When they hit the ground, Krycin rolled forward and came to a stop just past the general who had side-stepped at the last second. He got up off the ground and readied his sword for battle.

"Get these men out of here," Krycin said to the general.

He didn't wait to see what the general would do, but instead ran at Gladius before he could get himself up off the ground. Gladius had just lifted his head when Krycin swung his foot forward and booted Gladius in the face, sending him rolling away from him along the ground.

"That was for Cy," Krycin said as he continued his approach with his sword at the ready. He reached Gladius a few steps later and kicked him again, this time in the chest and sent him rolling once more. "And that was for all the other Lyecians you've killed."

Gladius came to a rest on the ground, wheezing, but laughing through the pain. "Oh, Krycin. I knew you would show up eventually." He pushed himself up off the ground, still holding the black steel sword. "But Morganath? That's a nice touch. How did you get that lazy reptile out of his lair?"

Krycin lost control of his emotions and rushed at Gladius, letting out an enraged scream. He swung the sword of light, aiming to kill, but Gladius ducked at the last second and flicked his own sword between Krycin's legs, tripping him and sending him sprawling to the ground. Krycin rolled and tried to ready his sword, but Gladius was already standing over him and ready.

A booted foot came down on Krycin's arm and pinned it to the ground. The tip of the black steel sword rested just under the left side of his throat. He could feel the heat radiating off the sword as Gladius looked down at him. "I hope you're ready to die," Gladius said as he pushed the tip of his sword against Krycin's neck.

"Not today," said a voice from behind. Krycin watched as the tip of a sword slammed into Gladius, pierced his chest plate and ran him through. Gladius stumbled back from the impact with the hilt of the sword still protruding from his chest.

Krycin rolled and got to his feet, catching a glimpse of the Findoor general in the process. He spun to see Gladius backing away from them, a look of intense concentration on his face. "Go," Krycin said to the general. "Run, now, while you have the chance."

"I won't leave your side," the general said, drawing a short sword and preparing to continue the battle.

"We can't win this, not here. Not now. Go, before the Narshuks have a chance to regroup." Krycin held his hand out and summoned the power of light, forming it into a ball of energy.

Gladius looked up at Krycin with hate filled eyes. "You should be dead five times over already."

"But I'm still here," Krycin said. "Let me show you something an old friend once taught me." He threw the ball at Gladius and blasted him in the chest, sending him stumbling back a few steps. Krycin looked around behind Gladius and saw the flames from the dragon breath were dying down and the Narshuks were again advancing.

"Friend. Ha!" Gladius said, breaking into a fit of laughter that made the protruding sword bounce, which in turn sent Gladius into a coughing fit. When he regained his composure, he said, "You were a lost puppy, and I saw a chance to get away from that infernal island. You weren't my friend any more than that incompetent fool Cy was."

The words struck Krycin to his core. Cy had told him this before, but to hear it right from Gladius's own mouth caused a wound that would never heal. "You're a bastard," Krycin said, raising his sword to attack again.

"One of us is going to have to die, because I will hunt you, Krycin. To the ends of this world and beyond. So long as you and I both draw a breath, I will never stop."

Krycin was about to launch himself at Gladius, and was in mid-stride when he spotted the black haze around Gladius's hand. In a split second, he willed himself out of existence, only to reappear several hundred paces away, just behind the now fleeing Findoor troops. He watched as a ring of black energy radiated out from Gladius, vaporizing everything in its path, including several dozen Narshuks before it dissipated. He looked up to see Morganath providing cover fire for the Findoor men as they ran, taking out any Narshuks that had made it past the initial blast. Other blasts were going off as well, and Krycin saw a great mass of robed men and women joining the Findoor troops and aiding in their retreat. *The Council wizards,* Krycin thought, smiling to himself. Fatigue set in all at once, but he refused to leave the Findoor army until they were back to the castle, and so he ran toward them, firing his own spells at any remaining Narshuks and blasting them away.

⊙

Gladius raised his hand to signal the Narshuk army to stop. Those near him obeyed, and the order spread out through the rest of the army. When he was sure they would go no further, he dropped to his knees and let the black steel sword fall to the ground. Pain flooded through him, starting from his chest and radiating through the rest of his body. The sword protruding from his chest punctured one of his lungs and came dangerously close to ending his life. Had it not been for his expertise with the element of water, it would have.

With both hands, he grasped the blade of the sword and carefully removed it, feeling blood rush from the wound as he did so. The pain was intense, but he managed to block it out and clear his mind enough to draw the power of water once more. Warmth filled him, easing his pain and mending the wound that the sword had inflicted. He tossed the blade aside like it was a poisonous flower and grasped for his black sword with a hunger he hadn't known before.

Narshuks gathered around him waiting for orders as he stood up and sheathed his sword, leaving his hand resting on the hilt. "Fetch me Scrag. I have a job for him," Gladius said and smiled as several of the creatures scrambled to fulfill the order. "The rest of you, rest for the night. Tomorrow, we march on Findoor once more, and burn their castle to the ground."

Chapter 31 - A Hasty Retreat

When Cy made it back to Findoor, the castle and surrounding city were calm and quiet. There was a palpable tension in the air as the residents awaited news of their armies to the south, but people continued on about their business regardless. Cy walked through the front gates carrying the Lyecian text under his arm and went unquestioned by the guards. While making his way to the castle, he found a runner and sent him ahead to inform Merek of his return. He would have run himself, but he'd been running for days and was too tired to bother.

By the time he made it to the front gates of the castle proper, Merek was waiting for him just inside the door. "I trust you were successful?" Merek said with a smile.

"Of course I was," Cy snapped at him. "Have I ever failed at anything before?"

He walked past Merek, and as he did, he slammed the book into Merek's chest, startling the old wizard. He let it go and continued walking, not bothering to make sure Merek had a grip on the book.

Merek followed behind him. "Is everything all right?"

Cy stopped and spun on his heels to face Merek. The action caught Merek off guard as he had to struggle not to run into Cy. "I've been running for days. I'm tired, and would like some well-deserved rest. If you don't mind, I think I'll get it now while I still can," Cy said. He returned to his original route and stormed away from Merek.

A few minutes later he was stepping through the door to his room in the castle. There was no sign of Merek, or anyone else for that matter, which suited Cy just fine. He walked to the wardrobe in his room and started rifling through it for night clothes when something struck him as odd. He looked at his bed and saw a small silver mirror that called to him, though it didn't make a sound. He walked over to his bed and picked up the mirror. It was just larger than his hand and rectangular with a brushed metal edge. The inner surface was polished so as to produce a perfect reflection, though when Cy looked into the mirror, what he saw startled him.

The image in the mirror was that of a Narshuk looking back at him. Before he could act or speak, the Narshuk spoke. "Gladius has a job for you."

He was about to make a smart remark back, but a pain in his head flared up suddenly and made him think better of it. "What is it?"

"Find out where Merek is sending the rest of the Lyecians. Not one can survive," the Narshuk said.

Cy considered what that would mean for his people. *Total extinction. But they're not my people anymore,* he thought. "Can he really defeat Krycin?"

"He almost did in the battle today, but he held back because killing Krycin too soon would cause the remaining Lyecians to go deep into hiding. He wants them all, and you will help him."

"I will," Cy said, and tossed the mirror away like it was a piece of trash. It clattered across the floor and came to a rest at the far end of the room. Exhaustion took over, and he lay down in bed without bothering to change. He was asleep the moment his head hit the pillow.

⊙

Cy awoke to a commotion. There was a rumbling sound approaching the castle, and cheers and hollers could be heard through his open window. He wasn't sure how long he had slept, but the sun was up and to the east, so it had to be morning. It took him minutes to find some clean clothes and get changed so he could see what all the excitement was about.

The mood in the castle was uplifted as he walked through the hallways. Everywhere he heard rumors swirling about the Findoor army returning victorious, but he doubted the source of these rumors. When he arrived at the front gates of the castle, Merek was already waiting for him.

"Good morning," Merek said with a smile. "I trust you feel better today? I can't tell you enough how much your task has helped us. The book you've returned to us is indeed quite valuable, and dangerous in the wrong hands. I can see why the Council was keeping it hidden away in the forbidden library."

"Spare me your pleasantries," Cy said walking past him. "What's all the noise about?"

Merek didn't react to his manners, but followed him out into the city where the buzz about the Findoor army was even more exaggerated. "Krycin returns with the Findoor army, though I've not heard from any runners, so I know not what news they bring."

Cy scoffed and walked faster through the city toward the front gates. The massive wood doors were open for the day with various carts being pulled in and out. Beyond the gates was the Findoor army marching toward the city with banners held high. Along with the Findoor banners, there were also banners for the Council. Leading the army was Krycin marching in plain clothes, and the Council who wore robes, each the color of their magic. One additional figure marched alongside Krycin. A tall man in steel full plate armor. He carried no longsword at his side, though a short sword remained on his other hip, and he carried a shield with the mark of a Findoor General. None of them looked happy, and the air about the army was grave, not celebratory like the rumors conveyed.

"Something's wrong," Cy said over his shoulder to Merek.

Merek sped up to walk beside him. "Indeed. Where is the king?"

Cy noticed an edge to Merek's voice that sounded like a hint of panic. He smiled internally, but didn't show his amusement on his face. When they arrived at the gates, Krycin and the rest of the leaders met them there.

"What news have you?" Merek asked, looking at Krycin for answers. Cy said nothing, but listened intently.

"Nothing good, I'm afraid," Krycin said, sparing a glance at Cy. He looked surprised, but the look was fleeting. "We should discuss it in private." His eyes drifted around to all the people waiting in anticipation for any scrap of news they could gather. More gathered by the second, and some of them were starting to cheer.

Merek nodded in agreement. "Come, we shall meet in the throne room in a half hour."

All the leaders of the army walked through the gates, leaving the army waiting just outside the city. Cy followed behind them and watched as the citizens of the city began cheering and clapping and congratulating them. About half way to the castle, Krycin spun to face the crowd who was now following them.

"What's wrong with you people?" he shouted. "We lost. Our army retreated. We've got nothing to celebrate. Even as we speak, Gladius and his army continue their advance. Our king is dead, most of the Lyecians have been destroyed, and our army is a fraction of what it should be, and you cheer us on? Go back to your homes, spend the day with your families, and pray to the gods that tomorrow isn't your last."

He walked away toward the castle with the rest of his companions giving him a wide berth. Cy remained at the back of the congregation with a smirk on his face.

⊙

Krycin led the way to the throne room and stood at the front of the room as the Wizard High Council, Merek, Cy, and the Findoor general filed into the room. Merek took his usual place beside the throne, and the rest of the men and women took seats on the benches that lined the room. Cy closed and barred the doors to ensure that no prying ears would hear what they discussed.

"Before we begin," Krycin said, "I'd like to introduce you all to the hero of the day. Jhet Corsair, general of the Findoor army. He saved my life, and the lives of many other good men, and deserves to be celebrated as a hero."

Jhet stood up with a smile on his face so that all the leaders could see him, but waved off what Krycin said. "Nonsense. I do my duty to Findoor, and nothing more. I would expect the same from all of my men."

"Regardless, if it weren't for you, I would be dead, so thank you." Krycin paused to allow the rest of the leaders to applaud, then continued. "As you all know, King Valerra died at the hands of Gladius during the battle. There was nothing anyone could have done to save him. He fought valiantly and led his people well. Gladius and his Narshuk army continue their advance on Findoor castle, though their numbers are reduced thanks to all our hard work. That said, they still outnumber us by a sizable amount, and we can't ask the remaining Lyecians to help us any further. They number less than a hundred and we need to preserve what remains of them."

Serrin nodded in agreement to this, and others clapped their approval as well.

"Where will they go?" Cy asked. Krycin hadn't expected to hear him speak, though he knew Cy was there.

"They will be taken somewhere safe," Merek said, saving Krycin from having to answer the question.

"Somewhere safe? That's all you're going to give us?" Cy asked. "I hold a stake in this as much as any of you. Serrin and Krycin as well. I think we deserve to know where our people are being taken."

Serrin stood up and looked to Merek. "I agree with Cy. We're all in this together. Let's not keep secrets at this already tense and difficult time."

Merek nodded. "The Fioraden have agreed to take them into their homes to the north and offer them protection until the war is done."

"That's a wonderful idea, Merek," Krycin said with a smile. "Serrin, you and Catrina should go as well. It's critical that all Lyecians are kept safe."

"You know as well as I do that I can't do that," Serrin said. "The wizards need all eight on the High Council, and with Catrina so close to giving birth, I don't think it's wise to transport her."

"I will take her," Krycin said. "I'll teleport her, safe and sound, straight to the Fioraden. You can't keep her here, Serrin, it's too dangerous." He looked at Merek. "We should move everyone in the city either inside the castle, or send them away to the country until the threat is past. The more people in the city, the more innocent lives we risk."

Lebriel stood up and spoke for the first time. "I agree with Krycin. Serrin, allow him to take Catrina to safety. You are required here, she is not. The more Lyecians we can save, the better, and this is no place to give birth to a child, with so much death and war around us."

Serrin sighed, his shoulders falling as if he were deflated. "You are both right, of course. Yes, Krycin. Take Catrina to the Fioraden. They will be more than capable of tending to her needs."

"Good. With that settled," Merek said, taking control of the meeting once more, "what are we going to do with this?" He removed the white Lyecian book from his robes and held it up. "Cy recovered this from Gladius, despite not having his Lyecian powers. He did well." There was compassion in his voice as he spoke. Krycin approached Merek and held his hand out for the book, which Merek handed to him. "What do you plan on doing with it?"

"I'm going to hide it," Krycin said.

Cy spoke up once more, to the surprise of all in the room. "Let me help. I know a few tricks to keep things hidden."

"Help me then, we need to make sure Gladius will never find it."

Cy approached the front of the room as Krycin placed the book on the seat of the throne. They both held their hands over it. The book opened and began to flip its pages. When the pages had flipped to the end, they divided and merged with the pages next to them creating a whole new book with blank pages. On each page, High Lyecian symbols formed in perfect lines. Page after page flipped and filled with symbols until the book closed. The white cover was masked by a new brown leather cover that grew from the spine, and metal formed around the corners and along the spine to reinforce it. When it was almost done, a steel band formed across the opening of the book and a lock appeared on the cover. Cy and Krycin looked at each other and nodded. Krycin picked up the finished book and held it up for all to see. "To the untrained eye, this will appear to be a book of children's stories. Only a Lyecian can open it, and only a Lyecian can determine the book's true nature. I leave it in your care, Serrin." Krycin walked over to him and gave him the book with a knowing smile on his face. "Perhaps you can read your child the stories within and inspire him to greatness."

Serrin accepted the book without question. "Thank you. I can only hope that I survive the battle to do so."

Merek spoke up once more, addressing the entire room. "With that taken care of, what is our strategy for the coming battle?"

"Bring them in," Cy said. "Bring the army into the city. The Narshuks are far too dangerous to confront on the open field. We need to rely on Findoor's natural defenses to keep them out, reinforced by magic of course. And while they siege us, we will assault them with spells and destroy as many as possible without a direct confrontation."

The rest of the leaders nodded their agreement to that plan, though none had an answer for what should happen if they breach the outer wall. Merek spoke above them and posed the question none of them wanted to deal with. "And what of Gladius?"

They all fell silent at this. Krycin looked around to see if anyone would speak up, but none did, nor would they. "I'll take care of him," Krycin said when he was sure nobody else would respond. "I'll destroy Gladius."

Cy scoffed. "What makes you think you'll be able to handle him this time?"

"I can do this, Cy. You know it," Krycin said.

"Do I? Because the last time I checked, you'd already made four unsuccessful attempts to destroy him. How will this time be any different?"

"I've seen the future, Cy. I know how this turns out. This is how it *must* happen."

"Or what?" Cy screamed with a sudden rage that made all of them jump. "Or the world will end? The sky will fall? Or perhaps, our *hero* Krycin won't get his fair share of the attention. Never fear, Krycin will save the day. Well, I'm waiting, Krycin. I've been waiting for you to destroy Gladius since he started this conquest. If you really had the ability to destroy him, why haven't you already? Or are you letting the Lyecians die intentionally?" He paused to approach the front of the room where Krycin stood. "If you can really see the future, why didn't you save them from a death you knew was imminent? Why didn't you stop Gladius before he became the most powerful wizard Galadir has ever known?"

Krycin felt his heart break one sentence at a time. Tears flowed from his eyes by the time Cy finished. He looked into Cy's deep dark eyes and saw something familiar. The man he once knew, the man he tried to save, was gone forever and replaced by a darkness that wouldn't be lit by any amount of magic. "Because I couldn't. I tried, and I failed. Everything I've done to change the future has just ended up creating the future I know. I didn't want this. I certainly never asked for it, and if I could walk away now and leave this world to its own ends I would, but I can't now. I couldn't save the Lyecians and I couldn't save you. I'm sorry. My only hope is that I have the strength to do what has to be done to save Findoor."

"I hope for all our sakes that you do," Cy said, and walked out of the room.

The doors to the throne room slammed shut behind him and everyone in the room remained silent for a long time. Krycin looked at the floor, unwilling to make eye contact with any of them. The silence was broken by Merek, who approached Krycin, laid a hand on his shoulder, and said, "Pay no attention to his words. You've done well, Krycin. Nobody here ever expected you to take on Gladius on your own, and we don't now either."

"I must. I have no choice," Krycin said.

There was a moment of silence in the throne room. Nobody looked up from their thoughts, but they all knew that each of them felt the impending doom weighing down on them. Merek was the one who finally broke the silence. "Some, and possibly many of us will not survive this battle. I want you all to know it has been a pleasure serving with you."

All of them gave their approval of the sentiment, and then left to start preparations for the coming battle. Krycin stayed back with Merek, a troubled expression on his face. His thoughts lingered on all the things people told him about 'the hero, Krycin' when he first came to Galadir.

"Something the matter?" Merek's voice startled Krycin out of his thoughts.

"No," Krycin said. "Well, a little. Is there a way to change a person's memories?"

Merek glanced around the room as if he were making sure nobody else was present, and then spoke. "Were you any other man, I would lie, and tell you no. There are powerful spells that a wizard of shadow could cast, but it can be dangerous as well. Alter their memories too much, and it could create too much mental stress, permanently damaging their mind. Why do you ask?"

"I was curious, that's all," Krycin said.

"This is not something one is normally curious about. What are you planning?" Merek asked, moving to block Krycin from leaving the room.

Krycin smiled and put one hand on Merek's shoulder. "Relax, old friend. I couldn't cast shadow magic even if I wanted to." He sidestepped around Merek and left the room, leaving him to ponder the meaning behind the question.

⊙

Cy returned to his room with his temper boiling over. Every door on the path to his room had been slammed, and now he took out his frustration on the wall behind his door, pounding his fist against it. It didn't help ease his anger toward Krycin. Instead he walked to the far end of the room where he had thrown the mirror earlier and picked it up. Despite having clattered across the stone floor earlier, it didn't have a single scratch or mark on it. He touched a finger to the center of the mirror and watched as a ripple ran across the surface like a water drop had fallen in a tiny pool. The mirror did the same again when he lifted his finger.

An image came to life in the mirror, dispelling his reflection. Scrag's face appeared in the mirror once more, and he didn't look happy. "Do you have the information?" Scrag asked, dispensing with the pleasantries.

"The remaining Lyecians are to be moved to the North to stay with the Fioraden."

"You've served the Dark Lord well," Scrag said, and severed the connection.

Cy sat down on his bed and dropped the mirror to the ground. The presence inside him surged against his consciousness and a voice spoke inside his head. *Having regrets?*

The voice surprised Cy and left him lost for words.

Speechless? Gladius's voice said with a tinge of amusement. *Since when is the great Cy Cooper speechless?*

Cy ignored the voice in his head and instead laid down. He tried to sleep, but ended up staring at the ceiling for hours.

Chapter 32 – Massacre

Night had fallen by the time Krycin and Catrina arrived at the Fioraden Mountain Range. The moon was up and full, and the sky was clear, allowing plenty of light to fall down on them. Catrina hobbled beside Krycin as he escorted her to a ground-level hut that had been set up for her. When she was safe inside and resting on the bed, she looked up at Krycin. "Thank you. You're a gentleman."

"It's nothing. Hopefully, the war will be over soon. Until then, the Fioraden will take good care of you," Krycin said with a smile.

"There's never been a war on Galadir in my lifetime," Catrina said. She looked at ease, but there was a hint of worry in her green eyes.

"I know I shouldn't ask a woman her age," Krycin said, "but how old are you?" His curiosity about his mother was getting the better of him. He knew her as a devoted housewife. She was always a strong woman, and raised him by herself after his father disappeared. He'd had no reason to question her, and they never talked about his father.

"Two hundred thirty years, give or take a few." Catrina's response startled Krycin out of his thoughts and surprised him at the same time.

"You're over two hundred years old?" Krycin said.

She gave him a curious look that had a hint of amusement. "Yes, though I can't be certain of exactly how old. I know you lost your memories, but I thought you regained them. You speak like you know nothing about our kind." She let out a little laugh, one that Krycin had heard hundreds of times growing up. It was familiar and made him feel homesick.

"Where I come from, there are no Lyecians. I only just discovered my lineage. I've only heard of a few people living past a hundred years old, but nobody as old as two hundred."

"I don't know exactly how old Lyecians can live to. Until Gladius began his massacre, I'd never known a Lyecian to die of anything. We tend not to worry too much about age. I've been with Serrin for over a hundred years and this is our first child together." She smiled and rubbed her enlarged belly like it was a reflex. "We still haven't picked out a name."

Krycin nodded, his thoughts going in every direction. He wanted to keep asking questions, but knew he didn't have time. He wanted to stay with Catrina, but he knew he had to go. He stood up and smiled at Catrina and said, "Thanks for everything. I know I ask a lot of questions, and I appreciate your patience. For now, I have to go."

"Indeed. There is a war to fight. Take care of yourself," Catrina said with a warm smile on her face.

"You as well. I know the Fioraden will take good care of you," Krycin said and walked away from the bed. When he reached the door he looked back with a half-smile on his face. "Oh, and as far as names go, I've always been fond of Seth."

There was a pause as Catrina thought about it, then said, "Seth is a fine name. I'll see what Serrin thinks. Thank you."

Krycin grinned to himself as he walked out of the hut and was met by Ferron and Tersca who waited patiently outside the door. He bowed low before them and then stood up before speaking. "Is everything ready for her?" he asked.

Everything will be fine, Ferron's voice spoke inside his head. *We are creatures of life and gifted by Anam. She, and all the other Lyecians are in good hands.* He motioned up to the sky where Krycin saw a number of fully armed Fioraden doing rounds to watch over the mountainside, and then to the sheer cliff face and the forest around it where more Fioraden marched and flew around. It appeared that Ferron had assembled every able-bodied warrior to help out with the protection of the Lyecians.

"Thank you," Krycin said and made another deep bow toward him. He focused his mind on an image of Findoor castle and was about to teleport back when he heard a commotion at the far end of the encampment. Snarls and growls could be heard, and Ferron took flight faster than Krycin had ever seen him fly.

Narshuks, Krycin heard in his head. It was Ferron's voice, but it was panicked and distant. He ran toward the sound to see what was going on. As he ran he spotted other Lyecians running in the same direction. "No, you fools, stay away," Krycin shouted through his quick breaths, but he couldn't get his voice to project far enough for them to hear.

The whole scene slowed to a crawl as he came near the commotion. Dozens of Narshuks were invading the Fioraden mountainside, flowing from several rifts that crackled with electricity in the forest. He saw the claws coming toward him in time to duck below them, and then time resumed its normal flow. Krycin stopped and spun on his heals. Behind him was a Narshuk bearing down on him, snarling and slobbering as it ran.

Krycin braced for the charge, empowering his fist with the power of light and life. When the Narshuk was within striking distance, Krycin surged forward and slammed his fist into the Narshuk's lowered head. There was a flash of white light, and a scream of pain right before the Narshuk collapsed to the ground. Krycin checked to make sure the creature was dead and saw blood oozing from a large split running the length of its head.

More Narshuks poured from the rifts, faster than Krycin and the Fioraden warriors could dispatch them. *I have to get those rifts closed,* Krycin thought as he took off running again. The first of the rifts was only a few seconds away at a full run. Krycin drew energy to him and released it in a pulse at the open rift. A Narshuk was half way through when the tear slammed shut, shearing the creature in half.

A second rift was several hundred paces away and surrounded by Narshuks who were trying to fortify the position. Fioraden warriors were having trouble breaking the Narshuk lines as they weren't able to fly through the trees and lacked the space to use their full combat abilities. Krycin ran straight for the rift, summoning his sword of light and his armor. Light flooded from him as he ran, and his armor wasn't totally formed before he struck the first Narshuk with his sword. It cleaved through the creature, who wasn't prepared for an attack that was so fast and powerful. Krycin continued to push, firing orbs of light to stun the creatures and slashing at them to cut a path to the rift.

When he was less than twenty paces from it, he summoned another pulse of energy and fired it into the tear. Again it slammed shut, leaving the Narshuk who was passing through it missing one foot. Blood poured from the stump of its leg as it collapsed to the ground howling.

Krycin drew in more power and focused it into a pulse that he fired in every direction around him. The Narshuks closest to him were vaporized in the blast. Others who were more distant were sent flying to the ground where Fioraden warriors descended on them without mercy. There were still a number of Narshuks around him, but Krycin ignored them. Instead he scanned the area and found a third and final rift.

Lyecians surrounded the rift and took turns firing pulses of energy into the rift to try and close it. Krycin took off running as fast as his feet could carry him. "No! Get away from the rift," he shouted, but it was already too late. A dark figure stepped out of the rift wearing polished black armor with a red emblem on the chest plate; a lily with a snake wrapped around the stem. *Gladius,* Krycin thought, and summoned up a ball of white energy in his hand. He threw the ball ahead of him and watched as it struck Gladius in the chest, exploding in a flash of light. Krycin blinked a few times to try and clear the spots it left in his vision. When he could see clearly again, Gladius was standing tall against a barrage of magical attacks from all the Lyecians standing around him. His hand was surrounded with black fire and he appeared to be concentrating.

Krycin pushed himself even harder, but as he arrived beside the first of the Lyecians, Gladius unleashed a wave of black energy that flowed out in a circle around him. Krycin focused all his strength and magic on a shield in front of him that blocked the wave and caused it to flow around him, but the other Lyecians weren't fast enough. The wave of energy struck them and vaporized them, leaving only Gladius and Krycin.

"God damn you, Gladius," Krycin said, still approaching the dark wizard. "Damn you to hell."

Gladius laughed and looked Krycin in the eye. "Isn't this fun? Just you and me, just like old times, right?"

"You think this is funny?" Krycin stopped in his tracks. He sensed something was wrong, but couldn't put his finger on it.

"Funny? Oh yes, I find it hilarious. Heroic Krycin, and the Dark Lord, Gladius facing off once more. I wonder who will win this time?"

"You've already won. They're all dead. The entire Lyecian race is nothing but a few scattered individuals," Krycin said. "All you wanted was me. Why did you have to kill all of us?"

"Because Lyecians are a stain on this world. High and mighty, always thinking you're better than all the others. Immortal. Humans once called you immortal. But I've proven them wrong." Gladius took a step toward Krycin. His hand rested on the pommel of his black steel sword. "The only thing I haven't found yet is the Traveler."

There was a look in Gladius's dark eyes that startled Krycin. There was no remorse, no hesitation, and no pain in his eyes. The darkness flowed on forever and led to nothing. An emptiness that Gladius sought to fill with power.

"The Traveler is just a legend," Krycin said, his voice calm. "You're chasing a dream that can never be fulfilled. The void inside you will consume you, and you'll never know the taste of that power you seek."

Gladius was several paces from him now, and still approaching. "We'll see about that. There's still a few of you left." Without warning, Gladius lashed out with his fist and slammed it into Krycin's chest. The attack was fierce and powerful and struck with enough force to send Krycin flying back through the forest. He struck a tree, his head slamming against the trunk, and everything went black.

Krycin opened his eyes and found himself staring up at the dark canopy of the forest in the foothills near the Fioraden mountain range. His head ached and his chest burned. He tried to move, but pain flooded through his body and caused him to gasp as if he had been robbed of air. His thoughts were a confused mess inside his head as he tried to make sense of what was happening. *Who am I,* he thought, and another wave of pain shot through his head.

Krycin, a voice said in his head.

"No," Krycin said, "That's not right. That's my father's name."

John Alkirk is your father, the voice in his head said. There was a familiarity to the voice he couldn't place.

"Krycin is my father. Merek said so, and he's never wrong."

Krycin waited a long time, laying on the ground staring at the trees in the quiet forest. His senses were still off and all he could hear was the whispering of the breeze in the trees. Pain still moved through his body in waves, but centered on two places: his chest and his head.

Serrin is your father. But John is what you know him as. The voice was female, and soft. Soothing almost.

"I'm confused," he said. "I'm not Krycin."

Bits and pieces of his memories fell back into place. His thoughts started to clear.

You hit your head. You are healing. Things will become clear. You are Krycin. The voice was more insistent this time. There was no edge to it, no anger, but an urgency to it.

Krycin lifted his head and looked around. His hearing became more acute and he saw a blue light pulsing in the forest about thirty paces away. Pain seared through his head as he heard a snapping down and felt something move in his head. It wasn't a thought, but a physical movement. He reached up with his hand in time to feel the second movement. A piece of his skull shifted again and fell back into place. Pain flowed through his head and made him cry out as his skull mended. He felt the power of water flowing through him for the first time since he woke up on the beach in Arda.

"Are you doing this?" Krycin asked. He looked around again, conscious that the pain in his head was now gone. His remaining thoughts cleared and his memories came back together.

No. You are, the voice said.

"But Krycin can only wield the time and life elements."

You are not Krycin.

Krycin's mind reeled. *No, I'm not Krycin. But I am.*

You understand now, the voice said. It wasn't a question, but a statement of fact. It was a voice that was not to be doubted. Soft, female, but powerful.

"I'm Seth. My father was John Alkirk. Why does everybody think I'm Krycin?" Krycin said.

Because you told them you were Krycin.

Krycin sat up, most of the pain now gone. He looked down at his clothes and saw them in tatters. A new scar was present on his chest, where there had been a large wound. He thought back to when he first woke up on the beach. "You're right. I did, didn't I?"

You must finish what you started, the voice said with the same urgency it had before.

"I want to go home. I want to go back to the way things were. I loved my life, even if it was boring. I was never cut out for any of this hero stuff," Krycin said. He looked around once more and listened again now that his hearing was cleared and working again.

The immediate area was calm and quiet. All around him were bodies. Some Fioraden, many Narshuks, and more that appeared human, though Krycin knew they weren't. The rift in the forest crackled with electricity that arced from the edge and struck the ground all around it. In the distance, for the first time, he heard the sounds of battle. Swords clashing, people screaming, the howls of the invading Narshuks, and the blasts of powerful magic.

You have a choice, the voice in his head said.

"I never wanted this," Krycin said. "I never wanted to fight. I didn't want people to die."

Death is a natural part of life, the voice said. There was little compassion in the voice.

"Natural? You think this is natural?" Anger crept up on Krycin. It clawed away at him, trying to come out. With a deep breath, he pushed it back down. "Gladius needs to pay for this. He destroyed them. He killed all of the Lyecians, and why? Because he's gone insane. He's mad for power, and I'm the one he's looking for."

Then give yourself to him. Satisfy his hunger.

"If I do that, it will break the time line. Everything I remember must happen as it did before. Isn't that what Tyriel said?" Krycin asked.

At last you understand. You have a choice. Go on, defeat Gladius as you are destined and forge your legacy, or walk away now. You will live, but the rest of Galadir will cease to exist.

"That's not much of a choice," Krycin said. "Who are you? Why does your voice sound so familiar?"

This is the first time we've met, yet we shall meet again in the future, though for you it's the past. I am your goddess, Lyecha, and as goddess of time I see all things no matter where or when they occur.

"So you already know what I'm going to choose," Krycin said, getting to his feet.

I do, Lyecha said. Krycin could almost hear amusement in her voice. *You learn quickly, my child. Defeat Gladius, as you know it must be done.*

"What about the future? What about the barrier between worlds? What about Malia? She's the reason I came back, to save her future. How do I fix the damage that's been done?" He began walking toward the battle sounds. "If I return to the future without an answer, it will all be for nothing. What do I do?"

He continued walking and waiting for an answer, but none came. He searched for her presence with his mind but felt nothing. Lyecha was gone, and he was on his own. Krycin made no effort to hurry back to the battle until he remembered Catrina in the little hut at the base of the mountain. "Mom," he said, and broke into a run.

⊚

When Seth reached the edge of the Fioraden village, most of the Narshuks were already slain. The last few who remained were battling Fioraden outside the hut where Catrina was being kept. Seth marched up to the hut and fired multiple balls of energy into the group of Narshuks, vaporizing any he hit. One Fioraden warrior leapt into the air, charged at a Narshuk at the front and at the last second, spun in the air spreading his wings so that the blades on his wings struck the Narshuk over and over. When the warrior came out of his whirlwind attack, he struck the Narshuk in the chest with his longsword, impaling the beast on it. Hundreds of cuts over the Narshuk's body bloomed with blood as it collapsed.

Seth ran at the rest of the creatures. One of them barked something at the hut and then ran. As soon as it ran, the rest of them scattered. The Fioraden followed them, continuing their assault. Seth ran for the hut.

He was twenty paces from the hut when a golden light flashed from the entrance. Seth had seen the light before, once, when they fought Gladius the first time at the border of the Eastern Badlands. "No!" He screamed and pushed himself faster, charging both fists with white balls of energy.

Gladius burst from the entrance to the hut with a smile on his face. The smile faded when he saw Seth charging at him. It took a moment for Seth to process that Gladius was directly in front of him, and by the time he got his head straight, Gladius had side-stepped and Seth fell past him. As he fell, Seth spun himself and launched the energy balls at Gladius. They burst as they hit him and sent him flying through the air back toward the rift he had come from.

Seth expected him to get up and rush back to battle him again, but instead, Gladius scrambled to his feet and ran for the rift. For a moment, Seth was torn. Chase down Gladius, or check on his mother and let Gladius run. It took only a split second for him to decide to enter the hut.

Inside was a bloodbath. Several Fioraden healers had been dismembered, their limbs tossed about the hut like random pieces of meat. Every surface of the hut was coated with splattered blood except the bed in the middle of the room. Not a single drop of blood was on the bed. Seth stepped through the hut with care so as not to step on any remains. Lying on the bed was Catrina, her eyes closed, her body peaceful, but not breathing.

"No," Seth said, rushing to her side. "No, no, no. This isn't right." He took one of her hands in his and felt the warmth draining from it. He pressed his other hand against her swollen abdomen where the baby rested. He summoned the power of life and projected it into her body to see if the baby was okay. He felt no heartbeat and panic seized his heart. "How? How can she be dead if I'm alive?"

There was a long silence in the room. Whether it was because the battle outside was done, or because Seth was ignoring everything else, he heard nothing. He stared at the lifeless body of his mother for what felt like an eternity before a thought crept into his head. "I brought Cy back. But I couldn't do that to her. I couldn't do that to my own mother."

A voice behind him startled him out of his thoughts. "You must. There is no choice."

Seth stood up and spun in one fluid motion, summoning attack magic to him and readying himself for combat. When he saw who it was, he let out a sigh and dismissed the power. "Tyriel. You'll get yourself killed sneaking up on people like that."

The black robed figure standing at the door approached him. "Before it's too late."

"You don't understand what you're asking of me. She won't have her powers. She'll be human. I saw what that did to Cy. I won't do it again."

"We all must do things we don't like to accomplish the greater good. You must bring your mother back to life, or everything we have worked for will be for nothing." Tyriel continued his approach. His robes drifted across the floor like he was floating through the air and wisps of black smoke drifted from them as he moved. His hood was pulled over his head and hung forward, hiding his face. "You know what it will mean for all of us if you are never born."

Seth thought about it for a long time. There was commotion outside the hut, and the door rattled once as somebody tried to get in, but it wouldn't budge. Seth didn't remember locking it, or it even having a lock, but he guessed that Tyriel had a hand in that. "You're right. I have to bring her back. I don't want to do that to her, but I have to."

Tyriel lifted his head to look directly into Seth's eyes. He couldn't see Tyriel's face, but he felt his gaze, and it was heavy, like it was trying to push into his head. "Do you ever remember your mother having powers?"

After a moments thought, Seth said, "No. But our powers were suppressed. Or rather, mine were. I just assumed she had done the same."

"She never had them to suppress. If she tried, she could still cast spells, but it would require great effort, like Cy, and she would require a focus to cast the energy out. She will never have Lyecian powers again, but she must live." Tyriel's voice urged Seth to turn around and get on with the spell.

"I understand," Seth said. He knelt down beside Catrina and placed a hand on her arm. The warmth was leaving her body fast, and so he had to hurry. He focused his mind on drawing the power of life and called to Anam to bring her back. The magic came and grew inside him, flowed through him, and poured into Catrina's body. Light flooded from him and Catrina as the magic infused her body with life once more. She gasped for air as her heart began beating again, but her eyes didn't open.

Seth slumped over and leaned on her now warm and breathing body. Catrina lifted her head and opened her eyes. "Krycin?"

Seth looked at her and saw only his mother's worried face. "Yes. It's me. You were slain by Gladius, but I brought you back."

There was a moment of silence in the room, and then she spoke again. "Is my baby all right?"

"Yes. You are both alive and well," Seth said, holding her hand tight. "I need you to do something for me."

Catrina turned to face Seth and said, "Anything, Krycin. Just name it."

"When your baby is born, you and Serrin must take him to the dead world and make a new life."

"The dead world?" Her face was tired and confused.

"I'll take you and Serrin there. It will be a better life for both of you. There's no magic there. You can live as a family and raise your child in peace." Seth's voice was excited as he said this, but Catrina seemed drained, like she just wanted to sleep. "Think about it, anyway."

The corner of her mouth raised in a half smile, and she closed her eyes as sleep overtook her.

Tyriel drifted forward to see her and offered Seth a hand up. Once Seth was on his feet, he moved to the other side of her bed and looked down at her. "Something's wrong," he said.

"What do you mean?" Seth asked. "She's alive, I'm alive, what could be wrong?"

"It's you, but not you. Something is missing."

Seth shifted his gaze from Catrina to Tyriel, and then back again. "What could be missing? I brought her back, and now everything is fine, right?" He paused and waited for Tyriel's reassurance, but it didn't come. "Right?"

"I thought you were born with it. I just assumed this whole time," Tyriel said.

"Born with what? Come on, Tyriel, tell me what's wrong."

"The reason you can travel through time where no other Lyecian can. The reason you are special, and more than just a Lyecian. You have something called a fatespark. Moving through time is taxing on a living being's body. Were a normal person to attempt it, the temporal forces would tear them apart. The fatespark protects you and grants you the power of the Fates."

The admission surprised and confused Seth. He remained silent for a few moments while he processed the information. "So, I wasn't born with it, but I have it now. Where did it come from?"

Tyriel reached up and pulled his hood back, revealing his red hair and crystal blue eyes. He stared at Seth with an intensity that startled him. "It was granted to you. But not by the Fates. The situation is so rare, it may never have happened before. See, there are others who hold a fatespark. Most are reapers who work for the Fates, souls who died before their time who are given a second chance. But a few rare souls are born with it. They exist outside of the Fates' control. They can travel anywhere and do almost anything."

"Like gods?" Seth asked, trying to make sense of it.

"No, even the gods are subject to the Fates' control. Those born with a fatespark are something else entirely. But for somebody to be granted a fatespark who wasn't born with it, and who didn't receive it from the Fates, it's unheard of. Those who have a fatespark, never part from it." Tyriel looked down at Catrina who remained motionless other than the slow, steady rise and fall of her chest from her breathing. "This must be it."

Seth raised an eyebrow at Tyriel. "Must be what?"

"My punishment for defying the Fates. My brother was supposed to die, and thrice I have prevented it. I was informed that I would be punished for my defiance, but I was not told what or when that would be. I must give up my fatespark to you. That's the price I pay." His voice was calm, but there was a sadness to it.

"What will that mean to you?" Seth asked. He suspected the answer before Tyriel said it, but he had to hear the words.

"Mortality, and eventual death. But I will be free from my obligation to the Fates. I will live out the remainder of my days by my brother's side, just make me one promise."

"Anything, just name it," Seth said.

"Do not kill Gladius. There is another force at work here. Gladius does not act on his own, though he doesn't know it. He is being influenced by something else. Something much more powerful. His soul has been corrupted by an outside force that is twisting his thoughts and goals to some other end."

"What does that mean? That Gladius doesn't know what he's doing?"

"No, he knows what he's doing, and he believes that what he's doing is right, but his original intentions are being pushed into something darker. The Fates have not figured out what it is, or what's doing it, but I do not believe Gladius deserves to die."

"But he's killed so many," Seth said. His mind was in conflict now. Part of him wanted to destroy the evil that was Gladius, but another part of him felt compassion for the man. He remembered their friendship, and longed to have that bond back again. "If what you say is true, then there still may be part of the old Gladius left. Can we save him?"

"I don't know. But isn't it worth a try?"

Seth thought about the young man who found him on the beach. The one who healed him, and taught him to use his magic again. It seemed so long ago. "Okay, I'll do it. I know what to do. There's been enough death in this war already."

Tyriel extended a hand and held it palm down over Catrina's abdomen. He closed his eyes as if in deep concentration. Moments later, his entire body glowed with an inner silver light. The power flowed from Tyriel's body and collected in his hand, throwing beams of glittering light out into the room. The light was warm and refreshing, and made Seth feel at peace.

When the light completed its transfer into Tyriel's hand, it looked like a crystal pulsing with silver light. The structure of the crystal was in a state of flux and no matter how Seth tried to focus on it, it never took on a constant shape. It was more beautiful than anything he'd ever seen before. Slowly, the crystal lowered itself into Catrina's abdomen, into the baby that rested in her womb. The light flooded out from the unborn child causing her abdomen to glow for a moment, and then it faded. Tyriel stood up, pulled his hood back over his head, and walked around the bed toward Seth. "We must go now."

Seth could tell something was missing from Tyriel, and felt it inside himself for the first time. It had always been there, but now he was conscious of it. "Your powers," Seth said. "They're gone."

"Not all of them," Tyriel said, "but most. I retain some basic abilities that were not tied to the fatespark."

Seth walked to the door of the hut and emerged from it into the field. Outside, Ferron waited with a battalion of warriors with their weapons at the ready. Ferron lowered his weapons and approached Seth. *Is she safe?* he asked.

"Yes," Seth said. "Sleeping comfortably, but safe and well."

She is no longer Lyecian, Ferron said inside his head. His voice sounded troubled at first, but when Seth heard his voice again, whatever troubled him was gone. *Her child is safe, and still Lyecian.*

"Gladius took her soul. I fixed it the best I could. The power of Anam does not restore a Lyecian's powers, only their life."

The child will come soon, I can feel it. Ferron stepped past Seth and approached the door to the hut. *I will have her moved. You should return to Findoor. Your presence is required there.*

Seth nodded and looked at Tyriel with a smile. He put his hand on Tyriel's shoulder and said, "Let's go and win a war."

The two men blinked out of existence leaving a void the surrounding air rushed to fill.

Chapter 33 – Battle Plans

Seth and Tyriel appeared on the battlements of Findoor castle just as the city was being evacuated. Merek was there as well, overseeing the business of keeping the castle safe. A great many wizards were stationed on the city walls casting protective spells to ensure the city and castle would withstand a lengthy siege. Seth took a deep breath of fresh air and savored it like it would be his last for a long time. "How are things coming?" Seth asked Merek without warning.

Merek spun to face Seth and appeared more startled to see Tyriel with him than he did in regard to the sudden voice. "The city will be empty in the next few hours. Many people are leaving for the hills to the north. The rest are taking up residence inside the castle." He looked at Tyriel and said, "My friend, I didn't expect the Fates to take any further interest in our affairs. Are things not in order?"

There was an awkward silence between the three men. When Seth opened his mouth to say something, Tyriel raised a hand to stop him and said, "Everything is in order. I am simply here to ensure all goes according to plan."

"Ah, good," Merek said and looked back toward the city.

"Merek, there was an attack up at the Fioraden mountains. Gladius knew. He knew the Lyecians were being kept there, and he was ready for it." Seth thought he had come to terms with the situation, but the emotion threatened to overwhelm him. "He killed them all. Every one he could find, and I couldn't stop him."

"By the gods," Merek said, taking a step back. The news appeared to deal a physical blow to the old wizard, who now sought something to grasp to keep him from falling over. "How could he have known?"

Seth looked to Tyriel for an answer, but he had stepped away from them unnoticed and was nowhere to be found. "I think we've been betrayed."

Merek's expression turned from shock to horror. "Who would do such a thing? There were only a few who knew where we were moving them."

"It was Cy. I have no evidence to back that up, but I know it was him."

"That's a dire accusation. We must tread carefully. If it truly was Cy, he will become desperate and dangerous if confronted." Merek turned and walked to the edge of the battlements. "You said Gladius killed them all. What of Catrina? And the child?"

There was a long pause between them as Seth tried to regain his composure. "He took her life as well, though I restored her to life like I did Cy. She's not a Lyecian anymore, but the child is fine."

"Perhaps we can do a search of Cy's chamber," Merek said, still looking out on the city. "I'll need some time."

Seth thought about this for a moment, then said, "I'll talk to him. Distract him while you search for the evidence we need. Send him to my room when we're done here."

"It shall be done. Now we have preparations to make. Runners are reporting that the Narshuk army is less than a day away."

Seth walked over to the wall and stood beside Merek. "Where is Serrin? I should be the one to break the news to him."

"I will send a runner to fetch him at once. Where shall I have him meet you?"

"No, I'll go and find him. It's too important to wait. When I'm done talking to Serrin, I'll return to my quarters to talk to Cy. Have him wait there." Seth walked away and left Merek on the battlements to continue prep work for the impending battle.

⊙

Tyriel walked the halls of Findoor castle for a long time before he decided to go and find his brother. When he did find Lebriel, it was outside near the front gate where he was supervising the reinforcements to the doors. He approached the red-robed wizard with quiet reserve, taking caution in each step. When he was not more than ten paces from Lebriel, he opened his mouth to speak. "Brother," he said and took a step back when Lebriel whirled to face him.

"What do you want?" Lebriel's face revealed nothing of his thoughts, though his tone of voice was unpleasant.

"I thought we could catch up. Perhaps I could help you with preparations for the battle ahead?" Tyriel felt awkward proposing it, and Lebriel's reaction didn't help at all.

"Catch up? Help out?" Lebriel said, raising his voice a little. "Don't you have business to do for the Fates?"

Tyriel lowered his gaze to the ground to avoid his brother's intense stare. "No. I am no longer in their service. I thought..."

"You thought what?" Lebriel asked, taking a step toward him. "You thought you could stroll back into my life after over twenty years of me thinking you were dead? You thought we could just patch things up and be good friends? You may be my brother by blood, but make no mistake, Tyriel. I know you no more than I know a stranger on the street. Who you are now is not who you were then, and you never will be again."

"I'm sorry," Tyriel said, dropping his shoulders.

"Sorry? I thought you were dead. I watched you die. I wouldn't even believe it was you now, were it not for the fact that I feel like I'm looking in a mirror. It too me many years to get over your death." Lebriel heaved a sigh and went back to his work at hand. "No. It's going to take time. Time to accept your fate, and time to heal from the wounds I have spent a lifetime running from."

There was a long pause between the two men which ended with Tyriel heading back toward the castle.

Seth's stomach was in knots as he approached Serrin's door and knocked.

"Come in," Serrin said.

Seth pushed the door open and stepped in. Serrin was sitting on his bed with his legs crossed and eyes closed. He was so still, Seth might have mistaken him for a statue. When Serrin opened his eyes, he looked surprised.

"Krycin, what brings you here?" Serrin said.

"When I defeat Gladius and the battle is done tomorrow, I need you to come somewhere with me. You and Catrina."

"I'm certain that can be arranged, but why?"

"I can't tell you where we're going, or why," Seth said looking down at him. A tear rolled down his face and fell to the floor. "I just need you to trust me."

"I can see that you're troubled, my friend. Speak to me. What has gotten you so upset?"

"I," Seth said. His voice hitched and he had to swallow a lump in his throat before he could continue. "I have news from the north."

Serrin walked over to the bed and sat down beside Seth. "What is it?"

Seth closed his eyes and took a deep breath to calm himself. "We were betrayed. Gladius knew where we were keeping the Lyecians. There was an attack, and he killed them all." More tears ran down his face as he spoke. Serrin took a handkerchief out of his pocket and passed it to Seth, who accepted it. "I couldn't stop him. I couldn't save them."

The shock was apparent on Serrin's face. All the color drained from his skin and his jaw dropped open. A strangled gasp came from him as he processed what he had just been told. "Catrina," he said after a long silence. "What about Catrina?"

Seth couldn't look at him. He couldn't bring himself to face his father and tell him, but Serrin wouldn't give up. "Krycin, tell me what happened to my love. I must know."

"Gladius took her. He took her soul," Seth said. A flood of emotions washed over him and he burst into tears. "I couldn't stop him. I couldn't save any of them. I couldn't even keep him from leaving. He's too strong. All I could do was restore what life I could to her."

"She lives?"

Seth nodded, but couldn't make another sound.

"And my child?"

"He is fine," Seth said without thinking. By the time he realized his slip, Serrin had already caught it and was opening his mouth to speak again.

"He? I have a son? Why didn't you tell me he was born already? I expected a message right away," Serrin said without humor.

"He is not born, but he will be soon, and he will be a son. I need you to do me a favor." Seth now looked up at Serrin through tear clouded eyes. "Sit this battle out. There are so few of us left, and Catrina needs you now more than ever. When it is done, I will take Catrina and your newborn son somewhere safe."

There was a long silence between them. Seth watched Serrin for any signs that he was going to agree or disagree, but Serrin gave nothing away.

"And what will the Council wizards do? I am supposed to be their leader," Serrin said.

"Explain it to them. You and I might be the only two Lyecians left on Galadir. Listen to reason, and sit this one out. There is nothing you can do that will change the tide of this war. I know it sounds strange, but I know how to defeat Gladius now. This time will be different. But you have to stay back and out of sight."

With some reluctance, Serrin said, "All right. I'll sit this one out. Lebriel will be appointed the head of the High Council until such a time as I can resume my duties. I hope, for all our sakes, that you are right. If you fail to defeat him again, there won't be any more last chances."

"I understand. I won't disappoint you."

Both men stood up and left the room. Seth went to his room to talk to Cy, and he guessed that Serrin would be rounding up the Council to inform them of his decision.

⊙

When Seth reached his room, Cy was standing outside his door leaning against the wall and tapping his toe on the floor. Neither man said a word until Seth was standing right in front of him. "You wanted to see me?" Cy asked, with a snide hint to his voice.

"Yes," Seth said. "I just got back from the Fioraden's mountain village. There was a massacre. Gladius knew where we were hiding the Lyecians. He killed them all."

"By the gods," Cy said. "That's terrible news. What of Catrina? Serrin will be devastated."

"Catrina is fine. I revived her, just the same as I did you. The baby is fine too. He will be born full Lyecian." He paused and thought for a second, and then said, "Come in my room, Cy. We should talk in private." He opened his door and walked inside, listening for Cy's footsteps behind him. When he heard nothing, he stopped and turned to face the door. "This conversation is best had in private. But if you want to talk about how you betrayed Findoor and your people where everyone can hear, so be it."

Cy stopped tapping his toe and took a step away from the wall. His movements were slow and measured. "Have it your way," Cy said, as he walked into Seth's room. When he closed the door behind him, the anger was apparent on his face. "How *dare* you. How dare you toss an accusation around like that with no evidence to support it. Is this another of your 'feelings'? Another hunch from the all-knowing Krycin?"

"No," Seth said, recoiling from the verbal assault. "It's a statement of fact. I know what you did, and when the rest of the

Council and Merek find their proof, you will be convicted. All I want to know is, why?" His voice was calm, despite the turmoil of emotions inside him. He wanted to shout and scream back at Cy, but knew it would do no good.

"Why? Because I've lost who I am. I was Lyecian, a master of time and space. Better than a human by far. But that's been taken from me, and I would do anything to get it back. Anything." Cy took a step forward and stared into Seth's eyes. The darkness they held disturbed Seth. "And if that means teaming up with the most powerful wizard who ever walked the face of Galadir in order to get it, then so be it. I'll do what I need to do, because I'd rather be dead than human."

"Then go back to him, and stop masquerading as one of our allies. You are no longer welcome here. Once Merek and the Council find the evidence they need, you will be put to death. And if you don't leave, I'll kill you myself."

Cy took a step back and looked from the door to Seth and back again.

"Go," Seth said, turning his back on him.

He heard the door shut behind him, and sat down on his bed, lost in his own thoughts.

Chapter 34 – Showdown

Krycin and Merek stood atop the battlements, surveying the land before them. The smell of death hung in the air. Rank upon rank of Narshuks waited outside the city walls. They wore leather straps and what pieces of armor they could gather, but were equipped with nothing more than their teeth and claws. Shouts from soldiers stationed on the city walls rose up to their heights but became mere background noise as they mingled and lost all definition. Buildings set ablaze by Gladius billowed with smoke, filling the air with the acrid taste of burnt wood. Constructed of dense gray granite, the castle held firm against any magic cast at it. "So this is it then, our last stand," Merek said, turning to Krycin. His face was lined with concern.

"It was good knowing you," Krycin said. He looked as if he faced the gallows, but Merek sensed something more in his voice. He wasn't ready to give up just yet.

Gladius paraded in front of his army on foot. His battle cries goaded his troops into a frenzy. Their shouts and howls reverberated off the stone walls and shook the Findoor people to the bone. Krycin took a step toward the front of the battlements and paused, as though he might jump. Merek approached him and asked, "You're not going to do anything stupid are you?"

A glimmer danced in Krycin's eyes, a light in the darkness that surrounded them, and he smiled. "You know me..."

"That's what I'm afraid of." The old wizard watched Krycin take one final step to the edge of the wall and hesitate. Clothed in loose-fitting black pants and an off-white tunic, Krycin looked more like a commoner than a powerful wizard or warrior. Tilting his head to the sky, he inhaled a deep breath and held it for a long moment before letting it go.

Merek watched his friend at the edge of the wall. "Are you sure you won't reconsider? Taking on Gladius alone before all those Narshuks is a dangerous gamble." Merek's gray robes fluttered in a light breeze. A deep hood covered most of his brown hair, and the sleeves extended to the middle of his hands. Every edge of his robe was embroidered with a silver trim that gleamed in even the dimmest light.

"I know how to defeat him now. I can't risk any more lives with what I'm about to do," Krycin said. "When Gladius took the king, he took Findoor's heart and soul. The soldiers will fight with little spirit, and our resources will dwindle fast. I must act now, or there will be nothing left to save."

Krycin's words stung in the old wizard's ears. "You're sure you can defeat him?" Merek asked. He took a step closer to Krycin, raising his voice. "He's already taken so many of your kind. What makes you think that you will succeed this time? Give us just a little more time, and we will find a way to destroy him and his army. I have my best and most powerful students searching for a way in my library."

"Time? What would ever make you think that we had any more time? When Gladius marched from the Badlands with his army, then we had time. When he traveled across the Losteron Plains, then we had time. We had time when he killed the king, and when he destroyed so many of my people. But now? Now we don't have time." His voice grew in volume with each sentence, and by the time he finished all the commanders could hear the exchange between the two men.

Merek opened his mouth to provide a rebuttal, but before he could, a black figure burst from the front gates and caught his eye. "Cy," Merek said, pointing to the field and the man running toward Gladius.

"There's nothing we can do for him," Krycin said.

"Perhaps not. I'll not waste resources trying to save him."

The pair watched as Cy approached Gladius and bowed before him. Gladius appeared to laugh, which was picked up by the rest of his army. In seconds, the entire contingent of Narshuks was roaring with laughter. Without warning, Gladius drew his sword, and swung it, slashing it across Cy's throat and spilling his blood on the field.

"No," Krycin cried, and stepped off the edge of the battlements. He drifted down like a feather on the wind, where Merek had expected him to fall straight down. Dust stirred into small clouds around him as he landed just outside the castle walls. With the city between himself and Gladius, he took off running. A few quick strides later he was lost among the buildings that surrounded the castle.

Shaking his head at the display, Merek thought to himself, *Since when can Krycin summon the power of air?* Merek shouted orders to provide cover fire for Krycin. A small contingent of archers and shield bearers marched out onto the city walls to stave off enemy troops and provide an opening when Krycin emerged. Narshuks carried Cy's body away and out of sight.

(⊛)

Seth thundered through the city, moving past buildings so fast he couldn't tell a tavern from a smithy. The smell of burnt wood strengthened as he approached the city walls where some buildings still burned. Despite the continued onslaught of enemies, the front gates, reinforced by the power of earth, held fast.

As he made his approach, Seth lifted his hand and summoned the power of time and space. He charged at the front gate at top speed, but the gate showed no sign of opening. Seth continued on without a worry. Just before he struck the solid wood obstruction, he let loose the magical energy he had summoned, and disappeared, reappearing on the other side of the gate.

Scanning the battle field, he spotted Gladius. Seth held his hand out to the side, as if holding a weapon. A sword of pure light materialized in his hand. The sword shone so bright that those looking on shielded their eyes to avoid being blinded. From the hilt of the sword, streamers of light spread up his arm and over his body. As the light encased him, it solidified into crystal creating a complete suit of armor around him. Seth let out a battle cry and ran toward Gladius, who ignored the blinding light of his sword.

Gladius readied his own weapon, the black steel sword, that erupted with flames. The air around Gladius wavered in the heat, and the interlocking plates of his black armor made him look more like a construct than a man. In his off-hand he held a large black shield. Seth saw his eyes glowing red with magic but did not stop his advance.

An instant after both men readied their weapons, they clashed together in an explosion of power. Their swords collided, raining sparks down onto the field. The blades sang as they separated and

Seth drew his sword back to swing again. His second attack connected with Gladius's shield, leaving a giant gash through the center of it.

Gladius returned the attack and shoved Seth back. With all his might, he swung the blazing sword in an overhead stroke. It crashed down on Seth, who wielded no shield. Calling upon the power of time and space again, Seth blinked out of existence and reappeared behind Gladius. The blade continued through empty air, causing Gladius to stumble forward. Catching himself with one foot, he used the momentum to swing his sword around the other way in a spin that would have impressed even the most seasoned gladiator.

The move caught Seth off his guard, leaving him flat-footed to bear the full force of the attack. The black sword roared through the air and struck his left shoulder. The crystal plates gave out and shattered, allowing the sword to bite into his flesh. It seared through muscle and tendons, stopping when it struck bone. Seth cried out, but choked back the pain and swung upward with his sword. Having Gladius's weapon mired in his shoulder gave him the advantage he needed. His sword flashed up in an arc and caught Gladius's left arm as he tried to steady himself. The pure light of the sword penetrated his armor and separated his arm from his body at the elbow. The black shield pulled the severed arm to the ground with an ominous thud.

Gladius howled with rage and struggled to free his sword from Seth's shoulder. "You've already lost," Gladius said as he heaved at the blade, pulling Seth with it. "Even if you kill me, my army will wash over this land and annihilate Findoor. All of Galadir will tremble at their might." He pulled again at the sword but couldn't budge it. "All the Lyecians are now dead. It's just you left. Are you ready to spend an eternity alone?"

Seth dropped his sword and reached up to grab the black sword that sizzled and smoked, still cooking his flesh. The pain was almost unbearable, but he gained a good grip on the blade and looked into Gladius's eyes. Through clenched teeth he said, "What makes you think I'm going to kill you?"

A look of confusion washed over Gladius's face, and changed to terror as Seth called upon the power of his people, the element of time and space. He drew the energy not from the world around him, but from Gladius, using the sword as a conduit. A torrent of magical energy poured from Gladius, robbing him of his strength and of all the power taken from Seth's people. As Seth harnessed it, his eyes blazed with inner light and the black sword glowed white-hot, fusing it with both men's armor. A flood of energy moved from Gladius to Seth, and as it did, Seth felt something else. Another presence inside Gladius, struggling to hold onto the power. He redoubled his efforts and drew more still.

The world around Seth melted away into darkness. The struggle, the war, and even Gladius disappeared, leaving only a feeble old man standing before him. A red robe with strange silver symbols embroidered into it covered the man's frail body. The symbols looked like runes of all shapes and sizes, and the more Seth looked at them, the more familiar they looked. He was hunched over, and teetered back and forth as he looked up into Seth's eyes. He stroked his long white beard and said, "You can't have him. He's mine."

"Who are you?" Seth asked.

"That's none of your concern. Go back to your time, fatewalker." His voice grew agitated as he spoke, making Seth nervous.

"What do you mean by fatewalker? And what's going on?"

"Get out!" the old man screamed, his face contorting with rage. "You don't belong here. You should have stayed where you were. I need this one. He's mine. You can't have him."

Seth prepared to defend himself as he watched the old man's hands light up with blue fire. There was little time before a stream of flames came toward him. He raised a shield, deflecting the flames to either side of him, and prepared an attack of his own. Calling on the power of water, he held a hand up and launched several spears of ice toward the old man. One of them struck the old man's robe and knocked the edge loose, revealing what was underneath.

Bright golden lights, hundreds of them, all flickering and flashing with inner strength filled the old man's robe. There was little doubt in Seth's mind what they represented. "Lyecians," Seth said, in awe. "It was you. You killed them all and took their souls."

"What of it?" the old man said. "They were wasting their potential on this miserable world. I can use them. I can do so much more with them."

An overwhelming rage came over Seth at seeing his people reduced to nothing more than a utility. He fired blasts of raw magical energy at the old man, over and over, dislodging the souls a few at a time. The old man made several attempts to defend himself, but the power of Seth's attacks overwhelmed him. When the last of the Lyecian souls were freed, Seth stood over the old man and shook his head, trying to catch his breath.

"You don't deserve to live," Seth said.

"Then kill me," the old man said with a slight smile on his face. "If I don't deserve to live, then kill me, and end my torment."

Seth raised his fist, white light flooding out from it as he summoned up the energy that would finish the old man. He was about to drive his fist down when he hesitated.

"What's the matter? Can't stomach it? You'll get used to the killing. Go on, take my life. It gets easier after the first." The old man cackled which turned into a fit of coughs. Tears ran from his eyes, though Seth doubted they were tears of sadness or pain.

"Who are you, really?" Seth asked.

"A long forgotten remnant, imprisoned in a deep dark place. Had it not been for you, I would be freeing myself right now."

"Why Gladius? You could have picked anyone. Why did it have to be him?"

"You ask too many questions, fatewalker. It's going to get you in trouble some day. Had I known you were this powerful, I would have taken you instead. No matter. I'll get you eventually. It's only a matter of time, and all I have is time."

"I'm taking my friend back," Seth said. "This ends now."

He lifted a hand and channeled energy from all eight elements at once. The old man squirmed and fought under Seth's grip, but he maintained his hold as the energy started to flow from his hand out, surrounding the old man in a crystal prison. The crystal was transparent, with threads of every color woven through it.

"Go back to your deep dark place," Seth said, and blasted the crystal away with a pulse of raw energy that sent it flying into the void around him.

The darkness receded, and the battlefield reappeared, with Gladius before him, and the sword still lodged in his shoulder. No matter how Gladius tried, he couldn't remove his hand from the sword. Smoke rose from his eyes, nose and mouth as the flow of magic heated his body, cooking him from the inside out. The smell of burning flesh filled the air as his super-heated armor blistered and charred his skin. Still he screamed with an inhuman strength.

The flow of energy stopped and a hush fell over the battlefield. Seth stood like a beacon, his entire body blazing with light, and stared down at his opponent. Gladius met Seth's gaze, his eyes filled with pain. A light breeze blew, cooling the surface of his armor. Seth spoke, his voice strong and clear, "Say goodbye to Findoor, Gladius."

$(\ast)$

Merek watched as Krycin's body erupted like a volcano, unleashing a wave of energy over the entire battlefield. Most of Gladius's army was caught in the white dome, but those unlucky enough to be near the edges were disintegrated, their bodies dissolving into dust. A shock wave traveled out from the energy curtain that knocked any remaining troops off their feet and shook the castle walls. Merek held the edge of the wall to remain on his feet. The energy bubble extended out from Krycin and spared nobody in its path. Panicked troops made feeble attempts to run, but only the farthest troops stood a chance of avoiding it. Merek could see nothing inside the crackling shell until it stopped growing.

For the seconds it remained, vague shadows moved around inside it, then it wavered and shrank down to where Krycin had stood, and dispersed. All that remained on the battlefield were a few scattered soldiers scrambling for their lives, and empty grass where the black mass of the army had stood.

The land remained quiet only for a moment, both sides staring in disbelief at what they had just seen. Merek broke the silence and shouted out to the remaining Findoor troops, "Attack! Purge this land of their filth. Every one of them."

The Findoor troops responded without question launching arrows and spells from the city walls at the remaining Narshuks who were now a mere few hundred. Scattered and confused, at least half of the remaining Narshuks perished in the initial wave of attacks. Those who survived ran from the castle as far and as fast as they could to the south. There was no call for retreat, nor any howls to indicate they were working as an army. It was every beast for himself as they ran.

Merek smiled at the victory and called on several runners. They lined up before him, waiting for their orders. "Organize all the runners you can find. Get the word out to all the outer holdings and neighboring kingdoms: Findoor is victorious. Krycin has defeated Gladius and his army. The Arch-Magus, myself, shall retain the kingdom until such a time as the king's heir is of age to take the throne."

The runners left the battlements as fast as their feet could carry them, leaving Merek up there alone. After a moment, Merek too left the battlements to inspect the battlefield.

Smiling faces were everywhere as he walked through the castle. The celebrations were already starting as the news got around.

Merek continued out the front doors of the castle proper, through the city, and out the front gates. A blackened circle remained where the two men had fought their battle, and Merek made his way there.

At the center of the circle, just poking out of the ground, was the hilt of a sword, charred and black. "What's this," Merek said out loud as he approached it. He reached down, wrapped his fingers around the hilt.

The moment he touched it, he knew it was his sword, the black steel sword that Gladius had stolen from him. There was an aura of intellect about the sword, and it felt displeased. He drew the sword from the ground and wrapped it in his robe to carry back to the castle. "Easy now. We'll find the right master for you yet."

By the time he made it back to the castle, Lebriel was waiting for him at the gate.

⊙

A hush fell over the battlefield as the dome closed over Seth, Gladius, and most of the Narshuk army. When the stream of energy ended, Seth called on the power of water and focused it into his shoulder. The bone that had been cleaved by the black steel sword fused together and pushed the sword out. Muscle bound back together and flesh closed, leaving only a faint scar.

The black steel sword fell from his shoulder and hung from Gladius's limp hand. Smoke rose from every crevice of his black armor, and Seth could see his dark eyes through the slit in his helmet. The red glow had left them now, and the whites of his eyes were bright under the dome of white energy. Seth reached down and took the black steel sword from his grip. "I'll take that."

Gladius groaned a protest, but couldn't move. The surge in energy through him created enough heat to fuse his armor plates together, preventing him from moving, and turning him into a living statue. Seth could see he was in obvious pain, but had to deal with the Narshuk army first, as they were now approaching the two men, and most of them looked angry.

The dome of energy around them wavered and began to shrink, and Seth brought up an image in his mind. A great gaping hole in the earth where a mountain had once been. The Fioraden mountain range that was now an endless pit. As the white dome collapsed, the Narshuks under it were transformed into pure energy and transferred to their new location. Seth took the black steel sword and drove it into the ground so that only the hilt was left showing, and then placed a hand on Gladius's shoulder. The dome collapsed in on them, but Seth and Gladius disappeared before it took them.

(◦)

The energy dome reappeared over the former Fioraden mountain range and spread out to cover the entire hole, plus some of the ground around it. Narshuks appeared under the dome at the center first, but with no ground underneath them, they fell into the endless abyss that Gladius had created. The last of the Narshuks appeared on the edge of the hole and could do nothing but watch their brethren fall to their doom, their screams echoing for several minutes before all went quiet. Scrag was one such Narshuk who was lucky enough to land on the edge of the hole. He looked around at what remained of his army and lowered his head.

"Lord Gladius will return. We must be ready for him," he said in the Narshuk tongue. "So long as the vessel lives, we can restore him to life."

A small contingent of Narshuks gathered around him as he began going over their plans, and several hours later, the remnants of the Narshuk army began their long trek back to the Eastern Badlands.

Chapter 35 - A Lyecian is Born

At the base of the mountains in a clearing about a ten minute walk from where the Fioraden had set up their village, a blue light appeared and split open, sending arcs of electricity cascading to the ground all around it. It was around midday, just after Gladius and the Narshuk army arrived at Findoor castle. Cy stepped from the rift into the cool, fresh air that was warming up as the sun reached its peak. *Having Gladius play those fools at their own game was genius,* he thought. *His illusions worked like a charm.* He took his bearings as the rift closed behind him and started his trek toward the mountain.

It took him close to fifteen minutes to get to the hut where Catrina was being cared for, and when he arrived, he could hear her cries from within. He rushed to the door only to be blocked by two Fioraden warriors.

"I've been sent by Arch-Magus Merek to watch over and protect the Lyecian within. Allow me to pass," Cy said. The two warriors stared at Cy with an intensity that felt like they were tearing him apart with their eyes. They looked at each other for a brief moment, and then lifted their weapons and allowed Cy to pass.

He walked through the door and into the room where several other Fioraden were working with tightly folded wings so they wouldn't interfere with each other. Catrina lay on a bed with a blanket draped over her legs. *The child is coming,* Cy heard in his head. He looked at the Fioraden nearest to her and met her gaze. *It should be an easy birth. She is strong.*

"I'm just here to make sure she makes it back to Findoor in one piece," Cy said.

Catrina lifted her head during a moment of calm between her contractions. "Cy, please, come hold my hand. Help me welcome my child into this world." The next contraction came and she cringed and gritted her teeth against the pain. Cy approached her and offered his hand, which she accepted once the contraction passed. "They tell me it will be a boy." She went quiet and looked like she was concentrating on something, then looked up at Cy. "One or two more pushes and he will be..." Her sentence was cut off by a powerful contraction that she pushed with. Cy watched her abdomen convulse and push down on the child within her. The Fioraden kneeling before her worked with great haste preparing water and towels and soft blankets. Catrina let out a cry as she bore down on the child and squeezed Cy's hands.

When the contraction let up, she relaxed, but lacked the breath to speak. Cy stood next to her, holding her hands. "It will be over soon," he said. "Be strong, my friend. Be strong."

She looked to him with warmth in her tired eyes and Cy knew she was grateful for his company. She opened her mouth to say something when another contraction struck and all that came out was a cry of pain. She pushed as hard as she could, and moments later the room was filled with the cries of a newborn baby. Catrina relaxed back onto the bed as the Fioraden placed the baby in her arms wrapped in a soft blanket. "He's beautiful," she said with a weak smile.

"He's a Lyecian. He could be nothing but," Cy said.

"Seth," Catrina said. "Say hello to Seth Alkirk, Cy."

"What an unusual name. Did Serrin come up with it?" Cy asked.

"No. Krycin suggested it, but it fits. I think he is very much a Seth, and he will do great things for Galadir some day."

Cy scoffed. "He'll be the last of his kind."

"Almost. Serrin and Krycin still live. Let's hope for the sake of our people that they are successful in defeating Gladius. Krycin says he can do it, though I don't know how."

"How can you still have faith in him after all of his failures?"

Catrina held her child close and closed her eyes. Cy wasn't sure if she was in deep thought, or sleeping, but then she opened her eyes and looked at Cy with a serious expression. "He saved both our lives, even if we lack our Lyecian powers. We owe him that much. No ordinary wizard can raise the dead, only one finely attuned to the gods could accomplish such a feat. Yet, further to that, there's something about him, something that tells me he knows more than he's telling us. I think he's been waiting for the right time."

"I think he's gotten lucky," Cy said, narrowing his eyes at her. "He knows nothing of our world but what he's experienced since he appeared. He's failed time and again to protect Galadir and the Lyecian people from a dire threat. If he had the ability to defeat Gladius, why didn't he do it before thousands of us died? No, I don't think he's a hero. I think putting our faith in Krycin is the greatest mistake the Lyecian people ever made." He turned away from her and stormed out of the hut.

(•)

Merek and Lebriel were on the battlements discussing city repairs when a Fioraden messenger arrived. The air had cleared of smoke and workers were milling through the city doing what clean up they could. The appearance of the messenger over the city had many residents looking up and letting out startled exclamations. He landed at the edge of the battlements, the wind through his feathered wings the only sound he made. As he walked toward Merek, the old wizard approached the messenger with a smile. "Please tell me there's more good news."

He heard a voice in his head speak clear and strong. *The child is born, safe and well. Catrina Alkirk eagerly awaits her time to return.* The messenger looked around at the castle and surrounding city. *The battle is done?*

"Yes, my friend," Merek said. "Krycin defeated Gladius and his army, yet, we have heard nothing from Krycin. He disappeared at the end of the battle along with Gladius. If Catrina is anxious to come back to Findoor, I know Serrin will be happy to see them. I shall send Morganath to bring Catrina back."

The messenger bowed to the two men and said, *Very well.* He walked to the edge of the battlements, spread his wings, and dropped off the edge, pumping his wings to gain height before settling into a glide that would take him back to the mountains in the North.

Lebriel spoke up from behind Merek. "Did you find the evidence you needed to prove Krycin's claim about Cy?"

Merek looked at the red-robed wizard. "Indeed. A search of his room turned up this," he said and produced a small silver mirror from his pocket. "It is paired with another. When I activated it, it showed me a Narshuk at the other end. I believe it is all the evidence we need. Cy was receiving orders from Gladius, and betrayed the kingdom of Findoor and the Lyecians. Not that it matters now."

"Do you really think he's dead?"

"I don't know. We never found a body, but you saw yourself what happened," Merek said. "Cy may have been angry about the loss of his powers, but he would never have willingly betrayed his people. I think there was another force at work, something that was working against Cy's will, or twisting it. Like Krycin, I can't prove my claim. I simply had a hunch."

"We'll never know, now," Lebriel said.

"I suppose not," Merek said, and returned to watching the workers below until the sun set.

⊙

Morganath lowered his shoulder to allow Catrina to climb up on his back. She carried a specially crafted basket that held her child and she guarded it as she made her way up. Cy tried to offer her a hand, but she brushed him away and managed on her own. Once she was settled and her basket secured, Cy climbed up and settled in behind her.

Ferron approached the pair now sitting on the dragon. *Take care,* Cy heard in his head. *The skies will be safer with Gladius defeated. May Anam smile upon you, always.*

Cy gave him a silent nod, but Catrina spoke up. "Ferron, you've been too kind to us. I wish there was something we could do to repay you."

It is our duty to bring light to those shrouded in darkness. Raise the child to embrace the light, and that will be all the thanks we need.

"I will," Catrina said, and waved to the other Fioraden who came out to see them off.

Cy nudged Morganath's neck and the dragon took a step back, spread his wings, and launched himself into the air. Both passengers held on tight as they gained altitude. The sun was approaching the horizon when they reached a good flying height. There was a small line of smoke in the distance that faded as they flew and they could hear the sounds of night birds just waking up in the forest below them. Cy broke the silence between them about twenty minutes into their flight. "It looks like the battle really is over."

Catrina didn't turn to face him, but shouted over the wind. "Indeed. The smoke has stopped."

"Serrin and your boy are some of the last Lyecians now. What will you do? And just what do you plan to do with him?" Cy asked, motioning to the basket with the baby in it.

"Take him to the dead world, just like Krycin said."

"You think your boy will be safe there? The Dark Lord isn't really dead you know. All Krycin did was destroy his body."

"He's never led us astray. He knows what he's doing."

"If that's what you want to believe, I won't stand in your way. But if he comes hunting for you," There was a pause as he considered his words carefully, "Gladius that is, don't think that Krycin will be able to get you out of a bind a second time."

"He knows what he's doing Cy. He's seen the future."

Cy let out a laugh and shook his head. "If he has. If you truly believe that Krycin has such a marvelous skill, then why did he let so many of us die?"

Catrina shifted in her seat and let out a sigh. "It was Gladius who killed our people, not Krycin."

"But if you think about it, if you take it right back to the beginning, and add in that Krycin has seen the future and knew what would happen and when, who is really to blame? He traveled with Gladius all the way from the beaches of Arda to Ducain's Keep. He could have ended this before it started at any time. But he didn't. He did nothing." Cy's voice increased in intensity as he spoke. "So tell me, who is *really* the villain here?"

Cy couldn't see her face, but he could tell he was getting to her. A voice inside Cy's head spoke up. *Go on, Cy. Turn her against him. Exact your revenge.*

He leaned in close to her so that his lips were close to her ear and whispered a suggestion, drawing on the dark force living inside of him. "Hate him. Hate Krycin with every ounce of your being."

"What did you say?" Catrina said, shifting in her seat.

Cy was startled at her resistance to his suggestion. "Nothing. Don't worry about it."

"No," Catrina said, looking into his eyes. "That was *not* nothing. What are you trying to pull, Cy?"

"Revenge," Cy said with a wide smile. "Sweet revenge at the cause of all this madness. Krycin may have destroyed Gladius, but he will not go on living like nothing has happened. They all think I'm dead, and now I'll turn everyone against him. One by one." He focused all the power he could draw from the dark force within him and said, "Hate him, Catrina. You will hate Krycin."

Catrina pushed him back in the riding harness and punched him in the chest. He felt the magical power emanating from her when she did and tried to release his harness, but he was too late.

"Restringuntas," she said, and hit him with a bolt of black energy that seized control of his body and froze it in place.

"Morganath," Catrina called out. "Stop for a moment, would you?"

Their forward movement slowed, and then stopped as Morganath beat his wings to hover in place. "Something the matter?" the great dragon said, his voice rumbling through his back and the harness.

"Not at all. Just getting rid of some refuse."

Cy watched through frozen eyes as Catrina spoke the words to open a rift below them. She then reached over to Cy's riding straps, unhooked them, and tossed him over into the rift. The feeling of falling didn't scare him nearly as much as where he might end up on the other end of her rift. When the hole closed above him, his body relaxed and he was able to move again, though he was still falling. The dark force inside him came to life and slowed his descent so that he came to a stop on the ground unharmed. *I can't have you dying on me, now can I?* The voice inside his head said.

Cy landed on his back in a puddle with rain falling on his face. All around him was darkness and mud. Explosions rocked the landscape now and then and there were fences running along the ground made of wire with bits of metal on it that looked like razors. Thunder rolled through the sky and lightning flashed around him. He heard a group of people approaching and looked around for somewhere to hide, but had nowhere to go.

When the person in the lead reached him, Cy cowered away from him. The man pointed a long piece of wood at him that had a metal tube mounted on the top. He guessed it was a weapon of some kind, though it was like nothing Cy had ever seen. He was about to raise his hands in resignation when the man said, "Wenn bewegen Sie sich, sind Sie tot."

Chapter 36 - The Dead World

Seth and Gladius appeared at the center of the Arvok Caldera. Serrin's manor remained intact at the edge of the burnt out volcano, and his lab, or what was left of it, stood in the center, surrounded by lush green grass. Seth looked Gladius in the eyes once more, and saw not hate, but fear. "I'm not going to kill you," Seth said to him.

He called on the power of earth and focused it into Gladius's armor, willing it to bend and fold away from Gladius's burnt and broken body. Seth's magic alone was holding the young wizard up, as he couldn't have stood on his own. Gladius was naked, and much of his flesh had been burnt off, exposing the muscle beneath it. There was little blood, as any blood vessels that had been severed were cauterized by the heat. Seth looked at him with pity, and saw a young boy, scared and confused, rather than a vicious tyrant.

"I'm going to heal you," Seth said to him. "Whatever the corruption was inside of you, it's gone now. You need to remain still though, it's going to be painful."

He called on the power of water and poured the energy into Gladius's body, causing new flesh to grow over his body. As he did, Gladius screamed in pain as new nerves grew, and fresh blood vessels ran through his body. It took a long time, and all the time Gladius screamed, tears ran down Seth's face. When the process was complete, Gladius dropped to his knees. Seth called on the power of earth and formed the energy into new blue robes that wrapped themselves around Gladius, covering his newly formed skin. His entire body was covered with scars, but he was alive.

"We were friends once," Seth said, and lowered himself to one knee. The wizard before him was nothing more than a kid, seventeen or eighteen years old.

Gladius lifted his head and looked into Seth's eyes. "I remember," he said.

"You helped me once. You didn't have to, but you did. Without knowing who I was, or where I came from. There's good in you, I can see it. Can it be like that again?"

"I don't know," Gladius said. He shifted his gaze to the ground and stared at the grass for a long time. "I knew what I was doing. I killed your people, and I enjoyed it. Something kept telling me they were dangerous, that they were going to destroy Galadir." He looked up at Seth again. "And you. Who are you? You told me your name was Krycin, but something is different now."

"I am Krycin. I've accepted that now, though it wasn't intentional. Galadir is in danger, though not from me. I came back to try and save it. It was you who caused the damage that I'm trying to repair now." Seth reached down and offered Gladius a hand.

Gladius took it and stood up. "Tyriel said it was you who was the threat. I'm confused."

"Maybe I was before I accepted my fate. I wasn't supposed to be here, and I changed the time line as a result of coming here. But to me, nothing changed. Everything happened exactly the way it was supposed to happen, though not for the reasons I thought it would."

"Who are you, really?" Gladius asked, confusion clouding his face.

"You can call me Seth. Seth Alkirk. In my time, I'm the last Time Weaver."

Gladius's eyes lit up. "Alkirk? Then you're related to Serrin?"

"Serrin is my father," Seth said.

"Blessed Philana. But how did you travel through time? Even Lyecians can't do that."

"I still don't fully understand it myself. What I do know is I need help. I still don't know how to repair the damage caused in the future. The boundaries of this universe are crumbling, and all of Galadir, and everything else in this universe will be destroyed if I can't figure it out." Seth walked away from Gladius toward the manor.

Gladius took a step to follow him. "Maybe I can help you. Take me with you."

Seth paused and looked at him. "I don't even know how to get myself back. I'm not sure if I could take you with me even if I wanted to. Besides, what makes you think, after everything you've done and all the lives you've taken, that you'd have a place in this world now, or in the future? This isn't the first time I've fought you. I fought that thing you put inside Cy, and destroyed it as well."

"Please," Gladius said, his eyes pleading. "The Council will put me to death if I stay here."

Seth watched Gladius's face carefully and saw the young man he once met on the beaches of Arda. The hate and malice was gone from his eyes, and all that remained was a boy who wanted to live, and was pleading for his soul. "I'll think about it. We need to keep you out of sight," Seth said, and led Gladius to the manor. "If you are seen by anyone here, there will be nothing I can do to help you." The two men entered the manor where Seth stopped in the front hallway. "This wasn't all your fault," Seth said. "Tyriel told me there was something else influencing your actions. I saw it, and fought it, but I didn't destroy it. I couldn't become what it was. I don't know if it was fully controlling you or not, but whatever it was, I've broken its grip on you."

"I feel better. Free. Thank you, Seth."

"I have a couple more things to take care of," Seth said. "Wait here for me, and stay out of sight."

Seth concentrated and disappeared, leaving Gladius in Alkirk Manor by himself.

(*)

Serrin waited in his chamber in Findoor castle for a long time while the battle was fought and won outside. He tried to convince himself that he was doing the right thing, but felt like he was turning his back on his responsibilities by staying out of harm's way. He was about to leave his room when he heard a sound behind him like a sudden rush of air.

He spun to see what it was and saw Krycin standing behind him. "You startled me," Serrin said. "Shouldn't you be out there, winning a war?"

Krycin smiled and said, "The war is won. Gladius is gone. So is Krycin, as far as everybody out there is concerned. Is Catrina back yet?"

"I've heard nothing. Not even a runner to tell me what's going on. Everything went quiet about an hour ago."

"I'm early then," Krycin said and crossed the room to Serrin. "Go. Be with your family. Come back here with Catrina when it's time to go, and I'll take you and your family to safety. Nobody will be able to hurt you or your family there."

"Thank you. Should I let Merek know that you're here?"

"No," Krycin said. "Nobody can know that I'm here."

Serrin gave him a funny look, but nodded. "If that's what you wish."

He left the room and made his way to the main floor, passing by the front doors of the castle before heading up to the throne room where Merek would be waiting. He stopped for a moment at the bottom of the stairs and admired the tapestry that hung on the wall. It was large and hand-crafted with a red background and a golden crown with a sword through it. The crest of Findoor. "I'm going to miss this place," he said to himself, and then moved on up the stairs.

When he arrived at the throne room, Merek was in his customary seat beside the king's throne and discussing something in a hushed voice with a woman Serrin had never seen before. She looked up as he entered the room, dried her red, puffy eyes, then left through a back door without saying another word. Serrin approached the front of the room and dropped to one knee before Merek. "Steward," he said as a show of respect to Merek.

"Get up," Merek said, sounding somewhat exasperated. "I have no interest in being treated like royalty. I'm the Arch-Magus and until the prince is of age, this kingdom shall remain headless."

Serrin stood up and said, "Apologies, Arch-Magus. Has there been any word from Catrina?"

"She is on her way back with your newborn son. She should be here shortly after dark." Merek gave him a comforting smile. "Stop fussing, Serrin. The war is over now. Gladius is gone."

"And Krycin?" Serrin asked.

Merek's voice filled with sadness as he said, "We've heard nothing."

"Thank you," Serrin said, and walked away before he let his secret slip. He made his way up to the battlements where he could see the land around the kingdom and watch the northern sky.

Morganath made it to Findoor castle just before midnight and landed in the courtyard in front of the castle. Serrin met him there as he touched down after having been alerted by the night watch. The massive dragon folded his wings to his back and lowered his neck to allow his passenger down. Serrin rushed forward to take the basket that held baby Seth. Catrina slid down the moment he had a firm grip on it. "I've missed you, my love," she said.

"I've missed you as well. Come, we must go now."

Serrin led Catrina into the castle and walked toward his chamber. "It's time to go. We have a new life to make." She followed close behind him, carrying Seth in the basket.

"I know Krycin said we have to, but I don't want to go anywhere with him. Who is Krycin to say where we should live?" Catrina asked.

"Krycin knows what he's doing. It's for our safety and the safety of our son. We're the last Lyecians on Galadir."

"No," Catrina said, her tone growing angry, "you and Seth are the last Lyecians on Galadir. I'm human now, or did you forget that? Krycin is trouble, and we're walking right into it by doing what he says."

Serrin stopped just outside his chamber door, spun around and looked Catrina in the eye. "What's come over you? You've never been this hostile toward anyone before. Krycin knows what he's doing. Our move will only be temporary, until things get settled here on Galadir, and then we can return."

"All right. I'm sorry. I'll go for you, and for Seth, but not for him."

Serrin opened his chamber door and led her inside where Krycin waited. "Ready to go?" Krycin asked, standing up to greet the small family with a smile.

"As ready as we're ever going to be," Serrin said.

Catrina said nothing, but Serrin noticed the hate in her eyes as she glared at Krycin.

Krycin approached the pair and looked down at the sleeping baby in the basket. "He looks so peaceful. Take good care of him and keep him close." He looked around the room one last time, then back at Serrin. "Do you have the book?"

"Right, the Lyecian book," Serrin said. He walked over to the wardrobe and pressed two fingers against the seam between the doors. The wards responded to his will and allowed him to open the doors that no other wizard could open, and then removed the book from the top shelf. "I have it right here."

Krycin smiled and placed a hand on Serrin's and Catrina's shoulders. "This might be a rough ride. I've never taken this many people with me before."

"Is it safe?" Serrin asked, his voice showing his concern.

"Oh sure. It's just going to take a lot out of me."

Krycin closed his eyes and concentrated. Serrin looked around and saw the room melt away around him into blue aether. He recognized the space around him as the aether that exists between worlds, but grew confused when even that melted away, leaving only darkness around them. He tried to speak, but heard nothing. Krycin was still in front of him with his eyes closed, more focused than he'd ever seen a wizard.

It felt like an eternity passed as they floated through the blackness, unable to speak to each other. Serrin closed his eyes for a second, trying to calm his nerves, and when he opened them again, he was blinded by sunlight.

When his eyes adjusted to the light, he looked around. The three of them stood in a flat area with yellow lines drawn on the solid ground. A large building stood off in the distance with many metal boxes on wheels resting before it. People walked back and forth from the metal boxes to the building and back again. Serrin looked up at Krycin, who was smiling back at him. "Welcome to the dead world," Krycin said.

"It doesn't look very dead to me," Serrin said, taking another look around. A mild breeze caused his gold robes to flutter, but nobody in the area payed attention to the small group.

"Dead refers to the lack of magic here. They don't know what magic is, and it needs to stay that way. Find a job, get a house, and raise your family. When Galadir is safe to return to, I'll come and get you."

Catrina remained silent through the exchange, but didn't break her gaze from Krycin. Serrin gave him a nod. "Thank you, Krycin. For everything."

"Don't mention it," Krycin said, and took a step back. A moment later, Serrin and Catrina were left in a strange world, all by themselves.

Chapter 37 – Crossroads

Seth focused his mind on reaching the same point in time that he left Galadir. Reaching a precise point required a much greater effort, and the exertion of drawing so much magical energy caused his head to ache and made his muscles burn. He appeared in Serrin's room just moments after he left, walked to the door and latched it, then lay down on the bed. The ache in his head grew to a tearing pain as he drifted off to sleep.

It was a knock on the door that startled him awake. He sat up and looked around, not sure of where he was until he organized his thoughts. The knock came again and the person outside tried the door, only to find it locked. Seth got up, not sure of what to do. It was only when he saw the black smoke passing through the door that he knew who it was. "Tyriel," he said.

Tyriel looked surprised. "This isn't your room."

"It's not Serrin's room anymore either."

"What have you done with him?" Tyriel asked.

"Sent him forward, and to the dead world. To Earth."

There was a moment of silence between them before Tyriel spoke again. "You're getting the hang of it then. Of moving through time."

"I think so. I have one more trip to make forward, but something must be set right here first."

"Set right? I thought everything was right," Tyriel said, confused.

"Not quite. There's still one more job to do. Someone is waiting at Alkirk Manor. He'll be coming with me when I go."

"A friend?"

"Sort of. A certain young man who lost his way. Whatever was controlling him is gone now." Seth looked down at his hands, which were shaking.

"You're tired. You need to rest," Tyriel said. "If you push yourself, you won't have the strength to make the trip again."

"I already slept. I'm fine. I want to get back to my own time, and Malia," Seth said. He clenched his fists trying to get himself under control.

"Krycin," Tyriel said, raising his voice. "Seth, you're not fine. Do you remember what happened the first time you attempted it while drained? You nearly killed yourself, and temporarily wiped out your memories from the temporal stress. Go to Alkirk Manor. Sleep. You mean more to this world, and Malia, alive than dead."

Seth let out a sigh. "Okay, you're right. I'll go and rest."

"One more thing."

"What?" Seth said, snapping at him just a little.

"Take me with you. There's nothing for me here. I thought I could come back. I thought my brother would accept me, and maybe I could try to live a normal life again. But Lebriel isn't ready for this, and I don't think he ever will be."

"Okay, but on one condition," Seth said, giving him a sly look. "You tell me your story."

Tyriel breathed a sigh and looked away. Seth could see the pain in his face before he turned. "Lebriel and I are twins. I was the first born, by only a few seconds. Our mother died in child birth, and we were raised by our father. When we were very young, only ten years old, Lebriel knocked an oil lamp over while we were playing. It set the house on fire and trapped both of us inside. We should have both died that day, but the gods intervened. Lebriel was saved from the fire, and I was left trapped inside to die.

"I once told you that the Fates make mistakes. It's rare, but it happens. Even the Fates could not tell us apart, and it was Lebriel who was supposed to die in that fire. As a result, the Fates gave me a choice. I could move onto my next life, or I could serve them and earn a second chance. For over twenty years I have served the Fates, ushering souls on to their next life, but I've never been back to the living realm. It was your arrival that prompted the Fates to send me here."

Tyriel turned back to face Seth, the pain apparent in his blue eyes. Seth took a step forward and placed a hand on Tyriel's shoulder. "And now you can't even go back. I'm sorry. I had no idea,"

Seth said. "Okay, come with me. I have a feeling we'll be able to use you. The future of Galadir isn't safe yet. I still have to find a way to keep the universe from crumbling."

"After you rest, of course," Tyriel said, cracking a smile.

Seth rolled his eyes and shook his head. In his mind, he formed an image of the Arvok Caldera with its green pastures growing in volcanic soil. The two men disappeared and reappeared just outside Alkirk Manor. When Seth let go of Tyriel's shoulder he felt the world shift and spin around him. The ground came up to meet him and the bright sunlight of the day faded to black.

(∘)

Seth opened his eyes to a white ceiling and a quiet room. His head ached, but the dizziness was gone. He couldn't remember getting himself inside the manor, let alone to a room or a comfortable bed and guessed that it must have been Tyriel and Gladius who moved him there. *Guess I was more tired than I thought.*

He sat up and looked at his hands again. The shaking had stopped and he felt refreshed, despite the headache. Across the room there was a dresser with fresh clothing and a bowl of water laid out on it. Seth examined his current clothing and scoffed at the torn and dirty rags. He got up, undressed, washed himself down, and put on the fresh clothes. They were a bit big and Seth guessed they must be some of Serrin's, who was a taller man than he was.

"Not exactly fit for a king," he said, cracking a smile.

Seth walked to the door and opened it. Through the door was not what he expected. There was a clean octagonal room with a floor tiled in black marble covered with silver runes of all shapes and sizes. White marble walls closed in the room with a door on each of the eight walls. The surface of the white marble was covered with gold runes that matched those on the floor. An elegant wood table rested in the center of the room with eight chairs surrounding it. Table and chairs were made of some kind of exotic wood that was dark with a golden grain. On each chair sat what looked to be a human. Four men and four women. Nearest to Seth was the goddess Lyecha, her dark hair cascading down her back. She was exactly as Seth remembered her from the last time he met her. When she stood up, Seth held his breath, though he didn't mean to. She was more beautiful than anyone he'd ever known. Lyecha lifted a hand and motioned for him to enter. Seth obeyed and walked into the Crossroads, closing the door behind him.

"It is good to see you again, Seth," Lyecha said with a smile.

He wanted to say something in return, but found he was still holding his breath. When he let it out, he blushed. "On better terms this time."

The rest of the people in the room looked back and forth at each other with confused expressions. Seth looked at them, and then back to Lyecha, who winked at him. *Right*, Seth thought, *they don't know yet.*

"The one you seek sits opposite me," Lyecha said. "Take my seat and make your request."

Seth was the one confused this time. "My request?"

"Yes, to Hadra. You were going to set things right?"

"Right. I can hardly think through this headache. What I would give for a Tylenol," Seth said. He approached the table and sat down in the chair meant for his goddess. Across from him was a young woman with short, straight brown hair, narrow yellow eyes and thin lips. She wore a black leather vest over a white tunic and looked at Seth with a half smile.

When Seth sat at the table, the rest of the Gods and Goddesses shifted in their chairs as if they were uncomfortable being there. None of them said a word, but Grishtor glared at Seth as if he were meeting an old enemy.

Hadra stared into Seth's eyes and waited for him to address her. He cleared his throat and said, "I've never been a believer in gods of any kind. Being raised on Earth, I know a whole different pantheon than what Galadir has. I've had to learn quickly, and I'm still coming to terms with all of this." He paused as the deities in the room all looked at each other and then back to him. "Still, I know that if there is anyone with the ability to do what I need done, it would be you. Serrin Alkirk has no place in history. As far as Galadirian history is concerned, he never existed. Instead, many believe that Krycin was in fact my father. I need this to be the case. I need everyone on Galadir to remember Serrin as if he were Krycin, but retain their memories of Krycin as well."

There was a long silence as Hadra considered his request. She narrowed her eyes at him and said, "You understand what you're requesting?"

"Yes. I know it will make it as if he never existed. The only people that remember my father are myself and my mother, and even we only have sketchy memories of him at best. I'm still not sure why Serrin left us when he did."

"This will not come without a cost," Hadra said. Her voice was strong and clear and sent a shiver down Seth's spine. Nothing she said was threatening, but he felt threatened by what she said and how she said it.

"What is the cost?"

"A favor," Hadra said, after a long pause. "Some day I will ask you to do something or change something, and you will do it, without question. You will be in my debt, and until you repay that debt, you will carry the mark of Hadra."

Seth thought about this for a long time, staring at the surface of the table with the strange gold grain in the wood. When he decided, he looked back up into Hadra's eyes. "Okay," he said. "I'll do it. Make it happen and I will be at your mercy until my debt is repaid."

Hadra smiled. "It is done. Nobody on Galadir now, or ever, will remember Serrin Alkirk. Instead, the memory of Krycin shall take his place."

"Thank you," Seth said, and slid away from the table. He went to push himself up and saw a mark in gray on his wrist that looked like a tattoo. It was an eye made of small arcs, the mark of Hadra.

He rose from his chair and found Lyecha waiting for him. She said nothing, but leaned in and gave him a kiss on the cheek, then allowed him to pass. Seth smiled in return and made his way to the door. When he opened it, the other side was the hallway of the manor outside his bedroom door. He stepped through the door and closed it behind him just in time for Gladius to appear at the end of the hallway.

"By the gods, you're awake. I thought we'd lost you for good," Gladius said. He smiled, which made the scar tissue on his young face pucker. Seth noticed some of his hair starting to grow back in patches, and some of the scar tissue had been smoothed and faded.

"You've been working hard I see," Seth said, pointing at the scars. "How long did I sleep?"

"Three days. We were starting to get worried. We can't save the world without you, can we?"

On the surface, Gladius's voice sounded good natured, but there was a bitterness to it that Seth caught at the end. "No, I guess not. When do we leave? I want to get this over with."

"Tyriel said that we could leave as soon as you were well rested. That was three days ago, so I guess it's time to go. There's been no sign of the Council or anyone else around here the whole time."

"Good," Seth said. "Let's go then. I'm as rested as I'm going to get."

Gladius walked the other way down the hall and said over his shoulder, "By the way, I poked my head into your room earlier today to see how you were doing, and you weren't there. Care to talk about where you went?"

Seth hurried down the hall to catch up to him. "Nope."

"I thought not," Gladius said with a sideways smile.

⊙

Tyriel was in the library when the other two found him. Seth noticed his clothes first, which were a black tunic and pants rather than the usual black robes he wore. The walls of the room were lined with books from floor to ceiling and a small set of steps rested on one side of the room that allowed access to the top shelves. Tyriel sat in an old red chair, reading a black leather bound book. He looked up and smiled at Seth, his face looking more relaxed than Seth had ever seen him.

"You look better," Seth said.

"Likewise. After three days of rest, you look as though you could take on Gladius again."

Seth looked at Gladius, who was staring at Tyriel with a blank expression. There was a moment of tense silence between the three of them before Gladius broke down laughing, followed by the other two.

"By the gods," Gladius said. "I didn't know reapers knew how to tell a joke."

Tyriel nodded. "But I'm no longer a reaper. We've been over this. The Fates must find another to do their dirty work from now on, and I'm certain they will."

"All jokes aside," Seth said, getting himself under control, "we should get going before somebody notices us here. The future of Galadir is still in trouble, and I want to get back to Malia." Seth looked at Tyriel. "When I left, there were too many rifts opening for me to close. I got the largest of them closed, but it was too much for me. Do you know how to close a rift?"

"Yes, but my powers are limited now that I've severed my connection with the Fates," Tyriel said. "Give me a moment to get ready." He walked out of the room and returned a moment later in his full robes with his scythe strapped to his back.

"Gladius, I need your healing abilities to keep me going. That's what I was missing before. I couldn't seal all the rifts and keep myself healed at the same time."

Gladius offered his hand to Seth. "You have my word. I shall do what I can to help."

Seth took his hand, placed his other hand on Tyriel's shoulder. "Are we ready?"

Both men nodded and Seth closed his eyes. As he concentrated, the three men disappeared from Alkirk Manor. Seth visualized Findoor castle as he had last seen it; with the great wall raised before it, and with the field before it littered with bodies from the battle. He tried to bring them to the precise moment he left, but the stress of such a distant jump was too much. When the three men arrived, a drop of blood was running from Seth's nose and his headache was worse than ever before.

The field around them was quiet and still. Dark clouds rolled through the sky, broken only by the occasional blast of blue lightning. The stone wall remained in front of Findoor castle, though something looked different. Seth searched the landscape, but couldn't put his finger on what was bugging him about it.

Gladius looked at Seth and offered him a handkerchief. "Are you all right?"

Seth nodded and said, "Yeah. I'm fine. Feel like I've been run over by a bus, but otherwise, fine." His two companions gave him a look of confusion to which he responded, "Never mind."

He looked up at the clouds and pointed at one of the blue flashes. "See those? They're wild rifts, opening and closing because the barrier around this universe has gotten too thin. We need to reinforce it and stop this from happening before it tears this universe apart."

Gladius looked up with wide eyes. "I've never seen a wild rift before. Opening a rift is complex magic. Something must have set this in motion. No ordinary wizard would do this."

"No," Seth said. "It was you. Or rather, whatever you put in Cy. It was almost you. I destroyed it, but I couldn't repair the damage it did."

"It was a simulacrum. A piece of my soul intended to keep Cy in line and working for me. If somebody used the right spells and gave it a physical form, it would have the same motivation that I had at the time that I made it."

"Kill Lyecians and destroy Findoor," Tyriel said. The sound of his voice startled Seth, but he didn't get the chance to respond before Tyriel pointed to the field around them. "We have company."

Seth looked around at the landscape and saw a mix of Narshuks and soldiers making their way across the field toward them. The soldiers bore the Findoor crest on their chest plates, but made no move to attack the Narshuks. "Something's not right here," Seth said as the group drew closer. His heart jumped in his chest as he watched the horde approach. "Malia should have slain all the Narshuks by now. Where is she?"

Gladius narrowed his eyes like he was trying to see more detail. "Blessed Philana," he said. "What defilement is this."

"They're dead," Tyriel said, drawing his scythe in one quick, fluid motion. "They're all reanimated dead. Go. The two of you. Do what needs to be done, I'll hold them off."

"Climb on my back," Seth said to Gladius. "Can you still cast spells if we fly?"

Still shaken by the sight of the corpses walking toward them, Gladius didn't respond at first. Seth put a hand on his shoulder and startled him out of his daze. "Yes," he said. "Yes, of course I can. Let's go."

Gladius wrapped his arms around Seth from behind over his shoulders and hopped up into a piggy back position. Seth found him lighter than he expected, and using the power of air, lifted them both up into the sky. Several wild rifts opened and closed around them, sending arcs of lightning flying through the sky. Seth dodged around them and drew in magical energy to seal the rifts as he went. Each rift they sealed opened two more and made the sky more unstable. Seth could feel the healing energy flowing into him from Gladius, which made sealing the rifts easier, but he couldn't keep up with the crumbling dimensional barrier.

"It's no use," Seth shouted to Gladius. "I can't seal them all. I need more help."

"You need another Lyecian," Gladius shouted over the thunder in the clouds.

Seth began his descent and saw Tyriel battling the dead creatures that gathered in the field. His scythe flashed as he cleaved them in half and spun to meet the next one. He'd laid waste to at least twenty of them but there were twice as many more coming from the direction of Findoor castle.

When his feet touched the ground, Seth let Gladius down and ran to help Tyriel, sending a wave of fire across the field and reducing the front six to ash. "I need to go and talk to an old friend," Seth said. "Keep these things busy, I'll be back with more help."

Tyriel looked at him, his breathing heavy. "Easy for you to say."

He returned to the battle just as Seth disappeared once more.

Chapter 38 – Twenty-five Years Ago

"And so, flags were raised for archers and infantry, and the front gates of the city were opened. The Findoor army swept the land and chased the remains of the Dark Lord's army back to the eastern Badlands from which they came.

"Merek ruled the kingdom until the young prince came of age, and peace settled over the land. A peace that saw the kingdom of Findoor thrive and grow into the greatest kingdom Galadir had ever known."

Five-year-old Seth frowned and looked up into Serrin's eyes. "And what about Krycin? What happened to Krycin?"

"Neither Krycin, nor Gladius were ever seen or heard from again," Serrin said, closing the cover of the old leather-bound book. "It's time for bed now."

Seth frowned and squirmed on his bed. "Aww, but Dad! Are you sure there isn't just one more story there? Krycin can't be gone." His eyes lit up at the prospect, but Serrin shook his head, dashing his hopes.

"That's all there is. Tomorrow we'll go out to the library and pick out a new book to read, okay?" Serrin smiled at Seth and tousled his hair.

"Tomorrow? But you'll work late again. And if you work late," Seth said, his lips curling into a pout, "we won't have time to go to the library, and then we won't have anything to read before bed."

"I know Seth, and I won't work late. I'll get home just in time, you'll see. Get some rest." He tucked Seth in and kissed his forehead. "Goodnight buddy."

"G'night Daddy." Seth sighed and nestled down into his blankets.

Serrin got up from the bed and left the room, turning off the lights and closing the door behind him. When he got to the kitchen, Catrina was sitting at the table waiting for him. A deck of cards was laid out on the table with a seven card hand dealt. "Finished that filthy old book at last?" she said.

"It's not filthy. And yes, Seth quite enjoyed the stories." Serrin sat down and picked up the cards. All four suits, no pairs, and only a three card run in different suits. "Really now, how am I supposed to beat you when you deal me a hand like this?" He flashed her a smile which she returned.

"What, I'm supposed to make it easy for you? Not a chance."

The two played several hands of Gin and talked quietly about their day, laughed about who was beating who, and discussed the fact that Seth would be starting school in September. They were getting ready to retire for the night when there was a knock at the front door.

"I'll get it. It's probably a salesman," Serrin said, sliding his chair back away from the table.

"At ten at night? Tell whoever it is to go away." Catrina stood up and walked around the table toward Serrin. She reached up and traced one finger along his neck. There was a hunger in her eyes that Serrin hadn't seen in a while. "It's almost our bed time."

He smiled back at her and said, "Okay, I'll get rid of them and be right there."

They always kept the door locked at this time of night, and on his way to the door, there was a second knock. "Okay, okay," Serrin said, turning the knob of the deadbolt. "Hold your horses."

He pulled the door open and looked outside. Standing on the front porch was a young man in an old fashioned tunic and trousers that were slightly too big for him. He had short brown hair that was growing a little too long, and a face that looked like it hadn't been shaved in weeks. Serrin might have mistaken him for a homeless man had it not been for the man's green eyes. They were the same green eyes Catrina had, and it startled him now that he took a good look at them.

"Krycin," he stammered, taking a step back.

"Serrin," Krycin said with a smile. "Sorry to bother you, I know this isn't a good time, but I need you."

"Oh no. Not now. We're happy here. I don't care if Galadir is safe, we're staying here. We can live quietly, and without all the politics.

It's taken us these last five years just to get settled and figure out our lives again."

Krycin laughed. "Five years. Then I missed my mark. I don't have the energy to do it right, but now that I think about it, this makes sense."

Serrin opened the storm door and stepped outside, pulling the front door shut behind him. "You're *not* making sense."

"Look, I know it's going to be hard. It's going to be hard on everyone. You have to leave. Galadir isn't safe, and neither is your family so long as you stay here. Cy is somewhere in this world looking for you, and your powers give you away. Galadir is in trouble, and I need another Lyecian to help me repair the damage that's been done."

There was a long silence between the two men before Serrin finally spoke again. "How long until Cy finds us?"

"I don't know. As long as you remain here, he could be here in days. If you leave, he might never find you."

"What about Seth? He's Lyecian, and a mighty powerful one I'd wager. Won't Cy find him as well?"

"Let me take care of that," Krycin said. "He'll be fine."

"How can you possibly expect me to pick up and leave my family? I won't have my son growing up without a father."

"Serrin, your son *did* grow up without a father, and he turned out just fine." Krycin gave him a half smile and for the first time, Serrin saw in him something he'd missed in all the time he'd known Krycin. The green eyes and half-smile he'd seen on his wife's face thousands of times.

"Seth?" he asked, confused.

"It's me, Dad," Krycin said. "I need you. We're the only two left. It has to be us."

"And what about your mother? How do I leave her behind?"

"I don't know. What I do know is this: If you stay, you'll probably live a happy, comfortable life with them, and billions of people will die. If you go, one woman will raise a son without her husband, and one boy will grow up without his father. He finishes high school, goes to university, and gets a great job at a high-tech company called Griffin Technologies. He's happy, even if he does miss his dad."

Serrin took a deep breath and held it for a second, then let it out slowly. "How did you get mixed up in all this then? And how are you here, now?"

"The details are a little hazy. Tyriel could tell you better, but I know that when I turn thirty, my powers return, and all hell breaks loose. I am powerful. Merek once told me that I'm the most powerful Lyecian who ever lived. Come with me, help me save Galadir, and we can come back for mom then."

"Okay. I'll do it. But let me talk to your mother first. She's not going to take this well."

"Let me know when to come in and suppress my powers," Krycin said. "That way Cy will never find them. But don't tell Mom who I really am. She doesn't know, and never knew. Maybe, someday, I'll have the courage to tell her."

Serrin nodded and went back inside. Catrina was waiting for him in the kitchen doorway with her arms folded over her chest. "Some salesman."

"The man out there isn't a salesman." Serrin tried to hide his feelings behind a cold expression but suspected he was doing so poorly. "Remember what we talked about when we first came here five years ago? The time has come. Krycin needs me, and Cy is here and getting close to finding us."

"Krycin? That's who's at the door?" Catrina said, walking over to the window to get a clear look. "Tell that wretch to crawl back under the rock he came from."

"Catrina," Serrin said, looking at his wife with loving eyes. "Krycin saved our lives. Besides, Galadir needs me."

"Why does it have to be tonight?" Catrina shouted.

"I've been discovered. It's not safe for me to stay here. You knew this day would come," Serrin said in a matter-of-fact way.

"That doesn't make it easier, and you know it."

"Five years ago, when we came here, we discussed this, and I told you then that this was only temporary. I can't let him find you, and he's so close."

"I just wish there was another way, I don't think I can do this without you." Catrina was crying now, her tears rolling down her cheeks. She looked up into Serrin's eyes.

"If he comes, use the book, and utterly destroy him. Come now, I have precious little time to waste." Serrin walked toward the hallway to go to his room and saw young Seth standing off to the left. "Seth, what are you doing out of bed?"

He thought for a second as if he couldn't remember why he was there, and then perked up. "Oh! I have to pee!" Seth ran for the bathroom and did his business, then went back to bed. Serrin tucked him back in and went to pack his things.

Catrina stood in the doorway waiting for him, still crying. "You're really gonna go, just like this? Not even a word to Seth?"

Serrin looked at his wife. "Billions of lives are at stake. If I don't go, I'd never be able to live with myself. Don't make this any harder for me than it already is. Krycin and I are the only Lyecians left. We're the only ones powerful enough to repair the damage that's been done."

"Fine then. Go," Catrina said, and walked over to Serrin. "I trust you, and love you with all my heart and soul. Please come back to me."

"I will," Serrin said. He wrapped her in a warm embrace and gave her one last kiss. Then finished packing his things and went to the front door. He waved Krycin into the house and said, "Go and do what you have to do. Make sure they stay safe."

Krycin nodded and walked to young Seth's room. Serrin watched him enter the child's room and waited a few minutes. When Krycin emerged, he looked sad, but Serrin said nothing about it.

Catrina remained in her bedroom, and Serrin said nothing further to her. The two men left the house and walked out to the sidewalk. Krycin placed a hand on Serrin's shoulder, and both men disappeared.

⊚

Seth was gone for only a few minutes, but when he reappeared, both Tyriel and Gladius looked ready to collapse. They fought hard against the relentless undead monsters, but couldn't gain any ground on them. More and more of the creatures were reanimated Narshuks who were much heavier and stronger than the fallen Findoor soldiers. Seth and Serrin positioned themselves back-to-back and raised their hands. Both of them unleashed a wave of fire that flowed across the field in opposite directions. The flames consumed the undead around them, reducing them to smoldering piles of charcoal. Still, hundreds of the undead approached, ready to tear them apart.

"It's about time," Gladius shouted at the two Lyecians.

"It feels good to do that after five years," Serrin said with a smile. He gave Gladius a strange look, like he was surprised to see the young man there, but shifted his attention to the others.

Seth wiped another drop of blood from his nose and shook his head. "We need to fix that," he said, pointing to the sky where wild rifts continued to tear open and close.

"By the gods, what's happened here?" Serrin looked to the sky in astonishment. "It's like the universe itself is weeping."

Tyriel took a step to the side to close the gap between the two pairs. "The barrier that holds this universe together has been damaged. It's up to you two to repair it from the outside."

Seth nodded at Serrin and said, "Come with me, we can do this together." Serrin offered his arm and Seth took it, linking the two men together with a tight grip. "You two, run," Seth said. "Get as far away as you can. You can't defeat this many of these things on your own."

"Go east," Serrin said. "Toward Ducain's Keep. We'll catch up to you later."

Seth called on the power of air once more and lifted the two men up into the sky. Several rifts above them opened at once sending waves of lightning toward them. Both of them created a white shield of energy before them that deflected the lightning. Seth motioned at the largest of the rifts, and the two men changed direction, heading for the center of it. "Quickly," Seth shouted. "Before it closes."

The edges of the rift quivered and shifted, closing as the two men approached it. Seth drew energy from the rift and used it to hold the rift open long enough for both men to get through it. As they entered the space between worlds, the rift slammed shut and sent a shock wave toward the two men. The force was enough to break their grip and they each flew in opposite directions. Seth looked toward the edge of the Galadir universe and saw a large area where the barrier was scarred with black energy that moved around like a series of worms or ribbons. It was like a disease that consumed the aether and left wild rifts in its wake. He spotted Serrin not far from him and motioned toward the holes.

Serrin put his hands together before him and sent a blast of white light at one of the black energy ribbons. The blast destroyed the ribbon, leaving the wild rift to close on its own. Seth repeated the same spell, calling on the power of life to destroy more of the ribbons. The two men worked hard together, patching the damage that had been done, and destroying the cause, but Seth could feel his strength waning, and the pain in his head was nearly unbearable.

Slow down, Son, a voice in his head said. Serrin's voice. Sound would not travel through the space between worlds, but Serrin used his magic to communicate with his mind. *We need you to get us home. Much more of this, and you'll kill yourself.*

Seth turned to face Serrin and pointed at the last remaining rift. One ribbon of black energy worked its way across the barrier, consuming the power that held the universe together. Serrin sent a blast of white energy at it and destroyed it, but Seth hadn't realized how much they had both exerted to accomplish their task. Serrin slumped where he was, having drained himself. His eyes were closed and he no longer moved. Seth moved himself over to Serrin and took hold of him, focusing his mind on the one place they both had in common. The two men disappeared from between worlds and reappeared on a large field of tall grass.

The weight of Serrin's limp body was too much for Seth to hold up, and both of them collapsed. Seth felt pain rage through his head as he looked at the manor standing before them. It was old and run down, with peeling paint and holes in the roof. Most of the windows were broken and the front door had long ago fallen off of its rusted hinges. Seth tried to lift himself up off the ground, but the world shifted around him, and he fell again, this time into unconsciousness.

⊛

Tyriel and Gladius ran for the only opening they could find in the undead horde. Gladius paused, turned, and summoned the power of water. "Congelascas," he said as he focused a wave of blue energy at the horde that turned into water, and then froze into a wall of ice.

With the undead held off for a short time, he turned back to Tyriel and ran after him. It was several miles before either of them stopped to catch their breath.

"That *was* Findoor, wasn't it?" Gladius said to Tyriel through labored breaths.

Tyriel couldn't catch enough breath to respond, and so he just nodded, and then broke into a fit of coughs.

When Gladius had recovered enough to stand up straight, he pointed back at Findoor castle in the distance. "Then why is it flying my banner?" he asked.

Tyriel looked back at the castle. The sky above settled and the rifts closed, but no sunlight broke through the clouds above it. The land that was once green and lush was now gray all around the castle. The hills were stained with blood and the banner flying above the castle was not a red flag with a golden crown and sword, but a black flag. Embroidered on it in silver was a lily with a snake wrapped around the stem.

A Word From the Author

I've learned a great deal over the last year. Writing is a journey for which there is no destination. There is always something to learn or something new to discover, a new book to write or a new idea. Anyone moving through this journey in parallel with me who is expecting a finish line will be sorely disappointed.

Nothing about this journey has let me down though. Sure, there have been high points and low points, but in the end, I'll never regret starting it.

The support I receive from the people I choose to surround myself with is amazing. Never in my life have I met such a wonderful, supportive group of people. Even my fans (O.M.G.! I have fans!) are here for me in a way I never thought possible. It makes this endless journey worthwhile.

I consider everyone involved with the production of this book part of my team. I wouldn't be able to do it without you. While I may write the words, it's the rest of you who make it great. My editors (Frederic Mora and my wife, Claire), my beta readers, my family, fans, reviewers, bloggers, you are all a part of this, and I thank you.

Visit http://thomasaknight.com for the latest news and updates on Thomas A. Knight